I0589261

Books by Brenda S. Anderson

_________________________________

Where the Heart Is Series

*Risking Love*
*Capturing Beauty (coming February 2017)*
*Planting Hope (coming Fall 2017)*

Coming Home Series

*Pieces of Granite*
*Chain of Mercy*
*Memory Box Secrets*
*Hungry for Home*

# Capturing Beauty

A NOVEL

Minneapolis, Minnesota

Vivant Press
Capturing Beauty
Copyright © 2017
Brenda S. Anderson



ISBN-13: 978-0-9862147-5-2

Scriptures taken from the Holy Bible, New International Version®, NIV®. Copyright © 1973, 1978, 1984, 2011 by Biblica, Inc.™ Used by permission of Zondervan. All rights reserved worldwide. www.zondervan.com The "NIV" and "New International Version" are trademarks registered in the United States Patent and Trademark Office by Biblica, Inc.™

This novel is a work of fiction. Names, characters, places, and incidents either are the product of the author's imagination or are used fictitiously. Any resemblance to actual events, locales, organizations, or persons living or dead is entirely coincidental and beyond the intent of either the author or the publisher.

Cover Design by Think-Cap Design Studios

Printed in the United States of America

17 18 19 20 21 22 23   7 6 5 4 3 2 1

*To the One who makes all things—all people—beautiful!*

*Never lose an opportunity of seeing anything beautiful,*
*for beauty is God's handwriting.*


**~ Ralph Waldo Emerson ~**

Chapter One

nxiety curdled in Callie Beaumont's stomach while her heart—and her hopes—twisted in knots. *Please, please may this pre-sunrise jaunt to witness God's artistry in action be the soothing balm she needed for today.* If she didn't hurry to her prime viewing location, the sun would edge above the horizon and she and her little follow-the-leader buddy would miss its arrival. She tugged her newsboy cap snug on her head and jogged away from the lighthouse at Duluth's Canal Park, young Reece already lengths ahead of her, and prayed the sunrise wouldn't bring a red sky along with it. A red sunrise was breathtaking, but it all-too-often foretold stormy weather.

Her announcement would conjure up its own storm at home. She swallowed back a spike of acid burning up her throat. *No!* She would not allow worry to steal peace from this morning. This was a time for worship.

She flung out her arms, tossing aside her concerns, and sped toward her best friend's son. Catching up to eight-year-old Reece without either of them getting hurt would be a miracle. That kid could run faster over Lake Superior's rocky shores with his prosthetic foot than Callie could jog with healthy limbs. She reached the end of the lighthouse's pier, and cupped her hands around her mouth. "Hey, slow down there, bud."

Rather than slow, Reece raced down the walkway beside the canal, and toward the lift bridge. *What?* He was supposed to go to the beach. The doofus was going to make them late! Well, she'd just have to run faster! And next time, *she'd* be the leader in this game.

9

With gulls swooping and cawing around her, she ramped up her speed.

And then braked to a stop, grabbing onto the concrete barrier to prevent a face-first collapse. A boat sat silent in the harbor, just beyond the Aerial Lift Bridge. A man lay on the bow, a large camera in his hand. Aimed in her direction.

Goosebumps broke out on her arms, and perspiration prickled down her back. *Get a grip, Callie girl. He's aiming at the lighthouse, not you.* She swiped her hand across her forehead then shook out her arms. No way was she going to let the sight of that photographer make her late to the sunrise.

She inhaled a lungful of air and took off toward Reece, who now aimed for the water. In only two steps, he leapt across the Lakewalk and landed on the pebble-and-boulder-strewn beach. He must be completely oblivious to the fact that this was the same shoreline that took his foot away. At his age, he couldn't care less about the sunrise. Yet. For him this morning was all about besting her, and she loved him for it. But with the dazzling light show birthing around them, God would change Reece's mind.

She shot up a quick prayer of thanks for this opportunity to kidsit her best friend's son overnight, and to show him God's paintbrush in action. If he sat still long enough to enjoy it.

Crossing the Lakewalk took her short legs three steps, then she began navigating the rocky shoreline, following Reece, who did a one-eighty, heading back in the wrong direction. The goofball! Shaking her head, she followed him up the rocky incline. Until the lift bridge snagged her attention. Or rather, the boat beneath grabbed it. Her stomach tossed like waves in a November gale. The man with the camera was still there.

*He's not filming you!* With trembling fingers, she wiped her forehead. Reece doubled back and scampered past her then began climbing over the sharp-angled boulders. The kid had no fear. He slipped, landing hard on his prosthetic foot, and pain wrinkled his eyes closed.

With a gasp, she ran toward him, but he laughed—he laughed!—and tried again, this time ascending without incident. Oh, to have that level of confidence and stamina. What a day brightener he was. She cupped her hands around her mouth and shouted to him, "Who do you think you are? Michael Johnson?"

He slowed and teetered for a second on a sharp rock, but quickly regained his balance. "Who?" The kid gave her heart more jumpstarts than she used to give her old Chrysler.

She yelled out, "Michael Johnson. Famous Olympic runner, won a boatload of gold medals?"

"Special Olympics?" He actually remained still!

She climbed over rocks and a couple of felled tree trunks before catching up to him, then laid a hand on his shoulder. "I guess he's a few years before your time." Probably about twenty years before Reece's time.

"I'm gonna be in the Olympics." He flexed his skinny, eight-year-old arms.

And she laughed. "Yeah, I bet you will be." She looked toward the horizon then glanced at her watch. About five minutes left before the sun would finally peek over the lake's edge. Plenty of time to do a little agate hunting and reach her spot, but not if she was chasing the wild wanderer. "But for now, this follow-the-leader game is done, and I need to get to my viewing spot. Join me."

She picked her way across the pebbly beach while Reece took the hard way over the boulders. The two of them were no longer alone on the beach either. The shore, illumined in shades of gold by the sun's imminent arrival, was smattered with a handful of other sightseers, many with phones at the ready, others with handheld cameras, and a couple with tripod setups. All aimed away from her and toward the east, thank goodness, but their mere presence still made her shiver. She'd never understand why someone would narrow God's morning hello. What could be seen through a small lens would only capture a miniscule portion of His greeting. She preferred taking in the entire picture.

Seagulls cawed around her, their calls sounding like laughter as if they too were delighted about the dawning day. Whispering waves licked the rocky waterfront and she raised her hands upward in praise. These calm rollers were so different from the storm-powered waves that had hurled boulders onto shore, pounding many into mere pebbles. This beach was a perfect example of God's gentle love and awesome power.

She breathed in the morning's fresh air and relished this gift from God, a gift that made her forget all her worries.

Well, not completely. Holding her breath, she turned around and her gaze drifted toward the lift bridge and beyond. The boat was still there, a mere speck to her from here, but she had no doubt the man was still prone on top. Every cell in her body zapped with electric fear. She shook her hands out, but the tingling clung tighter. With all the cameras on the beach, why that particular shutterbug upset her made no sense. He wasn't even aiming her way, but tension zinged through her fingers.

She knelt and dug through the pebbles, hoping to chase her strain. "Bud, come here. Help me find an agate."

He leapt off a Smart-car-sized boulder, turned a somersault, and stuck the landing. His Duluth Bulldogs baseball cap toppled off, revealing a towhead so different from his mother's auburn. He must have gotten that DNA from his father.

An absentee father.

She flicked on the penlight on her keychain and picked through the stones until she found a quarter-sized rock. Rubbing her thumb over its pitted texture, she examined the rust-red stone. A slight fissure revealed a glossy, tree-like banding. The tell-tale sign that beauty lurked beneath its exterior. It wasn't pretty by any means. Ordinary. At least on the surface. Beneath that plain surface was heart-stopping beauty. Straight from God's hands.

It was always important to look beneath the surface.

"Didja find one?" Reece ran toward her and craned his neck to see what she held in her palm.

"Yep." She rolled the stone around in her hand, and shone her small flashlight on it.

He wrinkled his nose. "It doesn't look like my agates."

"Oh, but it does on the inside. When we're done here, I'll take you back to my place and polish her up. What do you say to that?"

"Cool. Can I do it?"

"You bet you can." A perfect opportunity for him to learn and understand that beauty went far deeper than the surface. She flipped the rock in the air, and he caught it. "Before that we'll have breakfast, play a game or two, then get you back to your mom's."

He huffed and kicked at the ground, scattering pebbles. "Like Mom really wants me now that Bill's around." He took a flat stone and side-armed it into the lake, toward the line of boat-sized rocks a home's-length away. It skipped once and sunk well before it reached the line.

"Listen, bud. She loves you, but she's flying a little high with this new guy, and Bill treats her right." She ruffled his hair. "What do you say you give her a little time to float back down to earth?" At least Bill had better be treating Mandy right.

Yeah, Reece's mom was a bit love struck right now, but her first love was and always would be Reece. He'd realize that again. Probably later today, after Callie dropped him off, and Mandy smothered him with hugs and cooked his favorite meal.

Callie stared off toward the horizon. Smothered with hugs . . . What did that feel like?

Once she dropped Reece off, she'd go home and tell her parents her new plans. Rather than wrap her in hugs, they'd likely chide her foolishness.

Well, tough. She looked around toward Duluth's restored warehouse area and the building where she'd worked since she was a teenager. If her prayers were answered, in a few weeks she'd break free from the stale air of that aging brick building and work permanently amidst God's creation. *Lord, help them understand.*

And help Reece understand that he was ferociously loved by his mom.

He kicked at the pebbled shore. "I wish I could stay with you."

Oh boy. *Lord, what do I say?* She scratched her head, then a smile threatened to show. "Well, you know what happens at night at my house?"

"What?" His eyes grew large as the agate she'd discovered.

She wiggled her fingers in his direction. "The tickle monster comes out!" She tickled his stomach, and he doubled over in giggles.

"You're silly, Aunt Callie."

"That's what they tell me."

She got up and nodded toward her rock. "Coming with me?" She hadn't expected the deep conversation with Reece and time had slipped away. The sun would sneak out any second now.

The goof scampered off.

Heaving a big sigh, she started up the rocky incline toward her special spot. She should make it just in time. She attempted to pull herself up onto her boulder, but her hands lost their grip on the dew-covered stone, and she fell bottom first on rocks still damp from the evening's mist. "Oh, crud on a cracker!" That was going to leave a mark.

"You okay, Aunt Callie?" He hurried back to her, not a hitch in his step.

Grimacing, she stood and wiped the back of her cropped jeans, her bum already tender. "Super great and getting better."

He giggled. "You're too funny."

"Glad I amuse you." Rather than trying to scale the waist-high boulder again, she found a natural stairway of rocks leading to the stone's summit, hoping she'd make it in time. A second later she plopped next to Reece and let her legs hang over the side. "You ready for a breathtaking light show?"

"Yep." He scooted tight against her. "I'm glad Mom and Bill wanted a date last night. You're my best sitter."

She hugged him as she stared off toward the already-bright horizon. God was moments away from announcing the birth of a new day, a fresh beginning with bursts of color unique to this morning.

Now, if her parents would cheer on her news later today, her heart would burst with its own unique colors of joy.

She snuck a glimpse behind herself at the unmoving boat beyond the bridge and its camera-wielding occupant. Slapping down the nerves fighting in her stomach, she prayed again, as she'd prayed for too many years, for peace and a way to banish her irrational fear of photographers.

HAVEN CARLYSLE LAY ON his stomach on the bow of his dad's Hullcraft Nova and aimed his Nikon D7200 toward Duluth's famous lift bridge. Capturing the sunrise from this angle would be the perfect way to begin his first professional assignment.

Just to the left of the bridge rose the lighthouse. A smattering of clouds hid the stars. Precisely the perspective he was shooting for.

With no wind, the boat sat fairly still, but was it still enough? Bracing his camera on a towel by the railing, he switched the shooting mode from full-auto to aperture priority mode and then focused his wide-angle lens. The lighthouse wasn't as clear as he'd hoped it would be. But a longer lens wouldn't allow him to take in the entire bridge.

He checked his watch. Five ten. In just a few minutes the sun would proclaim a new day. Hopefully new beginnings for him too. God wouldn't have led him to Duluth otherwise. Would he?

A wine-red ribbon of light split the horizon from the red-tinted sky, and Haven began clicking the shutter. Purple and yellow hues invaded the red and fought for dominance then exploded into a kaleidoscope of color.

Yes, this was a definite sign from God that today was a day of fresh beginnings. He snapped shots, while slowly raising the exposure, until the sun completely escaped the water's edge and bathed the world with hues only God could dream up.

He kept shooting as the sun arched upward then hung in perfect alignment above the lighthouse, almost creating a cross-like effect. The sun continued to rise above the lake, and the colors of the sky transformed to a brilliant blue. Only then did he lower the camera. He sat back and took in the rest of the sun's ascension, without viewing it through the narrow scope of the lens, and warmth coursed through his body. What amazing artistry! Now, if his camera recorded a smidgen of that beauty, he'd be ecstatic.

He picked up the camera and rifled through the digital images. And bit back a curse. Blurry and too dark. Who was he to think he could capture such an amazing shot? Apparently, some things were meant to be enjoyed in memory only. His gaze went back to the brightening horizon and he smiled. He couldn't ask for a more breathtaking memory.

This wasn't a setback, but rather an opportunity to seek beauty elsewhere.

He packed the camera and supplies into an eight-year-old Snoopy diaper bag that still had a pink bottle of baby lotion showing through the front mesh pocket, and hefted it over his shoulder before crawling back inside the boat.

His dad had fallen asleep in the captain's chair, a Bulldogs cap pulled over his eyes.

"Time to go, Dad." Haven lightly shook his father's shoulder.

"What?" Roland Carlysle startled in his seat and his hat fell to the boat's floor. He shook his head and blinked. "Guess . . . " He cleared the sleep from his throat and ran a hand over his whiskered chin. "Guess I fell asleep there."

"Guess you did." Haven handed him the cap. "I'm done."

"Did you get what you wanted?" His dad stretched his neck from side to side, then rotated his shoulders.

Haven dropped into the passenger seat. "Not this time." He might be foolish believing he could make a career out of this hobby, but God used fools too. Still, it was a good thing his new job at the bank started in a couple of weeks. This photography-hobby-turned-hopeful-career was taking a serious bite out of his cash reserves.

"Next time, then. You're darn good with that camera."

"Thanks," Haven said over the rumble of the motor, and slapped his dad on the back. It was his father's wholehearted support that made this dream seem possible. Precisely what a father-son relationship should be like.

His dad steered the boat toward the docks on the south side of Duluth's Park Point peninsula, a place Haven had called home for the first twenty years of his life.

Until Amanda had coaxed him away.

And then kicked him out.

He'd deserved it.

But that was six years ago, and he wasn't the same man who'd ruined their son's life. He patted the AA Medallion he always kept in his pocket. Sober over six years, just like his dad. That had to mean something to Amanda. Besides, not once had he missed a support payment. He'd even given far more than was required, always accompanied with a letter.

He ran a hand over his whiskered chin. Had she read his letters? Did she realize how much he'd changed? Did his son know how much he loved him, missed him, and ached to hold him?

Not once had he heard back from Amanda, though his checks were always cashed. Maybe a face-to-face would make the difference, and she'd let him come home to be the father he should have been at the start.

Just like his dad was doing.

The Nova sidled up against the dock, and Haven tied her up. He grabbed the diaper bag and pulled out his hand-sized Canon PowerShot, a perfect camera to carry on his daily jogs. His dad stepped onto the dock, and Haven stuffed the camera into a waist pack that already held a bottle of water. He clipped the pack above his hips, hiding it under his T-shirt. "I'm going for a run." He handed his dad the diaper bag. "Would you mind?"

"Not a problem." He flung the bag over his shoulder and Haven winced. That unconventional camera bag hid thousands of dollars' worth of camera equipment and irreplaceable shots.

*Lighten up, Haven.* The camera equipment was replaceable, relationships weren't.

He'd give anything to restore the relationship with his son.

That started with prayer, and there was no better time for prayer than when out running. He waved to his dad and jogged off the dock while offering up gratitude and praise to the one who created the morning. He followed South Lake Avenue and crossed the lift bridge just beginning to bustle with morning travelers. He sprinted past the marine museum and down the concrete walk to the lighthouse. Blue sky brightened around him, and deep blue water sparkled below. A slice of heaven.

On the shore, a beret-wearing woman clambered over the rocks trying to keep up with a young boy, maybe seven or eight years. Or was the child older? Younger?

Didn't matter. It was beautiful, and that was precisely the unique beauty his editor wanted. He pulled the camera from his waist pack and followed the two—probably mother and son—on the LCD screen, capturing their frolic in still motion. It was obvious the two cared for each other. He prayed daily he'd soon have that kind of relationship.

Keeping his lens focused on the duo, he backed away from the shore. He crawled up the rocks a few yards behind them, sat down, and snapped shots as they flung stones into the lake.

Yep, now that was beautiful.

The woman turned around, giggles shaking her shoulders. Then her gaze met his lens, and she stilled, her mouth draped open, and eyes narrowed. "What do you think you're doing?"

He shut off the camera and lowered it into his lap. "I'm, uh, doing an assignment for a local magazine."

"Well, I don't take kindly to being photographed without my say-so." Scowling, she grabbed the child's hand, and the boy looked up at her bewildered.

"I'm sorry." Haven stepped off the larger rocks and walked toward them. "I didn't mean anything by it. You two made such a beautiful picture of a family having fun, I couldn't resist trying to capture it on film. I promise not to show the pics to my editor."

"Not good enough." She stepped closer and made a stabbing motion toward his camera. "Delete them. Now."

"But—"

"Now!"

He blew out a breath and rifled through his shots, deleting them one at a time. What a waste. These pictures were precisely what his assignment was about: capturing beauty along the North Shore. He got to the last photo and his finger hovered over the delete button but he didn't press it. Keeping one for his memory wouldn't hurt. Besides, it would be an encouragement for him, reminding him that a relationship with his son was worth pursuing regardless of the pitfalls along the way.

"That's it." He shut off the camera, and a tingle of guilt flashed through his brain. But he was the only one who'd see the photo. She'd never know the difference.

Still scowling, the woman tugged on the boy's arm. "Let's go, Reece."

Reece? His gaze snapped in her direction. Did she say Reece? He stared at the boy as the duo ran off. Towheaded and a barely-noticeable limp in the boy's step. Long pants and socks hid the boy's leg. Nah, it couldn't be. Could it? That would be too much of a coincidence.

But wasn't God the architect of coincidence?

He watched them until they disappeared among parked cars. Could it be? Why hadn't he taken a closer look at the boy's face?

And who was that woman? Definitely not Amanda, which meant he was being foolish. His desire to see his son was making him see things where they weren't.

Still . . .

He resisted chasing after them. If that was his son, he'd know for sure tomorrow morning when he met with Amanda for the first time in six years. Maybe soon, he'd be the one on the beach skipping stones.

# Chapter Two

"BANANA!" CALLIE NODDED AT the yellow Hummer coming toward them on the busy two-lane road. "That gives me three. Gotcha by one."

"But I beat you last time."

"Beginner's lu—"

"Banana. Banana." Reece pointed at the store parking lot on his side of the car.

"What? No way." Callie shot a quick glance to her right. Sure enough. There sat a yellow VW Beetle and a yellow Jeep. "Oh, pickles on meatloaf."

Reece giggled. "You're funny."

"Gee, thanks." Although she hadn't been too funny minutes before when she'd raged at that poor photographer. He hadn't done a thing wrong. How was he to know she hated—despised—having her picture taken? If she could go back and apologize she would, but then she'd become tongue-tied because he belonged in that same beautiful category as her parents and sister.

The category she'd flunked out of.

"We're gonna polish my agate now?" Reece tossed his stone in the air.

"Yep, after breakfast." But did polishing bring out the magnificence or only mask it? Her family would say polish away, but in matters of beauty, they weren't always right. Just mostly right.

She pulled into the driveway of the Tudor she shared with her parents and younger sister and parked her steel gray Nissan Cube behind the house. The lights were still off in the first floor, her parents' level. Good, then she could sneak up to her second-floor apartment without facing them yet. That would come later.

She opened the door that led to her separate apartment and tiptoed up the wooden stairs. Reece followed, his eight-year-old limbs pounding like a rhinoceros on a rampage. She turned and put a finger to her lips. "Shhh. Jess is still sleeping." He continued up, his steps quieting to Great Dane-sized noise. Oh well, if Jess didn't get her beauty sleep, she'd still look better than any of the other famous Jessicas seen in the movies.

The stairway led to another door which opened into her living room, where one hundred-year-old windows faced the lake. Sunlight streamed through, highlighting dust mote-filled air.

He ran past her to the kitchenette and tugged on the refrigerator. "Whatcha got to eat?"

"Hey, slow down there, bud." She cuffed her hands over his shoulders and led him around to the breakfast bar. "Have a seat and I'll whip you up some pancakes. How's that sound?"

"Got chocolate chips?"

"Well, duh. Of course, I've got chocolate chips." She bopped the top of his head. "What's a pancake without chocolate chips?"

"Sweet! My mom makes me use blueberries."

"Well, blueberries are good too." But berry picking season was a couple months away yet and she refused to use store-bought berries.

"Chocolate chips are better."

"You betcha." She combined pancake-making ingredients in a bowl. "You want your chips cooked in the batter or do you put them on afterwards?" With a plastic whisk, she blended the concoction.

"Can you make faces?"

"Can I make faces?" Shaking her head, she waggled a finger at Reece. "I'll have you know that I am the queen of making pancake faces."

He giggled. What an incredible sound.

She put a griddle over the only two burners on her stove, spritzed it with cooking spray, and turned on the gas.

"You gonna use those bullet-stopping gloves?"

"But of course." She opened the drawer next to the stove and dug out her Kevlar-coated oven mitts. She slipped one on each hand and angled them over her heart. "There," she said in her lousy British accent. "Now I can save you from all the bullets speeding through my home."

He giggled again.

She could spend the whole day hugging him, but then she wouldn't get the pancakes made and they'd both starve. "Bud, why don't you go through my bedroom to the porch? I've got my agate collection there. I'll call you when the pancakes are ready."

He ran into her bedroom, his footsteps probably sounding to her parents living below like she had a romping rhino. Did that kid ever walk?

With a chuckle, she removed her oven mitts and poured four cups of batter onto the griddle, puddling the batter into four separate circles. She waited a half a minute then created mouth lines out of chocolate chips on each. After they bubbled and dried around the edges, she flipped the pancakes. Delectably golden brown. While they cooked, she took her bottle of home-tapped maple syrup out of the refrigerator.

Maybe next March she'd be teaching others, especially children, how to tap maple trees and make their own syrup. Nothing would be more fun.

Humming, she flipped the pancakes onto plates. The smiles were perfect. She added a strawberry to each for the nose. Kiwi slices made large eyes on two of the pancakes. She used bananas on the others. Fun and delicious and even somewhat healthy. She sliced a Gala apple, took two pieces and glued them together with peanut butter, forming lips, and then added mini marshmallows for teeth. Breakfast was much more fun with kids around. It was bound to taste better too.

She set the plates on the bar along with glasses of orange juice. Now that was a good breakfast. Although it probably wouldn't be near enough food for that eating machine who was being too quiet on her porch. She walked through her bedroom and out French doors onto a windowed porch.

Her place of respite.

The table to her right was filled with well-worn jeans that would soon undergo a resurrection. Next to that was her agate collection. To her left, angled in the corner, stood her easel. And Reece. He'd discovered her charcoal pencils and was creating what looked like a monster truck.

"Hey bud, you hungry?"

He whipped around, his eyes wide. "It's ready?"

"And getting cold."

He threw his pencil toward the easel and zoomed out of the room. The pencil bounced off the paper and danced on the hardwood floor. He'd probably be seated with the first bite in his mouth by the time she placed the pencil back in its tray. Oh, to have that kind of energy and enthusiasm.

With her new job, she just might.

She joined Reece at the breakfast bar and nudged him with her elbow as he forked the final bite of one pancake, a piece with a banana eye. "Did you pray?"

"Oops. Forgot." He folded his hands and squeezed his eyes shut. "ComeLordJesusbeourguest . . . "

Callie's mind swirled with the speed of his prayer. It was as fast as his feet.

"Amen!" In a single motion, he had that pancake in his mouth and then washed it down with orange juice.

"Did you even enjoy that or did you just inhale it?" She popped the first bite into her mouth and savored the maple syrup. God hid so much sweetness behind the maple tree's bark.

"It was the best ever!" He coated his next pancake with butter then smothered it with maple syrup. Well, the way the kid ran, he could do that and still stay skinny as a sapling. "Mom never makes anything fun."

"That's not a mom's job, but it is mine." She scooped her second pancake onto Reece's quickly-emptying plate. "I'm guessing two isn't enough."

"Uh-uh," he said with his mouth full, and spewed small chunks onto the counter.

"Dude, that's just nasty."

"Sorry, Aunt Callie." More chunks flew, then he took his napkin and smeared the mess over the butcher block bar top.

She cocked her head to the side. "Why don't you let me clean it up? You worry about eating with your mouth closed."

"Mom says the same thing." He looked at her, spitting more pancake.

"Oh, fudge on the floor!" She drew a napkin over her face. "You have got to be the messiest kid north of Minneapolis."

"Uh-uh, Julio is."

"Julio?"

"My best buddy. We have dirt contests, and he always wins."

She couldn't help but giggle, and covered her mouth before she had more to clean up.

Less than a minute later, a plate with syrup remnants sat in front of Reece. "Can I be excused?"

Ah, so the kid did have some manners. "You betcha, but go wash your hands and your face first, stickyman. Then we'll polish up your stone."

She enjoyed the remainder of her pancake in silence. Someday she'd have a kid just like Reece. At least that was her prayer. But first she had to find a man who truly saw her.

"Snap out of it, Callie girl." Terrific, now she was talking to herself. Shaking her head, she gathered up the plates and silverware and arranged them in her tiny dishwasher. "There's more to life than romance." Unless romance with God's creation counted. She was completely in love with that and couldn't wait to work with it full time. But first, she had to tell her parents.

Later today. After she took Reece home. For now, she would enjoy the child's non-stop energy.

She joined him on her porch where he stood by her rock collection of mostly unpolished agates.

"Are you going to polish these?" He picked up a thimble-sized stone and tossed it from hand to hand.

"Some, maybe." She chose another rock and let it rest in the palm of her hand. "I like polished rocks but . . . " With her thumb, she rolled the stone around. "But sometimes I want to remember that beauty isn't all about polishing off our rough edges. I figure it's God's job to do that.

My job is to see beauty in all of His creation."

"Oh." He stood still, chewing the lower left side of his lip while squinting down at his rock.

"Want to polish it now?" Callie pointed to the rock tumbler.

His mouth shifted, but his squint remained. "Nah. I think it's perfect already."

"That's my boy." Now, if only she could get adults to see the same thing. Specifically her parents once she relayed her news later today.

She prayed they'd be as accepting as Reece.

HAVEN PARKED HIS BUICK Lucerne in front of the 1920s two-story he and Amanda had chosen ten years ago. He rubbed perspiring hands on his jeans while praying for guidance, praying Amanda would see he was a changed man, and that he deserved a second chance with Reece. With her too, if she'd allow it. Not that he had feelings for her anymore. Those had all been washed away when she'd banished him from their home and from a relationship with Reece. But if anyone could mend their broken family, God could.

He got out of his car and studied their once worn-looking house now updated with tan siding and reddish shutters. Amanda had turned it into the picture-perfect home they'd dreamed of. The stone retaining wall abutting the sidewalk looked new, and colorful perennials now skirted the home's foundation. Flowering plants hung from the eaves of the porch where he used to enjoy a beer or three. Or more.

But back then, Amanda had partied right along with him. Hopefully, single motherhood had mellowed her, as loss of fatherhood had certainly molded him.

He retrieved the purple flowers from his passenger seat. Amanda had always loved her perennial gardens. Maybe this small token would soften her a bit. He strode up the sidewalk, across the open porch, and poised his hand by the door.

Would Amanda recognize the changes in him? Would that be enough for her to give him another chance? To give their family another chance? Their son deserved to have a two-parent family.

He swallowed the grapefruit-sized lump in his throat and rapped his knuckles on the door.

"One second." A muffled voice called from inside. Amanda's voice.

He held his breath until the door opened.

Then held it some more. His absent years had treated her well. She'd cut her hair to her chin. Auburn waves added fullness to her narrow face. A face with chestnut eyes, high cheekbones, and full lips that still looked enticing even with her frown. A fitted T-shirt that read Nurses Rock hugged her curves, as did her jeans. And those jeans were painted like a mural with scenes spotlighting music, medicine, and nature, those very things she'd had a passion for years before. The things that had drawn him to her.

He could learn to love her again, couldn't he? For their son, he'd do anything.

Her precisely shaped brows rose. "Are you just going to stand there and stare?"

He blinked. Wonderful way to begin. He handed her the flower arrangement. "I see you still like flowers."

Her lips hinted at a smile. "You never used to notice."

Oh, he'd noticed. He just hadn't cared. Back then, life had been about him alone. Until he realized how lonely selfishness was.

"That's not the only way I've changed." He looked past her into the house, hoping to catch a glimpse of his son.

"He's not here."

Oh.

"I felt it important that only you and I talk first." She motioned him in.

He stepped across the threshold he'd once carried Amanda over, though without the benefit of marriage. Back then marriage had been an old-fashioned idea. Why bother when he got all the privileges of marriage without the hassle or expense? Back then, Amanda had wanted a wedding merely to be a princess for the day, not because she wanted to be married. If they had been married, his eviction would have been much more difficult, so she was likely happy that they'd never made it official.

"I see you've made all the changes we'd talked about." The living room's hardwood floors had been refinished, and the walls had been stripped of that hideous velvet wallpaper. They were now painted a light taupe, just the way he'd always wanted. "It looks great."

"Thanks." She stood by the couch, her arms crossed over her chest. "It really has become my dream home."

A dream home without him in it.

Would she want it to remain that way?

The Yamaha piano they had once played side by side still sat against the wall opposite the picture window overlooking the porch. He walked over to it and played a few measures of Mozart's Fugue in C-minor. Perfectly tuned. He glanced over his shoulder. "You still play?" That could be a starting point for their reconciliation.

"A little." She shrugged.

"And Reece?" When Amanda was pregnant, they'd dreamed of their son becoming a concert pianist.

"No interest. He'd rather be outside running and climbing."

Like the boy he'd seen at the shoreline yesterday.

She gestured to the couch that had been their first major purchase for the home.

He settled in and rested his hand on the leather arm. A stone fireplace was centered on the wall across from him. On the mantel sat an eight-by-ten picture of a boy wading in a creek, grinning, clearly unashamed of the metal prosthetic foot that started just above where his ankle should have been.

Excitement tingled through his body. It was the same boy he'd watched climb the rocks yesterday. The very same rocks that had mangled his foot beyond saving. Amazing. Clearly, Amanda had done an exceptional job as a single mother.

He prayed she'd consider sharing those parenting duties. But that part of the conversation needed to be worked in gradually. He nodded to the portrait. "Reece looks healthy. Happy."

"He is." She sat on the coffee-colored chair next to the fireplace and tucked slender legs beneath her. "But that's not your point coming today, is it." Typical Amanda. No beating around the bush.

"Thanks for finally seeing me." Focusing on her, he rubbed his palms on his jeans. "It's time we talked about what happened."

She folded her hands in her lap and looked down at them. "I've been wanting to talk too. For a while. I couldn't get up the nerve."

"You have?"

She nodded. "I appreciate that you've never missed a support payment. And I could tell you've changed, by your letters. Maybe I just needed to see that in person. You do seem different."

"I haven't had a drink since that night." And temptation was always drowned out by the image of what he'd done to his son.

"I'm proud of you." A twinkle sparked in her eyes. "I gave up the party scene too."

"Glad to hear it." He didn't want his son growing up in a home where getting drunk was an acceptable form of entertainment.

"And Reece is doing amazingly well. He's better adjusted than I ever was."

Haven leaned toward her. "Tell me about him." For six years, he'd hungered to hear the slightest snippet about his son.

"I want to know about you first. Why are you back here? Didn't you have a good job in Minneapolis?"

"I did, but a friend convinced me there was something more important than making money. And then I got a freelance photography offer for the area. I took that as a sign from God."

She laughed and shook her head. "So, you came to beg me to lower your child support. Of all the—"

"No! That's not it at all." He brushed both hands through his hair. "I'd rather starve than renege on that. Besides, I've got a new job, starting in a couple weeks."

"Still collecting?"

He shrugged. "I'm good at it."

"I know. You once sweet talked me." She set her jaw. "You should know, it won't work anymore."

Closing his eyes, he gritted his teeth. This was not going at all like he planned. "Amanda, let me start over."

She crossed her arms over her chest. "By all means."

"I'm sorry. I know those words are inadequate for what happened six years ago, but they're all I've got. I'm sorry I shirked my responsibilities. I'm sorry I chose to drink over watching Reece." He glanced upward and blinked the burn from his eyes. "I'm sorry I wasn't there for him." He clenched his fists to silence their tremble. "I'm sorry I've been gone since then."

She picked at her fingernails. Apparently, still her nervous habit. "You didn't have a choice about that. I didn't want you anywhere near him." She stood and walked to the fireplace. With a sigh, she picked up Reece's picture. "I forgive you," she whispered.

"You do?" Tears stung his eyes.

"It could have happened to me too. Life was one big party. We were horrible parents."

"Were, Amanda, were." Haven joined her at the fireplace and took the picture from her. "Tell me about him."

"He's eight now."

*I know that.* He clamped his mouth tight to avoid a retort.

"Just finished second grade. He loves being outside and anything Duluth Bulldogs—"

"Like my dad."

"Yeah, just like your dad." She touched the prosthetic in the picture. "And he runs everywhere."

"Runs." Haven shook his head. And climbs rocks. Activities Haven had always assumed he'd stolen from his son.

"I know. It amazes me. And in a few weeks, he's running in the children's Whipper Snapper race before Grandma's Marathon. I couldn't be prouder."

And Haven had missed all those precious moments leading up to this. Partly because Amanda had told him never to return. Partly because he knew he deserved his banishment.

But his son also deserved a father, and Haven had cheated Reece out of that.

"Amanda . . ." He took her hand and she didn't yank it away. "You've clearly done an incredible job, but he needs a father too—"

"I know." She drew her hand from his and returned to her chair. "That's why I agreed to meet with you."

"Really?" He sat back on the sofa, and tried to hold the grin off his face. Yes, God answered prayers, but this quickly?

"I've been seeing someone."

His grin slid away. "Is it serious?"

"He moved in a month ago."

"What?" He jerked up straight. "You're shacking up with someone in front of our son?"

"Excuse me?" Her eyes fired lasers across the room. "What do you think *we* did for three years?"

Touché. He sank into the couch, his hopes for reconciliation plummeting. "Living with you was wrong."

"That's right." She smirked. "You wrote that you'd gotten religion."

"I'm a Christian."

She pointed to herself. "And we go to church as a family."

"That doesn't make . . . " He clamped his mouth shut. Moralizing wouldn't help matters at all. At least they were going to church. "That's good then. I'm glad."

"Bill's a great father to Reece."

His stomach churned at the idea that someone else could claim that father role.

"And that's why I agreed to talk with you." Amanda folded her hands on her lap.

Foreboding roiled in his gut like rotten meat. He stared at her, his jaw tight.

"We want to release you from your financial obligations."

"What? Why?" He nearly growled.

She took a deep breath then puffed it out. "Bill and I, we're getting married. Bill's like a father to Reece and wants to adopt him. Then you can be completely free."

## Chapter Three

FREE? WHEN SHE'D JUST slammed shut the door to fatherhood? Haven jumped to his feet. "No way in—" He bit back the remainder of his sentence and continued with a tightened jaw. "There's no way I'm relinquishing my rights."

"You did that a long time ago."

"Not on paper, I didn't. We had a verbal agreement that I'd stay away." Accompanied with threats from her lawyer father. Back then Haven didn't have the means or the will to fight. That had all changed.

"An agreement I want to make formal."

Haven fisted his hands at his side. "It's not happening. As a matter of fact, I intend to get visitation rights."

"Good luck with that. Bill's an attorney, and my dad still practices."

"So what?" His tone rose. "You're not keeping Reece from me any longer."

Amanda stood, her gaze piercing his. "There's no way you'd win."

Haven stepped close enough to Amanda to feel her hot breath. "I may just go for custody."

She pushed him away. "Get out of my house."

"I'm not leaving—" Déjà vu slammed him in the chest. "No." He gritted out. He wasn't going to repeat that conversation, that behavior, from six years ago. This time he was going to do it right.

"No?" She raised her eyebrows.

"I won't be threatened by you. I'm not leaving. Not again." That was the coward's way out. He hated involving attorneys, hated what a legal fight would do to Reece. Amanda, of all people, should know better.

She'd never overcome her parents' split. But what choice did he have?

*God, where are you in this?*

Silence answered, but that didn't mean God wasn't there. It just meant Haven had to listen harder, and that couldn't be done here, not with this anger in the way. He strode to the door then turned around. "This isn't over."

"That's what you think."

"It's what I know." Hard to believe he once thought he loved this woman. And to think he came here to reconcile. He jerked open the door and jumped back, startled. The beret-wearing, camera-hating woman from Canal Park stood poised to knock.

And his son stood beside her.

Hot anger melted into near tears. More than anything, he wanted to envelop the boy in a hug, but the last thing Haven wanted was to frighten his son.

He nodded to the woman and smiled at Reece. The boy smiled back. An amazing smile. With a quick nod, Haven whisked past the two and jogged to his car.

He'd get his hug. Soon. Once Reece was ready.

Maybe Amanda had lawyers in her corner, but Haven had God in his.

He got in his Buick and slumped in his seat. Did God take sides in custody battles? Clutching the steering wheel, he looked down the street. The old familiar liquor store still sat there, seducing Haven with its offering of peace.

For the first time in years, his hands shook as alcohol's sirens sang out to him, promising to take away his pain.

He pinched his eyes shut, but the liquor store was imprinted on his eyelids.

"God, I need your help here." An O'Doul's would go down nice and smooth back at his dad's place, and his dad had gone fishing up north for the next couple of days. No one would know. Drinking wouldn't hurt Haven's chances with Reece. It would just medicate the pain. Just for today.

*Call Eric.*

He fingered the phone in his pocket. He hadn't had to call his sponsor in years, not as a sponsor anyway. He and Eric had become good friends. Eric could talk him out of this.

Trembling, he grabbed the phone and threw it onto the backseat floor. Not today. Today he was going to give in to alcohol's glorious forgetfulness and get rip-roaring drunk.

And if Amanda succeeded in stealing Reece forever?

Well, he'd no longer have a reason to stay sober.

CALLIE PULLED BACK THE drawn curtains of Amanda's picture window above the loveseat and peeked out. The surfer-cute photographer from the beach—Reece's father!—hadn't moved. His car hadn't, anyway. It still sat in front of her Cube. The man was shaking his head, and he seemed to be having a one-way conversation.

Callie'd had enough of those talks with God that she understood. It made her want to reach out and help him.

But that was foolishness. The man was a stranger to her. An enemy to her best friend. Still, God often used the foolish for His purposes. Biting on her lower lip, she took one more glance out.

"Is he still there?" Amanda returned from her kitchen, handed Callie a bottled water, and sat on the loveseat. With Reece in his bedroom, supposedly cleaning, they were free to talk.

"Yep." Callie twisted the cap off the bottle. "I take it things didn't go too well."

Amanda sighed. "I thought he'd be thrilled to give up his rights. Give him a fresh start with no obligations, but no, he wants visitation."

"Is that really so bad?"

"He hasn't seen Reece in six years!"

"By choice?"

Amanda looked down and muttered, "No."

"What happened, Mandy?" Callie sat beside Mandy and laid a hand on her friend's arm. "Why shouldn't he have visitation?" Callie knew what happened to Reece, but she didn't know what role Haven had played in it. In all their years of friendship, Mandy had said precious little about Reece's father. Callie glanced out through the curtains again. The man still sat there. Was he planning something? "Give me a good reason, and you know I'll fight for you."

"All right." Amanda picked at her fingernails. "I was out one night with my sister, and Haven promised to watch Reece—only he decided he had to celebrate a job promotion instead. He hired the next-door neighbor's daughter to babysit and went out drinking. Haven was out getting smashed at the same time Reece's little foot was getting crushed by a boulder on the beach." Amanda peered up with tear-glossed eyes. "It wasn't the first time he made that choice. That's why Haven can't see Reece. He always chose partying over his son, and it finally cost all of us. Especially Reece. I told Haven to stay out of our lives, and I meant it."

"But you didn't make it legal?"

"No." She kept picking at her nails. "All I had to do was threaten him with mentioning Daddy's law firm. We agreed on child support, and he always paid."

"And you always took his money."

Her head snapped up. "Of course, I did."

"Hasn't he changed since then? He doesn't sound like a louse to me."

"Should that matter? We had an agreement. Haven coming back in my life right now will mess everything up all over again."

"So, it's not about Reece, but you."

"Don't I deserve some happiness?"

"Don't you think Reece deserves an opportunity to know his father?"

"Bill is all the father Reece needs."

Callie put an arm around Amanda, tucking her friend's head against her shoulder. "Bill's a good man, but that man sitting out in his car, having it out with God, I have a sense he's a good man too."

"How would you know?"

"I met him before. Just this morning at Canal Park. And that man who opened the door, he's hurting."

"Whoa, back up there." Mandy jerked up straight and stared at Callie. "You saw him on the beach? What was he doing there?"

A vision of Haven's camera pointed at her made her shudder. She swallowed, trying to ease her nerves. "He was taking pictures of the sunrise."

Mandy grunted. "Right. Well, I don't believe in coincidences."

"I don't either." But she did believe in God-ordained moments. There had to be a reason both Haven and Reece were at the park this morning and at the same time.

Photographing her and Reece.

A chill slinked down her spine. Had he been stalking them?

No. That man she'd encountered this morning showed no signs of recognition, and he'd been very apologetic. Her toes tapping the floor, she swallowed her unease. "I could tell Haven had no clue who Reece was."

"Whatever." Mandy waved her hand. "Doesn't matter anyway. Bill thinks we should—"

"This isn't up to Bill." Callie pointed to Amanda's heart. "What's your heart saying?"

Mandy slouched, her jaw working back and forth. "Maybe you're right. Maybe he should get to see Reece once in a while. But . . ." Mandy looked toward the curtained window.

"Out with it, dearie."

Mandy's gaze bore into Callie's. "I'll let him see Reece if you're with them too."

HAVEN INSERTED THE KEY into the ignition, and the liquor store called to him. Six years of sobriety about to be thrown away because of Amanda. Right now, that didn't matter.

He turned the key.

Silence.

Not even a click.

He took a deep breath and tried it again.

Still nothing.

Stupid car. He rammed his fists against the steering wheel. Barely two years old and it was the third time this has happened. He retrieved his cell phone from the backseat floorboard and called his insurance company's roadside assistance number. After waiting on hold and listening to annoying Muzak, he was assured that a truck would be there within the hour to charge the battery.

Within the hour. Sixty interminable minutes sitting outside Amanda's house, a mere one hundred feet away from the son he might never get to know.

Haven pounded the dashboard then squeezed his head in his hands while gazing downhill at the liquor store. Three short blocks stood between him and mind-numbing relief. He could get out and walk. But then Amanda might see him, and her attorney father would make full use of that knowledge.

He closed his eyes and slunk down in his seat. "God, I'm—"

A knock sounded on his window and he cringed. Probably Amanda demanding to know why he was stalking her. Another point for her in the case against him.

Gritting his teeth, he sat up and opened his eyes, prepared to respond gently to her accusations, but another woman's face appeared at the window. The woman from the beach. So, Amanda was having someone else do her dirty work. Figured. Well, he could diplomatically send this woman away too.

"Can we talk?" She spoke loudly. And with a smile.

Oh brother. He pushed the window button. It didn't move.

Duh! If the battery was dead, then obviously, the windows wouldn't work either. After that service truck arrived, Haven would drive to the nearest dealer and trade this lemon in for a cheap car that didn't have all the electronic gadgets that could go wrong. What was wrong with hand-cranking a window anyway?

"Battery's dead." He yelled back. "I'll get out." And kindly tell her all communiqués would be between their attorneys.

She backed away.

And he stepped out of the car onto the blacktop and looked down on her. The top of her head barely came to his shoulders. "What do you want?"

Her eyes grew wide, and she drew back.

And he was being a jerk. He shook out his shoulders and took a deep breath. "I'm sorry, that was uncalled for." He pocketed his hands, determined to be the kind of man God called him to be. "How can I help you?"

Her body relaxed, and a slight smile drew on her face. "Hey, I understand. You've just had a meeting with mama bear, and she had her claws fully extended."

In spite of his foul mood, he laughed at the oh-so-true visual. "That's one way to put it."

She offered her hand. "I'm Callie Beaumont. Mandy's my best friend."

Mandy? Amanda had hated that name ever since her dad told her she was named after Barry Manilow's hit titled "Mandy." And why was Amanda sending her friend out to do her dirty work? Smelled like rotten fish.

Ignoring Callie's outstretched hand, he crossed his arms and planted his feet a foot apart. "Then I guess you already know who I am."

She retracted her hand, and her shoulders drooped, dragging her gaze along with them.

He groaned inwardly. Oh, he was a heel. Didn't matter that Callie was Amanda's friend, he was called to be a light, but all he was showing her was inky darkness. "I'm sorry. I'm being a first-class jerk. Forgive me?"

Her gaze lifted to his and she nodded, but her inviting expression had disappeared, stolen by him. He refused to let Amanda change the man he'd become since they broke up, so he took a deep breath and stuck out his hand. "Let's start over again. I'm banishing the jerk you first met. Hopefully he stays gone."

She graciously took his hand even though her smile hadn't returned. "Haven Carlysle. Reece's father."

"I see the resemblance."

"You do?" A burst of delight prompted a smile.

"The hair color. Your eyes when you smile."

He rubbed his chin, trying to make his pleasure less obvious. Callie had to be a salesperson. She'd effectively thrown him off his game plan to get a drink. Or was it God's perfect timing? Still, he had a message for Amanda, and if Callie was her go-to, then Callie would get the unfortunate task of delivering it. Forcing his lips into a straight line, he crossed his arms again, but kept his tone lighter, hoping to come across as matter-of-fact rather than crotchety. "Can you please make it clear to Amanda that my attorney will contact hers? Until then, I'll leave her alone."

Callie cocked her head to the side. "You'll be happy to know she's changed her mind about visitation. For now, anyway."

His arms fell to his side and he blinked, hardly daring to hope. "What do you mean?" Amanda was going to allow him visitation? Please God, let it be so.

"It means, for the moment, she's offering you a chance to reacquaint yourself with Reece. Now, I know she's fickle, and her mind changes as often as Minnesota weather—"

*Tell me about it.*

"—so, if I were you, I'd take her up on the offer, even with the caveat."

"Whoa." He raised his hands, palms outward. "What stipulation are we talking about?"

Callie looked at the ground and drew a figure eight on the blacktop with her foot. "She'll allow visitation as long as I come with you to chaperone."

He laughed. "Oh, that's rich."

She raised her hands. "Hey, I don't like it any more than you, but those are her conditions, and I'm certain you remember how obstinate she is."

Oh, he remembered. Her hatred of him had lasted six years so far and was showing no signs of waning. With his heel, he kicked backward at his car's tire. "What's the catch?"

"Catch?"

"Are you supposed to find dirt on me and report back to her? Or is she afraid I'll take Reece and run?"

She crossed her arms. "Cynical, aren't you?"

"Do you blame me?"

She sighed. "No, I guess not." She puffed out a breath and her bangs fluttered. "No, I'm not snooping into your life. But she hasn't seen you in six years. Would you send your son off alone with someone who'd been away that long? Isn't your son worth this little inconvenience?"

This woman was making too much sense. No wonder Amanda trusted her. He stuffed his hands in his front pockets. "Okay. Give me the details. I'll do whatever it takes. No argument."

"Awesome. I had a feeling you'd agree."

"How? You don't know me, and I'm certain Amanda hasn't painted a complimentary picture either."

She shrugged. "I have a sixth sense about people. I call it God's nudgings."

A smile crept to his lips. "God doesn't generally nudge me, it's more like a slap in the face to wake me up." And run from that liquor store. He shivered. To think he'd almost given in.

"I get that too." Her gaze drifted to the house then back to Haven. "Anyway, here's the deal. Mandy said take it or leave it. First, she has to talk to Reece and explain who you are. I have no clue what he knows about you, so be prepared for any reaction. You can see Reece every Tuesday night because she and Bill are taking an art class together. I'll meet you here at five, and he has to be home by seven."

"Two hours?" They could barely go to McDonald's in that time.

"Would you rather have nothing?"

"Two hours is great." He deadpanned.

"Thought you'd say that. Hold on a sec. I'll grab my business card." She stepped back, her foot caught in a pothole, and she started to topple.

Haven caught her arm, preventing her from falling on her backside.

And her entire face blushed, making a diminutive diamond in her nose stand out. "Oh, crackers and cheese!"

"Huh?"

She stood straight, and the crimson slowly faded from her cheeks as he released her arm. "Don't mind me. I'm the queen of goofy exclamations." She shook her head then nodded toward her car. "I'll get my card from the Seussmobile."

His smile became a grin. "Seussmobile?"

"Well, yeah. Look at its funky windows. It had to be inspired by a Dr. Seuss book."

He couldn't help but laugh. She was right about the car. And no wonder Reece seemed to enjoy Callie. She probably had a sixth sense about how to deal with kids too. Maybe it was a good thing she'd be there chaperoning them.

Because when it came to kids, he knew absolutely nothing.

# Chapter Four

*IDIOT!* CALLIE GRIMACED AS she hurried to her car. Crackers and cheese? Seussmobile? Why, when staring at those blue eyes and brownish-blond locks, did she have to go all sixth grade on him? Could she at least act her age until she got her business card to him? Was it any wonder men avoided her more than they avoided chick flicks?

And then he had to go and grin with teeth almost as perfect as her parents'. She was no better than Jess, drooling over a man's good looks without having a glimpse of his heart.

Okay, maybe she'd gotten a tiny glimpse of his heart, and what she saw she really liked, but—and it was a big but—men who won the DNA lottery never noticed a plain Jane like her.

And why, oh why, should that matter! She was just as superficial as the rest of her family.

Speaking of which . . .

She checked her watch. Almost four o'clock already. Almost time to share her plans with those perfect parents and pray they'd understand.

If they didn't, would she go against their wishes?

She pulled a business card from her car. It was time to get home and prepare for their Saturday supper, the one time each week the four of them would sit together and talk.

Rather, her folks would talk. Jess would agree. Callie would do whatever she could to keep from rolling her eyes.

She strode to Haven and handed him the card. "You can reach me at work most days, and I don't mind if you call there. It's a family business and they can't fire me." Although she wished they would. That would make her plans sooo much easier to follow through on.

"Thanks." He handed over his card.

Capturing Beauty Nature Photography. A freelance photographer, just like he said. So why was he taking pictures of her? The dude better have a keener eye than that.

"What is this place?" Haven held her card between two fingers and turned it over. "Superior Office Suites. Do you rent out office spaces?"

Arghh. Business on a Saturday. Time to turn on the professional marketer. Oh, she hated it, but she smiled anyway, just like she was paid to do. "Yes, we rent offices and secretarial services. It's perfect for the independent business owner who needs an office and the periodic assistant but can't afford to pay an employee. You just pay her per services rendered. And our location is the best you'll find. Not only does the first floor of our building house some of the best local small businesses in the city, but each of our offices has a view of Lake Superior."

"Interesting. Any type of business welcome?"

"Absolutely. Right now, we're renting to an interior decorator and a model, along with a website creator, cosmetics consultant, and landscape designer. A photographer would fit right in."

"Hmm." He rubbed a hand over his lightly-whiskered chin. "That's exactly what I've been looking for. My editor asked me to find a better location for her, looking to cut costs like everyone else. You've got office space open?"

"We have one empty office. It doesn't view the lake head-on, but you can see it."

"No big deal. When can I stop in and have a look?"

"I'll be there at eight Monday morning."

"Great. I'll see you then." He stuffed her card into his wallet then touched her arm. "And I really do appreciate what you're doing for me and Reece. It means more to me than you can imagine."

"I just want the best for Reece. He's my buddy."

"I'm glad for that." He nodded then looked beyond her. "Looks like my help is coming." He pointed down the street at the service truck chugging up the steep hill. "I'll see you on Monday . . . and Tuesday."

"Okie doke." Oh please, she did not just say that, did she? Get a grip, Callie girl. She kicked at the asphalt and bent back her toe. "Ouch," she muttered, shaking off the pain and reigning in another goofy phrase. Why did he have to go and be so nice? Before she knew it, she'd have a teenage-sized crush on the man, a photographer no less.

But she'd learned her lesson years ago, the very hard way. Photographers searching for beauty would always look right past her. No way was she going to repeat that lesson.

CALLIE FINISHED APPLYING HER makeup and smiled at her reflection. Not too bad. Creating the perfect façade to show her parents would help her delivery of her news. Maybe by the end of the evening they'd be cheering her on.

"You ready, Cal?" Jess appeared in the bathroom doorway, dressed in shimmery satin that highlighted her voluptuous figure. "Hey, you look terrific."

"You think so?" Callie looked down at her shapeless black sheathe that announced to the world she hadn't graduated from her training bra yet.

"Hey, I don't lie about beauty."

Callie chuckled. That was so true. As a model for plus-size clothing, Jess took outward appearances very seriously.

"Lead the way." Callie motioned toward the stairs. Their stiletto heels clicking on the staircase, Callie trailed her younger sister down to the first-floor landing. Separate doors led to their upstairs dwelling and to their parents' living space. Neither was ever locked, but her parents respected Callie's and Jess's privacy. For the most part, that made living here feel like she was on her own and not still living in her parents' home.

Jess pulled open the six-panel door and walked into their parents' apartment with the grace and confidence of a model walking a New York runway. Callie followed her into the dining room where the table was set for royalty with its Mikasa place settings and Lenox flatware on a lace tablecloth. Ice water already filled the crystal goblets. She'd be happy if this presentation was made to show how special their family was, that they deserved nothing but the best. But this table staging was as much of a façade as her makeup.

She sat in her usual chair with her back to the window, and Jess sat across from her.

"There you are." Her mother glided from the kitchen on three-inch stilettos. Her burgundy dress cinched at the waist and flowed outward. It looked like something Ingrid Bergman would have worn in one of those old-time movies. Her mother wore it well while carrying the first course: cucumber shrimp appetizers.

Her dad followed in his navy suit and tie, carting a bottle of white wine. Even nearing fifty, her dad still turned heads. "You ladies look lovely tonight." He filled her flute and gave her a kiss on the cheek, then did the same with Jess.

Jess raised her chin and smiled, showing off perfect white teeth. "And you look dashing as ever."

"Thank you, dear." He winked at Jess and then kissed their mom while pulling out her chair.

Their mom spread a cloth napkin in her lap, and their dad took his seat beside Callie.

They didn't offer a prayer of thanks for the food, like her grandma had taught, but Callie bowed her head and offered a silent thank you while her mother served up the appetizer. Then her mom dove right into their business for the week. "I see the office suites still have a vacancy."

Precisely the opening conversation Callie expected, but at least she had good news to report this time. "Someone's coming in Monday morning. A magazine is considering the space."

"A magazine?" Her dad held his fork midair. "Intriguing. Which one?"

"I didn't get the name, but I believe it's a local nature magazine."

"That sounds like a delightful way to round out our clientele, don't you think so, Kenneth?" Her mother dabbed a napkin at the corner of her lips.

Delightful. Callie resisted rolling her eyes. Gag me with a ladle.

"I quite agree, Mackenzie." He forked a piece of shrimp. "Jessica, dear, you'll be there to help make the presentation, won't you?"

Jess? Callie clutched her fork, wanting to slam it down. *Aren't I good enough?*

"I should be, I've got—"

"You will be." Their mother nailed Jess with a stare.

Well, if Jess wouldn't say no, Callie would do it for her. "I can do—"

"That is your sister's job." Mother waved her fork toward Callie. "We must make the absolute best first impression. People make their minds up in the first seconds of seeing the space."

*And just what kind of impression do I make?* Her chin quivered, and she clenched her teeth, trying to still it.

"Jessica, answer your mother please." Her father's gaze remained on his meal. For once, couldn't he stand up to their mother? Stand up for his daughters?

Jess stirred the food on her plate but didn't touch it. "Yes sir, I will be there."

"Very good. As for the next line of business—"

"I have something to add." Callie clutched the napkin in her lap. If she didn't speak now, she might never have the courage.

Her mother slapped her fork on the table. "That was rude, Callista. We'll pencil your business in at the end."

"Yes ma'am." She resisted slouching. Proper posture must always be maintained to make the best impression.

"This week I'll be going in for my Botox injection." Her mother pointed to the faint crow's-feet shooting from the corners of her eyes. "And Jessica, per your agent's suggestion, we've arranged a personal trainer for you."

Jess moaned, and her shoulders hunched. "I do fine on my own."

"That may have been true in previous years, but your agent says the demand for shapely plus-size models is dwindling."

"But not dead."

"Dear, if you ever want to take your modeling career beyond Minnesota, you must conform to the needs of the industry. If your father and I had taken that approach at the onset of our careers, we may have landed positions in a larger city rather than this little town." She spread her arms apart, holding palms up. "Is this what you want for yourself?"

Jess shoved her otherwise untouched food in circles. "I don't know."

*Stand up for yourself, Jess. Don't let them bully you into something you don't want. Or need.* Jess wasn't stick-bug skinny like the average runway model. No, she was normal, and that made her beauty stand out all the more.

Her mother patted Jess's hand. "This is for the good of your career."

"I guess." Jess jabbed her fork into a piece of shrimp.

"That's my girl." Their mom beamed, showing off impossibly white teeth. "And, Callista, we've asked Dr. Kallos about breast augmentation for you."

"You what?" Callie dropped her fork and it clattered on her plate, bouncing a piece of shrimp onto her parents' pristine hardwood. "I have no—"

"He says it's very helpful for those with self-esteem—"

Callie shoved away from the table and stood, wiggling but not toppling the wine glasses. "No." She crossed arms over her apparently too-small chest. "No way. Absolutely not." Tears loosed from her eyes, probably carrying dark streams of mascara down her cheeks. "I'm good enough just the way God made me." Now, if she could only convince herself of that fact. "And just so you know, in four weeks I'm starting a new job as a naturalist for the state parks. Out there, they couldn't care less if I'm a perfect Barbie doll."

Her mother dropped her fork, and her mouth gaped open.

"Callie girl." Her father reached for her.

She jerked away and ran from her parents' apartment, upstairs to her bathroom where she stared in the mirror. Just as she expected, black streaks began at her eyes and curved over her too-plump cheeks. The miniscule diamond nose stud was supposed to remind her that in God's eyes, she was more precious than priceless jewels. Today, like too many days, that reminder failed her. Why wasn't God's creation good enough for them? For her?

She lifted her breasts until the smallest hint of cleavage peeked from her dress. Would that raise her self-esteem? Would it make her more appealing to men?

Someone like Haven?

Right. She rolled her eyes. He wouldn't look at her twice once he met Jess on Monday. He'd look through her just like he had on their first brief meetings. Maybe her parents were right.

She heard a knock on the door. Sniffling, Callie glanced over at Jess, who offered a Hershey bar. "This always helps me."

"No thanks." Eating chocolate wouldn't make her acceptable to her parents. It certainly wouldn't make her beautiful.

Muffled footsteps echoed beyond her bathroom wall, two sets of hurried footsteps on her stairs. Shoulders slumping, she angled her head toward the ceiling. Figures, her parents couldn't let her be. She wet a cloth and wiped away the dark tracks beneath her eyes.

"Callista Lillian." Her mother appeared in the doorway, scooching in front of Jess, and their father stood behind Jess. Anger, not sympathy, tinged her voice and eyes. "What do you mean by—"

"Mackenzie." Her dad's voice held a stern warning, and her mom pinched her lips together. It was rare that her father spoke up against her mom, so it effectively quieted her. Dad hugged his arm around Jess's shoulders. "Jessica dear, would you mind cleaning up dinner dishes?"

She nodded and left the apartment without a word, leaving Callie alone to face the reprimand.

Feeling like a scolded child, she hugged herself and looked down at the black and white mosaic-tiled floor. Her hasty words at dinner had gotten her into enough trouble without heaping on more right now.

"Callie girl." Her father stepped past her mother and lifted her chin so she couldn't avoid looking in his eyes. "Your mother and I would like to talk with you, please."

Talk? All Callie wanted to do was hide. She shook his hand from her chin, stared at the floor, and mumbled. "Not today. Please."

"Sweetheart"—he laid a hand on her shoulder—"we've obviously hurt you, but if we don't know how or why, how can we stop from doing it again?"

She sniffled and grabbed a tissue to wipe her nose. How could she say no when her father was being so kind? Besides, by honoring her father and mother, even when she was angry, disappointed, and definitely disagreeing with them, she was hopefully showing Jesus to them. She nodded and gestured toward her living room.

Her mom led the way, cheeks taut and chin jutted in the air, her attempt to regain control over the situation. She settled on the padded rocker leaving the couch for Callie and her father.

She sat, squeezed against the arm. Thankfully, her father took the hint and sat at the opposite end of the couch.

He leaned forward, his elbows on his knees, hands folded, his gaze focused outward as he took an exaggerated breath. Then he turned his head toward Callie, his brows nearly knit together. "What did we say to upset you?"

She shook her head in bewilderment. How could they not know? "Why . . . why do you need to change me?"

"Change you?" His eyes narrowed and then closed. His broad shoulders seemed to wilt. "We thought that's what you wanted."

"What I wanted?" She shivered and barricaded her chest with crossed arms. "Where did you get that idea?"

"Callie girl." He took her hand. "It's obvious you're not happy with the way you look—"

"What?" It was obvious? She hugged herself even tighter. "How?" Her voice came out small and brittle.

"You think we don't notice when you put yourself down?" Her mom's voice still had an edge, but it had dulled. "When you compare yourself to Jessica?"

Callie kicked at the hardwood floor with her heel. She hadn't complained that much, had she?

Her father squeezed her hand. "And while your mother and I disagree with your assessment, we wanted to offer something, some way to help your confidence."

By getting a boob job? Proof that her parents didn't know her at all. She dared look into her parents' eyes. "All that does is make me more insecure. It tells me even you don't think I'm good enough."

Her father sighed, and he looked toward his wife.

She raised a brow, but the grim line of her mouth remained. "Fair enough. That topic is now off the table, but you've yet to explain your tantrum downstairs. What's this nonsense about quitting?"

So, just like that, their ridiculous offer was dismissed. It would be futile to try to state her point further, to try to express feelings they could never understand. And now she had the even more difficult job of convincing them this new position would be good and healthy for her, far better than any medically-changed outward appearance. She sat up straight, chin forward like her mother taught, hoping to demonstrate the same confidence her mother always showed. "It's not nonsense, Mom. I finally have an opportunity to use my degree, to follow my dream."

"Why haven't we heard about this before?" Her father's brows slinked close together.

With that seemingly benign question, her confidence fell to the floor. With her heel, Callie drew circles on the hardwood. She said, barely above a whisper, "You never wanted to hear about it."

The glare was back in her mom's eyes. "What are you talking about? We put you through college. Isn't that enough?"

"No, it's not." Callie's voice rose, and she returned her mom's glare.

Her mom waggled a finger. "You will not—"

"Mackenzie."

"You'll let her disrespect us like that?"

"Darling." He took his wife's hand. "It's time we listen."

Her mom's cheeks tightened, and she pressed her lips together. "Fine. Callista, why is this the first we're hearing about your new job?"

Callie sighed. "Because I knew this would be your response. You didn't even want me to go away for college."

"Oh, pish." Her mom waved a manicured hand. "If that were the case, we wouldn't have paid for four years."

"And every day of those four years you kept complaining how poorly the business was doing without me, that you were losing all this business because I was gone."

"That was the truth."

"So, is that what I'm going to hear again? You're going to guilt me into staying at Superior?"

"Guilt you?" Her father looked directly in to her eyes. "Is that what you thought we were doing?"

"Wasn't it? You didn't want me to go away in the first place, then all

I heard was complaints."

"Oh, fish on crackers." He sighed and wrapped his arms around her. "Mackenzie, I'm afraid you and I made a grievous error in judgment." Regret tinged her father's tone.

Callie pressed her head against her father's shoulder, wetting his silk jacket, waiting for a response from her mom. All she heard was silence as her father's chin rested on her head, and he circled a hand on her back. "You were so unsure of yourself back then, our intent was to encourage you, to let you know how special you were, that you were irreplaceable. We had no idea we were compounding that insecurity."

He pulled away, but clutched his hands on her shoulders. "If this job is your dream, then I couldn't be more excited about this opportunity for you. Yes, we'll miss you at Superior, you're gifted at what you do, but I want you to take this new job, with our blessing."

"Not so fast, Kenneth." Her mom leaned toward them. "Fine, go ahead and chase this dream, but I want to know what your plans are for Superior. You have an obligation to find a replacement."

Callie held in a smile. Her mom's blessing may have been slightly backhanded, but it was a blessing nonetheless. "I've already made plans. Come Monday, I'll put an ad online. I figure I need a couple of weeks to collect resumes. Another week to weed through the applications and set up interviews, and the final week to conduct those interviews." All while keeping up with her current duties, which meant putting in overtime, but it would be worth it.

"And training? If you're off pursuing this . . . this pipedream, who will train in the new hire?"

"I will. My first few weeks at the park are afternoon and evening only, so I can train them in the morning."

Her mom sat back in the chair, tapping burgundy fingernails on her leg, her facial expression blank. "It sounds like you have this all planned out."

Callie nodded, holding her breath. Her mother's approval wasn't necessary, but she still coveted it.

"Then go." Her mom flipped her hand in the air. "Go chase your dream." Then she leaned forward and wagged a finger at Callie. "Just remember, that sometimes sacrificing a dream is a blessing." Her eyes angled toward Callie's dad and stayed there. "Sometimes you have to sacrifice your dream. Oftentimes, when you use your gifts, you discover a better dream, your true path in life. Isn't that right, Kenneth?"

Her father said nothing, and looked away.

<h1 style="text-align:center">Chapter Five</h1>

HAVEN WALKED THROUGH REVOLVING doors into the rehabbed warehouse building in Canal Park, his handheld camera slung around his neck. What an absolutely perfect location. Close to the water and to all the dining anyone could possibly need. This first floor housed several quaint shops, all carrying locally-made wares and delicacies. No Starbucks or Ben & Jerry's here. Precisely the type of office setting he was looking for.

Problem was, this place looked too perfect to be affordable, but he'd check it out anyway. His editor wanted an office by the end of the week. Haven hoped to find a reasonably-priced rental by the end of today. Chances were, this wasn't it.

Regardless, he snapped photos of the old brick walls and aging hardwood floors for his editor, then strode to the elevators. He checked the office listings and found Superior Office Suites on the eighth floor. The top floor. Prime location for views. And no doubt expensive too. He'd likely be checking out that downtown location today too.

An art store across from the elevators caught his eye. He scanned the merchandise through the windowed wall. Ceramics, paintings, clothes, and more, all crafted by local artisans. Maybe they'd be willing to consign some of his photographs too. Definitely worth checking out later.

The elevator arrived, and he rode it to the top floor. It opened into a bright reception area. A leggy blonde zoomed past him into the elevator. "Someone will be with you in a minute."

"Thanks." He mentally paged through the clients Callie had said rented space: an interior designer, landscape architect, model . . . Yeah, that fit. The woman had no meat on her bones whatsoever. Not his kind of beautiful, but what so many of his photography-colleagues sought.

The doors closed behind him, and he snapped pictures of the lobby with its brick exterior and painted interior walls. Very inviting. He walked toward a mahogany reception desk across plush taupe carpet that cushioned his feet. An exquisite, lifelike painting of High Falls near Grand Portage hung above the desk. The colors were rich and vivid. Red, yellow, and orange tree leaves had a tactile appearance and looked to be waving in the fall wind. He could almost feel the spray of the water as the Pigeon River plummeted down over one hundred feet. He imagined the rich scent of autumn's air floating around him. The gifted painter had caught the Master Artist's creation perfectly.

Maybe next week he'd go up to High Falls and see what his lens could capture. He could spend the week trekking to the myriad of falls, all rushing toward Lake Gichigami. What he'd give to make nature photography his full-time profession. In time, if he kept honing his craft like the artist who painted the picture in front of him, that could come.

He started around the desk to read the name of the artist, so he could find additional works from the painter to hang in his home. Once he moved into his own place again, that is.

"Hello, may I help you?"

Startled, he turned his head toward the female voice. Another blonde beauty, although not exactly rail thin, maybe even a titch on the plump side. Still, she looked far healthier than the walking stick figure he'd just passed. "Hi." He offered his hand. "I'm Haven Carlysle. Callie Beaumont recommended these office suites."

"You're the photographer?" Her already large eyes widened, and she gripped his hand firmer and covered it with her other hand. "My my, Callie didn't tell me how handsome you were."

Whoa. Talk about forward. His ego appreciated it, but he wasn't here to build up his self-worth. He tugged his hand away from her cocoon. "Is Callie in?"

"Yes, she is, but I'll show you around first, and then we'll stop by the First Impressions office. That's Callie's domain." She flattened a hand against her clingy silk blouse, drawing attention to her healthy bosom. "I'm Jessica Beaumont. My family owns this building."

Beaumont? "You're related to Callie?"

"She's my big sister. Hard to believe, isn't it? I'm told we don't look at all alike."

He tried to bring a clear picture of Callie into his thoughts, but failed. Apparently, he'd been too obsessed with his son to really take notice of her.

"As you can see, you're standing in the reception area." She pointed a manicured finger toward his chest. "Your reception area." With an elegant twist of her hand, reminiscent of TV game show models, she gestured to the desk. "Ashley—you just passed her—is your personal receptionist. She's off running an errand for a client."

So, the pencil-thin blonde wasn't the model. Interesting. He couldn't wait to see what the model looked like.

"Here we offer phone answering, guest greeting, your personal mailbox, signing for packages. Think of Ashley as your very own secretary."

Sounded nice, but spendy. "I'm not looking for me, but my editor."

"So, I won't see you every day?"

"Not likely."

She stuck out her lower lip. "Now, that's a shame."

That it was. "I'd love to have my own space, but freelance nature photography doesn't exactly bring in a lot of money."

"Then maybe you should think of turning your camera elsewhere." She flashed a smile highlighted with cheekbones high enough to skydive off of. "But let me show you the space first."

He smiled back. Yeah, a little flirting wasn't bad at all for his ego. As long as that was all the further it went. He followed her around the reception desk, down a short hallway, and gestured to the second door on the right.

She walked through the first door and splayed her hands. "This is your editor's suite."

It wasn't huge, maybe twelve by ten and already furnished with a desk, chair, and credenza. But his editor wouldn't need anything larger than this. A window framed in the Duluth-Superior port. He walked to the window and looked out. As Callie had told him, it also had a view of the lighthouse, the lift bridge, Park Point peninsula, and the great lake itself.

He selected video-mode on his camera and turned in a circle, recording the suite. Then he snapped still shots of the view.

It really was an amazing space. He could easily imagine himself editing from this office, but his pretty tour guide was holding back on that key figure: cost.

"Nice, isn't it?" She stopped by his side and her perfume whispered *come closer*.

He stepped back. "Very nice." He cleared his throat. But very wrong. The last thing he needed right now was any kind of relationship. Amanda needed to see that Haven was committed to Reece and Reece alone.

"Let me show you the rest of your office."

And get him to fall in love with the space even more so he couldn't refuse it regardless of the price? He wasn't going to fall for that. He leaned against the desk and crossed his arms. "How about we discuss rent first?"

"Are you sure?" Her hand made a modelesque sweeping motion toward the doorway. "We've got conference rooms that face the water, our own little cafeteria—"

"That's all nice, but if it's out of my boss's budget, I'm just wasting your time."

"Believe me, you're not wasting my time." She tried that sexy pout on him again, but it no longer worked.

"I might be wasting mine."

Her pout turned real as she turned sharply away from him, her chin pointed upward. "I'll show you to Callie's office. She gets to do the dirty work."

She led him away from the vacant office and pointed at doors as they went along, talking up an attorney, an accountant, television news anchors, landscape architect, and the model. A man walked toward them dressed like he'd just stepped off the pages of a Neiman Marcus ad. The model?

"Haven, I'd like you to meet Jayson Grey, our resident interior decorator. He can make a shack look fabulous."

Jayson waved a hand at Jessica. "Oh, you're just saying that, Jessie dear."

"Well, it's true. He did the offices here."

"You've done a superb job." Haven offered his hand.

The man offered a limp-wristed shake. "I do my best."

"Oh, and Jayson," Jessica said, "I talked with Charlie earlier. The shop took in a '55 Chevy Del Ray today and wants Charlie to stay on late to work on it."

"Late, schmate." Jayson shook his head but grinned. "Looks like I'll have a cold bed tonight. Always choosing cars over me."

"And you're in love." Jessica squeezed Jayson's arm.

"Ah, that I am."

"We'll catch you later."

"See ya, doll, and nice to meet you too, Haven."

"Same." Haven nodded as the man walked into his office.

"What do you think?" Jessica gestured toward the reception area which lay ahead of them. "Will you be staying?"

So, they'd come full circle. The space wasn't large, but very cozy. After seeing this office, any other place would disappoint. Still, cost was the determining factor.

"It's very nice." He stopped by the desk and rested against it. "And I appreciate you taking me on the scenic route, but I can't make a decision yet."

"Well, a girl can try, can't she?" She flashed another grin showing off pearl-white teeth. "I'll take you to Cal, but I guarantee she isn't nearly as exciting."

Perhaps not, but he wasn't seeking excitement.

Jessica led him past the reception desk to a hallway behind the elevator, with him videotaping the tour. She pointed out a small cafeteria and a conference room then knocked on a door that read First Impressions. She opened the door without waiting for an invitation.

He turned off the camera and rested it against his chest.

"Hey Cal, this guy's a tough one. We're gonna need some of your magic to reel him in."

"I'll do my best." Callie's gaze remained on her computer. "Thanks,

Jess."

Jessica touched his arm on the way out. "I'll be out front. I'd love to show you the coffee shop on the first level. It beats any chain hands down."

"I'll consider it." For half a second. The woman had a one-track mind, and he had no intention of following that track.

"Please, have a seat, Haven." Callie closed her laptop and offered him a real smile that didn't reek of a sales pitch.

He sat opposite her and looked out the picture window beyond her desk. The bluffs rose away from the lake leading to Enger Tower. The popular Duluth landmark stood on top of a hill keeping watch over the lake and the hillside. From here, the tower looked no bigger than a thimble, but he knew from growing up in the area that the blue-stone structure rose a good eighty feet above the Duluth hillside, providing breathtaking views of God's handiwork.

"Enjoy my view?" She swiveled her chair toward the window. Her view wasn't of Lake Superior, but that didn't make it any less spectacular.

"Inspiring." He kept his gaze focused outward. In his youth, and even with Amanda, he'd spent many days climbing the five flights of stairs in the tower just to marvel at the area's beauty. Back then, even though he'd been unfamiliar with nature's Artist, he'd appreciated God's creation. Now, if only he could capture just a snippet of that with his camera.

Above the window a birch-bark plaque was nailed to the wall, the verse burned into it, "*I lift mine eyes to the hills, from whence cometh my help.*" *Psalm 121:1.*

He pointed to the plaque. "Quite appropriate."

"I think so, too. You don't know how often that view and verse have helped me."

"I can imagine." He stored the verse in his memory banks. Chances were, he'd need it again very soon. Tomorrow night, to be specific. Tuesday couldn't come fast enough.

"Did you like what you saw of the office?"

He jerked his gaze from the view as Callie laid a presentation folder in front of him. "I love it, and the help is quite"—he cleared his throat—

"friendly."

Distress tented her brows, and her shoulders slumped. "Please, please don't tell me Jess was flirting."

"I would, but I prefer not to lie."

"Oh, jelly on bagels." She muttered, shaking her head. "Sorry, but Jess knows that's not professional."

"Well, I can't say I wasn't flattered, but the last thing I want to worry about right now is romance. I don't want anything to get in the way of my relationship with Reece."

"Regardless, I'll have a talk with her and offer a gentle reminder." She tapped the folder in front of Haven. "Now, back to business at hand. Besides Jess, what's your opinion of our space?"

"I like it. Love it even, but it has to fit the budget I've been given."

"I understand." She flipped open the folder and tugged out a sheet of paper. "I also provide web services, logo design, brochures, graphics, et cetera, if you're looking for any of that."

"Hmm. Maybe for my photography business, but I really just want—"

"I know. The costs." She handed him a rate sheet. "This should answer all your questions. My father instructed me to make you our best possible offer."

He read the list itemizing the rent and all the services and fees. It wasn't inexpensive, but with all the services this place offered, it wasn't as bad as he'd imagined either. It might just be a go.

The phone rang as he tucked the page back into the folder. She raised a finger and picked up the receiver. "Superior Office Suites, Callista Beaumont speaking."

Haven blocked out her voice but studied her, really looking at Callie for the first time. She wasn't blonde like Jessica, and her hair was chin length. Her cheeks were rounder without defined cheekbones. Even her skin tone was darker. Jessica was right. The two sisters didn't look at all alike. But more importantly, unlike Jessica, with Callie there seemed to be nothing pretentious. How refreshing that was.

She hung up the phone. "Sorry about that."

"No problem."

"What do you think?" She touched the folder. "Do we fit your needs?"

"I think you might. The final decision isn't mine to make, but I'll talk with the editor today and get her opinion. Can I let you know tomorrow?"

"That would be fine." She stood and walked around her desk. "I'll see you out."

They walked the short hallway back to the reception area. Thankfully, Jessica wasn't in sight, but a woman dressed in gray overalls with hair pulled back in a tight ponytail stood by the reception desk, talking with Ashley.

"Hey, Charlie." Callie waved at the woman. "I hear you've got a new gem to work on."

Charlie turned to them, a grin lighting her entire face. "It's sweet, but I had to come see my honey before starting to work on it. Sometimes I get so caught up in fixing cars that I forget the time."

"Go on back." Callie nodded toward the hallway. "I don't think Jayson will mind the interruption."

Haven shook his head and grinned at Callie. "Charlie's a woman."

Cocking her head to the side, she shot him a half smile and a raised eyebrow. "Good observation."

He chuckled, his head still shaking. "I met Jayson earlier. He talked about Charlie the mechanic, and I made some assumptions."

"First impressions don't always tell the truth, do they?"

"That's for sure." He offered Callie his hand. "Thank your sister for showing me the space, and thank you for the recommendation. I'll let you know my editor's decision tomorrow."

"I'd appreciate it." Her soft hand slipped from his. "And I'll see you tomorrow night at Mandy's."

He grinned. "I'm looking forward to it."

Tomorrow he'd finally become reacquainted with his son. Hopefully, Reece's first impression of him this past Saturday had been a positive one. First impressions may not always tell the truth, but positive ones help smooth the introductions. Considering Haven's past with Reece, he needed all the help he could get.

# Chapter Six

TODAY, HE'D FINALLY GET to meet his son! Haven prayed Reece would like him. Or wouldn't be frightened of him. Or even just tolerated him. That would give Haven some positive foundation to build a relationship upon.

He parked his Lucerne behind Callie's little four-door . . . what had she called it? Ah yes, the Seussmobile. Its curved body and rounded windows did make it look like it could belong in a Dr. Seuss book.

It had been too long since he'd read Dr. Seuss.

Over six years.

And Reece was certainly past that stage now. So, what did eight-year-olds read? What did they do for fun? Why hadn't he done his research before coming today? Talk about making bad first impressions.

He got out of his car and walked around the front, giving the hood a pat. The mechanic said it was fixed, but Haven had heard that line before. Time would tell.

He climbed the steps leading to the front yard, and Callie, her head topped with a straw fedora, came out of Amanda's house. Alone.

Panic stewed in Haven's gut, and his feet froze to the sidewalk. Had Amanda changed her mind?

"Hey there." She jogged to meet him, a bright smile on her face. "You made my day this morning. You have no idea how good it felt to tell my parents that all the office spaces were rented."

"Glad I could help. My editor loved it." He glanced past Callie toward the house. "Where's Reece?" The front door remained closed, and no one peeked through the front window.

"Don't worry. He'll be out shortly. I just thought I should prepare you a little bit first."

Prepare him for what? This didn't sound promising. His heart amping up its speed, he gestured to the stone steps where he sat, his foot tapping out a nervous beat.

Callie sat beside him. "I need to tell—"

"What does Reece know about me?" That his father was responsible for his handicap? That his father was a coward who'd run from responsibility rather than fight for the right to see his son? "Does he hate me?"

"Hate you? Reece? Goodness no. That boy has a heart as big as Lake Superior. As for what he knows about you, Mandy's told him you're his dad, but he doesn't know why you two separated. He even thinks it's cool that you've come back. He's a little scared about spending time with you, so the two-hour limit is probably wise for now."

Haven kicked at the step with his heel. "He's not the only one who's frightened."

"You haven't spent a lot of time with kids, have you?"

"A lot?" He huffed. "I haven't spent any time with kids. I couldn't. I was afraid to be reminded of what I'd messed up."

"No nieces or nephews?"

"I'm an only child."

"Well, you're going to do just fine." She patted his arm. "Reece is a great kid, and Mandy's done an awesome job with him. Before you know it, the two of you'll be best buddies."

"You think so?"

"Absolutely." Callie glanced over her shoulder at the house. "He should be out in a sec. I hope you don't mind, but I told Mandy we're going to Lincoln Park. It's just a short way from here so you'll get to spend time with him instead of spending half your time driving. And there's that new little ice cream shop right down the road from the park. Their ice cream concoctions are to die for."

"I take it he likes ice cream?"

"Well duh, he's an eight-year-old boy. It's his favorite food group."

"Mine too, but it's been a while since I've indulged."

"Seriously? You gave up ice cream? Now, that's not right."

"I gave it up for a woman who's now engaged to another man, so you can see how well that worked out."

"Of course, it didn't work. True love is eating ice cream together, not giving it up."

He chuckled at Callie's wisdom. "Guess that was my problem. I'll remember that for future relationships."

"You better." She slapped her thighs and stood. "You ready?"

"A long time ago."

"Then let's go get him. No doubt Mandy's avoiding sending him with us."

Haven trailed Callie to the door, his heart picking up speed with every step. Callie let herself in, and they were immediately met by Amanda, who blocked his entrance.

She looked at Haven, her mouth set in a grim line, eyes narrow, and shoulders stiff. "You won't try anything."

Biting back a retort, he shook his head.

Callie rested a hand on her friend's arm. "You can trust him, Mandy."

Her shoulders relaxed . . . slightly . . . but her accusing eyes did not. "I trust *you*, Callie."

Haven clenched his jaw. He would not say anything Amanda could use against him, so that meant saying nothing at all.

"Reece." Amanda called without taking her gaze off Haven. She tapped her watch. "You have two hours from now. And don't think of being late."

"He'll be back on time." If not before. He wouldn't dare risk losing this privilege.

Reece appeared at the door and clung tight to Amanda. Fear etched his eyes as he looked up at Haven. "Dad?"

Haven had never heard a more precious word. "Yes, Reece, I'm your dad."

THE REUNION NEARLY HAD Callie in tears as Haven knelt to his son's eye level. He didn't reach out to hug Reece, although the arms pressed to Haven's side gave away his desire for more. Yes, Reece was afraid, and that was natural, but Haven's obvious love for his son came through his choked-out words, "I am your dad." These two needed each other, even if Bill was in the picture now. She silently prayed that nothing would stand in the way of father and son bonding today.

Reece's gaze darted from Callie down to his dad. "So, I get to play with you guys?"

"How does Lincoln Park sound?" Haven quirked a smile and stood.

"Sweet."

"Then let's skedaddle, bud. Don't want to waste any of this precious time." Callie put a hand on Reece's shoulder then looked at Mandy. "We'll take good care of him. Trust me."

Mandy crossed her arms, her narrow-eyed focus lasered on Haven. "Two hours."

Maybe Mandy was a good friend, and a good mom, but oh could she infuriate Callie. She didn't reply to her friend, or even say goodbye, she just took Reece's hand and led him down the sidewalk.

"We gonna take the Seussmobile?" Reece let go of her hand and ran toward her Cube.

"Whoa there, Eric Liddell. You've got to remember we adults are getting old and no way can we keep up with you."

Reece put on his brakes right by the retaining wall steps. "Who's Eric Liddell?"

"Who is Eric Liddell?" Callie propped her hands on her hips. "Bud, you really have to study up on your Olympic runners. Eric Liddell is *only* one of the most famous Olympic runners of all time. An awesome movie, *Chariots of Fire*, was even made about him."

Callie caught up to Reece, with Haven right behind her. "And you know why he ran?"

"Uh-uh."

"Because God made him fast. Just like you." She touched a finger to his heart. "And he ran because it made God happy."

"Really? So, when I run, I'm making God happy?"

"He's doing cartwheels, bud. He loves it when his children use the gifts he gave them." *So, why aren't you using those gifts, Callie girl?*

"Awesome!" Reece took off for her car.

"Hey, bud, maybe your dad would rather take his car. Your dad's got long legs, and if he sits in the Seussmobile, he might just be eating his knees."

"Callie," Haven's smooth baritone came from behind her, "I think eating my knees is worth the sacrifice for a ride in your famous car. Not everyone gets to ride in a Seussmobile."

"See Aunt Callie? My dad's cool."

"I agree." And she really did. So far Haven was proving himself worthy of the Dad title, but he was also on his best behavior at the moment. The real Haven could come out as time went on, but Reece didn't need to worry about that. "Your dad is the coolest."

As Reece climbed into the backseat, Callie felt a firm hand on her shoulder. She looked up into Haven's eyes. Eyes as blue as Lake Superior. Oh. My. Goodness, they could capture a heart.

He smiled, and his face lit up like Saturday's sunrise. Heaven help her. Why did he have to be so scrumptiously gorgeous?

"Callie, thanks for all you're doing. Reece obviously loves you."

She swallowed. And why did he have to be so nice too? Mandy had claimed otherwise. More than once. Besides, beautiful men were shallow, selfish creatures, weren't they? She gritted her teeth. She was just as guilty of judging by appearances as her mother. That had to stop. She dragged her gaze away from Haven and nodded to her car. "I just want the best for Reece. He's a great kid."

"I can see that, and I appreciate you helping me get to know him. I owe you."

"Oh pish." Pish? Seriously, Callie? After that little verbal display of patheticness—was that even a word?—he had to be laughing at her. No way could she look him in the face now. Really, that was safer anyway. She hurried around the car shaking off her teenage-like crush. "Let's get going. Don't want to waste your time, right?" She didn't stand a chance with a man like Haven. Even if she were as beautiful as Jess, it wouldn't matter. He'd made it clear yesterday that romance wasn't on his docket.

"I'll be right there. I've got to grab something from my car." Haven dashed to his Buick.

Too bad she couldn't scratch romance from hers. All her life she'd wanted a normal husband, a normal family, if there even was such a thing. Besides, Haven was an evil photographer. Any profession besides that and she might be enticed.

She sat down behind the wheel of her Cube and glanced through the windshield. Haven ambled toward them carrying . . . a diaper bag? And not even one of those new designer ones that looked like large purses. No, this was an old vinyl bag with appliqués of Snoopy. He didn't think Reece still needed . . . No. Haven was obviously smarter than that. Duh. Still, she couldn't wait for him to explain this. And people thought she was a little daffy.

He flung open the car door, stuffed his long legs beneath the dash, and rested the bag on his lap.

"Um . . ." She held back a smile. "I realize you haven't been around kids much, but when they're eight they don't need a diaper bag anymore."

"Aunt Callie! Gee."

Haven grinned as he unzipped the bag and pulled out his camera. "I don't go anywhere without it."

"Okay, this may be a silly question, but don't they sell camera bags at Target?"

"Sure they do, and those camera bags advertise to everyone I'm toting an expensive camera." He pulled a baby lotion bottle out of a front mesh pocket. "Who's going to want to steal this bag?"

"Ah, very clever."

"I am known to have a good idea occasionally."

Probably more than occasionally. "Well, now that we've got that settled." She started the car and pulled out from the parking space as a musky fragrance drifted toward her. Oh joy. One more reminder that she was sitting beside a living, breathing hunk of a bachelor, and that she was about to spend two hours with him.

And Reece too, of course.

Knowing that didn't make it easier.

"Banana." Reece yelled from the backseat.

"What? Already?" Callie searched for signs of a yellow car.

"Behind us."

She looked in the rearview mirror. Sure enough, a yellow Camaro was gaining on her. "Now, just tell me how you saw that?"

The little goof giggled.

"Mind filling me in?" Haven tucked his camera back into the diaper bag. "I missed the joke."

Shoot. For a few seconds, she'd completely forgotten about Haven. Then he had to go and talk with that velvety voice that made her stomach turn somersaults. She gave her head a shake and focused on the road. "It's a game we play when driving. If you see a yellow vehicle—can't be a business vehicle or a bus or a taxi—you yell 'banana!' If you see a purple car, you yell 'grape two.' And for a pink car, yell 'cotton candy three.' The rider with the most points by the time you reach your destination wins."

"And if you see a hot pink Hummer, you win for the month." Reece added. "But if you go by a used car lot, you lose all your points and have to start all over again. I beat Aunt Callie all the time."

"Well yeah, 'cause I gotta keep my eyes on the road, bud. Coming home, your dad drives so I can win for once."

"I'll still beat you."

"Just keep telling yourself that, buddy boy."

"Banana. Got one." Haven reached into the backseat and high-fived his son.

"My dad'll beat you too."

Callie wrinkled her nose and mimicked Reece in a high-pitched whiny voice, "My dad'll beat you too." She turned left on the next street. "I am surrounded with love."

"I love you, Aunt Callie, but I'm still gonna beat you."

Yeah, he probably would.

Five minutes later, when she drove into a parking lot near Lincoln Park, Reece had five points, Haven two, and Callie? Naturally, she had nothing. She'd hate this game if Reece didn't have so much fun beating the pants off her.

Reece leaped from the car the second she parked.

"Come on, guys, let's play."

Haven touched her arm before she stepped from the car. "Does he always have this much energy?”

“Hah. You haven’t seen anything yet. If that boy didn’t have the prosthesis, he’d be headed for the Olym—” Oh no. What did she just say? Could she be any more stupid? “Haven, I am so sorry. I didn’t mean . . .” *Just shut your mouth, Callie girl.*

Haven’s eyes took on a far-off stare.

Oh brother, her foot-in-mouth disease had done it now. She stared out the window, focusing on nothing. Good thing she wasn’t contagious. “I’m sorry, I—”

“Don’t.” A rumble marred his voice. After a long sigh, he gently touched her arm and she looked over at him. “Don’t ever think you have to pussyfoot around me.” He spoke low and slow. “Don’t ever wonder about my hurt feelings, got it? What’s important is that amazing kid out there. Nothing else matters. Nothing.”

And there he goes being all nice and thoughtful again. “I’ll remember that,” she said with a nod. Then she got out of her car, walked to the back, and tugged the hatch open. Her stash of Reece toys smiled at her. Which one should she choose?

“Got a Frisbee?” Reece snuck in front of her and rummaged through his toy box until he found a turquoise flying disc. “Sweet. Dad, are you good at Frisbee?” He flung it at his dad and Haven ducked, throwing a hand up. The disc sailed far beyond his reach.

“That answer your question?” Haven retrieved the toy then whirled it back on a perfect line to Reece who easily caught it.

“Hey, you can play.”

Haven stepped closer. “I can throw. My dog loved Frisbee.”

“You have a dog?” Reece clutched the toy to his chest. “Can I see it? Mom won’t let me have a dog. Says they’re dirty and too much work, but I promised I’d take care of it.”

“Your mom’s right. They are a lot of work.” Haven waved. “Throw it back. I need to learn to catch.”

Reece clutched the Frisbee tighter. “Will you let me see your dog?”

Callie laid a hand on Reece’s shoulder. “No bribery allowed, bud.”

“It’s okay.” Haven hurried to Reece and knelt down, making his eyes level with Reece’s. “Unfortunately, Schroeder died a little while back, but he was a great dog. A beagle like Snoopy from the cartoon. When you were a baby, he thought he was your watch dog, and he even saved your life."

Reece's eyes grew wide. "Really? Mom never told me about that. Are you gonna get another dog? I'll help you take care of him. I really, really want a dog. Please?"

"I tell you what, let's just give it a little time, and we'll talk about it again. Deal?" He held out his hand.

The boy scrunched his mouth to the side and eyed Haven's hand for a second before grasping it. "I guess."

"Great. Now no more wasting time." Haven jogged away from Reece and held up his hands. "Teach me how to catch this thing before we go get ice cream."

"Ice cream? You rock, Dad." Reece put more distance between himself and Haven.

"Schroeder?" Callie joined Haven while keeping an eye on her little buddy. "For a beagle?"

"Isn't Snoopy a little obvious?" The disc sailed toward Haven's midsection, and he trapped it against his stomach.

"Here, my turn." She stole the toy and tossed it toward Reece. At least that was her intention. It sailed about twenty feet wide of him, but that clearly didn't disappoint him as he took off running toward it.

"But why Schroeder and not Charlie Brown or Linus . . . or Pigpen?" She giggled.

"Well, Pigpen would have been pretty accurate, but I had an affinity with Schroeder."

"You play piano?" Be still her heart.

"I dabble."

"I bet." His definition of dabble was probably one step below concert pianist. "Like you dabble in photography?"

He shrugged. "Here it comes. This time I'm going to catch it." The Frisbee curved above his head. He jumped up and snatched it between his fingers. "Yes."

"Epic catch, Dad."

Haven grinned and snapped the toy back toward his son, but his face fell as Reece ran it down.

"What's wrong?" Callie touched his forearm. "Reece is having a ball.

You're doing well."

Haven stuffed his hands in his pockets then yanked them out as the disc sailed his way. He reached up and it nicked his fingers before teetering into the grass behind him. After retrieving it, he flung it back then looked at Callie. "Am I just purchasing his approval? Am I just going to be the fun dad so Amanda can be the disciplinarian mom? I hate that idea."

Oh, why does he have to be so considerate? Haven was blowing her shallow man theory into smithereens. "This is your first time out with him. You've got plenty of time to be more, but for today, go for it. These first impressions are vital. They're what's going to keep Reece coming back to you."

"Not if I don't follow up. I have so much to learn, Callie. I have no clue how to be a fa—"

"Watch out!" Reece yelled.

Callie looked up just in time for the Frisbee to connect with her face, sending her fedora to the ground. Her hands flew to her eyes which took the brunt of the force.

"Are you all right?" Haven took her arm and led her to a bench

"Aunt Callie." Reece ran to her and smothered her with a hug before cupping her cheeks between his dirty hands. "I'm sorry, I'm so sorry." He sniffled. "Are you okay? I wasn't paying attention. Mom says I need to pay attention better."

She nodded and slowly pulled her hands from stinging eyes. Everything blurred. She blinked repeatedly, and bit by bit everything came into focus.

Her heart felt like it stopped completely.

Kneeling in front of her, concern etched in the lines on his forehead, Haven's gorgeous blues connected with hers.

And stayed.

HER EYES WERE BLUE.

Not just any blue, but the layered blue of a dusky sky with the faintest of stars glistening in them. Pain-provoked tears magnified those stars. They were beautiful. Captivating, even. Why hadn't he noticed them before? His hand slid down her arm, and embraced her fingers. He whisked bangs away from those bottomless blue eyes. "Are you all right?"

Her mouth hung open, and she nodded.

*What are you doing?*

This wasn't a date. Today was about getting to know his son. He pulled his hand from hers and stood up, stuffing his hands in his front pockets, keeping his gaze away from Callie's. "Are you sure?"

"I'm fine. Really."

"Uh good." He swallowed and glanced at Reece. "What do you say to a walk up the trail? Let Callie's eyes recover."

"I didn't mean to hurt you, Aunt Callie." He smothered her with another hug. "I promise I'll watch next time."

"Reece, it was an accident, and let's face it, buddy boy, you weren't the only one not paying attention." She rubbed her eyes and kept blinking. "Guess I learned my lesson, huh?" She shot a quick glance at Haven then swept her gaze away. "I think I'm just going to sit here for a bit. You two take that walk, get to know each other."

Haven didn't move. "You'll tell me if there's a problem."

"Would you just get going?"

"Come on, Dad, there are some rockin' trails up here."

Haven shot one more glance at Callie. "We won't be long." He patted the phone in his back pocket. "Call if you need anything, got it?"

"Yes, mom." A slight smile hinted on her lips. "Now go."

"Guess she wants us to go, huh Reece?"

Reece took off toward the trail, barely a hitch in his step. Amazing. No one would ever guess his son ran on a fake foot.

Haven ran after him. Amanda obviously did something right in raising their son. Maybe he had to give her some time. Get her used to the idea of him being around again. Maybe he'd learn to like her again and vice versa, and Bill the fiancé would get kicked out of the picture. Then Reece would have the intact family he deserved.

But liking Amanda again was a long shot. He might as well try to scale a waterfall. If Reece could run on a prosthesis, though, other miracles could happen.

He caught up to Reece as he entered a wooded area, then ran alongside him. Now was as good a time as any to get to know this gifted young man. "Do you run track in school?"

"Nah, they don't have it 'til middle school, but I am gonna run in the marathon in a couple weeks. I'm gonna win it too."

"The marathon?" The famous Grandma's Marathon was two weeks from Saturday. The town was already showing signs of the coming invasion of runners and their families. Reece wouldn't be running in that, would he?

"Yep." Reece kicked at a stone and it scampered into the trees. "The Whipper Snapper, just for kids. Will you come watch me?"

Okay, the Whipper Snapper made more sense. He'd love to watch Reece, cheer him on, but would Amanda allow that? Or would she see that as breaking her rules? Haven slowed down and watched Reece run ahead. The kid was made for running.

If he hadn't lost his foot . . .

None of that. Feeling sorry for himself wouldn't change a thing. He hurried and caught up to Reece. "I wouldn't miss your race for all the ice cream in Duluth." If Amanda protested, he'd find a way around it.

"Awesome! Now I'll be just like my friends. I can tell them my dad's coming."

Haven blinked away the sting in his eyes. There was no way he'd miss the race. Amanda had to understand Haven was doing this for their son.

A brown squirrel skittered on the path in front of them then darted up a nearby oak.

Reece stopped and looked at the tree. "Did you know that an ostrich's eye is bigger than its brain?"

Huh? Haven stopped beside Reece. "Where did that come from?"

Reece giggled. "Squirrel."

"You're talking a different language, kiddo."

Reece sighed with his whole body. "When you see a squirrel, you gotta say something random, and when someone says something random, you yell squirrel. Don't you know nothing? You didn't know about banana. Now you don't know about squirrel. You got a lot to learn."

*Tell me about it.* Haven grinned. "Is it true?"

"Is what true?"

"That an ostrich's eye is bigger than its brain."

"The internet says so."

"Then it must be true." He might just have to look up a few of those random facts himself and be ready the next time a squirrel crossed his path. "I suppose Callie knows all these games."

"Well duh! Aunt Callie knows everything important."

Haven was beginning to realize that. It wasn't such a bad idea having her chaperone, after all. He was beginning to enjoy her company as much as Reece's. His phone buzzed as he trekked behind Reece. Not now! Still, he grabbed his phone and looked at the caller I.D. Callie. That couldn't wait.

He punched the answer button. "This is Haven."

"Hi, it's Callie. I hate to do this to you, but Amanda just called. She wants Reece home right now."

"What?" He glanced at his watch. "I've got an hour left."

"I'm sorry, but she says it's an emergency. They left their art class early, and she needs Reece home."

Emergency? That changed things. "We'll be right there, Callie."

He pocketed his phone. "Reece, your mom wants you home."

"But Da-ad . . ."

"Your mom says she needs you. Let's go."

"Fine." He shuffled his feet over the path, kicking at any stones or leaves that dared get in the way. "She's a party pooper."

Haven's feelings exactly, but Reece didn't need to know that. "She's your mother, she knows what's best for you, and you . . . we need to respect her wishes."

Besides, she had an emergency, and all he could think about was his lost time with Reece. How selfish could he be? He cuffed a hand over his son's shoulder. "How about we race to the Seussmobile? You win, you get double scoops of ice cream another time."

"Sweet!" Reece flew over the paved path, and Haven hurried behind him.

Maybe their time had been cut short, but every minute had been worth it.

Even though Haven had walked out on him, his son loved him. Haven prayed nothing would ever come between them again.

Callie appeared on the trail just in front of Reece. He walked toward her, and she smiled.

A pure smile with no motives behind it. One that made him smile back.

Why hadn't he noticed that before?

## Chapter Seven

CALLIE BROKE AWAY FROM Haven's gaze and studied the asphalt trail. Focus, Callie girl. Amanda. Emergency. She really had to get over this crazy, teenage crush. They never turned out good. Besides, now wasn't a time to worry about herself, not when Mandy had an emergency, whatever it was. Fire? Accident? Was Bill okay?

They'd find out shortly. Amanda wanted Reece home within—Callie glanced at her watch—ten minutes. Doable, but tight.

"What's going on?" Haven breathed hard. "Is Amanda all right?"

She looked up, gazing everywhere but at Haven's eyes. "She didn't say what, just that Reece needed to come home."

"Then we'll get him home." He aimed for her car, then stopped. "Are you okay to drive?"

"I'm fine."

"I'd be more than glad to drive. I've never piloted a Seussmobile before."

She giggled. How could she turn that down? She handed him the keys as they neared the car. "Treat her gently, now."

"Like she was my own."

"If I recall, your own doesn't always like to start."

He laughed. "So true. How about if I treat her better than my own?" He unlocked the car and held open the passenger door for her. "Does that suit you?"

The gentleman holding the door suited her just fine. "I feel much better now." She got in, buckled, and then picked up the diaper bag from off the floor and rested it on her lap. Her door closed softly, and she focused on breathing. These days with Reece and Haven were going to be a challenge. Next time, she'd be prayed-up beforehand that she'd keep her silly emotions in check.

Haven got in and started the engine. "Shoot, I forgot to take pictures." He slapped the steering wheel. "I can't believe I missed recording our first day together." He glanced in the rearview mirror. "Sorry, Reece. Next time, okay?"

"I had fun, even if you don't know as much as Aunt Callie."

"And that's why I'll see you next Tuesday."

"What are we gonna do?"

Haven shrugged and looked at her. "Any ideas?"

"Same place?" She patted her face. "I think I need to learn to catch a Frisbee."

"That okay with you, Reece?" Haven pulled out of the parking space. "Sure."

"I won't forget my camera again."

Callie looked at Haven's satisfied smile, then back at Reece who wore the exact same smile. There was no mistaking paternity. "Seems to me you recorded today just fine. Reece had a ball." She prayed again for Mandy and Bill, hoping this emergency wouldn't imprint bad memories on top of the good.

"I did. You're fun, Dad. Mom didn't think you would be."

*Oh, Mandy.* Why couldn't she just let Reece enjoy the time with his dad and not poison it? Didn't matter, really. Reece had fun, and so did Haven. That impression was the most important one.

Besides, Haven had recorded memories, just not the kind found on a digital camera. No, these were better. Callie ran her finger over the camera bag's Snoopy appliqué. "What kind of memories would you have created if you'd spent the last hour peeking through that teeny-tiny lens? Sure, you'd have still pictures of Reece, pictures without texture, without the laughter, and the scent of fresh air. Pictures devoid of love." She tapped her temple. "But instead you have memories that live. Most important, you and Reece created those memories together."

Haven shot a glance at her then focused back on the road. "Reece said you know everything important. I'm beginning to believe him."

"Oh pshaw. My little buddy is also prone to exaggeration, aren't you Reece?" She reached back and tickled the back of his knee.

He giggled and squirmed away from her.

Haven turned left, steering her Cube up Amanda's steep street. No emergency vehicles waited out front. That was a relief.

He tucked her car against the curb right behind his black sedan.

"Aw, rats, Bill's home too." A pout was evident in Reece's voice.

Callie looked toward the house. There sat Amanda and Bill on the porch swing, sipping tea or whatever was in their glass. No urgency in sight. She stole a glance at Haven. Judging by the flames shooting from his eyes, and his knuckles paling as he clutched the steering wheel, he was seeing the same thing.

What had Mandy done now?

Callie laid a hand over Haven's. "I think I know what you're thinking, because I'm thinking it too. I'll just remind you to maintain your cool. I have no doubt Bill can and will use anything against you."

"Then you better do all the talking."

"Do I have to go home?" Reece muttered from the backseat. "I was having fun, and Bill's no fun at all, and I didn't even get ice cream."

"Another time." Haven twisted at the waist to see Reece. "We have to abide by your mom's wishes."

"Fine." He got out of the car and slammed it shut then trudged up the sidewalk as if he'd just lost his best friend.

Callie put her hand on her car door.

"Why doesn't he want to go home?" Haven grabbed her arm before she could get out. "What's wrong with Bill?"

She should have expected that question. "Nothing's wrong with him, he's just not used to kids."

"I'm not either."

"But you have more to lose from this relationship, so you're going to try harder. As for Reece not wanting to go home, what kid wants to go home when they're having fun? Did you?"

He shook his head. "Hardly."

"On top of that, when Mandy's with Bill, he's taking precious time away from Reece, time that used to be solely devoted to him, and he doesn't know how to process that. It's tough on him, but it's all normal.

Mandy's a good mom, and she's the one who's given Reece the courage to run even with his handicap. I admire that in her." Even if she didn't admire Mandy's latest taste in men. Not that Bill was bad, he was just . . . boring. And Reece needed someone with more spirit than boring Bill had to give.

"Okay. I'll face them with a smile, and keep my thoughts to myself."

"That's perfect. Let's go find out what this emergency is all about. Remember, this is Bill's first impression of you."

"Right."

They both got out of the car, and Haven followed her up the sidewalk.

Bill looked at his phone. "Fifteen minutes. Not bad."

"I'm sorry?" Callie stopped at the porch landing and stared at the couple, then at Reece pouting by the door. "What's the emergency?"

"A test of sorts." Bill sipped his drink.

A test? What was Bill up to? And why did Mandy go along with it? It wasn't like her to be this unreasonable.

Bill tucked his phone into his back pocket, his expression poker-faced. He must use that in the courtroom. "I needed to see for myself that this man coming back from the dead was responsible. He passed."

Callie couldn't see Haven's face but she could swear she felt steam pouring from him. Or maybe that was her own steam. "You don't trust me either?"

"Reece, would you please excuse us?" Mandy nodded toward the door.

"Fine." He opened the door a crack, then turned and ran back toward Callie. He wrapped his arms around her waist. "I love you, Aunt Callie."

"Love you bunches, buddy."

He let go of her and held his arms open for Haven.

Haven's eyes misted over as he knelt and encompassed his son with a hug. "I love you, Reece."

"Love you too, Dad. See you next week. And don't forget about the race." Reece ran into the house and the door slammed behind him.

"Race?" Amanda stood, and anchored her fists on her hips. "What's this about a race? We didn't agree to anything else."

"We agreed to two hours on Tuesday." Haven shoved past Callie and tapped his watch. "I still have forty-five minutes coming today."

"If you want to see your son, you play by my rules."

"So, you can just make up new ones as we go along?"

"Perhaps you'd like no time at all."

Callie touched Haven's arm. "Shhh." She understood his anger, but he was going to blow this.

He shook her hand off. "I can't believe you."

"And there definitely will not be a race."

Not if he was confrontational. "Haven, let me—"

"This is important to Reece." He stabbed a finger at his chest. "He wants me to be there."

"Go ahead." Hands on hips, Mandy took a step toward Haven and whispered, her nostrils flaring. "Show up. I dare you."

He went nose to nose with Mandy, and Callie grabbed his arm. At first, he resisted, then his arm went limp. He retreated, holding his hands up. "Your rules." He stomped off the porch. "Callie?" Pain trembled from his normally liquid voice.

Callie turned toward him. His face was red, his jaw tight. "Tuesday?"

"I'll be here." He hurried to his car, got in, and sped down the hill.

How could Amanda do this to him? This wasn't the courageous friend Callie had come to love.

Arms crossed, she turned back to Amanda who once again sat on the porch swing, hand entwined with boring Bill. "You realize that was a lousy thing to do."

"Bill, would you mind checking on Reece?" She squeezed his hand then let go.

"Sure thing, babe." He pecked her on the cheek, stood, and then stared at Callie. "This is all about what's best for Reece, and we'll fight for that."

Callie clamped her mouth shut. All about what's best for Reece. Ha! What a bunch of horse manure that was.

As Bill entered the house, Callie wrinkled her nose at him, but resisted sticking out her tongue. Although he deserved it. Then she sat beside Mandy on the swing, took her friend's hand, and caught a whiff of Mandy's beer breath. Not that there was anything wrong with a glass of beer. If a single glass was all she'd had. She squeezed her friend's hand. "I didn't mean to jump on you, but I'm very disappointed in how you treated Haven. You're better than that, and you know it."

"But did you see how he reacted? Do you think I want him around my son?"

"Your son? Your son happened to fall in love with that man today. Yeah, Haven messed up in the past, but today, he did absolutely nothing wrong. He followed your stupid rules to a T, and you blindside him with a stunt like this. How was he supposed to react?"

"I don't know." Mandy picked at her nails. "I'm just afraid . . . "

"He's not going to take your son away, Mandy. He just wants an opportunity to know him. Is that so wrong?"

"Yes, Callie, yes, it is. I wish he'd never come back. And I don't want Haven at Reece's race." Mandy popped off the swing and hurried into the house without even a glimpse back.

Now, what was that all about?

HAVEN CARTED HIS LAPTOP and camera bag out of the elevator into his new office space. Rather, his editor's office. What he'd give to leave behind his nine-to-five and focus on his art. Ironically, if he didn't have Reece to support, that would be a possibility. He'd realize his dream, but lose everything that mattered. If Amanda got her way, that was exactly what would happen.

He walked past the reception desk and nodded to the stick-thin woman. "Good morning, Ashley."

"Good morning, Mr. Carlysle. Are you moving your editor in today?"

"Well, she's been called away for a few weeks so I get to set up her space, make it my own for a bit."

"It'll be nice to have you around."

"It's good to be here." He passed the desk to the right and entered his temporary office, which was naked except for a desk and chair. He may put up a picture or two to warm up the space for now, and keep them for the home he planned on purchasing soon after his real job began.

Hmm. He rubbed his chin. There was the painting he loved, hanging in the reception area. That artist had to have more works. Haven had completely forgotten to check who the artist was.

He set his laptop and camera bag on the desk and stepped into the hallway, aiming for the reception area.

"Good morning, Haven." A familiar female voice called from behind him, and he stiffened.

Forcing a smile, he turned around. "Morning, Jessica." Jessica walked toward him alongside an older woman who looked as if she'd just come in from gardening. Her hair was tucked beneath a baseball cap, and her face was lined with more wrinkles than the shirt he'd forgotten in the dryer the other day. But she was smiling, and all those wrinkles pointed to a face that had spent a lifetime smiling, not frowning. She definitely wasn't the model from the office suites, but she carried a cheerful countenance that would brighten even the Grinch's day.

"And good morning to you, Haven." Jessica, wearing painted jeans similar to those Amanda had worn the other day, offered her hand. "I didn't realize I'd be seeing you again. What a nice surprise."

"I'll be here until my editor returns in a couple weeks." He pulled his hand from Jessica, who'd held onto their shake rather than release it, and offered his hand to the older woman. "Haven Carlysle. I'm just moving in."

"Annabelle Scotland." She gripped his hand with the strength of someone who worked with the dirt. "It's lovely to meet you." She patted his arm. "But I must hurry on. My work is calling. I've got a world to beautify."

"Likewise." He smiled as she passed him, aiming for the elevator.

"Isn't she a hoot?" Jessica walked with him to the reception area. "If I need a smile, I just talk to her. She oozes this positive aura."

"I gathered that." He stopped in front of the desk and admired the painting behind it. "I was wondering, could you tell me—"

"Haven?"

He whipped around and smiled. Speaking of someone who could brighten his day. "Hey Callie."

"I didn't know you were coming in today."

"Well, I didn't either until last night. I got a text from Donna, my editor. She's been called out of town for a few weeks and offered her office to me for the time being. I couldn't turn her down."

"So, I'll get to see you on a daily basis." Jessica circled her arm around his. "My, what a treat."

Callie's mouth set in a line as straight as a ruler. "Jess."

She released his arm. "I'm just having some fun. Since when is flirting illegal?"

"Since Mom and Dad—"

The elevator bell dinged and the doors whooshed open behind Callie. She turned and her mouth dipped. "Mom. Dad."

The Channel 11 news anchors? They were Callie's parents? The owners of Superior Office Suites?

"Well, well, I see we're all hard at work here." The woman fired a hard stare to the girls, then she smiled as if a television camera had just flicked her way. "You must be our new tenant."

"Yes, ma'am." He offered his hand to Callie's mom first. "Haven Carlysle. I love your office setting."

"Mackenzie Armstrong-Beaumont." Her handshake was far stronger than he'd anticipated.

"Kenneth Beaumont." The father's hold was firm. "Welcome to Superior Office Suites. We hope you enjoy it here. We cater to long-term relationships. And don't worry about our First Impressions team. I'm certain we'll convince Callista to stay on."

Callie was leaving? He stared at her.

She ducked her head. "Dad, please—"

Mr. Beaumont held up his hand, and she clamped her mouth shut. "Isn't it time you get back to work?"

Her jaw worked back and forth. "Yes sir."

"Actually." Haven grabbed Callie's arm. "I was just taking her to lunch to discuss some business."

Her eyes widened, but thankfully she said nothing.

"I'm hoping she can throw together a website for me. We hoped to discuss it at Grandma's Sports Garden."

She cleared her throat. "Uh, yes, we were just leaving when you came up."

"Were you going too, Jessica?" Mrs. Beaumont waved her hand. "Our daughter has some fantastic ideas."

Jessica raised her pointer finger. "I would—"

"Just Callie and me." Callie clearly needed a break from these whirring family dynamics.

"Then perhaps you'll convince her to stay on. Her services are invaluable to our company."

To their company? Is that all they thought of? He took Callie's arm and tucked it around his. "It was nice to meet you both. I'll have Callie back as soon as we're done." Together they strode to the elevator and didn't turn around until the doors shut behind them. He released her arm as the elevator swooped downward. "I hope you don't mind my taking over like that."

"Mind? I could have kissed you." Her pale face pinked several shades darker. "I mean . . . Oh lollipops and licorice. That's exactly what I meant."

He felt his face warm, and he rubbed his hand over his chin. "I love your honesty."

"And it gets me into a heap of trouble, but I just can't stand pussyfooting around people. It's like trying to hide behind some verbal mask."

"You have nothing to hide from."

Gee, could he make her melt any more?

The elevator bell chimed and the doors slid open. They stepped into a retail center that was thriving with homegrown businesses. Coffee and candy shops. Clothing. Furniture. Hometown art. Jewelry. Knick knacks. Even ice cream. Reece would love that. This could be one of their Tuesday destinations.

Callie might enjoy that too.

Haven touched her arm. "I didn't mean to embarrass you, and if you're not up to lunch with me, that's fine, but I meant it when I said I wanted to talk business."

"No way are you going to take back your lunch invitation. I've been tasting that taco salad since you mentioned it."

"Then Grandma's it is."

CALLIE SAT ACROSS FROM Haven in the dining area that didn't hide the metal ductwork near the ceiling, giving the restaurant a warehouse atmosphere. A place that didn't have to be prettied up to be appreciated. Sure, it might be one of the area's touristy spots, but that didn't matter. She loved the food.

And today, she enjoyed the company.

The server took their orders, and then Callie searched for her purse.

Oh, shoot the can. In their rush to escape, she'd left it back at work. She didn't even have a pen to take notes. "I, uh, left everything back at the office."

He chuckled. "And I left my office door wide open with my laptop and expensive camera sitting right there for the taking."

"Oh no. We can head back." She pushed away from the table.

"It's fine, Callie." He pulled out his phone and punched some numbers. "Hi, Ashley . . . Yeah, would you mind locking my door for me? . . . Appreciate it." He returned the phone to his back pocket. "All taken care of."

"But . . . " How could she take notes on building his website? She stared at the table. Well, duh? The napkin, of course. World problems had been solved on those flimsy slips of paper; she could certainly plan a website. She unrolled the napkin and set aside the silverware. Now, for a pen.

The server carried over a round tray with their drinks. Perfect timing.

"Pardon me, would you happen to have a pen I could use, please? I'll return it before I leave."

"Not a problem." She handed Callie a cheap generic pen. "And if I don't get it back, I won't cry too loud."

"Thank you so much." Callie squared the napkin. "Okay, now, what's your vision for your business?"

"We're heading right into business talk then? No small talk? No getting to know you any better?"

"I, uh . . . " Oh, now he had her tongue-tied.

"I need to vet out the woman who holds my son's heart, don't you think?" He grinned.

Did he have to do that? Haven was quickly stealing her heart and her common sense. She should turn and run right now before he noticed her juvenile crush. But how could she do that when she'd made a promise to Amanda and to Reece that she'd chaperone Haven's visits? This was worse than pickles on a mustard sandwich.

She fingered her napkin and shrugged. "There's not much to tell."

"Why don't you start with why you're leaving your job? It'll be disappointing not seeing you when I pop in."

"I'm not really leaving completely. I mean, it's my parents' business, I won't leave them in the lurch, but my heart's not in it. I get tired of doing all this work to make businesses look good on the outside. What about what's in here?" She made a fist and pounced it over her heart.

"I checked out the websites you built, and you have captured the heart of the business. Sure, you make them look good, but it's more than that. There's a passion that shows in your work."

Oh, drat it all. Now a stupid tear wanted to fall. She blinked it away. "No one's ever told me that before."

"I wouldn't ask you to help me if I didn't mean it. I know you can create a site that'll show off the spirit of my work and, maybe, someday my photography can be more than an expensive hobby."

Yes, the perfect segue into a new conversation. "And what do you do when you're not taking pictures of sunsets?"

He looked down at the table and smirked. "I'm a collection agent. I'm the bad guy who calls people who are delinquent on mortgages."

"Really?" She wrinkled her nose. She always pictured the collection agent as some slimy Gollum-like creature that oozed out of a swamp. And Haven was so nice. He didn't fit that job description at all.

He looked her in the eye. "I do the job well, but the thing to remember is the good collectors are working for you, not against. The good collectors want you to keep your home and will help you find a way to do that."

"I never thought of it that way."

"Most people don't."

"But how do you deal with that side of it? Don't you get yelled at?"

He chuckled. "Yelled at, screamed at. Cursed out. Me and every member of my family and sometimes my best friend too."

"That sounds hideous. How do you take it?"

He shrugged and blinked a sad smile. "You want honesty or my pretend answer?"

"The truth. Always."

The server arrived at the table carrying Callie's taco salad and Haven's pepperoni bonotta, a rolled and stuffed pizza.

"Thank you." Haven nodded to the server then leaned back in his chair and stared up at the ceiling. "After what I did to Reece, I deserve every four-letter epithet spewed at me."

# Chapter Eight

"YOU CAN'T MEAN THAT."

Haven pinned her with his gaze. "I meant every word." Callie had no clue what it was like to live with the knowledge that his carelessness had crippled his son.

"What about forgiveness?"

"I know God's forgiven me, if that's what you're getting at, but I've earned the punishment."

"That doesn't apply to punishing yourself."

Touché. He smiled on one side of his mouth. "What was that I said about you being honest?"

"I'm sorry."

"Don't be. It's refreshing." He jabbed at his food with his fork. "Why don't we eat, then we can get down to business?"

"Sounds like a plan."

For the next twenty or so minutes they enjoyed their food mingled with small talk, but when the server removed their plates, it was time to get back to business.

Rather, Haven's business of finding out more about the mysterious Callista Beaumont. He leaned back in his chair and watched her wipe sauce from her mouth. How refreshing it was to be with someone who wasn't absorbed with appearances. She was one hundred percent genuine.

He folded his hands behind his head. "You never told me why you were leaving Superior Suites. Someone changed the subject."

"Gee, I wonder who that was." Biting her lower lip, she glanced toward the windows at pedestrians crowding the sidewalk.

"Yeah, I wonder."

"I don't like talking about myself."

"Then I get to fill in the blanks."

"Uh-oh."

"Let's see." He crossed his hands over his stomach. "You've signed on with the Peace Corps, and you're off to build septic systems and homes in third world countries."

She grinned. "Not a bad idea, but I'm not that altruistic. I'm just off to save my own little corner of the world. I've been volunteering as a naturalist at Gooseberry Falls State Park."

"A naturalist?"

"Working with the public, especially children, educating them about the wonders of God's creation. Teaching people to respect it."

"Sounds fascinating." He'd always loved nature, loved capturing it on film, and it disturbed him when people didn't respect God's handiwork. Callie would be the perfect person to educate the younger generation.

She leaned toward him, her eyes sparkling. "Oh, it is fascinating. Think about it. Your office is the wooded trails and grassy hills with real waterfalls as your backdrop. I get to fish and work with animals."

"Sounds like my kind of job."

"I knew you'd appreciate it, being a nature photographer and all."

"But apparently, it's become more than a volunteer position."

Callie toyed with her napkin. "And that's the problem."

"Why? Shouldn't your folks be thrilled you got a job doing something you love?"

"Don't I wish. They tolerated me getting a degree in biology."

"Just tolerated?"

"As long as I promised to return to Superior Suites after I graduated."

Haven shook his head. "I don't get it."

"Well, you see, the building housing Superior Suites has a family history. My great granddad was a furniture maker and that was his warehouse. Then my grandpa took over the business and ran it into the ground, not that I can really blame him. Business wasn't his thing, but he did what was expected of him."

"Just like you've been doing what's expected of you."

"Exactly. My mom inherited the worn-down building when Grandpa died, just as life was being breathed back into Canal Park. Mom saw the opportunity and ran with it."

"That's all great, but what does that have to do with you? It looks like Jess is more than willing to take over."

"Jess's job is, and always has been, to look pretty. She's the face of Superior Suites. My job has been to make everyone else look pretty, and I've discovered I'm very good at it. So good that I'm getting requests from beyond our little office suites and even beyond Minnesota."

"But that's not where your heart is."

"Exactly. But this service brings in a lot of money for the business, and Mom likes making money."

Haven huffed out a breath. "And here I am coming to you about my website. I'm sorry. I can look elsewhere."

"Please don't. Yours intrigues me. Anything that will show the world God's artwork is a worthwhile venture, don't you think?"

"Are you sure?"

She grinned. "Well, I haven't seen your photos, so I don't know if you're any good or not. You could be a tough sell."

"Then I guess our next step is to show you my work. I'd love to get your impression of it." He glanced at his watch. "I should probably get you back."

"Believe me, I'm in no hurry. Besides, I'm having fun."

"Me too." He shoved away from the table. "But unfortunately, work is calling me. I've got until the first part of July to create a portfolio to show my editor, and that'll decide whether I pursue photography as a profession or hobby."

He escorted Callie from the building. Crystal blue sky covered them as they walked along South Lake Avenue. Now this was the life. His six-year detour to Minneapolis had cured him of wanting to live in the big city. Duluth was plenty big for him. They crossed over Buchanan Street and passed the Morning Has Broken coffee shop and bakery. In spite of eating to fullness, the fresh baked bread scent wafted toward him begging him to enter.

Maybe some other time. Callie would probably appreciate another business lunch away from her office. To be honest with himself, he'd enjoy it too.

They stepped through the revolving doors leading into the Beaumonts' building and were greeted by a boisterous crowd. If Mackenzie Beaumont's concern was making money, by the looks of this purchasing throng, she needn't worry. But then tourists loved summers on the North Shore. For the next months, he'd be lucky if they could walk the streets without weaving through a crowd.

At the elevator, the doors opened before he had a chance to push the button. The interior designer stepped out with his mechanic wife and nodded to Haven. He greeted them in return then motioned for Callie to step in. A well-dressed older woman joined them before the doors closed.

"Hello again." The woman smiled at him. "Haven, is it?"

Again? When had he met her? "Yes, and I'm very sorry, I don't recall—"

"Forgive me." She patted her perfectly coiffed hair and shook her head as the elevator climbed. "Annabelle Scott. When you introduced yourself earlier today, I had yet to put on my face for the day. That marvelous landscape architect was giving dear Jessica and me lessons in gardening, and I had decided to learn *au naturel*. Believe me, it shan't happen again."

"Annabelle's our resident cosmetic queen. She can make lipstick look fabulous on a hyena."

"Dear, you are far too kind. Do keep it up. And, by the way, dear Callie, I have a pair of jeans in my office for you to pick up, if you don't mind."

"I'll stop by shortly."

Jeans? What was that all about? The doors opened before he had a chance to ask, and Haven trailed the women into the lobby. He was still shaking his head as Annabelle took a left around the reception desk. He and Callie veered to the right.

"She's quite the lady, isn't she?"

Haven chuckled and unlocked his office door. "I really have to stop making snap judgments. When I saw her earlier, I assumed she was the gardener, not the makeup expert."

"It is human nature." She led him into the office and walked right to the window. "And we live in an image-driven society. That's why I'm hired to create eye-catching websites. The businesses the sites promote may not be any good, but the website will get people in the doors."

"And that's why makeup artists and interior designers do their thing too."

"Exactly. I just wish I could get people to look at the heart first and not just the plastic veneer people put up."

"I wish I could say I was any better, but obviously, I'm not." He powered up his laptop.

"What are you going to do about Reece's race?"

Huh? He looked up, then grinned. "Squirrel."

She giggled and turned away from the window. "I see Reece has been teaching you."

"I'm getting quite the education." He joined her and looked out the window toward Bayfront Festival Park where the Whipper Snapper Race would take place. The park was too far away to watch the race from here, and if he watched down there, he'd have nowhere to hide but among the spectators. Callie's random musing brought up a good question. How would he watch Reece run? No way would he miss it, but he couldn't risk Amanda seeing him either, no matter how miniscule the chances were. "I'll come up with something." And he had just over two weeks to think of a plan.

Until then, it was time to work on his pictures. He returned to his desk and clicked on the slideshow. Hmm. The race could provide some unique shots. Maybe that was his angle. Something to think about anyway.

He pulled out his desk chair. "Have a seat. I'll show you my work, and I expect to hear that same honesty you gave me earlier."

Callie sat in his chair and watched the picture show run, mingling quiet with a periodic, "Beautiful" and "Amazing." Just the words he wanted to hear.

As the show played on, he rested his hand on the back of the chair, occasionally leaning forward to point out what he was trying to capture. The faint scent of coconut drifted toward him. He breathed in and leaned closer. It was Callie's hair.

Smooth, light brown hair untouched by bottled colors and curling chemicals. Hair that fell to just above chin level and gave a slight lift as if it were smiling. Hair as untouched and authentic as Callie. Why hadn't he noticed that before?

He fingered the loose strands that fell on the back of his hand. Soft enough to run his hands through and push back from her face and . . .

Whoa boy.

He released the chair and backed away, wiping his forehead with the back of his hand.

"Something wrong?" She spun the chair toward him and smiled. A smile as natural as her hair, a smile that made her blue eyes glitter.

What was she doing to him? He swallowed, and unhooked the top button on his rugby shirt. "Just feeling a little hot."

She nodded to the thermostat on the wall. "You can make it as hot or cold as you want."

"Thanks. I'll do that." But could he adjust the temperature on the unexpected feelings he had for Callie?

He had to. Reece was his priority. Period. He'd missed too much of Reece's life already.

Six years ago, when Haven had romanced the bottle, his son hadn't been a priority. Any romance now, anything that took away from his son, was forbidden.

CALLIE STARED UNFOCUSED AT the computer screen and worried her lower lip. That hadn't been interest in Haven's eyes, had it? An Adonis like him being interested in a plain Jane like her? She wanted to laugh at the absurdity.

Like a butterfly to lavender, beauty attracted beauty regardless if it was only skin deep.

She returned her attention to Haven's slideshow. Now, the beauty he caught on his camera, that was something else. He definitely had the artistic eye, a way of viewing nature through his lens that the average person couldn't see.

Pictures of the sun rising behind the lift bridge flashed on the screen. Probably from the morning they met. He'd captured the day's dawning beautifully with the sun arcing up the horizon, even if the pics were a tiny bit out of focus.

A picture appeared of two silhouetted figures playing on the beach, and Callie froze.

Her and Reece.

Anger tensed her fingers. He said he'd erased all the shots of her. This better be a mistake.

She slowly turned in his chair, her fists clenched in her lap, and glared up at him. "You said you'd get rid of those. I watched you delete them."

He blinked and looked over her shoulder then back at her eyes. "I kept one. I'm sorry, but . . . " He heaved a sigh. "Buts don't matter do they?"

"No, they don't. I want this gone." Her voice shook. "Period. Not for you, your editor or anyone else, do you understand?"

"Callie, it's a beautiful picture. I thought you'd love a copy. Reece too."

She shoved away from the desk and headed for the door. Yes, she was acting irrationally, but Haven had no clue what had happened to her before, and he never would.

"Callie, please. Help me understand."

"The only thing you need to know is if you don't delete that picture, I'm siding with Bill and Amanda, and you won't see Reece again."

## Chapter Nine

C ALLIE SPED DOWN THE hall, ignoring Jess's puzzled look as Callie brushed past. Now was absolutely not the time for a heart-to-sister talk. If she had any sense, she'd turn right back and apologize for her histrionics and for making that vacant threat. Reece needed to know his dad and she'd never intentionally come between them. Maybe she'd talk this over with Jess tonight, once rational thoughts returned to her muddled brain.

*That's what she gets for crushing on a photographer.*

A photographer of all things!

Hadn't one cruel lesson been enough?

She tugged open her office door and hurried inside, slamming the door behind her. Her jaw clenched, she sank into her office chair and stared at her sleeping computer monitor. What she'd give to be out in the wild right now, free from these confining walls, communing with God's creatures and teaching elementary school children.

Just two and a half more weeks.

Then her interaction with Haven would be limited to two hours on Tuesday evenings. And that time would be spent focusing on Reece. She could do that without making a fool of herself in front of Haven.

As long as he kept his camera lens on Reece and not her.

That shouldn't be a problem. After her drama queen demonstration moments ago, the guy probably wanted to stay miles away from her.

A rap on her office door broke her trance on the monitor.

"Callie, can we talk?"

Haven. Oh, toads on tree bark. Two and a half weeks seemed

infinite. A mature woman would invite him in and apologize.

Another rap, harder and faster.

"Callie? Are you all right?"

Just dandy. *I love making irrational scenes in front of gorgeous men. It's what I do best.*

A quieter tap. "Callie, I'm sorry."

Her lips puckered. Oh, why did he have to go and be so decent? "Come in."

The door opened slowly and Haven entered, stoop shouldered with worry forming a V in his brows. "I—"

She held up her hand, quieting him. "You have nothing to apologize for." She pointed to the chair in front of her desk. "Have a moment?"

"Whatever it takes." He closed her office door then sat across from her. "I—"

Again, she held up her hand. "I'm the one who needs to apologize. I completely overreacted, and I want to assure you that I won't say a word to Amanda and Bill. That was a purely mean thing to say and I am very sorry."

His shoulders and brows relaxed. "It wasn't my intention to hurt you. I thought you'd appreciate the picture. When I look at it, I see love."

Callie closed her eyes and visions of other pictures littered her brain. Hurtful and even hateful pictures. "I know." She tapped her foot beneath her desk and wished she could tuck the rest of herself under the desk too, away from his compassionate gaze. "I have my reasons, but I . . . I don't want to explain it. It's personal."

"Then I need to respect that. I'm sorry if I hurt you."

"Thanks for understanding."

He backed his chair up and stood. "I'll see you Tuesday?"

"Five o'clock."

"I'm looking forward to it."

*So am I.* What was she getting herself into?

WHAT WAS HE GETTING himself into? Kneading the back of his neck, Haven slipped out of Callie's office and down the hall. Jessica stood at the reception desk talking with Ashley as he strode through the lobby. If he hurried, she wouldn't see him, and he could get back in his office and delete that picture from his computer's memory.

Callie clearly had issues to deal with, and something inside him wanted to help her through those problems, but that wasn't his place. Or was it?

He curved his hand around his doorknob and turned it.

"Hey Haven, do you have a moment?"

Did that woman ever work?

With a sigh, he turned to face Jessica and forced a smile. "How can I help you?"

She invaded his space and shoved his door open. "We should have some privacy."

That wasn't happening. He leaned against his doorframe and crossed his arms. "Here is good."

She held up her hands as if in surrender. "I'm not coming on to you, I just want to know about Callie." And that wasn't a conversation for the hallway.

With a sigh, he nodded to his office. "Go on in." He left the door open and walked to his chair, keeping the desk between them.

She sat and looked him in the eye. "I haven't seen her this upset in years. She wouldn't tell me anything."

"Maybe you should give her time."

"It's your fault, you know."

He cringed. Yeah, he knew, but how did Jessica? "You want to elaborate?"

"She likes you." Her nose wrinkled ever so slightly.

"And I like her." But he didn't like the direction this conversation was taking.

Jessica folded her arms on his desk and leaned toward him. Her snug, scoop-neck sweater tugged tighter, emphasizing her physical assets. "Of course, you do. Everyone likes Callie, but I mean she really, really likes you, know what I mean?"

Backing his chair toward the wall, he shook his head. "I've known her for all of four days. We're friends, and she's doing me a huge favor. Don't read any more into it than that." Now, if he could convince himself of the same thing.

She leaned closer and her shirt dug lower. "I know my sister, and the only other time I saw her that mad was when a man rejected her."

He focused on his laptop. "That isn't why she was upset."

"Keep fooling yourself." She chuckled. "Listen, I'll tell her tonight you're not interested, and then maybe you and I can—"

"Jessica, stop." He slapped his hand on the desk. It was hard to believe these two were sisters. One was completely genuine, the other probably didn't have an authentic bone or skin cell left in her body.

Jessica's collagen-filled lower lip stuck out.

Oh brother. He ran a hand through his hair. This poor woman had issues too—emotionally and physically—that he had no desire to deal with. Sure, Callie had problems, but the difference was, she didn't display them for the world to see. Someone other than he would have to deal with Jessica.

"I'm here to work." He touched the camera bag on his desk. Maybe if he ripped an honesty page from Callie's book, Jessica would get the hint. "Look, Jess, it's not my intent to hurt you, but I've no interest in a romantic relationship with you or anyone right now so I'd appreciate it if you'd lay off the flirting."

Her entire face seemed to droop, along with her shoulders. "All right." She backed away, her lip protruding. Maybe it was permanently like that. "I'm just concerned for her. I love my big sister, and I don't like to see her hurt."

Finally, an unselfish thought. Hmm, maybe if he told Jessica what he and Callie had fought about, that would give him a little insight, so he could help Callie over this hurdle.

And maybe it would get Jessica out of his office. "The problem is, I took Callie's picture."

Jessica puffed out a lungful of air. "Oh boy, that explains it."

"Explains what? It was a beautiful portrait of her and Reece."

She sat back, her lip returned to normal, if there was a normal. "Callie hates having her picture taken."

There was an understatement. He worked his jaw back and forth picturing Callie's near-hysterical response. "She doesn't hate it, she's terrified of it. I want to know why so I can help her."

Jess shook her head and frowned. "We haven't had a family portrait done in years because of it, which totally tees Mom off, but it's the one thing Callie's been firm about. No one knows why. It started when she was a senior in high school and hasn't let up. If you can get it out of her, then you'll be doing better than I have."

Haven gazed at his camera, his lips scrunched to one side. "I'll see what I can do." Although he might need more than two hours a week.

"You're sweet." She flashed a perfect smile. A perfectly fake one anyway. "Are you sure you won't take me up on dinner tonight?"

He groaned. "Jessica . . . "

She tsked and stood up. "Your loss." She walked from his office swaying very curvy hips. Maybe once upon a time that would have intrigued him. What testosterone-filled twenty-something wouldn't have looked twice? But he was long past that kind of attraction.

He flipped open his laptop and brought up the picture of Callie and Reece. It was a shame she couldn't see the scene's beauty. His finger hovered over the delete button, but he couldn't bring it down. Instead, he dragged the photo to his personal photo file. No one else would ever see it.

Time to get to work. He shut the office door. Hopefully, that would give Jessica a clue. He had a queasy feeling she had more ammunition to fire his way.

But it wouldn't work on him. If he ever did date again, he'd want someone real and honest. Someone not afraid to be herself. Now that was true beauty.

Someone just like Callie.

HAVEN PULLED THE DULUTH Bulldogs cap down low on his forehead and adjusted his Ray-Bans as he threaded his way through the crowd at Bayfront Festival Park. If Amanda saw him here at the Whipper Snapper races, she'd threaten his visitation again. Just as she had this past Tuesday when Haven got in a full two-hour visitation with Reece—and Callie—this time at an indoor go-cart park. Man, that kid loved speed! And Haven was feeling really good about the day until he and Callie brought Reece home and Amanda reiterated that Haven had no business watching Reece's race.

No business. Hah. Legally, he was certain she didn't have grounds, but bringing in an attorney still didn't sit well with him. So for now, he planned to play nice.

And for today, he planned to remain hidden from Amanda and Bill's suspicious eyes because there was no way he was going to let his son down. His biggest obstacle had been taking time off a job he'd only started on Monday.

With the shoulder-to-shoulder crowd surrounding him, staying hidden shouldn't be a problem. He itched his Just For Men-darkened beard. Hopefully the unnatural color would help hide his identity. He navigated through the onlookers until he could see where the racers lined up. The Whipper Snapper, for runners ages fourteen and under, was far more popular than he imagined. He'd read just yesterday that over a thousand kids would participate, and Reece was among them. He couldn't be more proud.

He spotted Amanda and Bill in the front row. Callie, wearing a bright green baseball cap, stood beside them. He pulled to a stop several rows behind the trio. If Amanda saw him up close, she'd see right through his flimsy disguise, but it was the best he could do. No threat was going to make him break his promise to Reece, even if Haven couldn't run up and give his son a hug following the Whipper Snapper race. These past couple of weeks, Reece had brought up the subject every five seconds, along with making Haven promise on Callie's Bible that he'd be here.

Man, he loved that kid! And to think he'd missed the past six years of his life. Never again, no matter what restrictions Amanda placed on his visits.

She hadn't let up on her threats either. Whether those threats were legally binding, he didn't know. Family issues didn't belong in court, so he'd resolved to do whatever possible to avoid involving an attorney. Besides, she had two attorneys on her side, and he couldn't risk aggravating them.

So, here he was, slinking around like a criminal, just to watch his son do what he loved. The trick would be keeping an eye on Amanda and Bill, while cheering on Reece, to make certain they didn't come close to him.

The crowd roared as a field full of seven- and eight-year-old girls sprinted away from the starting line, all donning a black number one on their racing bib.

Reece would be in the second group, running with the boys. Haven pulled his camera from the case he'd purchased just for today. Amanda would recognize his diaper bag. He turned on the camera, adjusted the settings, and followed the determined young athletes through the LCD lens. Boisterous cheers and hoots filled the air from the first step until the last child crossed the finish line a quarter mile away where they got to slap hands with Minnesota Viking cheerleaders.

He zoomed in on the runners' exuberant and proud faces as they were each given a red ribbon for participating. It didn't matter if they won or not. They had competed and finished, and that made them victorious.

Haven couldn't be prouder of his son, not only for running but for not letting his prosthesis be a handicap. He focused back on the starting line where seven- and eight-year-old boys crowded, all wearing the number one. Through his camera lens, he located Reece and zoomed in. He snapped a few shots then settled the camera against his chest. As Callie had wisely stated a few weeks back, he didn't want to be the parent whose memories existed only as digital images. He wanted to remember the entire experience.

The crowd quieted, and the racers all leaned forward hoping to gain an edge. The gun sounded, and the crowd's cheers echoed in his ears. Amanda's "Go Reece" seemed to rise above them all. Determination steeled Reece's face as he sprinted across the grass toward the finish line, running well behind the front runners, yet far from the last.

Haven clenched his jaw and his fists, yelling encouragement in his head. The first runners crossed the finish line. Reece's limp became more pronounced as he ran, but his eyes remained on the goal. Ten more yards to go. Nine. Eight. Seven. *Go Reece, you can do it.*

Five. Fo—

Reece stumbled over another runner's foot and sailed face first into the ground, his prosthetic foot bending at an impossible angle.

And he didn't get up.

# Chapter Ten

HAVEN PUSHED THROUGH THE suddenly-silent crowd as Amanda and Bill rushed toward Reece. He broke through the first row, and a hand grabbed his arm.

"Let them take care of it."

Haven glared back at Callie and yanked his arm free. "He needs me."

"That's right. He does. And if you go running out there, you're going to cause problems. Amanda will take care of this."

He glanced over at Reece who was turning over onto his back. Grass and dirt streaked a tear-covered face.

"Reece, you can do it." Bill patted him on the shoulder.

Haven balled his fists. Bill was forcing Reece to run, after this? What kind of monster was that man?

Amanda rolled Reece's pant leg up and readjusted the prosthesis. "There. Just as good as new." She patted his leg and gave him a smile. "Now finish." She pointed to the goal line just feet away.

"But—"

"But nothing, young man." She helped him stand. "You're not a quitter."

Reece wiped his eyes and looked outward at the crowd, connecting with Haven's gaze. A wide grin spread on Reece's face, and he pushed back to his feet. Amanda shot a glance at the crowd, and Haven brought his head down.

"Did she see me?" he muttered to Callie.

"I don't think—Oh, there he goes!"

Haven looked up just as Reece leaped across the finish line, pumping his fists. Bill and Amanda engulfed the child in hugs, congratulating him for pressing on.

They had done the right thing. How could Haven have been so wrong? Maybe because he didn't know a single thing about raising children. Or maybe because he was intimately familiar with quitting, as he'd quit on his family years ago. He'd changed, hadn't he?

Maybe Reece was better off without Haven's intrusion.

Reece broke from his mother's hug and looked back toward Haven. More than anything he wanted to run to Reece and ensnare his son in a hug, but that would have to wait until Tuesday. Instead he gave a wink and a thumbs-up. Hopefully, Reece would understand.

Reece joined the line of participants and received his red ribbon. This, Haven could record. He aimed his camera and snapped shots.

Grinning at the camera, Reece grabbed his mother's arm and pointed toward Haven.

Oh no! Haven ducked and Callie stepped in front of him. *Please, God, don't let her see me.* His heart sprinted as he peered from under his cap.

Amanda was looking his way, her mouth set in a terse line. With her pointer finger she drew an imaginary line across her neck.

Dread curdled in his stomach. Maybe if he slipped away, Amanda would question what she saw. Hunching over, he wove through the audience, putting as much distance between him and Amanda as possible before the crowd thinned. From there he jogged to his car at the Great Lakes Aquarium.

He slunk down in his seat and took deep breaths, calming his heart, but not his thoughts.

Amanda was a good mother and, as much as Bill irritated Haven, the guy appeared to care for Reece and want the best for him.

Amanda had given Reece the stick-to-it spirit.

Haven had taught him to quit.

Maybe Amanda was right. Haven was nothing more than an unnecessary intrusion in his son's life. Who was he to waltz back into Reece's life after six years' absence and think he could claim father's rights? By quitting on Reece six years ago, hadn't he forfeited those rights, regardless of what legal forms claimed?

Whereas Amanda had stuck in there and raised their son to never quit despite his disability. She knew what was best for their son who seemed to be thriving. And that didn't include Haven.

Perhaps that was for the best.

REECE SKIPPED TOWARD CALLIE, clutching his red ribbon, his eyes darting back and forth. Amanda and Bill kept pace beside him.

Callie looked upward. *Please, God, let them understand.*

"Where is he? Where's Dad?" His eyes sparkling bright as the sun-glinted water, Reece held out his ribbon for Callie to see. "Dad?"

Callie's foot bounced nervously as she glanced at Amanda.

Amanda's lips smiled, but fire blazed from her eyes. "Yes, Callie, where is Haven?"

Oh, snickerdoodles and snapping turtles. Callie looked at the ground and drew a circle with her foot.

"I saw him, ridiculous beard and all."

"It wasn't ridiculous, Mom, but I saw him too, and I was so happy. I didn't think he came, and he promised he would, so I was really bummed when I ran, and I didn't try as hard, and then I when I fell I thought why get up, but then I saw him, and I knew I had to finish. So, where'd he go? I need to show him my ribbon."

Callie knelt and gave Reece a hug. The child could talk almost as fast as he could run. "Buddy, you are a wonder, do you know that?" She looked up at Amanda whose stern appearance had softened. "Haven just wanted to be here for his son. Was that so bad?"

"Yeah, Mom, why is that so bad? I wanted him here, and he kept his promise, and you always tell me it's important to keep promises, don't you?"

Amanda sighed. "Yes, it's important."

"So, where'd he go, Aunt Callie? I need to show him my ribbon."

"Bud, he had to take off." She bopped his nose. "But he burst all six buttons off his shirt when you finished that race. He'll probably be bragging to everyone he meets now about his brave son."

"You think so? You really think I'm brave?"

"Well, duh. You're probably the bravest kid I know. So, you just keep that ribbon safe, and on Tuesday when we get to spend an entire two hours with your dad"—Callie connected a stern gaze with Bill and Amanda—"then you can show him your ribbon."

"Sweet."

"And I'm guessing he got a few pictures of you too, that you can display right along with that ribbon."

"He's a good picture taker, huh?"

"I think he's the best."

"I think so too. Are you coming out to dinner with us? Bill said we need to celebrate, and I think so too, and I really want you to come."

"You know what, I have to finish up a job at my office tonight because I took this afternoon off, but I tell you what, next Tuesday we'll celebrate with your dad. Is that a deal?" She offered her hand.

He shook her hand like shaking an Etch A Sketch. "That's a deal."

"And that's my boy." She stood and placed a hand on his shoulder while focusing on Bill and Amanda. They wouldn't dare threaten to stop Haven from seeing his son now, would they?

Bill grimaced. "We'll see you on Tuesday."

"Two whole hours, right?"

Amanda wagged a finger at Callie. "Not a second more."

"Or less."

"Right." Amanda sighed. "Remind me why you're my best friend."

Callie hugged her. "Love you." And then whispered, "I knew you'd do the right thing."

At least she'd hoped Amanda would. It was a tough call now with Bill's influence. Callie waved to the family then began the trek back to her office. Without humidity, and with the breeze coming off the lake, it was a refreshing walk. She passed the freshwater Great Lakes Aquarium and the convention center and then rounded the William A. Irvin, an ore boat now permanently moored to a Duluth dock on the Lake Superior waterfront. Now a floating museum. So much history in one area.

History kept alive through artifacts and photographs.

Sometimes pictures lied.

She shook the thought from her head and cut through parking lots to South Lake Avenue and completed the short walk to her parents' office building.

It had felt so good to be outside during the day instead of stuck inside looking out a window at the world she longed to be part of. She might as well be looking at a photograph for all the good it did her.

But all that would change in a little over a week. She walked into the building, rode the elevator to the top floor, and wound her way past the conference room to her office. Her First Impressions, graphic design part of the family business was hidden in the back so as not to make a wrong first impression. Out in nature, no one cared.

She sat at her desk and awoke her computer. Time to get her work done so she could spend the weekend in fresh air. But with whom? She stared out her picture window up toward Enger Tower. Jess had plans all weekend, as did Amanda. Time spent alone was fine, but too much time alone—

Her phone buzzed and Callie startled.

"Haven Carlyle's on line one, Callie."

Haven.

She gnawed on her lower lip as she spun her chair toward her desk. Maybe he'd . . .

Right. Dream on, Callie girl. She picked up the receiver and hit the lighted button. "Haven, hi."

"Callie, have you got a minute?"

For him, absolutely. "Sure, what do you need?" She twisted the cord around her fingers and turned toward her window.

A heavy sigh came over the phone. "Reece. Where do I . . . ?"

Where does he . . . ? Oh. Stand. Shoot, she should have called him right away. He was probably worried sick. "You were the reason Reece finished the race today."

"Me? But I thought Amanda and Bill . . . they're the ones who told him to keep moving."

"You showed up. You risked everything and were there for him."

"But what about Amanda? She warned me to stay away."

"And Reece convinced her he needed you."

Silence talked back.

"Are you okay?"

He laughed softly. "Better than okay. I thought . . . I thought that was it. I thought I'd blown it again."

"Only if you fail to show up on Tuesday, and I promise you they'll give you the full two hours again."

"Thanks, Callie. Where would I be without you?"

"Oh, you'd be fine." She twisted the phone cord around her wrist, glad he couldn't see her blush.

"I'll see you Tuesday."

"I'm looking forward to it."

They said their goodbyes, and she hung up, rolling her eyes. *Way to go, Callie girl, you may as well have drooled all over him too.* Haven's interest in her was nothing more than a means to get close to his son. Once that was achieved, he'd forget she existed.

The problem was, she doubted she could forget him.

Chapter Eleven

CALLIE STUDIED GEMMA PATTERSON'S resume, one of three applicants she'd called to interview. The first two interviews today had gone well, but didn't overly impress her. She'd be settling if she hired either one. The third applicant would arrive any second now. Callie prayed she was the right one for the job. If not, Callie'd be going through this whole hiring process again.

While waiting, she added an image to a client's website and sat back to study the page. Eye-catching with a short, yet clever slogan to draw in potential business. Easy to understand and navigate. Mobile friendly and handicap accessible. Her client should be happy. They usually were.

Now she only had a month's work left to finish before her final full day here on Friday, a mere four and a half days away. Working twenty-four hours a day might give her enough time to finish.

But then she'd be starting her new job. Grinning, she did a little jig in her chair. One week from today, she'd be starting her dream job! With the exception of Tuesday, she'd be working the afternoon/evening shift that first week, so she could train in her replacement here in the morning. Gemma had better be the right one.

Her phone buzzed and Ashley's voice came over the speaker. "Your next interview is here."

"Send her in." Callie clicked out of her program and put the computer to sleep. A knock sounded on the door. "Come on in."

The door opened and Callie stood to greet her possible replacement.

A plump brunette with a round face and gray eyes.

Callie's parents would turn Gemma away faster than Callie could say *it*. Her parents probably wouldn't notice Gemma's pure smile that added a glow to those gray eyes.

Callie liked her immediately. "Good morning, Gemma." Callie walked around her desk and offered her hand. "I'm Callie Beaumont."

Gemma's smile broadened. "I'm pleased to meet you, Ms. Beaumont."

"Oh, please, it's Callie."

"Callie. Thank you so much for this interview."

"You're welcome." Callie gestured to the side of the room where two cushioned chairs were set for conversation. A pitcher of ice water and crystal goblets waited on an ottoman in between the chairs. "Won't you have a seat?"

Gemma sat, clutching a binder in her lap.

The gripping hands were the only thing that gave away Gemma's anxiety. Callie poured two glasses of water and set one in front of Gemma. "Why don't you tell me about yourself?"

Gemma smiled. "Well, I grew up in Two Harbors. My parents are both physicians, and my brother's a surgeon, so naturally I went to St. Scholastica for nursing, but I ended up at UMD for graphic design."

Interesting. "Now, that's quite a shift in focus."

Gemma shrugged. "It was more of me asserting myself and having the nerve to tell my parents I didn't want to go into medicine."

"I can relate to that." Callie grinned. Perhaps she'd found more than a replacement, maybe she'd gained a new friend. "How did that go over with your parents?"

"Much better than I anticipated. I always assumed I should go into medicine. But my heart was in designing. After taking my first college biology class, though, I knew I couldn't do it. So, I approached them with all my research of schools and employment possibilities and told them I wanted to change majors. My dad smiled and said, 'It's about time'."

"You're kidding." What Callie would have given to have had that kind of affirmation from her parents.

"No. They said they knew it all along but were waiting for me to know it myself. They said learning to assert myself was part of my education. I really learned how blessed I am."

That she was. Callie held in a sigh and pointed to Gemma's binder. "May I have a look at your work?"

"Absolutely."

Callie paged through Gemma's portfolio. The woman definitely had talent, but that didn't necessarily mean she could create what Superior Suites' clients wanted. It was one thing to be a talented artist and another to apply that talent to a specific need.

Callie asked Gemma a few more questions, then retrieved a binder from her desk. "I'm impressed with your work here, but now comes the fun part." She opened the binder and placed it in front of Gemma. "I've created a mock company here and your job is to use the information given to create a logo, letterhead, and website that fits this company's needs. I'm giving you until Friday to put this together. Keep in mind that people form an opinion within seconds of seeing something. Your job is to create a captivating impression, one that will prompt prospective clients to look further. Then, you need to layer in the pertinent information that makes the company look good."

"Okay. Do you mind if I look through this first and see if I have any questions?"

"Be my guest." Gemma paged through the binder, her mouth intermittently shifting sides. "If I have any questions during the week, may I call you?"

Hmmm. Gemma was the first to ask that. Showed she wasn't afraid to do whatever she had to do to get the job done right. "I highly encourage it."

"Wonderful. Thank you."

"Can you come back this Friday, same time?"

"I'll be here." Gemma picked up the books off the table and clutched them against her chest. "I appreciate you giving me this opportunity."

"Gladly. And I look forward to seeing what you can do." Callie escorted Gemma out then returned to her desk. She swiveled her chair to face out the window and look up at the hill. The blue-brick tower stood proud at the top of that hill.

Her parents *would* be proud of her for following her dreams. Just like Gemma's. Maybe not now, but someday they would.

One week from today she'd be out there amidst nature, no longer tied to the eight-to-five day. Of course, she'd still come in to Superior Suites to train her replacement, but the right person should have the initiative to take over.

Hopefully, Gemma was that person. That was what Callie's gut told her.

Now, to get through the week without any setbacks.

A LIGHT MIST FLOATED down as Haven walked up to Amanda's door. Figured, it had to rain again on his day with Reece. Their scheduled trip to Enger Tower would have to wait until next week, but the ice cream parlor wouldn't be a bad substitute.

He raised his hand to knock on the door and hit air as the door flew open.

"Hey, Dad."

Haven couldn't stop his grin. No word sounded sweeter than *Dad*. "Ready to go?"

"Yep." Reece pulled a rain poncho over his head. "Aunt Callie says we're going to Enger Tower."

Sure, now he gets to disappoint his son. "Well, it's raining. How about next—"

"Rain, schmain." Callie stepped next to Reece, also wearing a hooded poncho, and carrying a closed umbrella. "I'm not afraid of a few raindrops, are you Reece?"

"Uh-uh, and if it rains really hard we can have toothpick races and splash in puddles and—"

"Whoa there. Sounds like fun, but what would your mother say?" Haven looked inside the house. No sign of Amanda. "I don't think she'd appreciate it if I brought you home with pneumonia." That was putting it mildly. That would nix any chance he had with Reece.

"Oh, pshaw." Callie gave Reece a light shove onto the porch and followed him, pulling the door shut behind her. "A little rain never hurt anyone. Didn't you ever play in the rain?"

Haven scratched his head. "Can't say that I did."

"Reece." Callie laid a hand on Reece's shoulder. "We have a lot to teach your daddy, don't we?"

His eyes grew wide, and he gave an exaggerated nod. "That's for sure."

Chuckling, Haven took the umbrella from Callie and popped it open. "You're certain Amanda wouldn't mind."

"Who do you think taught Reece to play in the rain?"

Amanda? Ha! No way.

Callie skipped down the steps and onto the sidewalk into a mist that had become a drenching downpour. She shook off her hood, spread out her arms, looked to the sky, and opened her mouth. Reece mimicked her.

The Amanda he remembered would never have allowed that.

Haven glanced at his open umbrella then out at Callie and Reece dancing in the rain. Callie was nuts. Getting soaked to the skin didn't look like fun at all.

Maybe it wasn't Amanda who would have objected.

He puffed out a breath and closed the umbrella. It was time for him to grow up and become a kid again.

Closed umbrella in hand, he leaped over the stairs, away from the protection of the porch roof, and craned his head back. Drops pelted his face, and his rugby shirt velcroed itself to his skin.

Nope, not fun at all, but if this was what Reece enjoyed, he'd suffer through it.

He felt a hand on his arm and looked down at Callie. Her hair had begun to curl and mascara tracked down her face, but joy beamed from her eyes.

"Having fun?" she asked.

"You want the truth?"

"I thought so." She nodded toward her car. "Ice cream might just coax him away."

"Ice cream?" Reece stopped dancing, and his eyes lit up.

Haven pointed at his car with his thumb. "Let's go." Then he smiled at Callie. "Thank you." He could almost kiss her. "We'll take my car today. I might even have a rain jacket in my trunk." He aimed his key fob, and the lights flashed on his Buick.

"Ah, so you don't appreciate cramming those long legs into the Seussmobile." She hurried alongside him and Reece ran ahead.

"Now that you mention it." He opened the door for Callie. She stepped in, and he closed the door behind her.

The rain came down in buckets as he circled his Buick, not bothering to get the rain coat. It was a little too late for it anyway. He jumped into the driver's seat and turned on the car and the heat. No way was Reece going home with a cold.

He looked in his rearview mirror at Reece seated in the middle. "Buckle up. This car doesn't move until all passengers are strapped in."

Reece rolled his eyes. "Just like Mom."

"Your mom's right." After hearing the click of the buckle, Haven pulled out onto the street, his wipers fighting to keep his window clear. Again, he glanced in his rearview mirror. "You sure you want ice cream? Not hot chocolate?"

Reece's lip stuck out. "You promised ice cream."

"Then I better keep that promise."

"Banana!" Reece shouted.

Haven watched a yellow VW Beetle splash past, then looked over at Callie and raised his eyebrows. "He does this all the time?"

She nodded, grinning.

"And you taught him?"

"Guilty."

Haven took a deep breath and heaved it out. "I suppose I have to get used to it."

"You will." She rested a warm hand on his damp arm. "It's got to be hard, being thrust into fatherhood."

"It shouldn't be that way. I should have been there all along."

"You didn't have a choice."

"Not true. I didn't fight for him."

"You're fighting now."

"But will I win?" He looked in the rearview mirror again and regret clogged his throat.

Callie squeezed his arm, and her hand stayed there. "Stop looking back."

He laughed. "I've heard those exact words before. My mentor once told me that looking back only prevented me from moving forward."

"Wise man."

Haven stole a glance at Callie. What a wise woman.

He shifted his gaze back to the road while Reece chattered behind him. A few blocks later he spotted the red and white awning of the ice cream shop. Looking ahead was definitely better than looking back, even if the way wasn't clear. And if he had to get a little wet in the process, it would be worth it to be Dad to his son again.

CALLIE YANKED HER HAND from Haven's arm as he parked in front of the ice cream shop. What had possessed her to be so forward? She looked down at her offending hand. It still tingled from the touch. How immature could she be? Making goo-goo eyes at a guy who would never see her as more than a means to reach his son. Puhlease. Today was about Haven getting to know Reece better and vice versa. It had nothing to do with her.

Rain pelted the car as she tugged on the car handle.

Haven's hand on her arm stopped her. "I'll get your door."

Oh, why does he have to go and be so nice, so gentlemanly? This wasn't the man Amanda had described all these years. Not at all.

"I'm goin' in." Reece was out of the car and inside the shop before Haven had his door closed. That left her with Haven. Alone.

She shook her head. *Callie girl, you have one job and that's to supervise, got it?* And if she did her job right, Amanda would see that Haven had changed, and Reece would benefit from having his dad in his life. And then everyone would move on.

At least she'd be moving on to a job she loved.

Her car door opened, letting in a whoosh of rain. Haven offered his hand and sanctuary beneath an umbrella. Sure, completely erase the last few seconds of convincing herself Haven couldn't be a part of her future. She was a grown woman, for nature's sake, way too old for a teenage crush.

Regardless, she grasped his hand—a very strong hand—and he helped her from the car not letting a drop of water hit her.

He followed her to the restaurant, standing way too close beneath the umbrella. Even wet, the faint suggestion of his musky cologne was enticing. *Callie girl, you are a goner.* By the time Amanda made up her mind about Haven, Callie'd be completely infatuated with the guy.

And then he'd hurt her.

That was how life worked.

Although with Haven, she doubted the hurt would be intentional.

Not like Sean's.

Trembling, she opened the door and a bell jingled above her head. She stepped onto a black and white linoleum tiled floor that took her fifty years back in time.

"You're chilled." Haven pointed at her poncho. "See what happens when you play in the rain?"

She looked up into his gorgeous blue eyes, twinkling with his grin, and that alone chased her chills.

Oh, rain in the winter, she didn't have to worry about being infatuated in the future, the future was already here.

She looked away and focused on the menu hung behind the fifties-style soda fountain.

"Can I have whatever I want?" Reece tugged on Haven's damp shirt. "Mom never lets me have what I want, she says it'll ruin my supper, but I always eat everything, even when I eat dessert first, cuz I'm always hungry, and—"

"Whoa, there, can I get a word in?" Haven cuffed a hand over Reece's shoulder.

"I know, Mom says I talk way too much and she doesn't know where I get it—"

Haven laughed. Shoot, he had a nice laugh. "I guess I have to agree with her. Now, is there any other reason why she doesn't let you choose exactly what you want? Are you allergic to anything?"

"Nuh-uh. She just doesn't want me to fill up on treats, but I've already had dinner, so I don't have to worry about filling up—"

"What do you think, Callie? Would Amanda mind?"

"Go ahead and spoil him."

"Sweet!" Reece raced to the counter and got in line behind two other kids about Reece's height.

Callie started to follow, but Haven's hand on her arm stopped her.

"I don't want to just be the dad who gives him whatever he wants, Callie. I want to be more than Santa Claus to Reece."

Oh, now he had to go and get all wise on her even. "You're right. I think I'm guilty of that."

"The only thing you're guilty of is loving." His gaze met hers and held for an eternal second. His Adam's apple bounced, and he jerked his gaze away. Clearing his throat, he pointed to the menu. "Have whatever you want. Then I get to have whatever I want."

Callie gnawed on her lip as she floated toward the counter. What just happened there? She swallowed. Nothing. Just imagining what she wanted to see. He was just being nice and her infatuated mind had to go and make something big out of it. *Get a grip, Callie girl.*

She waited behind Reece as the server handed over a dirt sundae. Oreo ice cream smothered with fudge, marshmallow cream, Oreo crumbs, and to top it off—gummy worms. The treat looked nasty. There couldn't be a better sundae for Reece.

But now for her. She scanned the menu posted on the back wall. Banana split? Boring. Turtle sundae? Hmmm, maybe. Scotch and fudge? Oh, now that made her mouth water. Butter pecan ice cream topped with butterscotch, hot fudge, and pecans. Mmm, mmmm. She placed her order and moments later the server handed over a sundae in a tulip-shaped glass. She licked at the generous swirl of whipped cream before it dripped over the side, making certain not to upset the cherry. That she'd save for last. This single dessert would deplete her calorie quota for the day, but as long as it was a rare treat, she didn't care.

"If you can't eat all of that . . . " Haven nodded to her dessert.

"Don't even think about it." She held it away from him. "This one's all mine."

He grinned and then placed his order for a grasshopper sundae. Grasshoppers and gummy worms. Father and son were more alike than Haven realized. She carried her treat to the red Formica-topped, chrome-edged table Reece had claimed. She removed her poncho and hung it over a chrome chair padded with red vinyl then sat down by a window pelted with rain. A steady stream of water flowed down the sidewalk. Maybe Haven was right. Maybe they should forgo Enger Tower for the day.

But she'd been looking forward to it . . .

Well, it would give her something to look forward to next week.

"Can I have your cherry?" Reece reached across the round table, his spoon angled to steal it.

She pulled her treat to the edge of the table and swatted his hand away. "Keep your hands off."

"My, you're protective of your ice cream." Haven sat, forming a people triangle. He set down his glass that overflowed with mint ice cream, chocolate syrup, and chunks of Andes mints. His whipped cream swirled nearly as high as hers, but she still had more. And her cherry was bigger too.

"I have more whipped cream than you." She carved a spoonful of ice cream and delivered it to her mouth. Oh, *sweet* heaven. There had to be ice cream in heaven, didn't there?

"I didn't know it was a contest." Haven spooned a bite into his mouth and moaned. "Oh man, that is good."

"When it comes to ice cream, it's always a contest."

"Yeah, Dad, don't ya know nothin'? Can I have your cherry?" Reece scooped the cherry from Haven's sundae so quickly, Haven didn't have time to blink.

"Uh . . . " He looked down at his ice cream, then over at his son, his mouth open. "You . . . "

Reece began to giggle and Callie couldn't resist joining in.

"I feel like you two are teaming up on me." Haven clutched his glass and moved it to the edge of the table, far away from pilfering spoons.

"Now you know we take our ice cream very seriously." Callie took another bite and sighed with pleasure.

"Well, just to warn you, payback is coming."

"Is that a threat?"

"That, dear Callie, is a promise."

She grinned and her heart did a little jig. Oh, there she went again. She looked down at her sundae. Eat. Don't look up. Just concentrate on your ice cream. She nursed two more bites of heaven.

"Can I play a game, Dad?"

What? She glanced over at Reece's glass. Empty? Did the kid even take a breath or did he just inhale his ice cream?

"What do you think, Callie?"

Rats and rattlesnakes, now she had to look at Haven again.

"Would Amanda mind?" Concern narrowed his blue eyes. The poor guy was petrified of making a mistake, not that she blamed him. Amanda held that bar awfully high.

"Mandy'd be fine with it."

"Great." He dug into his pocket and pulled out a handful of quarters. "I came prepared just in case." He handed the quarters to Reece. "I'll join you in a minute, but I need to finish my dessert first."

"Sweet! Thanks, Dad."

Haven turned his head, following his son across the room to the games. "Do you have any idea how amazing that sounds?"

"Him calling you Dad?"

"I didn't expect it. I thought for sure he'd tell me to get lost, that Amanda would have filled his head with stories . . . "

"Mandy never spoke ill of you . . . to Reece anyway."

He laughed, but not out of amusement. "I take it she said a few choice words to you though."

Callie shrugged. "I've been her sounding board for nearly five years, so yeah, I've heard a thing or two, but . . . " Most of it wasn't true. At least of what she'd seen so far.

"But?" He set his spoon down, leaving ice cream in the lower third of his glass.

"You're not at all like I expected you to be."

He leaned back in his chair and crossed his arms over his chest. "Let me guess, she said I was stiff."

Callie worried her lower lip and nodded.

"Ah, but you see I had a cure for that. I was one of those people who turned into the life of the party when drinking. All my inhibitions sailed right out the door."

"She told me that too." Although it was difficult imagining the deliberate man seated next to her as being drunk.

Haven stirred his ice cream, but didn't take a bite. "I'm guessing she said I was selfish."

She nodded.

"Arrogant?"

She nodded again.

The right corner of his mouth edged up. "My guess is she said I thought I was God's gift."

Callie looked down at her lap. That was one of the most difficult things to imagine. Haven had to be one of the humblest men she'd met, but then, at home she was surrounded with physical arrogance.

"Funny thing was, when Amanda and I first started dating, that's what she called me, God's gift to her. Somewhere along the line it changed to me believing I was God's gift, and she threw that in my face more than once." He shook his head, his hand strangling the tulip glass. "And she was right, on all counts."

Callie covered his hand with hers. His hand was hot with tension. "But that's no longer true. I can tell."

"Can you?" His gaze found hers. "I never told you that you saved me that first day I met you."

She raised her eyebrows. "Me?"

"Amanda had just told me she wanted me to give up all rights to Reece, that she wanted me completely out of the picture. She had just taken away my reason for staying sober."

Callie closed her eyes, preventing tears.

"I hadn't been tempted to drink for six years, but that day I was ready to throw it all in."

"I had no idea."

"You were like an angel coming to me, offering this amazing, undeserved gift." He turned his hand over and grasped hers.

Oh, horseradish and bubblegum. She raised a napkin to her eyes and sniffled.

"You didn't have to do it, you know, and regardless of how this turns out, I'm indebted to you for giving me a chance at knowing my son."

She sniffled again. "I didn't do anything special, not really."

"Oh yes, you did." His thumb stroked her hand. "A little over five years ago, I learned that Jesus was God's true gift to me. Now, I'm thinking God may have given me one more gift."

HE DIDN'T JUST SAY that, did he? Haven looked down at his dessert, now a swirly mess. Any more comments like the one he just made to Callie, and he'd be in a mess he couldn't back out of. Not without hurting Callie, and that was the last thing he wanted to do. Callie deserved to be treated like a queen.

Something he'd failed to accomplish in any of his relationships so far, and probably why the relationships had floundered. Today was about laying a foundation for a relationship with his son, and he had a mere two hours to accomplish that. But as long as he got Reece home on time, he'd have another opportunity to build on that foundation next week.

Alongside this intriguing, fun-filled, loving woman.

He looked back at Callie who still clung to his hand. Or did he have a hold on hers? She deserved better than him, so he pulled his hand away. "I don't mean to give you the wrong impression."

She smiled, but her eyes didn't show their usual spark.

Just like that, he'd hurt her. "I mean—"

"Haven, you don't have to explain anything." She turned to look at Reece playing Whack-A-Mole. "He's what this is all about."

"You're right." So why did he feel disappointed? He looked out the rain-streaked window. The rain still fell, but had let up in its severity. Maybe a walk outside wouldn't be so bad after all. He nodded to the window. "Are you up for a walk around the area?"

She patted her stomach and grinned. "And wear off some of these calories? You bet."

"Then let's go." He pushed away from the table. "Reece, we're heading out."

Reece slammed a mole then spun around, his whole body pouting. "Aww, Dad, I'm just getting started."

Time to be firm, without anger. "Buddy, we're leaving now."

He crossed his arms over his chest, the mallet in his hand, and stomped his prosthetic foot. "But I don't want to go."

Haven swallowed and shot Callie a nervous what-do-I-do-now glance.

She raised her palms and shrugged her shoulders. A big help she was.

Haven scratched the back of his neck. They could stay and play—there was still time—but letting Reece talk back to him would set a bad precedent. Maybe a small compromise would work. "Tell you what, we'll make one of our outings a visit to Chuck E. Cheese's. Then you get to play the whole time."

"But they don't have this game. I wanna play now."

"Reece." Hand extended, Haven took a step toward his son. "We'll come back sometime soon."

"Fine." Reece slammed the mallet on the game. "Just when I was winning." He shuffled over to Haven, his lower lip sticking out and shoulders hunched. "I wanna go home."

"But we have more—"

"I don't care." He kicked at the tile. "You're just like Bill."

Haven's heart plummeted to his toes. "How about next week—"

"I don't want there to be a next week." Reece ran toward the door.

Haven rushed after him, whispering a prayer, "Dear God, please let this not be the end."

<h1 style="text-align:center">Chapter Twelve</h1>

JUST LIKE BILL? WHAT did that mean? For the umpteenth time during the drive home, Haven looked in his rearview mirror. Reece sat silent, brooding. Haven had performed the miraculous: he'd quieted his son. That was not the miracle he wanted.

Callie had talked the first few minutes of the car ride, but Haven hadn't comprehended a word, not when his focus was on his sullen son. He turned onto Amanda's street. Forty-five minutes early. Forty-five minutes he'd never be able to recoup. What could he have done differently, other than give in?

With a sigh, he pulled up next to the house. Reece was unbuckled and out of the car before Haven tugged the keys from the ignition. Wordlessly, he looked at Callie.

She smiled. How could she smile when his son hated him? "Remember, he's just a boy."

"Yeah? So?" He flinched as Reece slammed the door to the house.

"So, he's testing you. Seeing what he can get away with."

"But Reece is still mad at me."

"And tomorrow you'll be his best friend again." She smirked. "You're a guy, you should know that."

Jaw shifting from side to side, Haven mulled that over. Had Reece believed that Haven was going to be a Santa-type dad, one who said yes to everything? Today that would have been the easy thing to do, and the aching part of his heart regretted it. Even worse, now he had to face Amanda. Would she blame Haven for Reece's behavior and use this as another strike against him?

Dumb question. Of course she would. But having Callie on his side should help. He gripped the door handle. "Time to face mother bear. See how she can twist this around."

"She's not the monster you think she is."

Hmph. He got out of his car, hurried around it to help Callie out, then walked with her to the front door. It flew open as Callie was about to knock.

Amanda perched her hands on her hips and leveled a glare toward Haven. "What did you do?"

He spoke through clenched teeth. "I told him *no*."

"No?" Her brows raised.

"I said it was time to go. He begged to stay. I said no."

Her gaze flit to Callie. "Is that true?"

"Of course."

"Oh." Her hands fell to her sides, and she puffed out a breath. "He does the same thing with Bill," she muttered and waved Haven and Callie inside. She gestured to the couch, sat across from them, crossed her legs, and picked at her fingernails. "I'm guessing he has this glorified notion of what a dad is. So much of what he sees at school are dads that say *yes* all the time, dads who want to be their kid's best friend. What I see when I volunteer is a bunch of spoiled, disrespectful brats." Her gaze lifted and shifted from Callie and stayed on Haven. "I don't want that for Reece. Bill would have done the same thing."

*Just like Bill.*

Maybe being just like Bill wasn't so bad after all. Maybe Bill was the exact type of man Reece needed as a stepfather. But where did that leave Haven? Was intruding into his son's life the right thing to do?"

"Thank you for being firm," Amanda said.

Haven blinked and stared at her. Did she just compliment him?

She looked down at her hands.

Avoiding him. Why was she being so nice? She had to want something from him. He gripped his thighs, steeling himself against an attitude whiplash. "You're welcome." He tried to put a positive lilt in his words, but his doubt likely showed through. "Does this mean you have no trouble with me seeing Reece?"

"Well . . . " She pricked furiously at her fingernails. "I wanted to talk to you about that.”

“You’re not . . . ” He squeezed his thighs, reigning in his anger. Callie’s hand on his arm helped. “Then talk.”

“Um, about next Tuesday . . . ”

He shook off Callie’s hand. “Come on, that’s the Fourth of July. You won’t give me two measly hours?”

“No.”

He leaped up. “How can—”

“Wait.” She held her hands up, palms out. “I mean yes.” She sighed.

“Yes, what?” He crossed his arms. She had his insides completely pretzled.

“I mean, yes, you can have your two hours on Tuesday.”

That was way too easy. What was the catch? He squinted. “But?”

“You just won’t trust me, will you?”

“Like you’ve given me reason to.”

“Well, if that’s the attitude you’re going to take.” She drew her phone out of her jeans pocket. “We’ll find someone else to watch Reece next Tuesday night while Bill and I celebrate.”

Haven fell back on the couch, his mouth agape. “You want . . . ” His voice squeaked, and he cleared his throat. “You’ll let Reece spend the entire evening with me?”

“Not the night.” She scrolled through her phone. “And I’m having second thoughts.”

He ran his hand over his mouth, and took a deep breath. “Please, Amanda. I’m sorry I doubted you. Of course, I’ll watch him.” Just thinking about it, he wanted to do handstands. “But I’m living with Dad right now, until I find a place of my own. It’s okay if he meets his grandpa, isn’t it?”

Her mouth twisted. “I didn’t realize—”

“I get to meet my grandpa?” Reece’s voice came from the top of the stairs. He thundered down the steps, ran to Amanda, and gave her a hug. “Please, oh please. I’m sorry I talked back to Dad and Bill and you. I won’t do it again, I really want to meet my grandpa, please, Mom, you’re the best mom in the whole wide world.”

With Reece rambling on, Amanda looked over his shoulder and mouthed to Haven, “Does your dad still . . . ?” She raised a pretend glass to her lips.

"No." Haven mouthed back, shaking his head.

She tugged Reece from her shoulder and looked him square in the eye. "You can meet your grandpa, but you better behave."

"I will. I promise. Cross my heart, hope to die, stick a needle—"

"Reece." Amanda put a finger to his lips. He tore himself from her, ran to Haven, and squeezed his neck with a hug. "It's gonna be the best Fourth of July ever!"

Yes, yes it was. A tear escaped Haven's eye as he lifted a silent thank you to God.

ANOTHER VICTORY! CALLIE DID did a little Snoopy dance after she left her parents' office. The second victory this Friday. First Gemma had accepted the job offer, then she said she could start on Monday. Then the final victory, the best one of all: praise from her parents. No guilt trips for leaving, but compliments for a job well done and encouragement for her new career. It was time for a celebration.

She glided through the reception area and glanced at the clock. Five to twelve. Mandy would be here soon. Who better to celebrate with than her best friend? She prayed for one more victory, that Mandy would allow her to skip the Independence Day celebration with Haven and Reece next Tuesday. It was one thing to spend two hours with the guys, but an entire evening? She was crushing on Haven too much already. What would an evening of fireworks do to her? Mandy was reasonable—well, except for when it came to Haven.

Sighing, she walked into her office where chaos now reigned. To be honest, she didn't have time for lunch, but making time for friends was more important than work. And sleep.

She covered her mouth as a yawn escaped. These work-until-midnight sessions should be over soon. But first, she needed to free her desk from the mounds of paperwork. She sat in her swivel chair and began organizing, which included creating a to-teach list for Gemma. Just as she added number twenty, someone knocked at her door.

"Ready to go?"

Callie dropped her pen and smiled at Mandy dressed in green scrubs. "Just getting off shift, or taking a break?"

"Done for the day, thank goodness." She plopped in a chair opposite Callie and reclined back. "We've had more people come in with clogged arteries. I swear people are turning the Fourth into a let's-see-how-many-fat-laden-cholesterol-building-greasy-foods-we-can-eat holiday."

Callie giggled and grabbed her purse from her bottom desk drawer. "Is that why we're going out for cheesy, sauce-covered noodles?"

"Why should we be any different?"

Together, they left the building and waded among summer visitors flooding the sidewalks. Ten minutes later they were seated at a buzzing Italian restaurant, grateful they'd made reservations. Mandy seemed to be her old self today. Cheerful. Bragging on Reece. Rolling her eyes as she whined about the surgeon with no bedside manner, then wiping tears when she talked about witnessing a patient's miraculous revival. This was the friend Callie had grown to love.

She prayed that friend wouldn't retreat when Callie made her request.

The server took their orders then Callie sent up a silent prayer that Mandy would be open to her proposal.

She fingered her cloth napkin as she formulated her plea. "I was wondering about next Tuesday . . . "

Mandy's shoulders stiffened. "What about it?"

Oh boy. Callie cleared her throat. "I think it's time for me to stop chaperoning." After four Tuesdays, Mandy had to see that Haven was no threat.

"No." Mandy crossed her arms.

"Come on, Mandy. Haven's gone out of his way to bend to your rules. He's been nothing but trustworthy. It's time to give him some leeway."

"Our agreement was that he needed to be chaperoned."

"A verbal agreement. And agreements can be amended."

"And behaviors can change when you're not around."

"What if I had plans for the Fourth?" She didn't, but Mandy didn't need to know that. "Do I dump them to appease you?"

Mandy's face and shoulders slumped. "Oh man, I'm sorry, Cal. I didn't even think about that. Forgive me?"

"Of course. So, that means you'll let Haven and Reece share the evening without me?"

"Nope. It means I find a sitter."

Arghh. Callie wished she could shake some sense into her friend. "Fine. I'll stay until you pick up Reece."

"You'd do that for me?"

Callie laughed, but it wasn't from joy. "No, I'm doing it for Reece, Haven, and Reece's grandpa." She gulped down her water, preventing her from adding on a snide remark. What was up with Mandy? She'd never been so pigheaded about something before.

Well, best friends ask the tough questions. Maybe, just maybe, Mandy had a valid explanation. "Why are you being so obstinate? What are you afraid of?"

Mandy looked around the restaurant, her gaze flitting everywhere but at Callie. Even with the noise and voices echoing around them, Callie could hear Mandy picking at her fingernails. It was best to listen to her friend's silence rather than trying to coax her into answering, so Callie sat back in her chair and waited.

"You know how much I care for Bill, don't you?" Mandy toyed with her engagement ring.

Just care? "Yeah . . ."

"He's so good for Reece. The father figure Reece never had. Helping me with medical bills. He's even talking about getting Reece some of those running blades. Do you know how expensive those are?"

But what about love? "What does that have to do with Haven? He's accepted the fact that Bill's in your life. It hurts him, but he knows he'll always be second. And he'll take being second as long as he gets time with Reece."

Tears clung to Mandy's lower lashes. "You don't get it."

"Obviously." Callie reached across the table and clasped Mandy's hand. "Then help me understand."

Mandy gave an exaggerated sigh. Her gaze still didn't meet Callie's. "The problem is, I think I love him."

And that was a problem how? "Well, of course you love Bill, you're—"

"No." Lips trembling, she looked at Callie and whispered. "I never stopped loving Haven."

# Chapter Thirteen

"HEY, SLOW DOWN, BUD." Callie yelled over the top of her car as Reece zoomed toward Haven's home, backpack bouncing with each step. If she could make it through this grandpa-grandson reunion without tears, she'd be ecstatic.

Reece leaped onto the front deck, completely disregarding the steps. She laughed. Why even bother? Slow wasn't in Reece's vocabulary.

Besides, he had something to be excited about. If only she could share in his excitement. She kicked a stone across the asphalt driveway. Mandy should be here with Haven and Reece. She loved them both, for Pete's sake! And it didn't take a genius to know that Reece would like to see his mom and dad get back together. But no, Haven couldn't give the monetary comfort Mandy desired. Callie couldn't blame her for that—she'd struggled for years as a single mom to a disabled child, and had done a marvelous job. But it had worn her down, and Bill offered an easy hand up. How could Mandy resist?

Callie climbed onto the deck just as Haven opened the door. His entire face lit up as Reece launched himself into Haven's arms.

"I'm sorry, Dad, for being a brat. That's what Callie said I'd been—"

"Reece!"

"Well, you did! I won't do it again, okay? Can we go to the malt shop again? This time I'll listen. I promise."

"Just try and keep me away." Haven peeled Reece's arms from his waist. "Come on inside, there's someone who's dying to meet you."

Here was a man, heels-over-head in love with his son, a broken man doing everything he could do glue his family back together, and Mandy chose Bill?

Shaking her head, she followed the guys inside and slipped her flip-flops off. Shoot, it was hard enough for Callie to resist Haven, tonight with the lapping water, sand dunes, beach picnic . . . fireworks . . . Oy! Talk about a romantic setting! That would make spending time with Reece and Haven, without becoming more attached than she already was, even more difficult. Mandy was an idiot for not wanting to be here.

"Where's my grandpa?" Reece scooted across the hardwood floors, past a baby grand piano, toward an open kitchen. A fractured shadow of a man appeared outside the patio door, the textured and beveled glass obscuring his face, but she could still see the man wipe his eyes.

Haven caught up to Reece and perched his hand on his shoulder. Stillness bellowed through the room as they all waited for the door to open. She clenched her fists. She was not going to cry. Uh-uh. Nope.

Attempting to avoid the anticipated tender moment, she looked around the cottage living room. Cozy, and perfect for a couple of bachelors with its brown leather sofa and recliner. The room was brightly lit with the mid-evening sun streaming through trios of windows flanking the fireplace. The requisite man-cave-sized flat-screen TV was centered over the fireplace on sage-colored walls.

A photograph of grass-spotted sand dunes and an endless lake hung above the piano. Likely taken here on Park Point. One of Haven's shots, perhaps? If so, the man definitely had an eye for capturing light and shadow, for bringing out depth of color. The picture invited her in, and she longed to enter.

*Dear Lord, guard my heart.*

The patio door creaked open and Callie couldn't resist turning toward it. A man who shared many of Haven's features, but older with touches of grey in his hair, and permanent crinkles by his eyes, stopped in the doorway. The man's gaze never left Reece. "This is Ree—" his voice cracked.

And Callie wiped at her cheeks.

Haven rested one hand on his dad's shoulder and the other on Reece's. "Dad, I'd like you to meet Reece, your grandson."

HAVEN DREW A FINGER below his eyes. The only one not crying was Reece, and he just stood there looking puzzled at three adults who'd lost it. Haven hadn't realized how much losing Reece had hurt his father, not until last week when he'd announced Reece's forthcoming visit. That was the first time Haven recalled seeing his father cry. Not even when Haven's mother died had his dad shed a tear, at least that Haven saw, but he had witnessed his father drink to the point of passing out almost every night. A behavior that Haven had mimicked until Reece's accident. That had been a kick-in-the-gut wake-up call for both of them.

His dad cleared his throat and removed his Bulldogs cap.

"You like the Bulldogs too?" Reece pulled off his cap and held it next to his grandpa's. Same exact style.

"Why, you bet I do." He slapped the cap in his hand. "I'm even their official Zamboni driver."

Reece's eyes grew big as pancakes. "No. Way! That is like the coolest job ever! Wait 'til I tell my buddies. They're gonna be super jealous. Can you give me a ride?"

His dad chuckled and ruffled Reece's hair. "We'll have to talk about that."

Haven knew that phrase. His dad's way of saying no, but it still gave hope to Reece. For tonight, that was okay.

"Pardon my manners, young lady." His dad extended his hand to Callie who looked adorable with her navy sailor hat. She had more hats that Duluth had seagulls. "I've been wanting to meet my boy's hero."

Her eyes widened. "I'm not a—"

Haven slipped an arm over her shoulders. "Anyone who reunites families is a hero in my book."

"And a mighty pretty hero, at that."

Her cheeks bloomed red as an apple, and she dipped her face toward the floor. Haven's hand itched to lift her chin and look her in the eye, affirm his father's words. An intimacy that somehow seemed right, but he didn't dare breach the friendship they had. If broken, that could also snip that tenuous thread binding Haven with his son.

"It's nice to meet you, Mr. Carlysle." Her face still pink—an awfully pretty shade of pink at that—she extended her hand.

"It's Roland, young lady."

"Roland, it is. Please call me Callie."

"Well, Miss Callie, what would you say to helping me out with the burgers? Give Reece a chance to get his things settled."

"Be glad to." She scooted away from Haven's arm and hurried outside with his father.

"Well, Reece." Haven pointed to the open staircase in the living room. "Let's drop your stuff off in my room."

While Reece wouldn't be staying the night, chances were Amanda and Bill would arrive late to pick him up which meant Reece would hopefully get a little sleep in. Reece took off, clomping up the steps two at a time. Or maybe his excitement over being here would keep him awake until Amanda arrived. Haven wouldn't mind that one bit.

"Take a right at the top," Haven yelled up the stairs and smiled, picturing a little puppy trailing after Reece, fighting to keep up.

Someday.

Haven followed Reece up the stairs and hitched a right into his bedroom. The entire contents of Reece's backpack lay scattered on the bed. Pajamas, Hot Wheels, rocks. Probably some dirt too.

"You plan on sleeping with all that?"

Reece rummaged through his stones. "Yes!" His eyes lit up as he grabbed one that looked the same as the rest. He shoved his hand toward Haven, the stone lying in his palm. "It's for Grandpa. Think he'll like it?"

It was all Haven could do to keep from taking his son in his arms and holding him forever. Instead, he stuffed his hands in his shorts pockets. "I guarantee it'll be the best gift your grandfather's ever received."

"Sweet!" He crammed the stone into his pocket then stuffed his clothes, rocks, and cars back into the backpack. But not all the dirt. He dropped the backpack on the floor then zipped to the door leading to a deck. Did the kid ever stand still? Amanda certainly had her hands full, and she'd done an incredible job with those full hands.

Haven joined Reece on the deck, which was just large enough to hold two lawn chairs.

"Where's the lake?"

"Right out there." He pointed to his left, toward the backside of the house. Through the trees, a touch of blue from Lake Superior was visible. At night, he could hear it clearly. Nothing was more soothing than the slapping of the waves against the shore. Nothing was more romantic. He crossed his arms on the railing and stared outward. "Your mom and I used to spend a lot of time out here." And they'd shared the first of many kisses out here. "Here's where I first told your mother I loved her." And then proposed. But not marriage. Not when they could live together without the cost and hassle of a wedding.

How was he ever going to teach Reece to do things the right way, when he'd done it all wrong? When his mother was still doing it wrong?

"So, you loved Mom?" Reece clanged his foot against the railing.

"Yeah. I did."

"Oh." Dejection sounded in Reece's voice as he headed back inside, shuffling his feet along the way.

Haven scratched his head. Did Reece doubt him? Well, there was one way to prove he'd once loved Amanda. He hurried into his bedroom. Reece was already heading into the hallway. "Hey, wait, come here. Let me show you something." He dug into his top dresser drawer and pulled out a framed photo.

Reece slumped back into the room, his gaze directed toward the floor.

"See?" Haven shoved the frame into Reece's hands. "That's you as a baby." Sitting on top of the bronze piano statue in Rice Park in St. Paul, right between the bronze figures of Schroeder and Lucy from the Peanuts cartoons. Haven knelt by Schroeder who was hunched over, plucking his notes, and Amanda crouched by Lucy who lay on her stomach, gripping the piano, her head aimed in adoration toward Schroeder.

"If I wanted to make your mom smile, all I had to do was play the piano."

"Oh." Reece tossed the frame on the dresser and it clanked off the side, falling to the hardwood floor.

Haven winced at the sound of glass breaking. "Why did you . . . ?" He pinched back his frustration as he bent to retrieve the photo.

"You didn't love her!" Anger saturated Reece's voice and fired from his eyes as he glared at Haven. He kicked at the floor with his prosthetic foot. "If you loved Mom so much, why did you leave her?"

A punch in the stomach would have felt better. Haven left the frame on the floor and knelt in front of his son. He couldn't give the complete reason, not without speaking badly of Amanda. Instead, he grasped Reece's arms and looked him in the eye. As much as it hurt, he'd tell the truth. It might not be the entire truth, but it was the flimsy foundation for all that had happened. "I guess I didn't love your mother enough. I loved myself more."

Reece stilled completely, and fear snarled in Haven's gut.

"Is that why you left me?" Reece's voice trembled, and he sniffled. "'Cause you didn't love me enough?"

Haven's heart felt as if it shattered in more pieces than the family photo.

## Chapter Fourteen

A GASP CAME FROM the doorway. Haven's mouth agape, he stared at Callie who stood by the door, fingers splayed over her mouth. She didn't know what to say. She always had wisdom for him.

Voice failing, he looked at her, his thoughts begging, *Help me?* But she just shook her head.

Perhaps she was right. If Callie answered, Reece's questions wouldn't be resolved and would surface again later. Besides, this was Haven's responsibility, one he didn't need to handle alone. He looked upward and sent the same silent plea. *Help me?*

The silence seemed eternal, before a thought whispered through his thoughts. *Truth.* Yes. Of course. But would it make Reece hate him even more? Being truthful was a risk Haven needed to take.

Still on his knees, Haven gulped in a breath and turned Reece's face toward him. "Do you know what an alcoholic is?"

Reece shrugged, his face pink with simmering anger. "Someone who drinks beer all the time."

"That may be partly true." Haven stood and nodded toward the bed. "Come here, please."

Reece trudged to the bed and sat on the edge, his feet dangling, and arms crossed over his chest.

This wasn't how Haven wanted to have this talk. He prayed God would open Reece's heart, let him see and understand Haven's choice to leave, as lousy as it was.

He wheeled a desk chair in front of Reece and sat, facing his son.

Out of the corner of his eye, he saw Callie turn to leave. She couldn't. Her mere presence brought peace. "Please stay." His words came out barely above a whisper. "You should hear this too."

She cringed. "But I—"

"Callie, please." He patted the bed beside Reece.

She squeezed her eyes closed and nodded, then sat next to Reece.

"Thank you." He flashed her a weak smile then focused on his son. These next words had left his throat many times before, but never in such an intimate, personal manner. Somehow it was easier admitting to a roomful of strangers. He gulped and cleared his throat. "I'm an alcoholic."

Reece's face contorted. "But you don't drink."

"No. Not anymore, but I used to. For celebrations, disappointments, just because. And the night of your accident, that's what I was doing. I chose going out, getting drunk over watching you like your mom wanted me to."

Haven blinked and ran a fist below his eyes as the truth stared him in the face. It made him want to throw up. "You were right. That night, I loved drinking more than anything. More than you. More than your mom. Especially more than myself." Getting drunk had been his mistress who'd given him a sense of euphoria unmatched by anyone or anything else. A euphoria he would always crave.

"I knew it." Reece squirmed, trying to leap off the bed.

But Callie wrapped an arm around his back, pulled him to her side, and whispered, "Listen."

He stilled, all except his fidgeting hands which held his attention.

"I'm so sorry, Reece." If only Reece could understand the depths of that sorrow. Haven clasped Reece's hands between his. "That night made me see I had a very bad problem. The truth is, I didn't leave you because I loved you less. I left because I *did* love you."

"No, you didn't." Reece struggled to pull his hands away, but Haven held fast.

Now to tell the rest without blaming Amanda. That would be too easy, and it would likely hurt Reece even more. "I was sick, Reece, terribly sick, and I left because I was a danger to you. You were hurt because of me and I couldn't risk that happening again. Your mom agreed, so I left. I needed to find God, to trust in Him, because having faith is the only way I could remain sober. And He has helped me. I haven't had a drink since the night you were hurt."

Reece's lower lip stuck out. "Then why'd it take so long to come back? Huh? I missed you." His voice shook, and he sucked in that protruding lip as tears slipped over his cheeks.

Callie pulled Reece tighter against her side and massaged his arm.

*Lord?* Haven's Adam's apple moved up and down as he clung to his shivering son. "I missed you." He brushed a hand through Reece's hair, something he'd longed to do for years. "Every single day, I missed you. But God had work to do in my heart yet, in your mom's heart too. Even Callie's." He shot her a glance. "If I'd come back earlier, Callie wouldn't have been here, your mom probably would have chased me away, and with good reason. She loves you so much and couldn't bear to see you hurt again."

"Are you going to leave me again?" Some of the vibrato had fled Reece's voice, but a hint remained.

Haven grasped Reece's chin and forced it upward. He fired his gaze into Reece's eyes. Reece needed to understand. No, he needed to *believe* Haven's words. "Never. *Nothing* will make me leave. Not your mom, not a zillion lawyers, nothing."

"You mean that?"

"With all my heart, I promise you that."

CALLIE'S HEART NEEDED TO promise her not to fall in love. But after watching Haven bleed from his broken heart earlier in the evening, after witnessing grandfather, son, and grandson bond over grilled burgers, after listening to Haven's passionate piano rendition of *America the Beautiful*, Callie didn't know if her heart could resist. Especially with an evening of fireworks ahead of them.

But she needed to. With the sun striping the horizon in varying shades of orange and yellow, she spread a blanket on the boat dock just a few blocks away from the house. The men labored behind her, carrying out the cooler and a bucket of freshly-made, generously-buttered popcorn, plus extra blankets and insect repellent. If only it would repel her wayward feelings for a man who didn't—who couldn't belong to her.

A cool, brisk wind blew off Duluth's harbor basin, whipping up the blanket. She grasped for the edge, but the breeze flung it away.

"Here, let me get that." Haven caught the blanket and stretched it out. He set the cooler on one corner and the popcorn in the middle.

Ignoring the popcorn, Reece and Roland sat on the edge of the blanket, their feet dangling over the water. Well, she couldn't resist grabbing a handful of the buttered treat, even with the scrumptious view vying for attention. She moaned her pleasure as the others dug in. This was better than theater popcorn.

Haven began to sit between Reece and Roland, but he popped back up snapping his fingers. "Forgot something. Be right back."

With only jagged remnants of the sun remaining, he jogged down the dock, dodging families, dogs, and coolers.

With a happy sigh, Callie leaned back on her elbows and looked across the bay. From here, they had a front-seat view for the Bayfront Park Fourthfest. In the past, she'd always watched the fireworks from her bedroom balcony. It wasn't a bad view there either, but she was usually alone. Her parents always worked the festival, interviewing partiers eager for their fifteen minutes of fame. And Jess was never without a date.

For the first time Callie could remember, she was celebrating with family. Maybe this wasn't her own family, but she felt loved, welcomed, accepted by this family in a way she'd never experienced with her own. This family liked her for who she was and had no aspirations to change her. She could stay with them forever.

Breathing in lake-scented air, she lay back on the blanket, and listened to grandfather and grandson talk hockey and rocks and bugs as if they'd known each other all their lives. Those two were meant to be together. If only Mandy hadn't been so unforgiving.

Maybe that would all change now. Maybe, now that she'd given voice to her feelings for Haven, she'd act upon them and reunite this family.

Callie frowned. A restored family should make her happy.

"Hey, why the serious face?"

Startled, Callie stared up at Haven standing behind her, a boom box in one hand, and the Snoopy diaper bag slung over his shoulder. She sprung up, hugging herself, trembling. Of course, he'd bring his camera, she should have expected it, but still the thought of a camera pointed in her direction, had her shaking as if trapped outside in twenty-below temperatures.

"You're shivering." He knelt beside her and draped a blanket around her shoulders.

"Thanks." She pulled the blanket tight, letting him believe that she was freezing in this ninety degree, muggy heat.

After sitting next to her, he pulled his camera out of the bag and looked through the view screen while toying with buttons and knobs. As long as it was pointed away from her, she'd be fine. He snapped a few shots then froze, holding the camera in front of him. Slowly, he lowered it into his lap then looked at Callie, frowning. "You're not cold, are you."

She shook her head. No way would she look at him and see the tenderness, the care, and concern reflected in his voice.

"You have nothing to worry about." He rested his hand on her shoulder and nodded to his camera. "I promise."

How could he be so understanding?

She wrapped the blanket even tighter, and his hand slipped away.

Minutes later, Duluth's hill completely hid the sun. The first rocket screamed upward and was joined by a passel of other rockets that exploded in dazzling chrysanthemums. Haven turned on the radio and the fireworks danced to choreographed music.

"Neato, beano!" she squealed then slapped a hand over her mouth.

Reece stared back at her, his nose wrinkled. "What?"

She giggled. "Isn't that what you're supposed to say?"

"That's so lame." He shook his head and turned forward just as more color exploded in the sky.

"Neato, beano!" Haven shouted with his smooth baritone.

She broke out in giggles. "See, Reece? It's cool."

"It's so not cool." He shook his head which prompted her to shout it again, with Haven echoing.

Others around them joined in, squealing their own expressions of delight, and Callie grew silent. She'd teased Reece enough tonight. No doubt the kid would pay her back in the very near future.

Haven also quieted as he framed the harbor on his LCD screen and snapped shots of the show. Then he lay down on his stomach and aimed, catching silhouettes of Reece and Roland seated side by side with the lights streaking in the foreground.

What a cherished memory that would make! If only she could let him capture her alongside the other two. But the thought alone was nauseating. What she'd give to be over this ridiculous phobia.

After a few more snaps, Haven sat up, tucked the camera away, and placed the diaper bag between them. Even with the cordite-scented air, Haven's minty cologne floated toward her. What would it feel like to sit closer? To hold his hand. To—

Stop it!

*Sheesh*, this childish crush had to end. She inched away, hopefully slowly enough that he didn't realize what she was doing. Maybe the only way to combat this juvenile infatuation was to convince Mandy to end this silly chaperoning.

*Stars and Stripes Forever* boomed from the radio and showers of color rained from the sky. Oohs and aahs accompanied the music as the sky lit up with brilliantly-painted smiles, flowers, and fountains. The finale lasted the entire song, then the crowd around them responded with an ovation that likely reached the spectators across the bay.

"Neato, beano." Callie nudged Reece in the back.

He turned to her and rolled his eyes.

And they all laughed. Like a regular family. *Mandy, you are a fool.*

"Time to go." Roland stood on the dock and gave Reece a hand up. "You grab the popcorn, I'll get the cooler, and those two can clean up. What do you say to that?"

"Deal." Reece fist-bumped his grandpa then the two picked up their refreshments and joined the crowd heading back to land. Leaving Callie alone with Haven.

She jumped up and grabbed for the blanket, but caught Haven's hand instead. "Oh, sorry." She tried to pull away, but he held on.

"Thanks for the evening, Callie."

"Hey, what are friends for?" With him still clinging to her hand, she bent and tried scooping up the blanket, anything to avoid looking in his eyes. She couldn't let him see what her eyes would tell him.

"I'll take that." He gave the blanket a gentle tug.

With her gaze averted downward, she handed over the unfolded blanket. It was time to leave. Past time, even. She surveyed their area and, finding it clean, she aimed for land. But Haven's hand around her wrist stopped her.

"Callie, look at me."

Oh, fish out of water, what was she supposed to do now? Her gaze settled on his hand around her wrist, then it inched toward his face. The crescent moon shone just enough to spotlight his smile and the sparkling blue of his eyes.

"I can't remember when I've had a more enjoyable evening."

She shrugged. No way was she going to tell him how much fun she'd had.

"Tonight was the best gift anyone's ever given me. How can I repay you?"

*By kissing me?*

Oh, for Pete's sake. She swallowed and gathered the courage to look him in the eye, praying her voice conveyed the conviction she didn't feel. "By being a good father to your son. By restoring your family."

His grin grew. "I'd say tonight was a huge step in that direction."

"Then your next step is to involve Mandy." There, she said it, pushed Haven in the right direction.

But his eyebrows crouched together. "Amanda?" Tugging his hand away, he laughed but wasn't happy. "And spoil our evening?"

"You might have more fun than you think." She whirled away from him and hurried down the dock.

"Whoa." His footsteps stomped behind her, and then he caught her arm. "What are you talking about?"

She sighed and met his eyes. "Mandy. She still cares for you. Loves you."

His eyes blinked rapidly. "Say what?"

"You heard me." She started to turn away, but his hand landed softly on her cheek.

"And what if I don't care for her?"

"You did once."

He closed his eyes, and his chest undulated with deep breaths. Then his eyes opened and focused on her. "When I moved home, getting back together with Amanda was exactly what I thought I wanted, what I thought was best for Reece, but now, after fighting with her, and spending time with him . . . with you . . . and her not letting me see my son for six years . . . " Anger touched his voice. "Whatever we had is irreparably damaged."

"Even if that's what Reece wants?"

His shoulders slumped. "Does he?"

"Look at Mandy. She grew up in a broken family, being shuttled between parents. She's told me all she wanted was for them to get back together, to be a whole family."

He nodded. "You're right."

"Then don't you think that's what Reece would want too? What Mandy wants for her son?"

Defeat hunched his entire body, then he straightened to his entire six-plus feet and looked down on her. "I'll do anything for Reece."

But doing what was best for Reece would certainly break Callie's heart.

# Chapter Fifteen

REMEMBER TO HAVE REECE back in two hours."

Haven swallowed a scathing retort and averted his eyes from Amanda's fists-on-hips stance, guarding the door to her home. Yeah, he'd do anything for Reece, but get back together with this woman standing in front of him? He shivered. That would take a miracle God would have difficulty pulling off.

"He'll be home on time." He pulled the rain poncho over his head to mask his chagrin. He couldn't wait to step out into the drizzle and cool off. Reece and Callie were already dancing in the rain, sans ponchos. Oh, to be that carefree!

Without another word, he turned his back on Amanda and joined Callie and Reece. He didn't feel like dancing, but stomping in a few puddles did help lighten his mood. Besides, Reece deserved the best of him, not the wooden, grumpy man Amanda brought out in him.

His tennis shoes drenched, he waved Callie and Reece toward his car. "The clock's ticking, guys." If they wanted to spend any quality time at all at Enger Tower, they needed to leave now.

Thankfully, they piled into his car. Their dripping clothes didn't even phase him.

He gave Callie a quick glance and grinned. Her multi-colored rain cap matched her character. A little quirky. And a whole lot of fun.

Who knew he'd find that attractive?

But on Callie, it was beautiful. He couldn't ever remember smiling so much with anyone.

Whoa, there he went again. It was too soon to be caring so much for someone.

"Fat turtle jokes." Reece hollered from the backseat.

Huh? Squinting, Haven looked in the rearview mirror, appreciating the reprieve from his thoughts. Oh, it must be that game Reece and Callie played. "Squirrel?"

"No, silly, it's the license plate on that car that just zoomed past us. FTJ. Fat turtle jokes."

"Let me guess, Callie taught you that game."

"Well, yeah! She teaches me everything important."

"That's what you've told me." Red and blue lights flashed behind him and a siren squealed. Hands tensing on the steering wheel, Haven glanced down at his speedometer as he pulled to the side. Thirty-three in a thirty. They wouldn't stop him for three miles over, would they?

The police car sped around them and pulled over the car with the FTJ license plate. Haven puffed out a relieved breath.

"Ha ha." Reece giggled.

Being pulled over would have stolen more of Haven's precious minutes with his son. Haven veered back out onto the road, drove past the speeder, and read the new plate in front of him. ZTG. Zebras taking . . . No. Zebras talking. Yeah, that worked. Zebras talking. "Gibberish."

"Gibberish?" Callie giggled. "Now, that's a squirrel."

"Zebras talking gibberish." Haven pointed to the car in front. "See, I can play too."

"Good one, Dad."

Praise from his son. Now there was a sweet sound, even if it was for playing a silly game.

He slowed as he serpentined up Skyline Parkway, a few raindrops still wetting his windshield, and took care to stay far away from the road's drop-off to his right. Callie and Reece continued playing their car games. Just like a family would.

He wouldn't mind spending more time with this family, one that didn't include Amanda. That would make Reece happy, wouldn't it?

Whoa, it was way too early to think about that. Still, the thought whisked through his mind and made him smile as he turned onto Enger Tower Drive and followed the asphalt road to the parking lot. With the evening's rain, a near-empty parking lot awaited them. Perfect for their outing.

Reece hopped out of the car before Haven had it turned off. They'd have to have a little talk about that. Precisely what a father would do.

Callie pointed up the boulder-built hill at the stone tower Reece ran toward. "You go ahead, I'm going to sit by the cliff and enjoy the view."

"Are you sure? I like you joining us." Besides the thought of being alone with his son awoke butterflies in his stomach. Being a father was easy with Callie beside him, but alone? Would he know how?

"Go on. You two need some time alone together."

He looked at the stone hill. Reece had stopped climbing and was kneeling on a rock, studying something in the dirt.

Callie was right. The two of them did need some alone time, as much as it scared him. With Callie off toward the pergola-sided pavilion overlooking the cliff, he retrieved the diaper bag from his trunk then hurried toward Reece. He frowned at the boulders Reece had climbed, then headed toward the paved sloping path instead.

"Dad, watcha doing?"

Haven gestured to the path. "Heading this way. I'll meet you at the tower."

"But you'll miss it! This is way cool!"

Sure, killing himself by climbing up waist-high rocks was cool, but if that was what his son wanted, that was what he was going to do. Anchoring the diaper bag over his shoulder, he began the ascent. Reece made it look so easy. Huh!

He reached his son and knelt beside him. A night crawler? That was cool?

"Look at this." Reece suspended a worm over his finger. "Did you know that night crawlers help the earth?" He dangled the worm and started handing it to Haven.

Haven held up both hands and backed away.

"You're scared of a silly worm?"

Gritting his teeth, Haven took it, and it squirmed in the palm of his hand. He'd rather be yelled at by someone whose mortgage was late. "So, these help the earth, huh?" Then he should put it back down on the earth so that it could do some good.

Reece stroked the worm like he would a cat. "Uh-huh. They eat dead leaves and garbage and stuff and then poop it out and poof! The earth has more nitra . . . nitre . . . "

"Nitrogen?"

"Yeah, that's it. Nitrogen."

"From a worm's poop."

"Cool huh?"

"The coolest." When worms were in the earth where God purposed them to be.

"And they dig holes so that air and water can get into the earth."

"Amazing." And it was. Still one more reason this worm should be on the ground, leaving its nitrogen poop down there where it could do some good. He lowered his hand to the side of the path and nudged the slimy creature onto the dirt. "Let me guess, Callie taught you this."

"Uh-huh. She's the best teacher ever. Not like my school teachers. They don't know nothin', not like Aunt Callie. She knows every—"

"Everything important. So you've told me. Night crawlers are important?"

"Uh-huh. Did you know some people even put worms in their leaves at home and they feed 'em garbage?"

"Can't say that I did."

"But not night crawlers. They're not as good as redworms, and the redworms make comp . . . comp . . . "

"Compost?"

"Yeah, compost, and they spread it over the yard and the yard is happy all because of worms. Isn't that the coolest thing ever?"

"Absolutely." Totally cool. For an eight-year-old boy, anyway. Haven looked at his hand, wondering if the worm had left some of its poop behind. Thank God for diaper bags. He reached in the front mesh pocket and pulled out two hand wipe packets. He slit them open and offered one to Reece.

"What's this for?"

"To clean your hands."

Reece stared down at them. "I don't see no dirt."

"Yeah, well it's there, believe me."

"Whatever." He made two swipes over his hand and then threw the wipe on the ground. The kid had to be testing Haven just to see how far he could push things. Littering wasn't something he'd abide by. "Reece, buddy, where does that go?"

"In the garbage." His face twisted in anger, Reece grabbed the wipe. "You're as bad as Mom. But she's not afraid of silly worms. That's stupid." He kicked at a rock as he stuffed the wipe into his pocket. "I thought you were fun." He took off toward the tower.

What just happened here? "Reece, wait." With the camera dangling from his neck, he slung the diaper bag over his shoulder and climbed after Reece. Once on more level ground, he dashed after his son. He stumbled over a tree root and flew, camera first, toward the ground. He caught the camera between both hands just before Reece entered the tower. His elbows punched the dirt milliseconds before his chin scraped stone.

Ignoring the pain shooting through his elbows and face, he pushed off the ground and chased after Reece, into the tower. Reece's pounding footsteps echoed up the winding concrete staircase. Haven leapt up the steps two at a time. Level one. No sign of his son. He cupped hands over his mouth. "Reece, wait up." Footsteps answered, their pace quickening.

Haven scrambled to level two. Reece's footsteps neared, but still no sign of the boy. That kid was unbelievably quick. At level three, Haven stopped to catch his breath, but by the sound of Reece's feet on the stairs, the kid never ran out of breath.

Haven hurried to level four and finally spotted Reece midway up to level five. Maybe if he made this a game, Reece would mellow out. "You haven't won yet." He grabbed the railing and leapt up the stairs two at a time.

The kid climbed faster, if that was possible.

Five steps to catch up to him. Three. One. Haven lunged toward the fifth-floor observation deck, but Reece beat him. Unreal. Haven stood, held out his closed fist. Reece ignored it and slouched his way to the window.

All this because he made Reece pick up garbage? Dear God, was being a father always going to be such roller coaster? He joined Reece at the window, disregarding the tingling in his scraped chin and elbows, and looked out on Duluth's harbor. Any other time, he'd relish the beauty. Instead he knelt next to his son. "You want to tell me what that was about?"

Pouting, Reece kicked at the stone wall.

Scratching his head, Haven stood and gazed at the great lake. Storm clouds brewed off in the distance, pushed away by the blue skies now overhead. How come it still felt cloudy?

He rested his hand on Reece's shoulder. "I'm sorry if I was too sharp with you."

Reece shrugged his hand off.

*God, can I get some help here?*

Out on the lake a barge crawled toward the lift bridge. Haven stared at the boat, then an idea bloomed. He nudged Reece's arm then pointed at the barge. "Pirates!"

Reece shot him a puzzled look.

Haven made his eyes as large as they could go and spied the cliff-side pavilion peeking through branches. "They've come to get Callie!"

A smile sprouted on Reece's face. "They're climbing the hills, and they've got swords." He tugged on Haven's arm. "Let's go, Dad. We have to rescue her."

Reece turned toward the stairs but Haven caught his shoulder and made his expression as serious as possible. "You know who that is down there, don't you?" He pointed toward Callie.

Reece's eyes grew wide. "No, who?"

"It's, it's Super Girl." Lame. This playing pretend was harder than he remembered.

"No, it's not. It's Super Cal."

Haven grinned. "You're right. It's Super Califragilisticexpialidocious."

"And she needs our help. Let's go!"

"Wait. I have a secret weapon." Haven raised his camera. "It shoots a supersonic laser beam that knocks those pirates out."

"Then do it, Dad, quick, they're getting close."

Haven raised his camera and focused outward where he imagined Callie to be sitting. He zoomed in but couldn't see her with all the trees blocking the view. Still, he could imagine her sitting on a flat stone, overlooking Duluth's harbor. He'd like to join her. Alone.

What was she doing to his heart?

With a sigh, he lowered the camera, looked down at Reece, and whispered. "I think I knocked them all out. Let's go rescue Super Cal and be on our way."

Reece hurried down the stairs, but Haven followed at a slower pace. Two hours wasn't nearly enough time to spend with his son.

Yet, it was two hours longer than he'd had for all of six years.

He reached the bottom of the tower and followed the manmade path while Reece took the rocks again. No surprise, Reece beat him across the parking lot then climbed the stairs toward the pavilion. Callie sat just beyond it on a boulder, right where Haven had imagined. Reece was already at her side, making sweeping gestures with his arms. Oh, to record that picture forever. It would make great wallpaper for his laptop.

But with Callie's fear of the camera, recording it in his memory would have to suffice.

He walked toward them, tucking his thumbs in his belt loops. "Howdy, ma'am." He gave his best John Wayne impression, which was far from impressive.

Still, Callie smiled. That made it worth it.

"The boy here tells me them there pirates were about to kidnap you, so you needed some rescuin'."

With a giggle, she batted her eyes and waved a hand in front of her mouth. "I do declare, I've never had such a handsome rescue team in all my days."

Haven stretched out his arm and Callie laid her hand in his palm. It fit perfectly. "Well, Super Cal, we—"

"Excuse me?" She jerked her hand from his. "Super Cal? You have got to be kidding me."

"Now's not a time fer kiddin', Super Cal."

"Super Califragilisticexpialidocious." Reece giggled.

"Boys." Callie shook her head, but grinned.

"That's right, ma'am." Haven doffed his imaginary cowboy hat. "We best be goin' afore them there pirates wake up and get us in a heap o' trouble."

Reece groaned. "You two are silly. I was playing pirates."

"Well." Callie flicked a glance toward Haven. "How boring is that? Haven and I are playing pirates and cowboys and superheroes."

"'Cause Dad makes a bad pirate."

"Hey." He elbowed his son at his shoulder. "So, I'm not so good at the pirate accent. Ahoy there, matey is as good as it gets."

Callie giggled. "If you ask me, your cowboy accent needs a whole buncha work too."

"I think I should be offended."

"And I think it's picnic time." She shoved him toward the path. "I'll save our spot here, and you boys get the lunch."

"Yes ma'am." Haven tipped his imaginary cowboy hat, resulting in the desired giggle from Callie.

An hour later, an hour spent eating and laughing, a too-short hour spent playing pirates and cowboys and superheroes in the tower, it was time to go.

"Already?" Reece aimed his pretend bow and arrow out the top floor window at a barge on the lake. "They're coming to take over the town!"

"Nah, that's the ship coming to take the prisoners away." Haven tucked his air pistol into its invisible holster.

"And it's almost been two hours." Callie nudged Reece toward the stairs. "You don't want to get your dad in trouble now, do you?"

Reece shuffled his feet, his lower lip sticking out. "No, but we never get time together, and we were just starting to play, and I even like Dad's cowboy, and maybe next time Super Cal could come rescue us."

"I think that's exactly what I'm doing right now, buddy boy." She gave Reece another nudge. "And I'll bet I can beat you to the car."

"Nuh-uh." Reece sped down the steps, barely a hitch in his jog.

Shaking her head, she looked back at Haven. "I'm not even going to try to race. I swear he gets faster each day."

"He's amazing, isn't he?" Haven leaned out the window and aimed his camera at his son fleeing the tower. He captured a couple of shots of Reece climbing down the rocks.

"A walking miracle." Callie brushed his arm and nodded toward the steps.

That he was. Haven laid his camera against his chest and sighed. His hand itched to reach out to Callie's as she walked beside him down the stairs.

Maybe that wasn't such a bad idea.

He glanced over at her. A peaceful smile rested on her face. Would taking her hand steal that peace?

No, he better not try it. Today, anyway. There was always next Tuesday or the one after that.

They reached the parking lot, and he pulled his keys out of his pocket. He pressed unlock.

Nothing.

No click.

No lights flashing.

No horn beeping.

No. No. No! This was not happening.

He sped toward his Buick, repeatedly pressing unlock.

No response whatsoever.

*God, please . . .*

He reached his car, inserted the key into the keyhole, and turned it, unlocking the driver's door. At least that worked, but the lock had nothing to do with electrical charge. Clenching his jaw, he slid behind the wheel and inserted his key into the ignition.

Silence.

Not even a hiccup.

He pounded the steering wheel. Amanda was going to have his head.

And threaten to take away his son forever.

# Chapter Sixteen

CALLIE HURRIED TO CATCH up to Haven. She watched him punch the steering wheel and then rest his forehead on it.

*What now?*

She ran to Haven's open door. "What's wrong?"

He looked up at her, his jaw tight. "It's dead."

"Again?"

"Not even a hiss. The battery's deader than I'm about to be." He glanced at his watch. "Twenty minutes. No way can I get someone up here by then." He pulled out his cell phone. "But I'm not giving up. Not yet."

And neither was she.

Callie strode away from his car, drumming her fingers on her jeans. Although she could see Amanda's house from the tower, it was too far to walk. Calling Mandy and pleading Haven's case wouldn't do any good either. Mandy was probably waiting like a vulture to capitalize on any mess-up from Haven. No matter the circumstances, Mandy would be unforgiving because then she could get everything her way.

So, who did Callie know that lived close enough to give them a ride? She pulled her phone from her pocket and scrolled through the contacts.

A name finally caught her eye. Yes. Perfect. The shop was four minutes away, max.

Callie hit the speed dial number and waited.

A familiar voice answered. "Anton's Auto Repair."

"Charlie?"

"Yeah, who's this?"

"It's Callie from Superior Suites. I've got an emergency up at Enger Tower."

"Then dial 911, girlfriend."

"No, not that kind of emergency." She turned and looked at the car. Haven sat cheeks taut, with a phone to his ear while Reece dug in the dirt at the parking lot's edge. "It's my friend. He needs to be somewhere in twenty minutes, and his car won't start. I think the battery's dead. If Haven doesn't have his son home in twenty minutes, he could jeopardize his visitation rights."

"Oh my. I'll be there in a jiffy."

"Thanks, Charlie, I owe you."

Callie hustled back to the car just as Haven threw his phone down on the passenger seat. Red lightning bolts streaked across the whites of moist eyes. "This is it, Callie, this—"

"Haven, listen, Charlie's coming."

"Charlie?"

"Yes. Her husband, Jayson, is the interior decorator at Superior Suites."

He blinked. "The auto mechanic?"

"She's the one."

He slumped in his seat, closed his eyes, and rested his forehead on his fist. After a moment, he smiled up at her, his eyes still glassy. "Super Cal to the rescue, huh?"

"I'm not . . . " A hero. She looked down. With her foot, she drew an imaginary figure eight on the tar. She was just an ordinary woman trying to do what was right. That didn't make her special.

Haven got out of his car, laid his hands on her shoulders, and his musky aftershave drifted her way. "You are to me."

Her breath quickening, she peered at him through her lashes and swallowed. He was way too close, his aftershave too inviting, his lake-blue eyes too alluring. And those lips, *have mercy*, were way too tempting.

She backed away from his touch, licking her lips, and hugged herself. "I only did what anyone would do for you."

"If you say so, Super Cal." Smirking, he leaned his back against his dead car, placed one leg over the other, and crossed his arms.

Oh, brother. She couldn't take the pressure of balancing on a pedestal. "It's what friends do."

She heard the crunch of asphalt beneath tires. "Speaking of friends." She looked to her right and her shoulders hunched. Bummer. Not Charlie's tow truck, but a yellow Camaro with an invoice sticker still clinging to the window.

The Camaro parked next to Haven's Buick, and Charlie got out.

"Where's your tow truck?" Callie hurried to her friend.

"Cal, if I had to drive that thing up here, you'd still be waiting for me, and then it'd take me five minutes to give his car a jumpstart. We'll get your son home first, then we'll take care of your car." She opened her door to the backseat and nodded to Reece. "Hop on in."

"Sweet! Wait'll I tell my friends." Reece leapt into the tiny backseat.

"A Camaro, huh?" Callie walked around the front and opened the passenger door.

"A friend's giving me a test drive as a thank you." She sighed. "It's more of a tease. I'm afraid my little sedan's about all I can afford."

"Hey, Dad, since your car stinks, maybe you could buy this. It'd be epic."

Haven laughed and offered his hand to Charlie. "I'm indebted to you."

"You keeping your son is all the thanks I need." Charlie sat in the driver's seat, Callie squeezed in beside Reece, and Haven took the front. His legs would have been pinned to his nose in this tiny backseat.

"Major banana." Reece yelled as Charlie drove off.

"Does it count if we're riding in it?" Haven asked.

"Dad, it counts double. That means I get two points for every yellow car I see."

"You wouldn't be making up these rules as you go along, would you?" Haven looked back at Reece.

Giggling, Callie glanced at the watch she had synchronized to the clocks in Amanda's house. Fifteen measly minutes to go. Charlie would have to speed to make it, and down those wet, winding roads too. Oh, joy.

She closed her eyes and held her breath as Charlie navigated the turns with the ease of a racecar driver. A minute or so later, she felt a touch on her knee.

"We're safe now." Haven's voice held far too much joy, no doubt at her expense.

"Ha ha." She opened one lid and blew out a breath as she opened the other. No more cliff clinging. That road always bugged her—especially when wet. She glanced at her watch again. Two minutes to deadline.

The light turned red ahead of them, and Charlie screeched to a stop. "We'll make it, Cal. I promise." Charlie sounded like she was trying to convince herself.

A police car stopped on the cross street as their light turned green. Callie nibbled on her lower lip as the Camaro pulled through the intersection and accelerated down the street. She looked back and the police car turned their way. Oh, cops in a kettle, with Charlie driving the speed limit, they'd never make it in time.

Okay, God, it's miracle time, okay?

Charlie hung a right.

Holding her breath, Callie glanced back.

Lights flashed on the police car and Haven muttered something beneath his breath she was certain he didn't want Reece to hear.

"I'm sorry, guys." Charlie pulled to the side of the road and turned off the engine. "I don't know what I did wr—"

The police car zoomed past them, and they heaved a collective sigh.

One minute remaining.

Callie swallowed and held her breath.

One block to go. Five houses. Four. Three. Two.

Home.

"Go, Reece." Haven's voice sounded strained as Reece flew out the door and up the sidewalk.

Callie checked her watch. Two minutes late. Would that be good enough for Amanda?

Charlie turned and looked at Haven. "You go take care of your son, and I'll wait here."

"Thanks, Charlie. We'll be right back."

Haven helped Callie out of the car just as the front door of the house opened, and her breathing stopped.

Lasers beamed from Mandy's eyes toward Haven as she braced her hands on her hips. "You're lucky."

Haven stopped and wiped his mouth with the back of his hand. "Thank you, God," he whispered.

"Amen." Callie took his arm and walked with him up the sidewalk, feeling a slight wobble in his stride. This was too much for him. Mandy was being completely unfair.

And Callie was going to let her know.

But not now. Later, once Reece went to bed, she'd have a little one-on-one with his mom.

Reece grabbed his mom's arm and dragged her across the porch. "Look what I got a ride in."

Mandy pursed her lips, crossed her arms, and glared at Haven. "I never pictured you as a Camaro type of a person."

"It's not mine," he growled back, stopping at the base of the porch stairs. "But who knows, I am in the market for a new car."

"Sweet, Dad, really?"

He sighed, long and loud. "No, Reece, your mom's right, it's not the car for me. But." He aimed a forced smile at Mandy. "If it's all right with your mother, I'd love for you to come car shopping with me next Tuesday."

Callie put a supporting hand on his back. "With me, of course."

"Mom, can I? Please, please, please? I promise I'll keep my room clean and brush my teeth and wash my hands and—"

"Enough, Reece." Mandy frowned at Haven, raised her eyebrows at Callie, and then smiled at her son. "If that's how your father wants to spend his time with you, who am I to object?"

"Thanks, Mom." Reece hugged her waist. "You're the best."

"Right." She patted his back. "Now go on in and shower up."

"But I'm not dirty."

She ran a hand over his rain-matted hair. "Yeah, I can see that. Humor me, okay."

"Fine." He took a step toward the house then stopped and turned around. With a toothy smile, he ran back to Haven and opened his arms. "I love you, Dad. Thanks for an epic day."

Callie felt Haven shudder as he hugged his son.

"I love you too, bud. Thanks for helping me save Super Cal from the pirates."

Oh, cats on a rainbow. She looked up at a sky now awash with blue and wiped a hand over her eyes. *Thank you, Jesus.* Reece was right. This had been an epic day.

"Next Tuesday then?" Haven pinched out another smile.

"Tuesday." Mandy turned on one foot and strode into the house.

Haven's body seemed to cave, and he collapsed down onto the porch steps. "Is every Tuesday going to be like this?"

Callie sat beside him and laid her hand on his. "I'm sorry she's being like this. It's not the Mandy I know."

"Well, it is the Amanda I remember." He slapped his thighs, stood, and nodded toward the Camaro. "I better not take advantage of your friend any longer."

"Charlie's glad to help." Callie walked with him down the sidewalk. What she'd give to take his hand and squeeze her assurance, but as it was, she'd been too forward.

They stopped outside the muscle car and Haven looked down at her, bags darkening his eyes. "I can't thank you enough, Super Cal."

She rolled her eyes, and he smiled.

"I'll be in the office on Friday, meeting with the editor. Will you be there?"

"Until about noon, training my replacement and doing bookwork."

He tucked his hands in his front pockets. "Mind if I stop by to see you?"

Oh, dear. Did he know he was churning butter in her stomach? She sucked in her suddenly dry lips and nodded. "I'd like that."

He placed his fingers beneath her chin and lifted, "Callie, I—"

"Hey Dad, wait!" Reece hopped down the porch steps and ran toward them.

"What . . . ?" Haven's baritone voice pitched higher, and he snatched his hand from her chin. Clearing his throat, he turned to his son. "What do you need, Reece."

Callie held in her moan. Of all the lousy, rotten, stinkin—

"I have something for you." Reece tugged on his dad's hand. "Mom says you can come in for a second."

Haven looked through the open car window at Charlie.

"Go ahead. I need a moment with Callie, anyway."

"Thanks. I'll be right back."

Reece ran to the house and Haven jogged to keep up. That kid was going to keep them all in shape.

"Come sit." Charlie pushed open the passenger door.

Oh, boy. Callie bent into the Camaro. She was about to get an earful. She shut the door behind her and tucked her hands between her knees. "I suppose you saw that."

Charlie laughed. "Oh, sweetie, you are smitten."

"I know." She kicked at the floorboard.

"And you're not happy about it?"

Callie turned her head sideways and gazed at her friend. "He's all wrong for me."

"Wrong? Don't tell me that man's married." Fire shot from Charlie's eyes.

"No!"

"Engaged? Why I'll—" She made a fist that Haven wouldn't want to be on the receiving end of.

Callie raised her hands. "Charlie, he's unattached."

"Then what, pray tell, is wrong?"

"He's . . ." Callie stared at her knees. This was going to sound so silly to Charlie, but she was pretty, she'd never understand. "He's too good looking; he'd never go for someone like me."

"Excuse me, girlfriend? Someone like you? What, do you think you're yesterday's leftovers?"

Yeah, that about covered it.

"Sweetie, that gorgeous, Roman-chinned man almost locked lips with you."

Almost was the key word. Her lips still tingled from the wanting. And losing. "That's just it. *Almost*. It was an emotional moment. He's going through a tough time. I just happen to be convenient."

Charlie laughed. Laughed! "Cal, I know love. I see it in Jayson's eyes every day, and that hunky blond who just walked in the house? He's got those same eyes for you."

HAVEN WALKED INTO AMANDA'S house and watched Reece sail up the stairs. Stairs Haven hadn't touched since that night of Reece's accident. If he could keep his mouth shut and not heave any snide remarks toward Amanda, this could be another building block in their reconciliation foundation.

"You and Callie are looking awfully cozy." Amanda walked from the kitchen, wiping a plate with a dishtowel. Bill came up behind her and laid a hand on her shoulder.

Haven planted his feet and crossed his arms over his chest. "So, what if we are."

Her jaw clenched. It had been six years, but Haven still remembered that look, and it wasn't one of love. Callie was way off base on that assertion. No, Amanda was attempting to coax him into an argument he couldn't win. Well, he wasn't so easily coaxed anymore.

Amanda handed the plate and dishtowel to Bill and stepped toward Haven. She stopped within two feet of him and hissed in a near whisper, "Don't you dare use her to get at *my* son."

He fisted his hands beneath his arms. What could he say that she wouldn't use against him? Probably nothing. She'd always had a way of twisting his words. And living with an attorney probably heightened those skills.

Hoping to appear less confrontational, he lowered his arms to his side. "Callie's become a good friend. I would never use her."

Amanda's eyes locked with his as if trying to see beyond them into his thoughts. After what seemed like hours, she lowered her arms and nodded toward the stairs. "Go on up."

He aimed for the stairs, but she grasped his arm and stared him down again. "This is a one-time thing. Don't get used to coming in here."

Gritting his teeth, he strode to the stairway. Any comment would put her guard right back up and may cost him this opportunity. He wouldn't take this one-time privilege for granted.

He walked up the hardwood stairs, hanging onto a railing Amanda had painted white. Portraits of Reece angled up the wall, starting with his baby picture. Haven had that one, and the one year and two year pictures, but none after that. Stopping at the next portrait, he tried to mentally record the changes in his son. He did the same with each subsequent picture. Did he dare ask Amanda for copies?

Not today. But someday soon. She'd have to see that he'd changed, that he was no threat to her or to Reece.

More pictures lined the narrow hallway leading to Reece's room. Family pictures. Pictures he should have been in. Even a portrait including Bill.

That was going a little too far, now, wasn't it?

He stuffed down his frustration and walked into Reece's room. The last time he'd entered this room was when he'd rushed a goodbye before heading off to the bar.

And Reece ended up in the hospital where they sliced off what remained of his mangled foot.

Remembering that had always been Haven's greatest incentive not to drink and had kept him sober for six years now.

"Hey Dad."

Haven blinked and looked at his son standing by a desk littered with rocks.

"It's my collection."

Haven ambled over to the desk and studied the collection of polished agates. "These are great, Reece."

"I know." He picked up the one unpolished stone. "This is my favorite."

"Really?" Haven took the rock from his son and rolled it around in his hand. "Can I ask why?"

"Uh-huh. Callie said—"

"Ah hah, I should have known Super Cal was involved."

"Yeah, she knows everything, and she said that we're like this rock."
"We?"

"Yeah, you know, people. And God tumbles our lives around and poof, we're awesome."

"So, that's why we have all our problems, huh? Because God's polishing us?" Haven set the stone back on the desk.

"Yep. That's why I have a fake foot and you have a car that doesn't start and . . . are we really going car shopping next week? I've never gone car shopping and—"

"I promised you, didn't I?"

"It's time to go." Amanda's strained voice came from the doorway.

"Aw, Mom, he just got here."

Jaw tight, Haven laid a hand on Reece's shoulder. He would be agreeable with Amanda no matter how much it hurt. "She's right. I've already been given bonus time."

"But—"

"No buts, young man." Amanda strode over to the desk, her lips pursed.

Haven ruffled Reece's hair. "I'll see you next Tuesday, and I want you to be thinking about what kind of car I should get, okay? And no, not a Camaro."

"Ah, gee." He grabbed the unpolished stone from the desk and handed it to Haven. "For you."

"But it's your favorite." Haven stared at the ordinary rock that had become a precious treasure.

"It's so you can always remember me, and you won't leave me again."

Haven squeezed his eyes shut, but moisture still leaked from beneath the lids. He knelt and grasped Reece in a hug. "Son, I promise you, I'm never going to leave. Never again."

Amanda huffed. "We'll see about that."

Okay, that was all he could take from her. He stood and wheeled in her direction. "I'm not running again, it doesn't matter what you do to sabotage our relationship."

She said nothing as he marched from the room. He descended the stairs two at a time wishing he'd kept his mouth shut, praying he hadn't done irreparable damage.

FRIDAY ARRIVED WITHOUT A word from Amanda. Was it possible she'd let his departing comment slide? Or would she wait until the last minute to put a wrench in his plans to car shop with Reece?

That was a problem for another day. Today he had other things on his mind. He pulled his chair next to his editor, Donna Aster, and flipped open his laptop. Would she like what he'd done, or would it be the same old photography she saw every day? Did he have any kind of a future in photography, or would it always be an expensive hobby? Now was the moment of truth.

With his wireless mouse, he clicked on the icon for Nature Slideshow. "This is what I've got so far."

"Very well." She sat straight in her chair, her sole attention on the pictures as they floated past, not even offering a grunt to indicate what she thought.

He'd spent the last month and a half exploring the north shore, looking for a unique way to capture the area's beauty. Hopefully, some of his pictures qualified.

After going through what had to be a hundred shots, the picture he'd taken of the earthworm flitted past. Donna clicked the mouse, stopping the show. She returned to the night crawler and leaned back in her chair. She tented her hands over her chest and bounced her fingers.

What was she thinking? Probably wondering why he'd wasted good digital space on a silly night crawler.

She pointed at the worm. "This is precisely what I'm looking for."

*Really?*

"Enger Tower has been photographed ad nauseam, but never like this. There's a story here, and the reader will want to know all about it."

"And the other pictures?"

"Nice—"

Wonderful. He frowned.

"—but the same old thing. I want a story, Haven, not just a pretty photograph. Give me more like this one, and we may have a long relationship."

She restarted the slideshow and paused on a picture of Reece running up the path toward the tower. The picture his camera had accidentally shot when Reece had run from him after the wipe incident.

"Interesting." She zoomed in on his calf. The hem of his jeans had caught in the metal of his prosthetic foot, providing just a glimpse of Reece's handicap. "And this." She pointed at the screen. "I want to know the story behind this young man. This, Haven, this is what I'm looking for."

Was that a compliment, or a criticism that that was all he had?

She twisted her chair toward him and folded her hands in her lap. "Excellent job, Haven. I'm seeing great potential here."

Just potential? He rubbed his hands over his thighs.

"And now that you know what I'm looking for, I challenge you to go find it." She patted one of his nervous hands. "I'm confident you'll succeed."

CALLIE SAT AT HER desk, looking out toward the hill. She'd made a total fool of herself on Tuesday. And yet Haven had been kind to her. No, not kind. Charlie was right. The look he'd given her outside of Mandy's home was more than kindness. More than friendship.

She didn't want that, did she? Wouldn't it be better for all of them if Haven and Mandy could mend their relationship?

Arghh! She spun back toward her desk just as someone knocked on her door. Trying to flush Haven's smile from her mind, she arranged the bookwork on her desk—the final bookwork she'd be doing for Superior Suites. Hallelujah!—and looked toward the door. "Come in."

The door opened and Haven walked in, a smile glittering in his sweet blue eyes. Butterflies fluttered in her stomach.

"How's your last full day going?" He sat in the chair opposite her desk and reclined back.

"Busy." She gestured to the piles of work on her desk. "But that's okay because on Monday I get to start my dream job, full time."

"Sounds like you're up for a little celebrating."

"I am, but . . . " She stilled her chair and splayed her hands over her desk. "After my shift at the park, I'm going to be here until midnight cleaning up."

"Wish I could help somehow."

"You have helped. You added sweet sunshine to my day. Can you think of a better motivator?"

He smiled and warmth seeped across her face. Yeah, he added sunshine all right.

"I couldn't be happier for you." He rested his hands on her desk and leaned forward. "I have a reason to celebrate as well."

"Oh yeah?"

His smile blossomed into a grin. "The editor likes my work, especially a picture of a grimy earthworm Reece told me all about, courtesy of some remarkable teacher."

Oh, worms and weasels, why did everything he say make her want to blush? She studied her desk. "He loves the outdoors almost as much as I do."

"You're an amazing teacher, Super Cal."

Her head jerked up. "Would you stop that?" *Please don't.*

"Never." He rested his head in his hands. "You know, I was thinking I'd like to treat a very special friend to a thank-you dinner for all she's done for me." He leaned toward her. "Do you suppose she'd approve of Järvi's? I hear it has spectacular sunset views."

Järvi's? Oh my! Only the most romantic restaurant setting on the north shore. He couldn't be asking her, could he? "I think she'd love Järvi's."

"So, you'll come with me?"

Her heart stood still. He was asking her! It couldn't be.

Could it?

"Well?" He cocked his head to the side.

Her heart danced to the beat of a polka, while her foot tapped uncontrolled on the beige carpet. "I'd love to join you." This wasn't a date, though. It was a celebration and a polite *thank you*. Right?

"Great. Can I pick you up around seven thirty tomorrow night?"

"I'll be ready." But in what? Dress or jeans? She'd worn both to Järvi's, and neither had been out of place. "Um, this is a silly question, but can I ask what you'll be wearing?"

His brows leaped up. "A suit and tie."

*Oh, Lord, help me please.* She resisted the urge to pick up a piece of paper and fan herself. Nothing compared to a man in a suit and tie. "Then I guess I'll see you tomorrow night."

"I'm looking forward to it." Haven swaggered out of her office, and closed the door behind himself.

She couldn't tear her gaze from the door, where his confident gait stuck at the front of her memory. She was going to be completely useless for the rest of the day. If she didn't have the slew of work to finish, she'd head home after her park shift and lose herself in *While You Were Sleeping* for the umpteenth time. She'd imagine herself as Sandra Bullock and Haven as Peter Gallagher. No, Haven was far cuter than Peter Gallagher.

But just as out of reach.

Thank-you dinners did not morph into romance, especially for her.

*Way to return to earth, Callie girl.* She moved her computer mouse and the screen lit up with an image of Charlie Brown. Boy, could she relate to him!

She clicked Google Chrome just as someone else knocked on her door.

Now what? She'd never get anything done tonight. "Come on in."

Jess bounced in. "Hey Cal, how's it going?"

"Slow." She gave Jess a sideways smile. "I keep getting interrupted."

"Oh, hey, sorry about that, but I thought you'd want to know who's in town wanting to see you tomorrow night."

"Who?" Callie shook her head. "Doesn't matter, I have plans."

"Oh, you're gonna want to change them, believe me."

"Fine. Who do I want to see so badly?"

"Only the guy who discovered me."

Her blood seemed to freeze. No. Not him.

A quiver shook Callie's chin, and she whispered, "Sean?"

"Yeah, isn't it great? He wants to go out with the two of us tomorrow night, and I know you won't pass that up even if we have to tell Mom and Dad no Saturday family meal."

Callie bit into her lip and tasted metal. In her excitement over Haven's offer, she'd completely forgotten about the Saturday family dinner. Didn't matter. For once, she could miss it.

But not to spend time with Sean Porter, professional portrait photographer and human scum. Oh, she needed to tell him exactly what she thought of him, but she'd meet with him on her terms, not his, and tomorrow night was already taken.

After tomorrow night, she'd try to think of a Christian way to tell him off. Until then, though, not even Sean Porter could ruin her day.

## Chapter Seventeen

RESSED IN HER PAJAMAS, robe, and slippers, Callie rummaged through the dresses in her closet, all fine for her family meal, but tonight was special. She glanced back at the digital clock beside her bed. Only nine a.m. Plenty of time to find something. If only she had good taste in clothes. Why was it she could make businesses look good, but not herself?

With a huff, she closed the closet door and collapsed onto her bed. Nothing from her current wardrobe would work.

But . . .

Maybe dressing to impress wasn't her talent, but she was related to two women who excelled at it. With a slight skip in her walk, she hurried from her room and put an ear to Jess's closed door. Complete silence. Not a surprise there. It wasn't uncommon for Jess to sleep until noon on Saturdays and Sundays. Of course, if she'd come in at a decent hour, maybe she'd be up.

That left their mom.

Turbulence tossed Callie's stomach as she walked down the stairs to her parents' apartment. Her mom was not going to be happy about both of her girls missing their family dinner, but that couldn't be helped.

She knocked on their door then walked right in. Her father sat at the dining room table reading the newspaper and sipping coffee, wearing cheaters and loungewear, and looking not at all like Duluth's hottest anchorman. With his mussed-up hair and faint beard, he even looked normal. Like a dad.

He looked up and smiled. "Good morning, sweetheart."

"Morning Dad." She padded across the hardwood and gave him a kiss on the cheek.

"Come to join us for breakfast?" He tugged out the chair next to him.

"Sure." She ignored the chair and aimed for the kitchen. "I'll go help Mom."

"Oh, she can handle it. Maybe I'd like a little one-on-one with my daughter."

Uh-oh. Probably to try and tell her he'd changed his mind about hiring Gemma, or worse, to talk Callie out of continuing in the naturalist position. She sat in the chair beside him anyway, her arguments already prepared. "What do you want to talk about?"

"Can't I just want to spend some time with my daughter?"

Not without ulterior motives. She shrugged.

He laid the paper on the table and folded it closed. "Tell me how your new job is going."

Yep. Just as she thought. He was probably hoping she hated it, that she couldn't wait to return to the office, but nothing could be further from the truth. Now to convince him that she was right where she belonged. "I'm loving it. There's nothing more exhilarating than being out in nature, teaching, learning."

"It's your dream?"

She nodded while gnawing on her lower lip.

"Then I guess I need to be happy for you, don't I?"

"Really? You mean that?" She stared at him, looking for indications of a doppelganger.

He stretched an arm around her shoulders and tugged her to his side. "Sweetheart, I know it doesn't always seem like it, but your mother and I want the best for you and sometimes we forget that doesn't mean what's comfortable for us. You do such a marvelous job at Superior Office Suites, it's hard to imagine your passions lie elsewhere, but if they do, then you need to follow your dream." He winked and nodded toward the kitchen. "That's how I ended up here with your mother."

Callie looked down at the solid maple table.

He kissed her forehead and whispered, "We are proud of you dear."

"My, my, I hate to interrupt this moment, but I have hot scrambled eggs and toast all ready."

Her dad squeezed her shoulders and let her go.

Great, now she got to tell them that she was skipping out on tonight's meal. What a time for her dad to get all sentimental on her.

Her mom, looking like she was ready to go on air with her perfect hair, make-up, and pantsuit, set plates in front of them then sat across the table. "Lovely to have you join us this morning."

Callie cut off a bite-sized piece of egg. "Well, I came with a request." She stuffed the egg into her mouth.

"And what is that. dear?" Her mom reached for a carafe of orange juice. "Care for some?"

"Yes, please." Callie wiped her mouth with a cloth napkin. "Do you remember meeting Haven Carlysle? Our new tenant?"

"Of course." Her mother poured juice into two glasses and handed one to Callie. "Quite the handsome and accomplished young man. Just the type of gentleman Jessica needs rather than those rapscallions she insists on dating."

Callie dropped her fork on the Martha Stewart plate. Naturally, they wouldn't consider for a moment that Haven had no interest in Jess and maybe, just maybe he liked someone else. At least Callie hoped he liked her. She looked down at her food, now unappetizing. "He asked me out tonight."

"Excuse me?"

*Don't sound so surprised, Mother.* Callie's gaze fired bullets across the table as her mother sat down. "Yes, he did. So, I won't be here for our Saturday meal. He's taking me to Järvi's." So, what if it wasn't a date but rather a thank-you dinner.

"Järvi's, huh?" Her father began slicing his toast diagonally. The knife slipped from his hand, clanked on the plate, and then somersaulted onto the floor. "Oh, fudge on a stick." He picked up the knife and set it on the table. "Sorry about that, dear."

"You've got the clumsies today." Her mother handed him her knife.

"It seems I do." He completed the diagonal on his toast. "Now where were we?"

"Järvi's." Callie pushed her plate away. She wanted to save room for tonight.

"That's right. A lovely place. I took your mother there for our last anniversary. This young man must think you're pretty special."

"Well, it's not really a date but a thank you for some work I've been doing for him."

"Hmm." Her dad forked the eggs but didn't eat. "That's quite a nice thank you."

*Tell me about it.* "I know, but the problem is I don't know what to wear." She tucked her chin and peered over at her mom, not at all confident of the answer to her coming question. "Will you help me?"

A sincere smile spread across her mother's face, and she clasped her hands in front of her chest. "I can't think of anything I'd love to do more." She sat back in her chair and drummed a finger on her chin. "I know this perfect little boutique where they get the latest fashions. And then we could stop by George's Salon and have them give you an updo—"

"Mom, please, it's not a date. Just a nice style would—"

"Nonsense. If this young man is taking you to Järvi's, you will be dressed for the occasion. Perhaps it's not a date. Yet. But I guarantee once he sees you, a date is exactly what the dinner will become."

Callie blinked. Was that a compliment from her mother?

Maybe a mother-daughter outing wouldn't be so bad after all. Callie picked up her plate with barely-touched eggs. The butterflies tickling her stomach left no room for hunger. "I'll get dressed, then I'll be ready to go."

"Marvelous, dear. I can't wait."

Surprisingly, neither could Callie.

HAVEN CLUTCHED THE BOUQUET of wildflowers and pushed the doorbell marked with the number two. He tapped his foot on the porch as he waited. Why was he nervous? This wasn't a date. Not really. It was just a dinner thanking Callie for all she'd done for him, a stranger a mere six weeks ago.

Funny, it felt as if he'd known her forever. These weeks of knowing her had been some roller coaster ride, but she'd made that ride fun. Maybe tonight they could relax and not worry about the rest of their lives.

He heard footfalls inside the home and the inside door opened. Mr. Beaumont smiled at Haven and pushed open the screen door. "Nice to see you again." He waved Haven in and offered his hand. "Callista's looking forward to this evening."

"I'm looking forward to it as well."

Mr. Beaumont pointed at the door to his right. "She asked that I send you up. Her mother's nearly done futzing with her."

Haven reached for the knob, and Callie's father clasped a hand over Haven's shoulder. "I presume I don't have to tell you to treat our Callista with respect."

"I will, sir."

"My princess is awaiting." Mr. Beaumont winked and patted Haven on the back.

Taking a deep breath, Haven opened the door and climbed the stairs. For a second there, he thought he was going to be given the third degree.

Haven liked that in a father. It showed he cared.

Midway up the stairs, he stopped to admire a painting hung on the wall of Split Rock Lighthouse. The artist's style appeared to be similar to that of the painting behind the reception desk at Superior Suites. He squinted at the diminutive signature. Looked like a K and a B followed by a scribble. With the artist's gift, that tiny scribble was no doubt intentional. A painting from this artist would be the perfect piece to add to a home he planned to purchase soon. Callie would know where to find one. He'd love to go artwork hunting with her.

But not tonight. He hurried up the remaining steps and rapped on the door. Seconds later it opened and Haven stood mute.

Callie?

Her indigo dress clung to curves Haven hadn't noticed before and brought out the dusk in her eyes even more than usual. Her hair hung in loose, messy waves around her head, and that diamond stud in her nose had been exchanged for a deep blue-colored gem that matched her dress. Stunning.

"Hi." She looked toward the floor, but it didn't hide the pink in her cheeks. "Come on in."

He cleared his throat and handed her the bouquet. "You look . . . amazing."

"Thank you." She shrugged and the blush on her cheeks deepened. "So do you."

"Callista, darling, help me find a vase."

Haven shook his head. He hadn't even noticed Mrs. Beaumont scouring through cupboards in Callie's galley-sized kitchen. He'd had eyes for Callie alone.

"Right back." Callie walked gingerly on spike-heeled sandals toward her kitchen, the bouquet lifted to her nose.

He took a breath and smoothed down his jacket. His gray suit and burgundy tie paled next to Callie. He honestly hadn't expected her to look so . . . so . . .

Breathtaking.

Had he been blind these past weeks?

Callie added water to a crystal vase and then dropped the flowers inside. She inhaled another breath and then centered the arrangement on her kitchen peninsula. "Did I tell you I loved wildflowers?"

"I guessed." He crossed the hardwood floors toward Callie and fingered a yellow aster. "With your love of nature, it made sense."

She blushed an even deeper shade of red, if that were possible, as if she was unaccustomed to compliments.

Well, he'd shower her with them tonight. She deserved it. "Are you ready to go?"

"I'll grab my clutch."

She crossed the living room to what was likely her bedroom, her ankles wobbling slightly. With her job, she probably rarely wore heels, but those spiky heels sure emphasized shapely calves.

Haven tugged on his collar. It had been months since he'd been on a date. Too long, obviously.

Was this a date?

He hadn't planned on it. Even with their near-kiss the other day. A kiss prompted by an emotional moment.

Tonight was just supposed to be a nice evening for him to show his gratitude.

Callie came out of her bedroom, a sparkly black purse in her hand,

and she smiled.

A heart-abducting smile. Why had it taken weeks for him to notice how beautiful she was? He walked toward her and offered his arm. Maybe he should rethink the evening's purpose. Oh, he was grateful for her all right. She alone was responsible for giving him a chance with Reece and for teaching him little-boy games. But she was so much more than that.

He led her to the stairs and opened the door.

Yeah, this was definitely more than a thank-you dinner.

WITH SOFT PIANO MUSIC playing in the background, Callie bit into her Rönttönen, a pastry with lingonberry filling, and sighed. Sitting across from Haven, deliciously handsome in his gray suit and burgundy tie, and with his blond hair tickling his ears, made her believe she was in some fairy tale. *Beauty and the Beast* with the gender roles reversed.

He finished off his Vispipuuro, a dessert porridge made with lingonberries, then laid his spoon on the empty plate, but his attentive gaze never left her face. She could swear her cheeks wore a permanent blush.

"So, tell me how you know Amanda." He rested his elbows on the table, then his chin on folded hands.

"Art class."

"You're an artist?"

"I dabble."

"I'll bet. Like I dabble in photography." He half grinned. "So, that painting behind the reception desk at work, and the painting in your apartment stairway, are they yours?"

Didn't she wish! "They're my dad's." While she'd inherited a love of art from her father, she didn't inherit his talent. If only he would return to it someday.

"I see. So, KB scribble stands for Kenneth Beaumont."

She chuckled. "Dad would appreciate that description."

"I'm surprised I didn't know he could paint. With his celebrity status in Duluth, I'd think that would be a great marketing tool."

"Which is exactly why he doesn't make it known. Dad wants people to appreciate his art because it's great art, not because it's created by a local celebrity."

Haven raised his water goblet toward Callie. "Gotta give him credit for that. Not everyone would take that approach."

"When it comes to his art, he's very humble." Too bad he didn't take that same approach at the station.

"Like father, like daughter." He took a drink of his water. "Enough about your dad, I want to know more about you. What art medium do you work with?"

Her cheeks must be on permanent blush tonight. She couldn't remember the last time someone asked about her art. "I've tried a few different things. Watercolors on canvas. I'm testing out charcoal sketching. And this sounds rather silly, but what I really love working with is denim."

His eyes widened. "Denim? I haven't heard that before."

"It's done, but not widely. For a Girl Scout craft once we painted canvas tennis shoes, and I enjoyed that so much, I started looking through my closet for more canvases. I found an old denim jacket that had holes in the elbows and was frayed at the cuffs and decided to experiment. I patched up one elbow, but left the other and I painted scenes of my favorite things on it. It was so cool taking something old and ratty and making it new again. Jess loved it so much, she took it for herself and a little side business grew from that."

"Huh. I'll bet you paint jeans too."

How did he know? "People bring me their favorite, most comfortable old jeans that they hate to get rid of and I renew them. I ask the client all about themselves, getting a feel for their passions and talents, then I transfer that to their jeans."

"Interesting, so you're the one."

"I'm the one?"

"Amanda had on a pair of painted jeans when I first saw her this summer, and then I saw Jess wearing them a while back. What a clever idea. How come I haven't seen you wear any? That would be a terrific way to market yourself."

"Me?" She slapped a hand to her chest and shivered. "Goodness no. They're for people who crave attention. I prefer to stick in the shadows and let others do my advertising." But it was certainly nice being noticed for once, especially by Haven.

"Hmm." He reached across the table and grasped her hand. "I think I'm glad that you don't seek attention. I'm beginning to think I don't want to share you." He stroked her fingers with her thumb.

Good gracious heavens, Callie hadn't thought it possible, but her cheeks seemed to warm several more degrees. She looked down at his hand protecting hers. Maybe she should trust him to take her picture. Haven was seeking beauty, not fame.

He wasn't like Sean.

She looked out the window next to their table, across Highway 61, at the gentle waves slapping Superior's shore. The crescent moon was already visible in the blue sky. In an hour, it would reflect the sun's light, making it appear brighter.

That was all Haven wanted to do: reflect the Son's light, not shine his own.

Not like Sean.

She turned her hand over, entwining her fingers with Haven's and he didn't let go.

"What would you say to a walk on the beach?"

*Be still my fluttering heart.* Heels and all, it would be worth it. She nodded. "That would be nice." Super nice, actually. She couldn't wait to tell Man—

Oh boy, how could she talk to Mandy about this evening when she still loved Haven? That was a conversation for a calm day.

But Jess would be excited. Maybe even Mom.

Haven walked around the table and pulled her chair back as she stood. Then he tucked her hand in the crook of his arm as they walked toward the exit.

Whether or not his intention of inviting her out tonight was one merely of gratitude, the evening had become much more. For the first time in years she felt pretty. No, erase that.

She *believed* she was pretty.

The restaurant door opened and Callie stopped.

The pattering in her heart quit with a thump.
It was Jess.
Clinging to Sean Porter's arm.

## Chapter Eighteen

JUST SEEING SEAN PORTER again made her nauseated. She clung tighter to Haven's arm, praying they'd make a hasty exit.

But Haven stopped abruptly. "Sean?"

What? Haven knew the man who'd cemented scars on her heart?

"Haven, that you man?"

Callie released his arm as he strode forward and greeted Sean with a vigorous hand shake.

"In the flesh. What brings you up here?"

Sean winked and nodded at Jess. "Do I need a better reason than this?"

"So you know . . . " Haven looked around until he spotted Callie behind him. She had no desire to speak with Sean ever again.

But Haven reached out for her hand and drew her next to him, her legs reluctantly stepping forward. "You know Callie?"

Sean smiled, his eyes narrowing, and she shivered. "Callie, Jess, and I go waaaay back."

"That's right, I forgot you grew up in this area."

Sean kissed Jess's cheek, but his gaze remained on Callie. "I had the best scenery to work with."

Callie's stomach frothed like Superior during a storm.

"That's how I got into modeling." Jess squeezed Sean's arm.

"You . . . ?" Haven glanced at Callie, then back at Jess and smiled. "So, you're the model in our office. I didn't . . . "

Jess rolled her eyes. "I know. I'm not Kate Moss thin, but I model plus-sized clothing."

"And I wouldn't want you that skinny, babe. I have to photograph enough sticks with legs. I return home whenever I need to shoot someone healthy." Sean nodded toward Callie. "Callista even posed for me once."

The Rönttönen backtracked up her throat. She squeezed Haven's hand and let go. "If you'll excuse me, I need some fresh air. I'm not feeling very well."

Her whole body shaking, she hurried out the door into the parking lot.

Too many cars.

Too many people.

Swallowing back the dessert that wanted to pitch out, she hurried across the road, her feet and ankles complaining about her heels. She crossed grass and weeds to the rocky shoreline with heels sinking into the dirt. Dirty. Just like her. No! Just like Sean. The images of what he'd done to her leaped to the front of her thoughts, and she could no longer keep down her meal.

Her stomach empty and throat raw, she backtracked to a gnarly pine and sagged against it. Didn't matter that she might ruin her new dress. This evening was ruined anyway.

Tears trickled over her cheeks and her body trembled as if she were experiencing his abuse all over again. She yanked off her sandals, threw them out on the rocks, and massaged the balls of her feet, trying to calm her nerves, but failed.

She sniffled and wiped her nose with her arm. Why was Sean here? Why now when she thought she could move past what he'd done to her?

She tucked her head between her knees and let her dress soak the tears.

"Callie?"

And why did Haven have to see her like this?

She kept her head down as he sat beside her and circled an arm around her shoulders.

And said nothing.

She sniffled and listened to the waves slap the shore. Haven's musky cologne mingled with the breath of water carried by the wind. "I'm sorry." Her words came out like a boat dragged over a sand bar.

"Shhh." He tucked her head against his shoulder.

She felt the rise and fall of his chest, smooth and gentle as the waves. He didn't offer platitudes of "It's okay." He didn't offer to make it better. He just held her, protecting her, letting her know someone was there for her.

A good man who would never take advantage of her. A true gift from God.

IGNORING THE PAIN SHOOTING through his fist, Haven held on to Callie, hoping to soothe the mass of tremors from her body.

Tremors caused by that sleaze, Sean Porter. Haven hadn't worked with the man much, but it didn't take much to know Porter liked to take advantage of his position as a photographer.

No wonder Callie hated having her picture taken.

He didn't dare say anything, fearing his anger would seep through. His anger, stirred with whatever Callie was feeling, was likely a combustible combination. Back in the restaurant, it had taken all the strength he could muster, not to grab Porter up by the collar and demand to know what he'd done to Callie. Instead, he'd taken his frustrations out on the outside wall of the restaurant. He flexed his fingers, and they all still worked, but he'd likely have some nice bruising tomorrow.

Didn't matter. What mattered was being here for Callie. He caressed her shoulder and breathed in her coconut shampoo. She deserved to be cherished.

Her quivering slowly ebbed away, and her breathing deepened.

He relaxed against the tree's trunk, stretched his legs out, closed his eyes, and matched his breaths with hers.

The rhythm of the waves lulled him, calming his rage, ferrying it back out to sea.

He'd known Callie only a matter of weeks. How could he care for her this deeply already?

With Amanda, that relationship had been about breaking away from home and playing grown-up with a pretty girl.

And Lissa, the woman he'd proposed to before moving to Duluth? He'd promised his dying mentor, Lissa's father, that he would care for his daughter. It wasn't a difficult promise to make, and on paper they were a perfect match.

But relationships don't live on paper. While he'd cared for her, and wanted to abide by his mentor's wishes, true love hadn't followed and Lissa had graciously turned down his proposal.

What he'd felt for Amanda or Lissa didn't go anywhere near as deep as what he felt for Callie.

He removed his suit coat and blanketed Callie then loosened his tie. When she was ready, he'd listen. He twisted a strand of her hair around his finger. Soft hair he longed to feel more of. But for now, this was good.

Crickets chirping around them underscored the melody hummed on the lake breeze as night took over the sky. Callie stirred and snuggled in closer, wrapping an arm over his chest. With a smile, he closed his eyes and sleep finally took over.

CALLIE BLINKED HER EYES open and lifted her face from the hard pillow. She stared outward and stars blinked back.

Stars?

Crickets. Water.

Musky cologne.

Haven.

She smiled, but then the evening's memories returned, and she yanked her arm off Haven's chest. His jacket slid to the ground. How had he allowed her to get so close, especially after her meltdown at the restaurant?

She stood on panty-hosed feet and hugged herself, warding off the brisk air blowing off the lake. The water crept up the shore then leaped back as if burned by fire.

Years ago, Sean had crept up on her, and she'd bought into his flattery. She hadn't realized he was holding her next to the flames the whole time.

Did burn scars ever heal? Why did extinguished fires leave her feeling so cold?

Rubbing the chill from her arms, she stepped closer to the water and stones tore at her nylons. Now where were her sandals? She searched the shore. With the moon and stars providing the only light, her dark shoes blended in perfectly.

A groan sounded behind her. Seconds later, something blanketed her shoulders. Haven's jacket.

He stood at her side, his shoulders at her eye level. "How are you doing?"

"Super great and getting better." Her voice was flatter than a good skipping rock.

"I'm so sorry, Callie." He knelt and dug through the stones then flung one out toward the water. It made two leaps before sinking. "Porter taught a photography class I took. I admired him. At first."

She breathed in through her nose. "Then I don't need to go into details."

"Only if you want to."

She shuddered at the thought and rubbed her arms which were covered with goose bumps. She couldn't ever imagine wanting to discuss that. "I suppose we should be getting home."

"Your dad might not be too happy with me."

She laughed at the not-so-funny statement. "Or he might be thrilled. He's always worried because I'm home too early. A girl in her mid-twenties shouldn't be such a homebody, you see."

"Callie." Haven stepped in front of her and grasped her arms.

She looked down at the damp stones cooling her feet.

"He's not going to hurt you again." Haven released her arms and gripped her chin, tilting it up, but she refused to look him in the eye. "I'm not going to hurt you, understand?"

She nodded and finally glanced up.

His gaze searched hers, and she moistened her lips.

The heart Sean had brought to a stop, raced again like Reece during his Whipper Snapper sprint.

Haven released her chin and cupped her cheeks, his eyes focused on her, and his chest pulsed to the same beat as her heart. "Can I . . . ?"

Callie leaned toward him, raising up on her tippy-toes, and closed her eyes.

And waited.

Lips lightly brushed against hers then slipped away.

She opened her eyes wide. "You stopped?"

With his thumbs, he caressed her cheeks. "I don't want to take advantage."

She touched a finger to his lips and traced their softness surrounded by a slight prickle of whiskers. How would that feel against her skin? "I've never . . . "

His hands sprung away, and his Adam's apple jerked down then back up. "I didn't mean—"

"Kissed, Haven, I've never been kissed before." Twenty-five years old and no man had ever even come close. As a dreamy-eyed high schooler, she'd always imagined Sean would be her first. Thank God, he hadn't been.

A smile edged the corners of his mouth and the twinkle in his eyes matched the stars flickering above them. "Never?"

She sucked her lips between her teeth and shook her head. "I think I need lessons."

His smile grew. "If you don't mind hands-on lessons."

"That's how I learn the best." She curved her arms around his back and drew him closer, breathing in his masculine scent.

His strong, yet gentle fingers kneaded her shoulders, worked up the back of her neck, and combed through her hair.

And then his lips touched hers.

Tentative. Warm. Chasing the chills she'd had moments before. She shrugged the jacket from her shoulders as she savored his lips caressing hers. He walked his fingers back down her neck, over her shoulders, and down her back, pulling her in tighter, nearly melding their bodies together. Yet she wanted to be closer. Heat and goose bumps mingled together as his heart beat against her like Superior in a storm.

She loved him for being so gentle.

Her heart beat in rhythm with his, and she deepened the kiss, tasting the sweet and salty lingonberry dessert.

And hunger.

A hunger tempered with care. It couldn't be love. Not this quick, could it?

Once upon her childhood, her parents had taught her that a kiss had healing powers. She'd thought it a fairy tale. Haven was making her believe.

He backed away, sticking an entire hand into his trouser pocket, his breath coming in quick jabs, and smiled. "I think that first lesson went quite well, don't you?" he said between breaths, and then drew his shirt-sleeved arm across his lips. "As you said, it's time to go home."

"No more lessons?" Callie touched a hand to his chest.

He backed away again and fell bottom first on the stones. "Ow." He leaned over and then held up two spike-heeled sandals. "Missing something?"

"Oh, that's where they went." She took them from him and dropped them on the ground next to her feet. "Now, where were we?"

"Heading home." He stood and wiped his backside.

"But I need practice." She stuck out her lip.

"Oh, really." He took her hand and pulled her close. "Well, maybe one more lesson." He reached behind her head, pulled her toward him, and his phone buzzed. He puffed out an exasperated sigh. "Now, who . . . ?" He glanced at his phone and his brows formed a V. "It's your sister."

Jess? Why would she be calling Haven? Callie patted her left hip where she usually kept her phone and shook her head. It would be awfully difficult for Jess to reach her when her phone sat on vibrate in a purse a few feet away.

Still, what did Jess need so urgently that she had to call Haven?

And interrupt their romantic moment. Her sister was going to get an earful when she got home tonight.

Assuming Jess came home. With Sean, there was no guarantee.

Callie leaned over and tugged on a sandal, ignoring Haven's conversation with Jess. It wouldn't surprise her if Jess tried to make a move on Haven. She was probably insanely jealous. With an arrogant grin, Callie pulled on the second sandal. Good for Jess. It was time the tables were turned.

"Callie." Haven rested a hand on her shoulder. His voice had taken on a somber tone. "We need to go."

"Why?" Her chills returned. She didn't want to hear his answer.

"It's your dad, Callie. He's had a stroke."

## Chapter Nineteen

*P**LEASE, GOD, LET DADDY be all right.* Callie clutched Haven's suit jacket around her shivering shoulders as she hurried through St. Luke's corridors and into the hospital waiting room. Her ankles protested each step because of the stupid stiletto-heeled sandals. She found Jess, their mom, and Mandy sitting huddled together in the corner of the waiting room, as if they were praying.

But Callie knew better.

Mandy wore her scrubs, so she must be on duty tonight. And to think she was taking time to comfort Callie's family. That was the Mandy Callie knew and loved.

Callie cut across the room and knelt next to their chairs, not caring about her expensive dress. Besides, sitting on the beach had already ruined it.

"Callie." Haven touched her shoulder and then helped her into a chair he'd carried over and set down, creating a private circle for the women. "I'll be over there." He pointed across the waiting room.

"Thanks, Haven." She looked back at her mom and did a double take. Her mother never left her bedroom, much less the house, looking less than spectacular. Shadows had settled beneath red-streaked eyes that looked much smaller without the benefit of eye shadow, eyeliner, and mascara. Her hair was pulled back in a frizzy ponytail emphasizing cheekbones that weren't as high as blush made them appear.

Her mother actually looked human.

And broken.

Callie laid a hand on her mom's shoulder and looked at Mandy.

"How is Dad?"

"They're doing tests right now." Mandy gave Callie a side-armed hug then stood. "I've gotta get back to work, but I needed to be here for you."

"Thank you." She gave a little nod as Mandy hurried away. Then she looked at her family. "What kind of tests?"

"A CT scan, MRI, blood tests." Jess sniffled. "We're just waiting to hear the results."

"You don't know for sure it's a stroke?"

Her mother shook her head, raised a handkerchief to her nose, and wiped. "Dear, he was being so clumsy and then . . . " Her mother's chin quivered. "And then his face . . . " She closed her eyes and patted them with her handkerchief. "What else could it be?"

Callie circled her arm around her mother's back and whispered a silent prayer. It didn't make sense. Her dad was the epitome of health. Frequent exercise and excellent nutrition helped him maintain the youthful appearance that was so necessary in his profession. Certainly, the eggs he ate every Saturday morning wouldn't cause this, would they?

"Mackenzie." A male voice crooned behind Callie. An all-too-familiar voice.

Her mom didn't even try to hide her dissatisfaction as she turned at the waist to glare at Allen Eddings, the weekend anchor who'd do anything to usurp her dad's position.

"Allen." Her mom looked toward the man then jerked her head down, probably remembering she wore no makeup. "News travels fast."

"I am so sorry, Mackenzie." The man's words practically drooled like a rabid dog. The twenty-something reporter with his chiseled-for-TV face and deep vocal pipes may have garnered hero worship by a young female audience, but they were only looking skin deep. He and Sean were built from the same rotten material.

The slime dragged over another chair, inserting himself into the womens' once-intimate triangle. "The station sent me down to talk with you, find out how things are going."

"The station can wait."

"Come on, Mackenzie, don't insult me by saying you wouldn't be the first one hounding the hospital if I were admitted."

She worked her chin back and forth and swallowed. "I'm asking you to leave."

"Hmm." He flipped open a notebook. "If you're this upset, there's obviously a story here. I'm certain I can get someone—"

"Sir, the Beaumonts asked that you leave them alone."

Haven towered over Eddings, whose hair was too thick and perfectly coiffed and reminded Callie of chocolate frosting. "This is a private moment and, when they're ready, they'll issue a statement, but not before."

"And you are?" Eddings backed up his chair and stood, the top of his head barely reaching Haven's nose.

"A friend of the family."

Callie scooted her chair back and stood beside Haven. "Our spokesperson. Anything you want, you go through him." Callie prayed Haven would forgive her for this.

"So, that's how you're playing this." Eddings jotted a few notes. "And your name, Mr. Spokesperson?"

"Haven Carlysle." Haven pulled a business card from his wallet and handed it over. "Now, this family would appreciate some privacy. Oblige them, and I'll oblige you. It can be a symbiotic relationship, if you so choose."

The anchorman pinched Haven's card between two fingers and quirked a half smile that sent shivers down Callie's spine. "We'll be in touch, Mr. Carlysle."

They all watched him swagger from the waiting room and make a brief stop at the nurses' station. Callie prayed the nurses would see past the man's DNA and send him packing, but judging by the way the nurses batted their eyelashes, they'd give Eddings whatever he asked for. Why couldn't intelligent people learn to see beyond the face?

Finally, the man flung his business card onto the nurses' desktop, and he strutted to the elevator. The nerve of that man.

Once the elevator doors closed, Callie tried to shake off the heebie-jeebies Eddings gave her. What kind of slime-ball would intrude on a family's private moment? And then try to take advantage of their problems for his own gain?

Her gaze flitted to her mother who sat with her face cradled in her hands. Certainly, her parents hadn't done the same in their ascension to the weekday anchor throne.

Had they?

She shook away the thought. Her mother needed her support, not judgment.

Haven secured his arm around her shoulders, affixing her to his side. She'd never felt so cared for, so protected.

But she owed him a big apology. "I'm sorry, Haven. I didn't mean to get you so involved. It was all I could think of to get that weasel away from us."

"Yes, Haven, thank you for interceding." Her mother still looked to the floor. "We would be grateful if you would accept the position Callie offered. I can't deal with the station right now."

"I'll gladly take it off your hands." He kissed Callie's forehead. "Assuming that means I get to hang around you a little more."

More shivers tickled her spine, but these made her smile, temporarily taking away concerns about her dad. "As long as the family puts up with you, I suppose I can too."

"Mackenzie Beaumont?" A female voice intruded.

Great, another reporter. Callie turned to the voice and winced. A woman in scrubs walked toward them. Definitely not a reporter.

Both Jess and Mom stood, and her mom offered her hand.

"Dr. Rochelle Jalen." The doctor shook Mom's hand and then gestured to the chairs. "Please, sit."

Haven offered the doctor Eddings's empty chair and then walked away. Callie looked at him, planning on telling him to stay, but he shook his head and pointed to the doctor.

Considerate. One more adjective to add to her description of Haven. She mouthed 'thank you' then turned back to listen.

Dr. Jalen folded her hands in her lap and connected her gaze with each of them. "First of all, I wish to tell you, Mrs. Beaumont, that your husband has a wonderful attitude. He's got the entire staff smiling. That's the best medicine possible for him. I wish all our patients were as positive."

Callie smiled, but her mother's cheeks remained taut and her jaw clenched. "Would you please just give me the bottom line? Do you have the test results?"

The doctor looked down at her lap then back up, having installed a practiced faux smile on her face. "Yes, we have the results."

CALLIE WORRIED HER LIP as she followed her mom and Jess down the hall toward her father's room. How was she ever going to smile and be positive for her dad when her heart broke for him? Haven's jacket warming her arms helped, though she wished he walked beside her. He'd made the right choice by staying back in the waiting room allowing them family time. Still, having him nearby was a surprising comfort.

Dr. Jalen had said her dad had a stroke caused by a blood clot in an artery that carried blood to the brain, and he was given medicine to dissolve the clot.

But that just dealt with preventing further harm. Months of therapy would be required to correct the damage that had already been done.

They stopped outside the door and her mother primped herself one last time. Before making the trek down the hall, she'd ducked into a hospital restroom to apply her face and tame her hair, insisting that Kenneth see the best of her right now. Her mother was right. Her dad didn't need to see their worried faces.

He needed hope.

Callie pinched her cheeks, glued on a smile, then followed Jess and her mother into the hospital room. Her dad sat up in his bed and smiled.

On the left side of his face.

The right half drooped in paralysis.

"My girls." Only the left side of his mouth moved and his words came out muffled, but her heart heard them clearly.

"Kenneth." Eyes blinking rapidly, her mother walked to the left side of his bed, took his functioning hand, and kissed his healthy cheek.

"Hi Daddy." Jess stood at the foot of his bed, failing to imitate a smile and failing to stop the trail of tears on her cheeks.

Callie stopped at his right side and took his weak hand. She kissed the lifeless cheek and smoothed hair out of his eye but couldn't think of a thing to say. All the typical small talk ice breakers, "How are you doing?" and "You're looking good," obviously didn't fit, so she remained silent.

She caressed the fingers that normally squeezed back.

"Callie girl." He angled his head toward her, his words came out slow and plodding as if speaking around marbles, his beautiful TV anchor voice stolen by a tiny blood clot. "I'm shorry 'bout your date."

"Oh, Daddy." Tears escaped her eyes. She hadn't called him Daddy for years, but then he rarely called her Callie girl anymore. She leaned over and kissed the sagging cheek, dropping tears on his face. Haven's kiss had healed her aching heart earlier. Wasn't that much harder to mend than her father's paralysis?

His left arm twitched as if he wanted to move it and the left side of his face wrinkled with agitation. "I can't . . . "

"Kenneth." Her mother patted his good hand. "Before you know it, you'll be as good as new. We'll have you home in a couple of days, and then we're putting together a schedule for rehabilitation."

Callie nibbled on the tip of her manicured pinky. A rehab schedule that would take her mother away from concerns at Superior Suites.

His good eye narrowed. "My job."

"Will be there when we're done, and the station will be lauded for supporting you."

Her mother was probably right about that, but who knew what magic Eddings yielded with the station manager?

As for managing Superior Suites?

Keeping her dad's limp hand in hers, Callie dropped into the padded guest chair. Running the office right now was out of the question, for both her dad and her mom.

A storm simmered in her stomach and threatened to rise up her throat. What did that mean for her new job?

She looked at her dashing and cocky . . . and loving dad, a man whose entire world had been flung around like a ball on the Tilt-A-Whirl. And then she studied her mom. Beautiful, arrogant, yet providing love through her strength. A woman willing to jump onto that Tilt-A-Whirl ride to hold Dad's hand while dragging her feet on the ground in an attempt to stop its maddening whirl. If anyone could encourage her dad's recovery, that would be Mom. She wouldn't let him fail.

Everyone was being asked to make a sacrifice.

Shouldn't she sacrifice as well?

But why now? When she was finally moving toward her dream?

And when she might have met that special someone to share in her dream?

Callie slumped in her chair.

"Callie girl." Her dad's hand made a slight movement beneath hers. "Don't be sad."

She sniffled and forced the smile back on her face. How could she think only of herself at a time like this? It was time to take lessons from her mother and move down this new path with confidence, even if it had taken a detour. She stood and kissed her father's cheek again and whispered. "I'm proud of you, Daddy, and I love you."

The left side of his mouth curled up. "I proud too."

Would he feel so proud if he knew she was bucking against making this sacrifice? She caressed his limp cheek. "I'll be right back."

"Bring boyfriend."

She nodded, and aimed for the door, but her mother stopped her.

"You'll confirm with Haven that we wish to retain his services as our family spokesperson?"

"I will." Haven had stepped into the role with grace, which wasn't at all a surprise. But would he want to continue that role?

"Do you agree?" Mom refocused on Dad.

He nodded. "Good . . . idea. Like boyfriend."

"I'll get him." Callie walked out the door, and then leaned against the wall.

*Boyfriend.* She sniffled and pushed away from the wall. She wiped her face dry, straightened her shoulders, and strode down the hall.

Haven wouldn't like the sacrifice she was making. Not at all.

But family always came first.

Haven, of all people, would understand that. Wouldn't he?

# Chapter Twenty

AVEN SAT ON THE edge of the chapel's unforgiving pew, his hands folded on the seatback in front of him. He closed his eyes, praying for healing for Mr. Beaumont and comfort for the family.

And discernment in this surprising bond with Callie.

Was it wrong to pursue a relationship with Callie when Reece was his priority?

Was it wise to be involved with Amanda's best friend?

He sighed and leaned back in the pew.

"How's he doing?"

*Porter.*

Haven clenched his jaw and stared straight ahead at the crucifix centered on the wall in front of him.

The bench creaked beside him as Sean Porter sat down. "Jess didn't know anything last I talked with her."

*And where have you been all this time?* Haven kept his gaze forward, so as not to show his distaste for the man, and stared at the pain carved into Jesus' eyes. The Son of God had been beaten and hung so that humanity would be forgiven its innumerable transgressions. Porter was the type of person who made forgiveness difficult.

But maybe he'd changed too?

Haven massaged the tightening muscles in his neck. "I don't know anything either. I left Callie with her family when the doctor arrived."

"Callie's quite the girl, isn't she?"

*Girl?* Haven fired his gaze into Porter's eyes. "She's an amazing *woman.*" Super Cal didn't come close to describing her.

Porter gave a nonchalant shrug then smirked. "The question is, has she loosened up since I knew her seven years ago?"

Haven balled his hands over his thighs. If they weren't in the chapel, he probably would have decked the man. If Sean could be called a man. "What are you doing here, Porter? Don't you have business back in the cities?"

"I'm taking a break." Sean leaned back, resting his head on his hands, and stretched his legs out on top of the pew back in front of him. "I'm tired of dealing with malnourished prima donnas. Thought I'd see what I could do with nature photography. That doesn't have an attitude. And can you think of a more picturesque area?"

A niggling tickled inside Haven's stomach. "Are you working for someone?"

Sean's lips lifted to the side. "*The North Shore Explorer.*"

The magazine Haven was shooting for. The tickling inside Haven's stomach turned to nausea.

"They're looking for someone who can capture this area's beauty in a unique way, and I'm up for the challenge." Porter stretched his arms out in front and cracked his knuckles. The sound echoed through the small chapel.

Nausea tunneled up Haven's throat. So, his editor didn't fully trust him to do the job alone. Clearly, she'd brought in Porter before she'd even seen Haven's work.

Well, now that he knew what she was looking for, he'd find it. But that took time. And with his full-time job, he had no extra time. Not with Tuesdays devoted to Reece.

And hopefully extra time alone with Callie.

He'd fit it all in. No way was he going to lose this job to Porter or—

"Haven?"

Callie's voice eased the war in his thoughts.

He stood and watched her walk down the aisle, her face pale and her styled hair a curly mess. She wrapped his suit coat tight around herself, covering her wrinkled dress. He squeezed past Porter and hurried to meet her. Tears slid over her cheeks. He pulled a handkerchief from his pocket and wiped the tears then swaddled her in his arms.

She sniffled, and her body shook.

What he'd give to insure her that everything would be all right, but that was a promise he couldn't keep.

She sniffled again, raised her head, and peered over his shoulder. "Sean." Her voice quivered. "I need to speak with Haven alone."

Sean breezed past them then turned and walked backward. "Tell Jess I'll catch her tomorrow." He saluted then walked from the chapel. Haven and Callie sighed together as if needing to expel foul air.

Keeping his fingers locked behind Callie's back, Haven backed away and looked her in the eye. "How is he doing?"

She wiped a hand across her nose. "It was a stroke, as Mom suspected." The faintest hint of a smile lifted the edges of her lips. "He's telling me not to be sad, and Mom is ready to jump into rehab. I have no doubt he'll fully recover. And fast."

"That's great news."

"It is. And he wants to see you before we get kicked out tonight."

"Me?"

She wriggled to escape Haven's arms, and he reluctantly let her go. "About you being our family spokesperson." She bit her lower lip and headed out of the chapel.

Haven hurried to her side. "You've changed your mind about that?" They entered a dimly lit hallway scented with bleach and antiseptic.

"Ha." She gathered his suit coat around her, and crossed her arms at her waist. "He likes the idea. Mom and Dad have a publicist, but this news coming from a family friend rather than a paid colleague will play better to the public. My question is, are you up to it?"

"I'll do whatever you need me to do." Did she need him to hold her? If he read her posture correctly, she didn't want his touch at the moment. He stuffed his hands in his front pant pockets to dissuade them from reaching out to her.

"The family really appreciates this." She led him into her father's room. "Here he is, Dad." Mrs. Beaumont sat to her husband's right and Jess sat beneath a television suspended from the wall. A monitor showed the rhythm of Mr. Beaumont's heart. He may have had a stroke, but his heart still beat strong and steady.

Haven clenched his jaw hoping to hide his shock at seeing the droop on the right side of the once modelesque man's face. He started raising his right hand to greet Mr. Beaumont, but forced it back to his side. "Callie says you're doing well, sir."

"Good as 'spected." His words garbled from the left side of his mouth and were difficult to understand. Mr. Beaumont offered his left hand. "You speak . . . for family?"

Haven accepted with his left. "I'd be honored."

"And now it's time for rest." Callie leaned over and kissed her father's paralyzed cheek. "Jess and I will be back tomorrow. Make sure you don't give the nurses a hard time, you hear?"

"No fun." The left side of his mouth lifted. "Love you."

"Bye, Dad." Jess stood at the end of his bed and made a slight waving motion with her hand then hurried from the room.

"That girl." Mrs. Beaumont mumbled.

Callie shot her a wide-eye, head-cocked, tight jaw look, then smiled back at her dad. "I love you too."

"I'll be praying for your family." Haven met Mr. Beaumont's gaze. The man gave a slight nod, but Mrs. Beaumont frowned. "We'll be in touch." He smiled at her anyway.

Callie took Haven's arm and led him from the room, shutting the door behind them. She sighed, and her shoulders sagged as much as her father's face.

"Hey there." Haven wiped hair away from her eyes and resisted saying her dad would recover, though Haven believed he would. The man emitted an indefatigable spirit. "I'm here for you." He shot a glance at Jess who leaned against the wall munching on a Mounds bar.

"I know." Callie looked toward the speckled linoleum and puffed out a breath. "I need to get home. Rest. Clear my mind."

"Okay." He looked over at Jess. "I'll take you home too."

"What about Sean?" she asked mid-bite of her candy bar.

"He said he'd see you tomorrow."

"Figures." She stuffed the remainder of the candy bar into her mouth.

Conversation halted as he walked with Callie and Jess from the hospital, and it remained silent as he drove them home.

He'd been a mere thirteen years old when his own mother had died from a heart attack, but he could still remember that night in the hospital waiting for a miracle that never came. It had zapped the life from both him and his father.

Until Haven found the false companionship of alcohol. He prayed for the strength to resist its call yet today when a good numbing would feel better than watching a loved one in pain.

He accompanied Jess and Callie inside the home, and Jess hurried up the stairs to her apartment without a thank you or a goodbye. He couldn't blame her.

Callie stood with him in the small entryway, again hugging her body, her head angled down. "Can we go for a walk?"

"Sure." Although the defeated tone of her voice scared him. "Wouldn't you like to change first?"

She looked down at her heels and chuckled. "I suppose I should, although I'm pretty used to these things by now."

"I'll wait here."

Callie pulled off her sandals and climbed the stairs.

Haven sat on the steps and brushed a hand over the top of his head. *God, help us through this night. Please be with the Beaumonts, and remind Callie she doesn't have to shoulder this on her own.*

Prayer was something he hadn't relied on seventeen years ago when his mother died. What a difference that would have made in his life, and Reece's, if he'd had the comfort of knowing someone else was in charge. At least Callie had that assurance, even if the rest of her family didn't.

He heard the door creak behind him and stood.

Callie hurried down the stairs wearing black jogging pants, a solid gray sweatshirt, and white running shoes. She handed Haven his suit coat. "Thanks for the use."

"Not a problem." He slipped on his jacket, wishing he had running clothes in his car. A brisk jog would be cleansing.

He offered his arm, but Callie ignored it and stepped outside ahead of him. That tickle awoke in his stomach again. Crickets serenaded them as they walked down the sidewalk. Unfortunately, they didn't walk hand-in-hand. Her arms swung close to her sides, her hands fisted. Haven kept his hands in his pockets, resisting the desire to grasp hers and warm it.

"Did you know that you can tell the temperature by the number of chirps a cricket makes?" Callie sidestepped a grassy crack.

"It's not a myth?"

"Nope." She kicked at a pebble and it skittered into the grass. "Take the number of chirps in fifteen seconds and add forty. The real equation is a bit more complex, and experts will disagree on other details, but that's close enough for me."

"Fascinating." Haven glanced at his watch and counted the chirps. Twenty-five plus forty. Hmm. Sixty-five sounded just about right. And that was about thirty-five degrees warmer than the vibes he was getting from Callie. He touched her arm. "Talk to me?"

She wiped a hand across her mouth and kept her gaze forward, increasing her speed. "I'll write up a press release for you before I go to bed and e-mail it to you."

"Who do I contact with that?"

"KQSR, Mom and Dad's station. They should have it first. I'm sure they're upset that Mom refused to talk with Eddings."

"What does the station expect? Can't they give your family time?"

"This is news, Haven. They don't let people's feelings get in the way of their scoop. Mom and Dad know that better than anyone."

*I wonder how they feel about that now.* "Okay, KQSR first, then what?"

"Give it thirty minutes then contact the rest of the area stations and newspaper, if they haven't gotten word already. Chances are they'll call you before you reach them."

"And I'll relay whatever information you provide me."

"See, you've got the hang of it already." She turned the corner and lengthened her stride going up a hill.

Haven reached ahead and grasped her arm. "Callie, what's going on?"

She stopped, looked down at his hand on her arm, then up at him, her face an impassive mask. "What do you mean?"

"I think you know what I'm talking about."

Her shoulders slumped, and she nodded. "Home's not far from here. We'll talk there." She took off jogging.

*Talk.* The tickle in his stomach turned into a nasty roiling. He hurried after her, blisters announcing their arrival on his feet, but that didn't slow him down.

Callie turned onto the curved sidewalk leading to her house and stopped beneath the gabled porch. She sat on the steps and stretched out her legs.

He sat beside her, his hands on his knees. "What aren't you telling me? Is your dad sicker than you're letting on?"

Hands folded in her lap, she looked outward at a sky tinged with orange. "They're going to need me, Haven."

"And I don't doubt you'll be there for them."

"But that means some things . . . " She closed her eyes. "May I borrow your handkerchief?"

He resisted the urge to wipe her tears and handed it over, the roiling in his stomach becoming a tornadic whirl.

"I can't stay on at my new job."

"But you can—"

"No." She held up her hands. "Don't try to talk me out of it. It's the right thing to do for now. Mom and Dad can't manage the office, and Jess wouldn't have a clue how to run it."

"What about your new hire?"

"Sure, in time, probably, but she wasn't hired to manage. Someone has to train her in, and someone has to manage the properties. If I leave, that'll be another worry for Mom and Dad, and they don't need that right now." She looked upward. "I just have to trust that God'll give me another opportunity."

"I'm so sorry." He rested his hand over hers. Callie was made for the outdoors. He'd do whatever he could to see that she realized her dream. "How can I help?"

"There's more, Haven." She tugged her hand away. "Dad's coming home Tuesday. I can't . . . "

Chaperone his time with Reece. Would Reece understand Haven's broken promise? Would Amanda use it against him? He inhaled a deep breath and blew it out. This wasn't a time to be selfish. He covered her hand again. "I understand."

"I knew you would, that's what makes this so doggety hard." She raised his hand to her lips and kissed it. "You've given me a gift these past weeks, and I've really treasured my time with you."

His pulse sped up as she returned his hand to his lap and released it.

"For the first time in years, I've felt pretty."

"Callie." He cupped his hand around her chin and turned her head toward him, his voice husky. "You are more than pretty."

She looked down and picked at her joggers. "Mom needs to keep working. She's afraid of what Allen Eddings will do if she doesn't."

"On top of caring for your dad."

"Exactly. So, I need to be there for Dad in the evenings."

"What about Jess? Can't she take some of the load?"

Callie chuckled, but it wasn't from being happy. "I'm afraid my little sister is a touch self-centered."

"What are you trying to tell me?" He rubbed his hands over his wrinkled trousers.

"Something's been happening between us."

"Something good, Super Cal."

"Please don't call me that. I'm just . . . I'm just . . . me." She dabbed at her face. "I can't do it right now. I can't do . . . us."

Panic awakened the butterflies in his gut. "I'm sure you're just overwhelmed. Sleep on it. Give it a few days. When things calm down you'll feel differently."

She touched his cheek, her look so tender. "You're so sweet. I don't know why Mandy ever let you go."

"Then why are you telling me to go?" He caught her hand and held it against his splintering heart.

"If I've learned anything from this tonight, it's how important family is. They have to come first. Give Reece your attention. He's who you need right now."

"And just how am I supposed to spend time with Reece if you're not there with me?"

"I have a feeling Mandy will change her mind." She tugged her hand away and folded it with the other one in her lap.

"Right. She's looking for a reason to keep me away from Reece."

"I know you find this hard to believe, but she does care for you, Haven. She wouldn't fight you so hard if she didn't."

He pinched the bridge of his nose.

"I'll talk to Mandy, tell her what's going on, remind her to think about what's best for Reece."

True, an intact family would have been best for him. Haven had even returned to Duluth with that very intention.

But then Callie entered the picture.

What was best for Reece? He gazed outward at the sliver of light glinting over rooftops. If Amanda had shown any sign of interest in them getting back together, that would have been one thing, but she had her plans all laid out. Plans that had nothing to do with him.

There was no future for him and Amanda, of that he was certain. But a future with Reece and Callie?

It made no sense arguing with her tonight. She'd been through enough already and didn't need him pressuring her. He slapped his legs and stood up. "Then I guess I better get going."

"I'm sorry." She stood, yet angled her face away from him. "And don't forget to pray."

"I won't." He kissed her forehead and then pulled her to him, caressing her stressed shoulders.

His mouth went dry from the wanting to taste her kisses again. "One thing before I go." He tilted her chin up and skimmed his lips across hers. "Be with your family now, but when your dad's better, I'll be here, waiting for you, and that's a promise." He squeezed her hands then walked down the sidewalk.

Away from the woman he was beginning to love.

Just like he'd walked away from Reece when Amanda had sent him packing six years ago. He'd been stupid, listened to her, and stayed away. A terrible life-altering mistake.

He had no intention of making the same mistake with Callie. Nothing would prevent him from coming back to her.

## Chapter Twenty-One

CALLIE STARTLED AWAKE TO someone rapping on her bedroom door. She blinked her eyes into focus and stared at her bedside clock. Two? Oh, butter on a stick. She'd slept through church and lunch and had to make that dreaded call to Mandy. *Please, God, let her say yes to Haven taking Reece without me chaperoning.*

Doubt soured in her throat as her door squeaked open. "Callie?" Jess peeked in then opened the door all the way. "You're still in bed?"

"No. It just looks like it." She clamped her lips shut. Jess hadn't earned that snarky retort. She sat up and rested against the headboard. "Sorry about that."

Jess crossed the hardwood floor and plopped down on Callie's comforter. "Are you feeling okay? You never sleep in."

"I'm fine." Physically anyway. Her heart was still splintered from sending Haven away, even if it was the right thing to do. If there was any chance that he could repair his relationship with Amanda, he should take it. That would be best for Reece.

Even if Haven's leaving broke her heart.

She blew upward and her bangs fluttered. Right now, she had more serious concerns than those of her broken heart. "Hear anything about Dad?"

Jess crawled next to Callie and snuggled against her, just like they used to do when they were younger. "Mom's home."

"Home? Did you go get her?" Oh brother, she'd really messed up this morning.

"She took a cab. She figured I'd be sleeping and that you'd be at church. To be honest, I thought you were at church too until Mom said your car was in the driveway. I can't believe you slept longer than me."

"It was a long night."

"Tell me about it."

"You never answered my question. Did Mom say how Dad was?"

Jess chuckled. "She said he was awake and giving the nurses grief."

"Any physical change?"

"None." Jess shook her head. "Mom had to get away from the hospital and clean up. Your press release alerted all the vultures, and they were circling. She sicced them on your boyfriend."

Callie clutched at her comforter. "He's not my boyfriend."

"Could've fooled me. But hey, if you're not interested—"

"Don't you dare." Callie flung back the covers and scooted out of bed. She grabbed her robe and wrapped it around her. "He's got enough on his mind without you throwing yourself at him."

"You do like him. I knew it."

"Yeah, so?" She strode to the mirror hung above her dresser and yanked a brush through her tangled hair.

"You haven't had a crush since Sean."

"And look how well that turned out." She yanked on a snarl and winced.

Jess slipped out from under the covers and walked to the open door. "Someone got up on the wrong side of bed today." She held the door handle then looked back at Callie. "By the way, Mom wants us down for lunch."

Callie resisted the desire to stick her tongue out as Jess slammed the door shut behind her. She threw her brush down on her dresser. Why did doing the right thing have to hurt so dabnabbit bad?

Was sending Haven away the right thing? Or had she spoken hastily out of fatigue?

No. Reece deserved an intact family, and Amanda cared more for Haven than she let on.

Or was Amanda really that angry with him?

Callie'd find out shortly when she made the call to Amanda explaining the situation. She couldn't possibly hold this against Haven.

Ack! Callie crossed the room to her closet and picked out a pair of worn jeans and a T-shirt. It didn't matter if her mom would remind her of dressing for meals. If she had to spend her days indoors at the office instead of outside, she'd be comfortable on weekends. It didn't matter what her parents said.

And now to tell her mom about her decision to stay on at Superior Suites. Her dad would be disappointed, but her mom? She'd probably applaud.

Callie pulled open her bedroom door and walked downstairs barefooted. Her mom wouldn't appreciate that either, but today it didn't matter. Jess already sat at the dining room table waiting to be served while their mom worked. No surprise there either.

The aroma of Chinese takeout wafted from the kitchen, and Callie's stomach growled. She strode past the dining table into the kitchen. Her mom pulled three plates from the cupboard and handed them to Callie. "Thank you, dear."

Callie grabbed silverware from a drawer and glasses from a cupboard and brought them out to the table where Jess sat studying her fingernails. Would it hurt Jess to lift a finger? Just once? Oh my no. She might break a fingernail.

*Sorry Lord.*

Maybe it would be best if she kept her mouth shut today. Nothing good was coming from her thoughts.

Her mom set the takeout containers on the table and sat across from Jess. She scooped a helping of shrimp fried rice onto her plate then handed the box to Jess. "Before we eat, we need to catch up on business."

Seriously? Mom wanted to talk business when Dad was in the hospital?

Appetite waning, Callie accepted the shrimp dish from Jess and spooned a miniscule helping onto her plate.

"Regarding the office, I—"

"I'm not taking the new job," Callie blurted out. She looked down at her food she had no appetite for.

"Well." Her mother unfolded a cloth napkin and spread it on her lap. "I must say this is a surprise. You did hire that young woman, did you not?"

Callie took a deep breath and looked her mom in the eye. "I did, but that's for the First Impressions business. I'll handle the management of Superior Suites so you can focus on Dad and not worry about the business."

Was that a tear in her mom's eye?

Her mother gazed at her food. "That's very thoughtful of you, Callista. I trust you've given considerable thought to this decision."

"Yes, I have." All the thought she needed. "Family comes first."

"Your time will come, Callista dear."

Yeah, when she was retirement age.

She winced.

Yes, her time would come, but that didn't make waiting any easier. She took one bite of her shrimp fried rice and choked it down. She shoved her plate aside. "May I be excused? I need to shower and change before we go see Dad."

"I'm not terribly hungry myself." Her mom nodded. "Go ahead."

Callie pushed away from the table and hurried up the stairs. Time to make the call to Amanda, then she could clean up without that worry hanging over her. Once in her bedroom, she dialed Mandy's number. Mandy would understand about Haven. She just had to. Reece needed his dad, and Haven needed his son. Even Mandy could see that, couldn't she?

One ring, then two.

"Hey Callie, how's your dad doing?"

Callie collapsed on her bed and closed her eyes. "About the same, but I have a favor to ask."

"SHE SAID WHAT?" HAVEN squeezed the hand brakes on his bike. He skidded into the elevated boardwalk and then bounced across the asphalt bike path onto sand mottled with grass. His front tire hit a rut, and he catapulted off the bike, planting his face in the patchy grass.

"Haven?" Callie's voice was distant. "Are you there?"

He pushed up on his hands and knees and adjusted the Bluetooth back over his ear. "I'm . . . " He spit grass and dirt from his mouth and wiped his hand across it. "I'm here."

"What happened? I heard a crash."

"That was me." He spit again, turned over, and sat on the grass, his legs tented in front, and gazed at Duluth's Lakewalk bordering Superior. "My bike decided it wanted to be a bucking bronco."

"Oh no, are you okay?"

No. At least his heart wasn't. It couldn't take much more bad news. "I'm fine." Physically, anyway. He probably had skid marks across his face, but no bones were broken.

"Are you sure?"

He studied his Schwinn. The rims looked straight, the chain remained on. Still, he'd take it in tonight and get it tuned up.

Too bad he couldn't do the same with his heart. "Now that I'm on safe ground, tell me what Amanda said."

A sigh came over the phone. "I'm sorry, Haven, but she was adamant that if you were to see Reece, I had to be with you."

"And she didn't care that you're unable right now?" He picked up a stone and hurled it toward the lake.

"I tried, and she told me to tell you that now's a good time to relinquish rights to Bill."

He bit his tongue, holding back a curse. No way was he going to let that man control his son.

"I'm sorry. I just can't get her to change her mind."

His jaw taut, he clutched at the ground, digging up grass. Amanda was heartless. How had he not seen it all those years ago? If he didn't have Callie on the phone, he'd turn the air blue with nasty adjectives for his ex.

"Go ahead. Get it off your shoulders."

"What?" He growled and wiped his hair away from his eyes. The back of his hand came back bloody. He felt his forehead and winced as his fingers brushed over a gash. Apparently, his forehead needed a tune-up as well. But that didn't make it okay for him to take it out on Callie. He pulled a tissue from his pocket and pressed it to his now throbbing temple. "I'm sorry."

"Don't be sorry. You're angry and rightly so. I know there are things you want to say, and you won't offend me one bit. Don't hold it in."

A dictionary of four letter words paged across his thoughts. All adequate descriptors of his feelings. But he couldn't force them across his tongue, not with Callie listening. "Da . . . Da . . . daggers and donuts."

Silence.

And then a chuckle that grew into full-blown laughter.

He laughed with her. "Now I know why you do that. Thanks, Super Cal. I needed that."

"Glad to oblige. You can credit my dad. He always told me to get it out in a creative way, and it's stuck."

"And it's one more thing that makes you special."

She said nothing.

Shoulders hunched, he looked out at the lake, its low rolling waves beating the shore with the regularity of a metronome. Now wasn't the time to push their relationship. With patience, that would come.

But it was time to assert himself with Amanda. He cleared his throat. "Did you just talk with Amanda? Is she home?"

"Don't do anything rash, Haven."

"I don't plan on it, but I need to take you out of the middle and deal with her on my own." He pulled the tissue from his head and grimaced. It was soaked. A trip to urgent care was necessary, but not before confronting Amanda. A little home first aid would have to suffice.

"You'll be kind?"

"If it kills me."

"She's home for the evening. Sunday evenings are reserved for backyard barbeques."

"Then I'll bring my own steak."

"I'll pray for you."

"Thanks. I'm going to need it."

He ended the call and righted his bike. His dad's place was a short two miles away. He'd go home, wash, and bandage up.

And then he'd make Amanda an offer she couldn't refuse.

Chapter Twenty-Two

HAVEN FINGER-COMBED HIS HAIR over his temple as he walked up the steps to Amanda's porch. That wouldn't hide the blood-soaked bandage, but he couldn't afford the time it would take detouring to urgent care, not when custody of his son was at stake.

After this visit, a trip to the clinic could be the one thing keeping him away from the lure of a bar. Somehow, being near Amanda revived urges he hadn't experienced for years.

He rang the doorbell and held his breath as he waited. If Amanda didn't accept his compromise, the desire to drink would become even stronger. His sponsor's number was on speed dial, just in case.

The inside door opened and Haven released a smile. "Hey there, Reece."

"Hey Dad, whatchya doing here? Do we get a bonus day?"

He wished. "Sorry, bud, I'd like it, but that's up to your mom." Haven looked over Reece's shoulder into the house. "Your mom around?"

"Yep. She just put a hamburger on the grill. She makes the best burgers and lets me eat it with chips even. Have you ever crushed chips all over your burger? It's the best ever. Do you want a hamburger and try that? I bet Mom would make you one."

*I bet not.* "Uh, not right now, but if you could tell her I'd like a moment to speak with her. Alone. I'd appreciate it."

"Sure. I'll go get her. I can't wait to see you on Tuesday. I told all my buddies I get to go car shopping with you, and I've even made a folder of all the cars we can look it. You'll love it."

"I know I will." He kept his smile until Reece disappeared, then he slammed his fist into the door molding, the same fist he'd used the other night. He held in a gasp as the pain radiated up his arm. But the pain was good. It would keep him from lashing out at Amanda for stringing their son on, for letting Reece believe that all was okay for Tuesday. He shook his fist and grimaced at his bleeding, bruised knuckles. Like this was going to help his cause any.

"What do you want?" Amanda's voice came from behind him.

He spun and found her on the sidewalk just below the first step, wielding a grill spatula like a sword, her eyes firing flames hotter than a barbeque.

He returned the glare. *You're not helping yourself, Haven.* He forced a smile through the glare and hid his bloody knuckles in his other hand. "I need a minute of your time."

"That's all I can afford." She cocked her hip to one side and crossed her arms, the spatula waving off to the side.

"Thank you." He walked down the steps and leaned against the railing. "About Tuesday . . . "

"Didn't Callie give you my message?"

"Yes, but I—"

"There are not buts. The rules are, if want to see Reece, you go with Callie."

"Listen, Amanda, I don't know what you're afraid—"

"What happened to you?" Her glare softened, and she reached up and brushed the hair from his forehead.

"I had a run-in with the ground."

"You should see a doctor."

"I needed to see you first."

She sighed and walked up the porch stairs. "Come on in. I'll butterfly it, but then you've got to promise me you'll go to the clinic."

He followed her into his former house and into a guest bathroom.

"Sit." She pointed to the toilet, and he obliged.

"You don't have to—"

"What kind of nurse would I be if I didn't care for the wounded?"

The kind that loved stabbing spears into his heart.

He held his tongue as she pulled off the bandage.

"Did you lose consciousness at all?"

"No."

"Headache? Troubles seeing? Dizzyness? Vomiting? I won't ask about mental confusion."

"Funny. And no to everything. It's just a cut."

"One deep enough to require stitches. Did you clean this out?"

"I rinsed it with water for several minutes."

"Good. But to be on the safe side." She pulled an antiseptic wipe from her medicine chest and cleaned the wound further, making him wince. "You promise you'll go to the clinic?"

"Sure. I promise."

She attached a butterfly bandage and then taped a gauze patch over it to catch the blood. "That should be good as a temporary measure."

He patted the gauze.

"Your hand too?" She grabbed his hand and examined his knuckles.

He jerked it away. "It's fine. Can we talk now?"

"Suit yourself." She led him out of the bathroom into the living room and pointed at the couch. She sat kitty corner from him on the loveseat. The hard glare had left her face. She pushed hair back from her eyes and pulled it into a ponytail. "What do you need?"

He swallowed the calcified knot in his throat. "I want to ask you for a compromise. I'd like to—"

"Mom." Reece bounded into the living room and offered a notebook to Amanda. "See? It's all the cars Dad should look at. We're gonna have so much fun. I've never gone car shopping before, and Dad's gonna help me choose."

Her eyes widened as she paged through the notebook, a picture of a different vehicle glued to each page.

Haven sat back on the couch, bracing his hands on his knees, holding back a smile. It would be interesting to see how Amanda explained that this Tuesday was out. Haven would not accept the blame for letting Reece down.

"I . . . " Amanda flipped the book closed and looked to Haven. If she thought he was going to help her, she was sadly mistaken. But there was a way to steer this conversation in his direction.

He waved Reece toward him and put his hand on his son's shoulder.

"I'm afraid we can't go out on Tuesday."

Relief spread over Amanda's face, but Reece's became dark. "But you promised." He stamped his prosthetic foot.

"I know, but, well, I'll let your mom explain." It was her decision. She needed to take responsibility.

Her mouth dropped open and her eyes widened as Reece whirled back to his mom. "Why? This was going to be my best day ever."

Haven hid his smirk by studying the hardwood floor.

"I . . . your dad . . . Um, I think he misunderstood, Reece. Your Aunt Callie can't go. She's taking care of her dad, remember?"

"I know, and I've got a Get-Well card for him too. When can I bring it to him?"

"Soon, okay?"

"Awesome, but I can go with Dad then? Just the two of us? Please, pretty please?"

Haven looked toward Amanda, holding his breath. Would she relent?

Her gaze flitted from Reece to Haven and back to Reece. She pulled him down on her lap. He tried to squirm away, but she hugged too tightly. "Bill is has a meeting on Tuesday night, and I don't feel like going to art class all by myself, so I'm coming with you and your dad. What do you think of that?"

A terrible—

"Sweet!" Reece gave his mom a hug and jumped from her lap. "That's the best news ever, don't you think so Dad?"

His lips curved into a sardonic grin, and he looked at Amanda who sat picking at her nails. Her eyes were closed and her jaw set. Oh, yeah, tons of fun. "Yeah, Reece, it'll be the best day ever." Any moment spent with Reece though, even with Amanda skulking around, would be a best day.

"THANK YOU SO MUCH." Callie's smile was so broad, it hurt her cheeks. "I will see you on Saturday then." Only four days away.

She hit 'end' on her phone and nearly floated out of her bedroom into the bathroom. Today couldn't get any better. Her dad was home. His therapy was going well. They were having supper together as a family, albeit an earlier meal than normal so her father could get the rest he needed. At work, Gemma was proving to be a great addition to the office. And now this phone call.

Well, the day could have been better if she hadn't sent Haven away. She looked in the mirror at her ordinary face. A face Haven had called more than pretty.

She applied lip gloss to her thin lips. All it did was accentuate that she didn't have the same full lips that Jess had. She added blush to cheeks trying—and failing—to give the impression of high cheek bones. Another trait Jess had received from their mother. She brushed a brownish tint on her eyelids, contoured her too-small eyes with eyeliner, and stroked waterproof mascara onto her too-short lashes, just as she had done before the date on Saturday.

Haven hadn't taken his gaze off her. She'd never felt so cherished.

She must be a complete idiot for breaking things off with him. But given her dad's stroke? The suites? And with her great news? He deserved more time than she could give him.

Didn't he?

*God, did I do the right thing by releasing him?* Something she had done on emotional impulse and without prayer. She should be with him right this moment, picking up Reece so they could go car shopping. Now what would happen to Haven and Reece's budding relationship? Had Callie doomed it? Was it too late to ask Haven for forgiveness?

Ugh! Why was she letting something bring her down on a day like today?

She straightened the straps on her sundress and then made her way downstairs praying her parents would rejoice with her news just as they were all rejoicing that her father was home.

Jess already sat at the dining table, across from their father who sat in a wheelchair. Callie blinked away the initial reaction of seeing her once-active father now confined to a wheelchair and where it could take him. She walked around the table, greeted him with a hug, then kissed his sagging cheek.

"Look lovely." Her dad grasped her hand.

"Thank you." She squeezed back and released. "I'll go help Mom."

She hurried into the kitchen just as her mother was pulling a dish out of the oven. Callie breathed in, and her mouth watered. "Chicken tenders are healthy?"

"Almond-crusted chicken fingers." She nodded to the bowls on the cupboard. "Could you bring the cucumber salad?"

"Everything looks delicious, Mom." She peeked in the fridge at the strawberry-citrus dessert made from berries she'd picked that very afternoon. If this was eating healthy, a mandate set by her dad's doctor, then they should have no problem.

Callie carried the salad out to the table and sat across from her mother. "Would you mind if I gave thanks?" She held her breath waiting for an answer. God had brought her dad home, and they were sharing a meal together, the least they could do was express their appreciation.

There was a first time for everything. Why not now?

Her mom looked at her dad, and he winked his good eye.

Callie exhaled. She grasped Jess's hands and reached across the table, taking her mother's. Worry wrinkled her mom's brows as she took her dad's limp hand, but he smiled, and her wrinkles eased. Her dad completed the circle by stretching his left arm across the table.

And they all bowed their heads. One more thing to be thankful for today.

Callie closed her eyes and raised her face toward the ceiling. "Dear Lord. Thank you for bringing Dad home and for letting us have the celebration of family here this night. We are truly blessed. Amen." Her parents would appreciate the brief prayer. She squeezed the hands she held, and their circle was broken.

"Now it's time for business." Her mom filled her dad's plate with the chicken and salad, then she filled her own. "Jessica, any word on the new modeling job?"

Jess took the smallest tender and five cucumber slices. "Sean said he knows this alpaca farmer who's looking to market a line of sweaters. He says the yarn is like silk."

"That sounds like a marvelous project." Their mom took a bite of chicken. "Mmm. This is amazing, if I must say so myself."

Their father fumbled with his left hand, but he insisted on feeding himself. "Very good."

Callie bit off the tip of the tender and felt her eyes roll back. "Amazing."

"Callista, how is the new girl working out?"

"She fits right in. I explain things once and that's it. I can see her running the whole office eventually." At least that was the hope.

"And the rest of the office?"

"Good." She laid her fork on her plate. "But there is something I need to discuss with you. It's not office related."

"Please tell us." Her mother tried the salad.

"I got a call just before I came down. From the DNR. They said there was a part-time opening for a naturalist since I had to turn down the full time. This would be mainly weekends and working with young kids."

Her mother sat back in her chair, her lips pursed, and her fingers tapping together in front of her chest. "And it would not take away from your duties at the office?"

"Not at all. The only problem is, I won't be around on weekends to help you."

"Is Jessica unable to help?"

"Not the weekends!" Jess held her cucumber-filled fork midair.

Her mother held up her hand like a police officer giving the stop sign. "Your sister has made her share of sacrifices. It's not too much to expect you to do the same."

"But I have a life."

"And I don't?" If Callie were still little, she'd have pulled one of Jess's bleached locks.

"Fine." A fork clunked on Jess's plate. Her food had been pushed around and cut up, but Callie doubted Jess had even taken a bite.

Dad raised a napkin to his mouth and wiped salad from the drooping side as he focused on Callie. "And boyfriend?"

Callie should have known this would come up. She looked down at her chicken. "We're taking a break from each other."

"Wh-what?" He dropped his knife and it clanked on his plate.

"Why?"

"Dad, there's just no time to devote to him right now. It wouldn't be fair to him."

"No." He fisted the table. "You make time."

"But—"

"And wasn't Tuesday your day to chaperone Haven with his son?" Her mom sliced off another portion of chicken.

"Well yes, but—"

"Then why are you here?"

"Because it's Dad's first day home. I needed to be with family."

"He's family." The words fumbled from her dad's mouth. "He's good for you. Makes you smile."

"Your father's right, Callista. We were just talking about it this afternoon, how we hadn't seen your smile in years. Not the one Haven brings out in you."

Callie blinked back a tear and averted her gaze from her dad. Her parents were both right. With Haven, for the first time in years, Callie had felt special. And she'd never imagined finding someone her parents would not only approve of, but encourage her to keep seeing. She'd be a fool not to attempt reconciliation. After all, he did say he'd wait for her. Hope added one more blessing to this already blessed day. "I'll go with him next week." Her heart smiled at the very thought.

"Dear," Callie's mom said. "It's just barely five o'clock now. It's not too late to call him, is it?"

"Are you sure?" Her gaze flitted from her dad to her mom.

She waved her hand toward the door. "Go before it's too late."

"Thank you." Joy overflowed as she pushed back in her chair and began picking up the plate of barely touched food.

"Just leave that. Jessica and I will clean up."

Callie rounded the table and gave both her parents hugs. Then she ran up the stairs to her apartment and dialed Mandy's home number. It would probably be best to clear the evening with her first, but Mandy had no reason now to say no.

"Hello," a male voice answered.

"Oh, hi, Bill. Is Mandy around?"

"Is this Callie?"

He didn't know her voice by now? What kind of lawyer was he anyway? "Yeah, this is Callie."

"I'm afraid you just missed her. I'm leaving for a conference in a few minutes so she made the fool decision to escort Reece with that man."

That man? What in the world did Mandy see in Bill? How could she think of choosing him over Haven? "That man happens to be Reece's father."

"Well, that's an argument for another day. I'm heading out the door."

*You do that.* Too bad it wasn't a permanent heading.

Callie stared down at the phone and gnawed on her lip. So, Mandy not only let Haven take Reece car shopping, but she went with him? Yay for Reece, but . . .

Did that mean Mandy planned on following through on her feelings? If so, good for Reece. He deserved an intact family. But Callie's heart seized at the thought of losing Haven for good. Maybe she should try calling Haven and meet them all somewhere. But then the three of them shopping together, without her tagging along, was probably good and healthy for their family, even if Haven and Mandy didn't get back together. After all, should Mandy decide to share custody with Haven, they'd be seeing a lot more of each other, and Haven would want to get along with her.

She set the phone on her bed and lay beside it.

Maybe she could surprise Haven at Mandy's. Apologize for making a hasty decision. They could make it up tonight over a berry dessert. Her parents would love to see him again.

She'd love to see him again.

Kiss him again.

Feel cherished again.

She hopped out of bed and hurried to the bathroom. Sure, she'd fancied up for supper, but this was Haven. She wanted to see that same wow in his eyes she'd seen on Saturday night. She prayed she wouldn't be too late.

AFTER REECE RUSHED THROUGH a prayer for their meal, Haven shot up a silent prayer that his makeshift family would survive the day. Miracles could happen. The fact that he was seated in Burger King across from Reece and Mandy was proof.

She sat silent, her mouth in a perpetual frown as she picked at her chicken salad. Who had salad when they went to Burger King? But at least she kept the peace. With Reece as a buffer between them, Mandy had retracted her mama bear claws and even treated Haven like a human being, not the worthless piece of trash he'd once been.

He finished off his Whopper about two minutes after Reece had finished his. That kid could put down an astounding amount of food and at a rate that rivaled his running speed. "Okay, bud, let's see that notebook. So glad you're letting me help choose my car."

A brief smile appeared on Amanda's face. Hmm. Maybe this evening would be tolerable after all.

Haven opened the cover and chuckled. "Bud, there is no way my long legs will fold into a Smart car. And where would I put passengers?"

"But it gets good gas mileage. Super Cal says that it's important to get a car that's good to nature."

"Well, I happen to agree with her there, but still, no Smart car." Haven flipped the page and laughed. "Now, didn't we just discuss good gas mileage?"

"But a Hummer is epic."

"I know, but I think we'll have to pass on that one too."

Reece slumped in his chair. "All right."

"I'm sure we'll find several to agree upon." Haven turned to the next page to a picture of a doorless Jeep Wrangler sloshing through mud. Now that could be fun.

Amanda craned her neck, glancing at the page, her mouth pursing. "A Jeep?"

"What do you think?" Haven turned the notebook in her direction.

"That thing doesn't have any doors."

"But that's what makes it cool, Mom."

"Oh, yes, real cool in the winter." She rolled her eyes like only Amanda could do.

"Easy fix." Haven waved his hand.

She looked at him, her eyebrows raised. "Like you're going to go off-roading."

He grinned. "I'm not opposed to giving it a try."

She harrumphed. "Now that would be a change."

"I'm not the same guy you knew six years ago."

"Right." She shook her head and did the Amanda eye-roll thing again.

He bit back a retort.

"No Jeep, Dad?"

He refocused on the book. Maybe if he had extra money to get a second vehicle. "Sorry, bud, but I don't think it gets any better mileage than the Hummer."

"You're not gonna like anything." Reece blew out a breath, puffing up his bangs.

"Oh, I think we'll find something here. You've got great ideas." Haven quickly flipped through the pages. Probably twenty-five or so filled with car prospects. Then he started back at the beginning, skimming past the Hummer and the Jeep. He stopped at the next page. "A Rogue?"

"A Nissan, just like Super Cal's Seussmobile. Then you'd drive brother-sister cars."

Brother-sister. Not exactly what Haven had in mind.

He studied the SUV, then looked the vehicle up on his phone. Decent mileage. Room for five. Cargo space. "Okay, Reece, we'll take a look at this one."

"Sweet."

Haven turned the page and rolled his gaze toward Reece. "A yellow Camaro?"

"No, Dad, it's Bumblebee, from the Transformers. Gee, you don't know anything."

"Reece, I don't think your dad is into Transformers."

Was that a dig? Haven squinted at Amanda, who wore a smirk.

He refused to return it. "Tell you what, Reece. Maybe in my next visit you can teach me all about Bumblebee and the Transformers."

"That doesn't mean you go spend hundreds of dollars buying him toys." She crossed her arms.

Was she going to find something negative in everything he said or did? Haven bit down hard, stopping a comeback. *Lord, give me a hand here, please?* Counting down from ten in his head, he cleared his throat and rolled the tension from his shoulders and focused on the reason the three of them were here: Reece. "You've got Transformers at home I suppose."

"A whole bunch."

"Well then, it's up to your mom if you show them to me."

"Please Mom, please?"

She jutted a finger toward the notebook. "One week at a time, young man."

"Okay, but can we look at a Camaro? Please? I loved riding in Charlie's and now I really want to ride in one again."

Haven ruffled Reece's hair. "Sure. Why not?" He'd always wanted to test drive one anyway, even if purchasing one wasn't in his budget. Today wasn't just about buying a car. "And if we see a yellow one, we'll give that one a try."

"Dad, you're the best."

Haven grinned as he flipped through the remaining pages. He added a few more vehicles to his list, then slapped the book closed. "Do you suppose we should go give those cars a test drive?"

"It's about time." Reece jumped up from his chair and ran toward the door.

Three hours and five cars later, Haven signed the final page of paperwork and slapped the pen down on the finance manager's desk. "I've got a son who's probably a little disillusioned about this car buying process now." He looked out the office window into the waiting room where Reece sat slumped over in a chair. Sound asleep. "I think it's the first time I've seen him sit still."

"You've got a nice family there, Mr. Carlysle." The manager stood and offered the key fob to Haven's new car.

"It's n—" Not his family.

Or was it?

"Thank you." Haven accepted the keys then shook the man's hand. He walked out of the office, juggling the keys in one hand. He sat next to Amanda and whispered. "I don't want to wake him. I don't think I've ever seen him still. He's beautiful."

"I know. There's nothing like a sleeping child." She wiped hair from Reece's face. "Otherwise he's constant motion. Feet and mouth."

"I suppose I should get you both home." He slapped his legs and stood then offered his hand to Amanda.

She took it, and his gaze met hers.

Vulnerability shone in her eyes. Or was it fear?

He pulled his gaze and his hand away and then picked up Reece, resting him against his chest like an overfull sack of flour. The boy didn't even twitch.

Haven carried his son out to his new palatial-ruby Nissan Rogue. Keeping silent, Amanda climbed in the passenger side, and Haven sat behind the wheel. Reece was right. This was the perfect vehicle to complement Callie's Seussmobile.

He turned the key in the ignition, and it purred to life. A car that started. Wow, what a concept.

Ten minutes later he turned onto Amanda's street and climbed the hill toward her home. If he hadn't messed up six years back, this would be a regular occurrence. This should have been his home too, and they'd be a family just like the finance manager assumed.

If only God removed the selfish gene when two people had children, then far fewer kids would be raised in broken homes.

"Are we home?" A groggy voice mumbled from the backseat.

"Almost, buddy." Haven checked Reece in his rearview mirror. The boy's eyelids practically drooped to his knees. "It looks like it's time for bed."

"But I'm not tired."

"Sure, you're not." Amanda smiled. The same sweet smile she used to give Haven when they first knew each other.

"Would you mind if I tucked him in?"

"I think he'd like that."

He startled at her surprise answer. *Thank you, Lord.* Reece wasn't the only one who'd like it.

BINOCULARS ON HER LAP, Callie rested on the bench at Enger Park. Not finding Amanda and Reece home yet, over an hour past Mandy's two-hour deadline, was a godsend. Callie had needed this trek up the hill, and this communing time with God, far more than she'd needed the company of people.

For the first time in years she felt at peace with her family. And with herself.

Exploring the possibility of a relationship with Haven excited her instead of inciting conflict.

God was good.

With a light wind whipping her hair, she raised the binoculars to her eyes and followed a barge as it neared the lift bridge. The bridge floor lifted as if Duluth were opening its doors and welcoming the stranger.

It was time to open her heart and welcome in Haven. Camera and all.

She floated the binoculars' view from the barge, past Canal Park and up the hill into a residential neighborhood, landing on Mandy's home. The house was still dark, and no car sat in front of the sidewalk.

Perhaps Mandy was finally seeing that Haven had changed and that Reece deserved to know his birth father.

A red SUV climbed the hill and stopped in front of the house. Haven stepped out and then gathered an obviously sleeping Reece and rested him against his shoulder.

They walked into the house looking like the perfect model of a family.

She lowered her binoculars and looked out at the lake, where dusky blue sky met frothing water. "Thank you, Lord."

If she hurried, maybe she could catch Haven before he left. Maybe the two of them could go for a walk, and she could apologize for her tired and hasty decision on Sunday morning.

She breezed to her Seussmobile, a smile tugging on her lips, and joy tickling her stomach.

Maybe they could end the evening with an uninterrupted kiss.

## Chapter Twenty-Three

NO MATTER WHAT HAPPENED now, nothing could spoil this day.

Haven carried his son up to his bedroom and laid him down on top of a blue-striped comforter. He pulled off Reece's shoes and froze. A metal post stood where a fleshy ankle should have been. Haven wiped the sudden perspiration from his forehead and looked for a place to sit.

Nothing but the floor.

He lowered himself to the ground, tented his knees, and tucked his head between them.

It had been so easy to forget his son's handicap, so easy to forget the pain Reece must have gone through and probably still experienced on a daily basis. Emotional if not physical.

"Are you okay?"

He felt Amanda's hand on his shoulder.

"I forget." Slowly, he lifted his head and studied his son who hadn't moved. "He never wears shorts." Was Reece ashamed of his prosthesis?

"He got tired of receiving special treatment. He wants people to see him, not his handicap so he started wearing long pants all the time. When he runs, he wants people to congratulate him because he gave his best effort, not because he's got an artificial leg."

Haven scooted back to the wall and leaned against it. He raised his chin and stared at the ceiling as Amanda sat beside him. "He's an amazing kid, Amanda. And I'm amazed by you. You've been a terrific mother."

She snorted. "I don't know how terrific I've been. Even with the challenges of his foot, he's been an easy child to care for. He gets his temperament from you."

"You're kidding, right?"

"No. He's easygoing, takes things in stride, doesn't get bent out of shape if things don't go well. Just like you always did."

"And he's got your tenacity. This is the stillest I've ever seen him."

"That's the way he is. He runs all day, then conks out at night. I don't think he moves an eyelid when he sleeps. A cannonball crashing through his room wouldn't faze him."

"So, it's okay to take care of his leg? Does it hurt? Won't we disturb him?"

"Nah, he's used to it. Bill carries him to bed all the time."

Bill.

It was easy to forget there was another father figure in Reece's life. Probably more of a father than Haven ever would be. But maybe after tonight, Amanda was finally seeing that Haven wasn't a threat. Haven shouldn't perceive Bill as one either.

"So Bill . . . he's good to Reece, right?"

"Very good, even though Reece objects. I don't think he wants to share me with anyone. It's been just the two of us for so long."

"Is there room for me in that equation?"

Amanda picked at her fingernails. "We'll see."

A smile edged up the corners of Haven's lips. She'd just given him hope.

"Let's get him settled." Amanda stood and returned bedside. "I'll show you how to take care of him . . . Just in case he stays with you sometime."

Haven swallowed and ran a hand over his mouth. That was more concession than he'd ever expected from Amanda.

She pushed up Reece's pant leg, revealing where the artificial limb connected with the remainder of his leg. "His limb is attached via suction." She pointed to a pin close to where his ankle should have been. "Press this."

He pushed the button and the prosthesis released. "That was easy." He held the bionic looking limb in his hands. The technology was incredible. "How often do you have to replace this?"

"It's been every two years. He's constantly growing out of them. I think he'll be as tall you."

"Where do I put it?"

"On top of his dresser, is fine."

"But what if he has to get up at night and use the bathroom?"

"The kid's a champion hopper too. Do you honestly think having one leg would stop him?"

"Guess not." Haven laid the metal limb on the dresser. "Now what?"

She pointed to a flesh-colored liner covering Reece's stump. "Roll this off so the gel faces outward, and I'll get a wash cloth."

Haven did as she told, finishing as Amanda walked back into the room.

"Set that aside for a second. We'll clean it once we've got him set."

Reece wriggled and stretched, his eyes blinking open. "Dad, is that you?"

"Yeah, bud, I'm still here."

"Cool." His eyes closed and again he was still.

"Now just pull this sock off and throw it in the dirty clothes. That keeps his residual limb—"

"His what?" He stopped mid-motion of throwing the sock into a hamper next to the dresser.

"His stump."

"Oh." He completed his throw, swishing the dirty sock into the hamper.

"That sock prevents too much perspiration. The liner doesn't allow the skin to breathe." She handed him the warm wash cloth. "Wash his limb, check for abrasion, and then he's ready for the night."

"No pajamas?"

"He'll be okay."

Haven gently wiped the cloth over Reece's rounded limb and swallowed the grapefruit-sized lump that had caught in his throat. Amanda handed him a towel, and he dried the leg.

"And that's it." She covered him with a blanket folded at the end of the mattress. "I'll wash his liner and meet you outside."

Outside. Yes. It was time for Haven to go, but he'd had an incredible evening. If he didn't blow it now, unsupervised visitation with his son could be a reality.

He walked out of the house and sat on the porch steps. The sun perched on top of the hill lighting a cloud-puffed sky. He breathed in the fresh air that swooped down the hill, rushing toward the lake. It had the distinct scent of hope.

"Father, thank you." He lifted his gaze upward, past the sun and the clouds. Once he got home, he'd share the day with Callie. She could use some good news.

How he missed the gentleness of her voice. Her quirky expressions. Her laughter.

He missed her.

How had he fallen so quickly? And for someone he didn't even notice at the start?

The screen door screeched open and closed behind him, and then Amanda was beside him. It felt all too familiar.

She handed him a bottle of Pepsi. "Remember when we'd sit out here, beer in hand, watching the sunset?"

"We thought we were so grown up, didn't we? With no worries." He twisted off the pop cap and took a swig.

"So, what's up with you and Callie?"

He spat out the pop. Him and Callie? Where had that come from? Reece would shout "squirrel." He shrugged. "I like her, but . . . with her dad's stroke, she's called things off for now. I have the feeling relationships scare her."

"With good reason. She's got a problem with good-looking men."

"You still think I'm good looking?" He quirked a smile.

She nudged him with her elbow. "Get over it." She took a sip of her pop. "I think I'm the only one she's told, but someone hurt her badly several years ago, and she's avoided men ever since."

"And because of you, she couldn't avoid me."

"Sure, blame me."

"I'd like to thank you." He took another sip. "For Callie, and for this evening."

She pushed off the steps and walked toward the road, then turned and strode back and nailed him with a glare. "Why did you come back?"

"What?" He set the pop bottle on the steps and wiped his mouth.

"Why now? Everything was going perfect and now you . . . you have to come and muddle everything up."

"All I want is some visitation time. How does that mess things up? I have no intention of stepping between you and Reece or Bill."

She balled her fists and pressed them on her hips. Her chin trembled. "And why did you have to be so dratted nice?"

"What's going on, Amanda?" He stood and braced his hands on her shoulders.

"You." She shrugged him off and jutted a finger into his chest. "*You* left me to take care of Reece all by myself. I had to face it all alone. His surgery. His crying in the middle of the night. Him telling me to stop the pain in the foot that was no longer there. Do you know how many hours of therapy we went through? Do you have any clue how hard this has been to go through on my own?"

He kept silent, absorbing her verbal darts. Her accusations were spot on, even if she had sent him away. The problem was, he'd listened to her then when he should have stayed and fought.

She fisted her hands and rammed them into his chest. "And now, now I finally have someone to share it with, someone to take the burden off me, and you show up ruining everything." She sniffled and a tear leaked from her eye. "Why couldn't you just come and give up your rights to Reece? That's all I expected from you. It would have made everything so much easier."

Haven circled his arms around her and pulled her against his shoulder, letting his shirt absorb her grief. "I don't understand," he whispered. "How have I ruined anything?"

She leaned back, her shoulders shivering, and looked him in the eye. "Because . . . I still care for you." Her lips parted, and she pressed them against his.

And he kissed her back.

<h2 style="text-align:center">Chapter Twenty-Four</h2>

A CAR DOOR SLAMMED and Haven jerked away from Amanda. What had he done? How could he betray Callie like this?

Amanda looked to her left and fear widened her eyes, then she turned back to Haven, her eyes narrow slits. "How dare you?"

How dare I? Haven's mouth hung open.

She raised her hand as if to slap him, but held it back then ran toward the car in the driveway. The car he'd failed to hear because he was too busy locking lips with an engaged woman.

"What's going on here?" Bill strode toward Amanda, but ignored her open arms and marched to Haven. He poked Haven in the chest as if daring him to retaliate. "I'm gone for a few hours and you're hitting on my fiancée?"

"I wasn't . . . " He looked to Amanda, hoping for some back up, but she stood still as a picture. "We were talking and—"

"You kissed me." Amanda grabbed Bill's arm and snuggled against him. "Trying to coax me into letting him see Reece unsupervised."

"Amanda, you know that's not what happened. Tell him the truth."

"The truth is, you had your chance, Haven, and you just blew it." She clung tighter to Bill's arm.

"What?" Haven forced his arms to remain at his side. He'd give anything to punch that smug grin off the attorney's face.

A car motored up the street, drawing everyone's attention. The Seussmobile pulled to the curb right in front of his Rogue.

Haven didn't know if he should be relieved or scared. He jogged to greet Callie before Amanda could slander him further.

He opened her car door and offered his hand.

"What's going on?" She inserted her hand into his and let him help her out of the car.

It would be better to tell her the truth now than let Amanda slant it. "Promise me you won't jump to conclusions."

She glanced over the car at Amanda and Bill, then back at Haven. "I can't promise, but I'll listen."

His hand shook, and he clasped the other hand over it, encompassing Callie's. "Then will you let me take you out somewhere after this? So, I can tell you the whole story?"

"You're scaring me, but okay."

*Just spit it out.* He swallowed, but that didn't remove the lump in his throat. "Amanda kissed me and I . . . " How could he say this to the woman he was falling for? His words eeked out as his eyes sought hers. "I kissed her back."

She slid her hand away from his, and she blinked. "I don't understand."

"That's what I need to talk to you about."

"Careful, Callie, don't let him spread his lies." Amanda came around the car, with Bill trailing her like a puppy. How could she turn on him like this? How could she offer hope then torch it seconds later?

Callie grasped the door handle. "I think I should go."

"Not before you know that your boyfriend made a move on me."

"Amanda, that's enough." Haven tased Amanda with his gaze. "Tell her the truth."

"The truth is, Callie, your precious boyfriend hit on me tonight—"

Haven clenched his fists at his side.

"—and we've decided Haven's had his chance, so you don't need to worry about chaperoning anymore."

He ground his teeth, stopping his mouth from spouting something he'd regret. Amanda would probably twist anything he said. A trip to the gym might be necessary tonight.

And a call to his sponsor.

He wiped an arm across his mouth that desired the bitterness of alcohol's oblivion.

Callie glanced between Haven and Amanda and sighed. "Mandy,

you and I need to talk. Not tonight, but this week. I'll call you tomorrow."

She wrapped her hands around Haven's arm. "And we're going to get a coffee."

"Don't let him—"

"Mandy, I said we'll talk. You'll have to be satisfied with that." She tugged open her car door and looked back at Haven's SUV. "How about you meet me at my place then give me a ride, show off your new car."

He could kiss her right here and now. He prayed she'd want to after their talk.

CALLIE PRAYED FOR THE strength to forgive Haven as she studied the Superior Sip'n menu. How could he have kissed Mandy? Wasn't that proof that he still cared for her? That Callie was just a temporary diversion? Her reflection stared back at her from the mirrored backsplash behind the bar, a dull reflection lacking beauty. But Haven's? She studied his somber reflection. Even lacking a smile, the man was meant to be in front of a camera, not behind it. Just like Mandy. The question wasn't how could he have kissed Mandy? Rather, it was how he could be attracted to Callie? Was that attraction more than Reece deep?

"What can I get you, ma'am?" The barista broke into her musing.

"Um." She shook her head, chasing the shadowy thoughts. "I'll have a dark hot chocolate with a spritz of peppermint and don't skimp on the whipped cream. Medium."

"Specific." Haven shifted his diaper bag to his other arm and laid a twenty-dollar bill on the counter. "Large coffee. Black."

"Boring." She nudged his side with her elbow and winked, hoping to mask her insecurity while attempting to coax a smile onto his grim face. "Come on, be adventurous. I know you can do it. You bought a red car."

The barista flattened her hands on the counter. "I'm with her. The Lemonade Cold Press is to die for, and no one makes an Iced Superior

S'more Mocha like I do."

"Fine." A trace of humor played in Haven's voice. "What's in a Superior S'more?"

"Dark or white chocolate with marshmallow syrup and espresso over ice, with a layer of marshmallow fluff on top. All my customers love it."

"You talked me into it. With white chocolate, please."

The barista gave him change for the twenty, and Haven nodded to a table that would offer privacy.

"Actually, I was thinking it'd be a good night for a walk." She glanced out the coffee shop window at lightning animating the sky above the lake. She loved watching God's light shows.

"It's supposed to rain."

"You afraid you're going to melt or something?"

"Don't you ever do anything the conventional way?"

"What's the fun in that?" She accepted her hot chocolate from the barista and took a sip. Sweet heaven. Chocolate could always make her problems go away. At least temporarily. Hopefully, it would chase some of Haven's away as well, and give him a moment of peace.

If only she could give him a sense of peace when it came to her feelings toward him. She'd give anything to overlook him kissing Amanda, but betrayal, no matter how small, couldn't be overlooked.

Yet, it could be forgiven.

"Where to now, Super Cal?"

Oh brother. Any other time she'd chide him for the over-the-top nickname, but a smidgen of a smile rang in Haven's voice, and she refused to steal more hope from him tonight.

"Canal Park?"

"Lead the way."

He walked by her side, maybe a half a foot between them, just enough so that their swaying arms didn't touch. More than anything she wanted to touch his arm, to take his hand and tell him it didn't matter, but that would be a lie.

They walked to the lakeshore just to the north of the lighthouse and climbed up on one of the massive boulders that Lake Superior had spewed onto the shore during one of its stormy rages. The wind blew now, making the waves froth more than her hot chocolate. She closed her eyes and breathed in the freshwater air tinged with a warning of rain. She could stay here all night and listen to God's voice whispering off the waves.

Haven sat next to her, respecting her need for silence, and pulled his camera from the diaper bag. As long as he kept the lens pointed away from her, that was fine. He clicked off shots of heat lightning reflected in the fuming waves.

She sipped her hot chocolate then balanced the cup on the stone by her feet. Avoiding talking would never solve their problem, but she'd rather ease into it. "Don't you just marvel at this shoreline? The huge rocks surrounded by all the fragments? It's like God's chiseling the boulder one skipping stone at a time, breaking off the rough edges, molding them into something better."

"I never thought of it that way." He picked up his camera and aimed where the boulders met the small stones, then laid his camera back on his lap. "Maybe someday I'll get to take pictures for a living and leave the office behind."

"Oh, that reminds me, I never told you my good news."

"I could use some good news today." He kicked at the gravel at the base of the rock.

"I've been hired as a part-time naturalist. They want me to work weekends. With children."

"Callie, that's great." He took her hand, but she avoided looking in his eyes. It was too easy to get lost in them. "And your family's okay with it?"

"Jess wasn't too thrilled, but she'll get over it." She tugged her hand away and folded it with the other. "How's your job going?"

"Today someone used every curse word they could think of and probably invented a few. I had three people hang up on me, but then I had one family I helped. That one makes up for all the rest. Besides, knowing I had tonight to look forward to, nothing bothered me today. It was easy to let it slide off."

"No one deserves to be treated like that."

"When people are faced with losing their homes, I can't blame them for spouting off. It's my job to take their abuse."

"Do you want to tell me what happened tonight?"

"No." He chuckled and heaved a handful of stones toward the water. "It was going so well. Amanda invited me in, let me take care of Reece's leg, let me tuck him in, and then she met me outside. All night she'd been hinting that I'd have more time with Reece. Unsupervised time even. And then . . . "

He expelled a breath. "When I quit my job in the cities, I had every intention of coming to Duluth and getting back together with Amanda. I thought I could woo her like before, show her I'm a different man. I thought that was the direction God had pointed me in. Tonight, it was almost like old times. We were getting along."

"And then she kissed you."

He nodded and hurled another stone toward the water. "I don't know why I kissed her back. Maybe it was remembering our old connection. Maybe I'm just a weak man."

Callie laid a hand on his forearm, afraid to ask the next questions, but she had to know the truth. "Do you still care for her? Do you want to get back together?"

He turned toward her and caressed her cheek with the back of his hand. "Absolutely not."

A drop of rain landed on her knee and she wiped it away. "I believe you here." She pointed to her head. "But here?" She patted her heart. "It hurts, and it shouldn't. I have no claim to you. I'd told you to go away. I have no reason to be jealous."

"No reason at all. Amanda is . . . she's become an ugly person . . . to me . . . but she's a terrific mom. I don't know how to reconcile that."

"I don't either." Light rain sprinkled over her bare skin, making her shiver. Haven reached for her, but she hugged herself, closing him off. "For some reason, you bring out the worst in her, something I've never seen before, and I'm not sure what to do with that."

"Do you think she planned the kiss? Is that why she said to meet her outside? So Bill could see me kissing her? And give her a solid reason to keep me out of Reece's life?"

"That doesn't sound like Mandy. I've never thought of her as manipulative."

"Yeah, well, if what she did tonight wasn't manipulative, I don't know what is."

"I'm sorry, Haven. I'll try to talk to her."

"I don't want to put you in the middle anymore. Don't let me ruin your friendship with her."

"She might be doing that all on her own." Callie stared out at the water and brushed the hair from her face. The wind had picked up, and whitecaps frothed at the waves' peak like a root beer float. More raindrops landed on her arms and legs. Just a light mist so far, but judging by the swirling wind, that could change any time now.

Haven picked up his camera and aimed it toward the lake, then the shore line, then he swerved toward her.

"Don't!" She shoved the camera away then clasped her hands together. "I'm sorry, I'm so sorry, but you promised."

He nestled the camera back into the diaper bag. "And I intend to keep that promise. I just had to see you through the lens. The camera loves you, you know."

"No. It doesn't." She looked down and let her bangs cover her face.

Haven gripped her chin and pulled her face toward him. "Why do you say that? You're beautiful."

She jerked her head away and jumped up, goose bumps breaking out over her body, and not from the cool rain. He was telling lies. There was nothing beautiful about her.

Haven hugged her from behind and rested his whiskered cheek against her face. "What's going on Callie?"

She sniffled and sucked in a breath, still shaking even with Haven's warm arms coating hers.

"Is this about Sean?"

Biting into her lip, she nodded one slow nod. The rain drops fell closer together. She turned in Haven's arms, rested her head against his solid chest, and whispered. "He once said I was beautiful."

"You are, Callie." He brushed his hand over the back of her hair.

"And he convinced me to model for him."

Haven rubbed his hands over her chilly arms. "You don't have to talk about this, Callie."

"But I do. You need to understand why." She sniffled and backed away from him.

"Do you want to go inside?"

"No. I need to be here, surrounded by God. It's where I feel safe. Where I feel wholly loved."

She led Haven to the boulder on which she and Reece had watched the sunrise all those weeks ago. Once settled, she wiped rain and tears from her eyes and finger-combed damp hair from her face. And dear sweet Haven allowed her silence.

"We were high school seniors and I had this massive crush on him." The words finally rushed out, words she'd kept imprisoned for too long and needed to free. "Every girl I knew had a crush on him. So, when he approached me and asked me out for a Friday night, it was better than winning the lottery. After seeing a movie, he said he wanted to show me some of his work. I was so smitten, I would have followed him to Antarctica."

Haven tucked her against his chest where she could hear his heart beating.

"He took me to his home where he had his own studio, and it was all set up to take portraits. He kept telling me how beautiful I was. No one had ever told me that before, not with my gorgeous parents and model-perfect sister stealing all the attention. I was the ugly duckling, so to have Sean Porter say I was beautiful?"

"You'd do anything for him."

She closed her eyes and nodded. "Almost anything. For nearly an hour I posed and laughed and I really believed I was beautiful, and then . . . "

The words caught in her throat, and tears loosed from her eyes while Haven caressed her back and took her hand.

"He . . . " She sniffled and swallowed the boulder-sized knot in her throat as shivers took over her body. "He asked me to take my clothes off."

"Oh Callie." Haven's grip tightened.

"But I couldn't. Not even for him. Not even when he said it was about art and showing off the beauty God created. I couldn't do it."

"I'm proud of you, Cal." He kissed her forehead. "I know how persuasive Sean can be."

"That would have been fine if that's how it ended. I went home proud that I'd stood up for myself."

"And you should have been proud."

"But come Monday at school . . . "

Her body shook with a heaving sob as the sky released its fury in a downpour.

"We can go in." Haven tried pulling her up, but she refused.

The rain felt good, as if God was cleansing her. "He'd . . . he'd Photoshopped pictures of me. Pictures of a pig's face on my body. Pictures with my face . . . "

"Callie, you don't have to—"

"With my face on a naked body and those pictures were all around the school, and everyone laughed, pointed fingers . . . "

She touched the diamond stud in her nose. Since then, no matter how hard she tried, no matter how many verses she read about God loving her and about how precious she was to Him, believing she was anything but ugly had become impossible.

## Chapter Twenty-Five

AVEN HUGGED CALLIE TIGHTER, but what he really wanted to do was plant his just-recovering fist right into Porter's face. To think that rotten excuse for a man would steal someone's innocence like that . . . He was an anathema to their profession. No, to the human race.

How could Haven convince Callie that she was truly God's masterpiece when Sean's horrific behavior had rooted insecurity into Callie's soul?

"I've never felt so ugly."

And he'd never wanted to hurt anyone like he wanted to hurt Sean. But that wouldn't solve anything. Getting Callie to see herself as God sees her was the best way to uproot that insecurity.

"Callie." The rain hurled downward as he curved his hands over her cheeks and forced her to look at him. "The only ugly one is Sean, do you understand that? You, Callie, you are the most beautiful person I've ever met."

"Oh really?" She shook his hands away. "Is that what you thought the first time you saw me here with Reece? Or when I ran into you at Amanda's house?"

Haven closed his eyes and thought back. When he saw Callie here with Reece, he'd witnessed a beautiful scene, but hadn't really noticed her. And at Amanda's, he'd looked right past her. Yet, he'd noticed Jess, and the Superior Suites receptionist, and even Amanda. It wasn't until he got to know Callie that he saw her beauty. How could he have been so blind before?

Here he was, on assignment to capture the North Shore's beauty, and he'd completely overlooked the most beautiful person he'd met. He was no better than anyone else, seeing with human tunnel vision only what the world described as beautiful. Looking only at the flower but not the worm that cultivated the earth. Seeing the waterfall but not the vegetation along the way that provided healing remedies for the sick.

He'd missed so much. He looked upward, the rain cleansing his face. *Lord, help me see through your eyes.*

"See what I mean? I'm the ugly duckling in the family. I'm the one they tuck back where customers can't see me. I despise the word 'beautiful,' and when anyone points a camera at me, all I remember is the ugliness. All I can see is a pig's face."

*Dear God, how can I undo Sean's damage and help Callie see the marvelous beauty you created in her?* "Callie, what he did was his way of getting back at you for standing up to him. What you did was amazing. He's the ugly one. What bothers me now is Jess dating him after what he did to you."

"Because to her, it was a hilarious, harmless high school prank. She has no clue how it hurt me. Besides, Sean pulled the same thing on her, only she had no trouble taking off her clothes."

Why didn't that surprise him? At least Callie had had the self-confidence to say no, something Jess lacked both then and now.

"She didn't understand what the big fuss was about." Callie wiped drenched bangs away from her eyes. "And look, it launched her modeling career."

Haven gripped Callie's arms, but she kept her head down. "Look at me, Callie." She peered at him between drenched lashes and raindrops. "I promise I won't aim my camera in your direction ever again." As much as he desired to capture her beauty. He traced his fingers down her rain-washed cheeks. "Callista Beaumont, you are an amazing creation of God. You couldn't be more beautiful, and the only lips I ever want to kiss are yours." He leaned toward her and kissed the rain from her cheeks.

And then her lips.

From today on, he would remind her of her beauty every day.

Until she started believing it.

MAYBE SHE WAS BEAUTIFUL.

The taste of Haven's kisses lingered in her memory as she stared down at Superior Suites' monthly fiscal report. Bookkeeping was so not her gift. She spun her chair around and looked out her parents' office window at Lake Superior. She sneezed and wiped her nose. That was what she got for staying out in the rain last night. She imagined Haven's lips brushing over hers, and her cheeks warmed. Oh, it was worth every sneeze.

But it certainly wasn't helping her concentration.

A knock sounded on the door, and she gladly looked away from the report. "Hey Jess, come on in."

"What you up to?" Her sister walked around the desk and peeked over Callie's shoulder.

She grunted. "My favorite."

"Bookwork, huh?"

"And I'm failing."

"Why don't you let me handle it?"

"Huh?" Callie squinted over her shoulder at her little sister. "You want to do the books?"

"Give me credit, will you? I've taken a few accounting classes."

Yeah, but that didn't make her any good. Still, it wouldn't hurt for Jess to look at it and give Callie an excuse to take a break.

She pushed away from the desk and gestured toward the high back leather chair. "Be my guest. Our revenues aren't matching up with our billings. If you could find the discrepancy, I'd be thrilled."

"Not a problem." Jess sat and put a finger to her lips as she studied the screen.

"I'm gonna go down and grab a smoothie. Need anything?"

"I'm good. Thanks."

Callie hurried out of her parents' office and past the other office spaces, sneezing as she went. She paused briefly at Haven's editor's room. Too bad photography wasn't his full-time profession, then she'd get to see him more.

Was that what she really wanted? Did last night make up for him kissing Mandy?

Mandy.

Callie gritted her teeth and strode toward the elevator. What was it about Haven's arrival that had brought out this demon in her best friend? This coming Sunday evening, they were going to talk over dinner, and Callie had no plans to hold back her opinion. How Mandy could be so vindictive, so manipulative, was beyond her.

She rode the elevator to the first floor and stood several customers deep in the line at Superior Sip'n. The threat of a sneeze tickled her nose, and she buried it in the crook of her arm just in time. Maybe another hot chocolate would be better than a smoothie, but when it was nearing ninety degrees outside, hot chocolate sounded nasty.

A strawberry-orange smoothie would have a little nutritional value, maybe some Vitamin C, wouldn't it?

She ordered her drink and carried it outside. The storms last night had ushered in July's overbearing humidity, but being outside was better than being in the manufactured cold air. She just needed some patience to wait on God's timing for her to exchange her indoor office for the outdoor one.

A siren whooped as Callie leaned against the building's brick, and she glanced up the block. A car—a Prius—pulled to the curb, and a police car parked right behind it. She giggled. There was someone who didn't quite get the concept of driving a fuel-saving vehicle.

She finished her smoothie just as the police car pulled back onto the street. Time for her to drag herself back inside.

With a sigh, she walked through the revolving doors back into cool air. To help walk off the calories from the smoothie, she took the three flights of stairs to the office and walked in just as the landscape designer stepped off the elevator.

Pinched lips seemed out of place on the usually outgoing man.

"Hi Lance, is everything okay?"

Frowning, Lance waved a piece of paper. "Just got another ticket."

"Another? That was your Prius?" Callie held back a giggle. Lance had to be the most adamant environmentalist Callie knew. An environmentalist with a lead foot. Too funny.

"You saw that? I suppose the whole office was watching too."

"Just me." She winked. "I'll keep your secret. Hope the rest of your day goes better."

"It can't get worse."

With a smile, Callie returned to her new office.

Jess sat in the chair nibbling her lip. She looked up and then pointed to the screen. "I found the problem."

"Oh?" Callie came around the desk and followed Jess's finger.

"Our landscaper is a little behind on his bills."

Callie studied the screen. Two months behind, as a matter of fact. Looked like Lance's day was going to get worse after all.

And now, instead of her mom being the heavy, Callie got the job. Or maybe Jess would like that too. "You want to talk to him?"

Jess held up her hands up. "Uh-uh. I did my job. I found the error."

"And I appreciate it too. If you wouldn't mind, I'd love it if you'd take over the bookkeeping responsibilities."

"You'll let me?"

"Of course. Why wouldn't I?"

Jess shrugged and backed the chair up. "I've got a few other things to take care of first, then I'll see what you need me to do."

"You don't think we trust you?"

Jess looked toward the floor and drew a circle with her foot. "Sometimes all I think you see is a pretty face." She looked up and met Callie's gaze. "But I'm more than that, Cal. There's more to me than what the camera sees."

"Jess . . . oh, fuzz on the carpet." Callie sneezed and grabbed a Kleenex off the desk. "I had no clue you felt that way. I'm sorry if I've treated you like that. Can you forgive me?"

"Will you take me seriously?"

"If you're willing to be honest when I don't."

Jess opened her arms. "Forgiven."

Callie wrapped her sister in a hug. "Now you be sure and tell me if there's more you want to do around here. I'll have absolutely no problem handing it over to you."

"Thank you, I appreciate that."

Callie backed away and grinned, her lips rising more to the right. "You're sure you don't want to talk with Lance?"

"A hundred percent."

"It was worth a try." Callie sat back at the desk then looked up at Jess as she was walking out. "Want to do lunch today?"

"Yeah. That would be nice."

Yes, it would. Jess walked from the office, her head held higher than normal. How could Callie have been so insensitive all this time? Thinking she was so much better than her sister? Hardly. She was just as bad as anyone else who rushed to judgments. And this was her little sister, for Harold's sake. Well, today she'd start making up for it.

But until lunchtime . . .

She printed off Lance's statement showing sixty days past due. Her mom excelled at this part of the job. She picked up her phone and punched in Lance's number. Too bad Haven wasn't here. Two rings. He'd probably sweet talk Lance into paying a year in advance. Three ri—

"Lance's Green Landscaping."

"Hi Lance, this is Callie again. Would you mind stopping by my office for a moment?"

Silence and then a sigh.

"I guess I know what this is about."

"Probably do."

"Give me five minutes?"

"See you then."

Callie wiped her forehead and sneezed again. Stupid cold. She yanked a Kleenex from the box and blew into it.

A knock pounded on her door. "Hey, Callie, I've got a delivery." Ashley, the receptionist, walked into the room carrying a vase with three variegated tulips and two yellow tulips surrounded with baby's breath. She set the arrangement next to the monitor.

"Who's it from?" Callie reached for the greeting card-sized envelope. It was extra thick.

"As if you don't know."

Heat flooded her cheeks as Ashley sashayed out of the office. Callie took in the tulips' fragrance as she slit the envelope open. Inside were five more envelopes, reading Wednesday, Thursday, and through

Sunday.

She couldn't stop the smile from blossoming on her face, probably as big as the tulips' bloom. She opened Wednesday's card and read, *"People are like stained glass windows: they sparkle and shine when the sun is out, but when the darkness sets in their true beauty is revealed only if there is a light within." Elizabeth Kubler-Ross*

*Callie, I love the way God's light shines from within you and shows in your eyes and your smile. Thank you for sharing that light with me. ~Haven.*

Oh, tulips and tomatoes. Callie sniffled and wiped her eyes and dropped into her chair. Now she'd be a sniveling mess for the rest of the day.

Another knock on her door. Yippee. Just what she needed her office mates to see: a blubbering fool. She pulled a tissue from the box and wiped her eyes and her nose then looked up at Lance. "I'm sorry, won't you have a seat?" She pointed to a chair pressed against the wall.

Lance pushed it closer to the desk, but examined the flowers instead of sitting down. "An admirer I presume."

There went her cheeks again. She looked down at the keyboard. "You could say that."

"You know what these flowers mean, don't you?"

"They mean something?"

"All flowers do. This guy must think you're something else."

She looked at her foot drawing circles on the floor and whispered. "Tell me."

Lance took his time sitting and relaxed back in the chair, his arms crossed over his chest.

"Come on, you're killing me here."

"Tulips, in general, express love, and my guess is, by the way your cheeks just turned bright as a red rose, you think this guy is something special."

"He is." Callie flattened her hands against burning cheeks. "I'm going to have to lock my door, or I'll be blushing every time someone stops in."

"It's adorable. And about time someone realized what a great catch you are."

"Flattery won't get you out of paying your bill, you know." Maybe if she brought business back to the conversation, her cheeks would cool off.

"It was worth a try." Lance fingered the variegated tulip. "Now this one means beautiful eyes."

Oh, my goodness. Callie blinked rapidly and sneezed. Now she had a reasonable excuse for using a tissue. "And the yellow one?" May as well find out now and get her weeping over with. How was she ever going to thank Haven without turning into a waterfall?

"Yellow. This dude has it bad for you."

"Would you just tell me already?"

"Yellow means there's sunshine in your smile."

Oooh. Sunshine that melted her heart into a puddle. Callie mumbled "Thank you" and wiped at her eyes again. Haven was in mucho big trouble.

"Glad to help." Lance winked and laid a check in front of Callie. "Sorry I'm late. You know me and organization."

That she did. The man knew flowers, but was clueless about anything else.

"That should take care of everything, right?"

"Until next month."

He sighed. "Great, although I think you owe me for my floral expertise."

Callie picked up the check made out for the exact amount owed. "Thanks Lance." She pulled the receipt book from the top drawer and hand wrote it. "Until next month." She handed the receipt to Lance without looking up. With her eyes still puddling over Haven's endearments, no way on this earth was she going to look up again. "Can you close the door behind you?"

"We'll catch you later." Whistling, he walked out and pulled the door shut.

Callie sat back in her chair and pinched her eyes closed. Haven's grin took front row in her mind. Shoot, he was gorgeous.

And to think he liked her plain self. The guy must be blind.

But he did indeed make her feel beautiful.

Next time she saw him, she'd thank him with a kiss that would definitely say "all is forgiven," but first she had to talk Mandy into changing her mind about visitation. Come Sunday evening, after her first two days of working her part-time naturalist position, she'd tell Mandy exactly what she thought.

WITH A SNEEZE, CALLIE followed the group of elementary school-aged children away from the education building, down a path designed specifically for teaching. It was vital to teach children to love and care for all of God's creation. Her second day on the job was nearly over, but she planned on making the most out of every minute, even with the remnants of her cold annoying her today. She probably should have called in sick, but if a person from this area called in sick every time they had a little cough, no work would ever get done.

"Hey, I found a caterpillar!" Derek, a rambunctious third grader who reminded her of Reece, plunged off the path into long grasses. The caterpillar clung to the blade of grass. How Derek spotted the insect, she'd never know. Like Reece, he seemed to hone in on nature's crawling creatures.

He picked up the fuzzy brown and black striped caterpillar and it tickled its way across his palm.

"He's so cute." Tracy, a pigtailed second-grader petted its backside. "Can I keep it?"

What a perfect teaching moment. A God-given one at that. "Let's all sit in a circle here, and I'll tell you all about this cute little guy."

The eight kids circled close to Derek, and Callie squeezed in across from him, tenting her legs in front. "This is called a Wooly Bear caterpillar. Can anyone tell me why?"

Janna, a petite little redhead, raised her hand. "'Cause it looks like a teddy bear, but it's cuter and it doesn't have big claws and teeth."

"I think it looks like a tiger." Tyler bared his teeth and growled at the girls.

Some shrieked, while others giggled.

"You're, right, Tyler, he does look sort of like a tiger, doesn't he?"

Callie loved how kids were able to stretch their imaginations. "Now, as to your question, Tracy, what will happen if you take Wooly Bear home?"

"I'll put him in a jar with a stick and punch holes in the top and feed him leaves and grass every day."

"Hmm." A sneeze tickled her nose, and Callie turned just in time to direct it away from the group. She wiped her nose with her overused handkerchief and turned back to the kids. "And what happens to Wooly then?"

"Oh, oh, I know." Derek waved his hand back and forth. "He becomes a butterfly."

"I love butterflies. They're so pretty." Janna smiled.

"Will he look like a tiger butterfly?" Tyler growled again and raised his fingers pretending they were claws.

He was probably thinking about the orange and black monarch, a very common butterfly in this region, that looked like a stained-glass window.

She reached into her pocket and fingered the notes from Haven, five days of beauty quotes beginning with the stained-glass image. Today's quote by Nate Dircks—"*Beauty . . . when you look into a woman's eyes and see what is in her heart*"—made her blush just thinking about it. She'd thanked Haven every day over the phone, but between their rushed schedules this week, he still hadn't received his proper thank you.

The one accompanied with the I Forgive You kiss.

A kiss she couldn't offer him with this silly cold. She wiped her nose again, a nose that was probably as red as a fire engine.

"Miss Callie, will he be a tiger butterfly?" Janna tugged on Callie's shirt.

"Oh, uh, no." Oh, tigers and tortoises, Haven was a distraction even when he wasn't around. She smiled at the little group and reached over to pet Wooly. "Not this little guy. He becomes an Isabella tiger moth, but he doesn't look like a tiger. He's brown, with some spots, and most people don't like moths. This caterpillar is even prettier before he becomes a butterfly than afterward."

"Then what makes the beautiful butterflies? Are those caterpillars ugly?" Tracy twirled one of her pigtails.

"Some people would think so, but I think they're all beautiful. The monarch caterpillar sort of looks like a zebra with black, white, and yellow stripes and it has big long antennae."

"Cool!" The Wooly Bear caterpillar wiggled up Derek's arm.

"Now, why do you suppose we have caterpillars? What do you think is their purpose?" To Reece she would have asked why God made the butterfly. One of the downfalls of working for a government organization was that God-talk wasn't allowed.

"To be pretty." Tracy smiled, revealing a wide gap in her top front teeth.

"Absolutely, Tracy, but they also serve another purpose. Can anyone guess?"

Her little group was silent. Even Derek.

"They do make the world a prettier place, in more ways than one." Callie stole a glance at her watch. Time was up, but she had one very important point to make. One Jess would appreciate. "Like bees, they carry pollen from one plant to another so that fruits and vegetables and flowers can make new seeds so new plants can grow."

As Jess had said, she was more than a pretty face.

Their parents were too.

Figures, it took nature to point that out to Callie.

She slapped her thighs and stood up. "It's time to get back—"

"Already?" Janna stuck her lower lip out far enough for a butterfly to land on it.

"I'm afraid so, Janna. The time goes too fast sometimes, doesn't it?" She patted the redhead's shoulder. "I'd love to have you back any time."

"Me too?" Tracy tugged on Callie's khaki shirt.

"As long as your mommy or daddy say so." Hopefully, she didn't just make life difficult for a lot of mommies and daddies or caregivers.

She urged the group back up the dirt trail to the education building where adults awaited their children. With a grin, she waved them off then sneezed into her handkerchief. This job was even better than she imagined.

"Callie, have you got a moment?"

Callie turned toward the voice. Her supervisor, Glynnis, gestured to a bench created from a split log.

"Sure." She sat next to Glynnis.

"First, I want to tell you that we've already received marvelous feedback regarding your work with the children's programs. When your father is better, I do hope you'll consider a full-time position again."

"Really?" Callie clasped her hands in front of her chin. "I'm thrilled to hear that."

"In the meantime, I have some fun news to share. *The North Shore Explorer* has chosen to do an article highlighting our naturalists."

*North Shore Explorer?* That was the magazine Haven was working for. "I'm familiar with it."

"I know you're new here, but I love your enthusiasm for the job, and we would love to have them speak with you."

"I'd be glad to." Anything to spread word of the wonderful programs the parks had for children.

"Just what I wanted to hear." Glynnis finger-waved toward her windowed office. "I've a photographer here right now to take your picture."

Anything but that. Callie froze and stared toward Glynnis's door. She gulped as an all-too-familiar figure walked out the door, and bile billeted up her throat.

And never with Sean Porter.

# Chapter Twenty-Six

... I ... " CALLIE SNEEZED and wiped her watery eyes as Sean neared, his brows rising in recognition of her. She stood and started backing away, trying to maintain eye contact with Glynnis. "I don't really like having my picture taken."

"Who does?" Glynnis smiled. "But we're not looking for head portraits. We want an action photo, one that shows you out in nature."

"But I ... " She tried holding back a sneeze but it exploded anyway. "I ... these ... " Did she admit she had a cold? Probably not, especially when she worked with kids. "These allergies ... I look awful."

Sean stopped next to Glynnis and smirked. "You have had better days."

Oh, if only she weren't a lady, she'd deck him right here and not feel an ounce of guilt.

Okay, maybe an ounce, but that was it.

She wiped her nose. "Another time please? Next weekend?"

Maybe by then they'd have all the photographs they needed, and they'd forget about her.

Glynnis heaved a sigh. "Perhaps you're right. But take care of yourself this week so next Saturday you'll be ready. Your cooperation will be recorded on your record."

"I promise." She sniffled and scurried away from her supervisor and the leering Sean Porter. They couldn't fire her for not having her picture taken, could they?

Maybe not, but they could make the job difficult for her.

The mere thought of Sean aiming his camera her way made her

stomach churn like the November gale that sunk the Edmund Fitzgerald.

She couldn't pose for Sean Porter. No matter the cost. And she had less than a week to talk her way out of it.

CALLIE PRAYED THE ENTIRE WAY to Mandy's house, pleading for a good excuse to get out of the photo shoot, but God remained mute. It couldn't be His will for Sean to photograph her again?

If so, that was one directive from God she could not follow.

And she refused to waste an entire week worrying about it either. That would give Porter way too much satisfaction. Besides, tonight she had more important things to do.

Like convincing Mandy to change her mind.

It was near five when she arrived at Mandy's home. Plenty of time for the friend-to-heart chat. She carried a gift-wrapped box up to Mandy's door and rang the doorbell.

Seconds later a droopy-faced Reece opened the door. "Hey Aunt Callie."

"Why the frown, buddy?"

He rolled his eyes. "Mom and Bill." He clomped away from the door and climbed the stairs, his limp more pronounced than usual, and his shoulders stooped.

Oh boy. That poor child. Couldn't Mandy see what she was doing to him?

She crossed the threshold and stepped onto the hardwood floors just as Mandy walked from the kitchen, a purse slung over her shoulder. The shadows around her eyes told Callie that Mandy wasn't any happier than Reece.

Well, she shouldn't be. She should be upset over her decision to expel Haven from Reece's life.

Callie forced a smile and offered her gift. "A little something before we go."

Mandy took the present to the couch and patted the seat next to her.

"What did you do?"

"Thought you needed a little cheering." Callie sat beside Mandy. Sometimes a little sunshine was all someone needed to see things in a better light.

Like Haven's bouquet. Just thinking about it made her blush. And sneeze.

She dug a tissue from her pocket as Mandy ripped open the shirt-box sized package and pulled out a pair of painted jeans. "Oh my." She held them up, the legs draping to the floor. A tree, still bare from winter, grew from the left hip pocket. A garden of flowers, their spring buds newly appearing, trickled from the tree trunk, spreading outward, and trellising down. The buds blossomed into tulips and lilacs, azaleas, and rhododendrons. Around the knee, they gave way to marigolds and lilies which jumped to the right leg. Snapdragons and sunflowers grew near the calf and cascaded downward with fall's mums near the hem. A maple tree grew from a frayed hem. The tree's autumn colors branched around the back of the leg where leaves floated down into snow, baring a few branches.

Not unlike the seasons of friendship.

Mandy pressed a hand to her chest. "They're exquisite, Callie. How did you get my old jeans?"

"Bill. A week or so ago. I planned on giving them to you for your birthday, but I figured you needed them a little more right now."

"You know me so well." Mandy hugged the jeans. "Do I have time to change before we go? I don't want to intrude on your family time."

"Go ahead." It's what she planned on. Mandy never could wait to wear her restored jeans.

Callie relaxed back into the sofa's cushion. As expected, the gift-giving had gone well. Now to keep up the momentum.

A few minutes later, Mandy jogged down the stairs, her step much lighter than when she first greeted Callie. The shadow had fled her now-sparkling eyes. She curved her thumbs around belt loops and turned slowly around. "What do you think?"

"Love them."

"Me too." She grinned and gave Callie a hug. "They're perfect. Thank you."

Yep, a little sunshine was exactly what Mandy needed. "Ready?"

"I am now."

They rode in the Seussmobile about four blocks to their favorite mom and pop café. Normally they'd walk the short distance, but she wanted more time to give her mom a break from caretaking tonight. Tomorrow, her mom was returning to work, and it just wouldn't do if she appeared on television with dark circles framing her eyes.

A waitress dressed in jeans and a T-shirt advertising Lampi's Café brought lemon-tinged water just as Callie and Mandy sat in their usual booth. "Menus today?"

"Nah." Callie waved her hand. "Just bring me my usual chicken sandwich."

"And I'll take the tuna melt."

"It'll be right up." The waitress tucked the pencil behind her ear and walked off.

Mandy folded her hands on the Formica table top, her thumbs twiddling. The smile had vacated her face. "Now I know this isn't going to be our typical girl's-day-out meal. What's up with you and Haven anyway?"

Shaving cream on a bun, there went her cheeks again. She was as bad as a high schooler with her first crush. "I like him, Mandy."

Mandy shook her head. "I don't get it. You avoid guys for years and then you fall for Haven? Seriously? Do you know how hard that is for me?"

"You're the one who thrust us together, remember? And why should it be hard for you? You gave him up six years ago. You're engaged. What's hard about it?"

Mandy pulled a napkin from a silver and black holder and fiddled with it, her gaze avoiding Callie's. "It complicates what we need to do with Reece. He loves you, and you've been so good for him, but if this thing continues between you and Haven, Reece is going to lose you too."

"Whoa. Let's back up a few steps here. First, you need to explain why you're cutting Reece off from his dad. I see no reason other than selfishness."

"You're completely off. This is all about Reece."

"Then enlighten me." Callie took a swig of her water.

With a spoon, Mandy swirled the water in her glass. "You have no clue what it's like to grow up in a broken family."

Callie narrowed her eyes, but kept silent.

"Bill and I do. We both grew up being passed from one parent to the other, both parents slandering the other. You have no idea what it's like to be the ping pong ball between feuding adults. I promised myself I would never do that to my child, and Bill agrees with me one hundred percent. We won't do that to Reece."

"What does that have to do with keeping Haven away from Reece?"

The waitress walked over with two plates of food and set them on the table. "Can I get you ladies anything else?"

"I'm good." Callie raised her brows and glanced at Mandy.

"Me too."

Callie took a bite of her sandwich and sighed. There was nothing like mom and pop restaurants. She looked back at Mandy who was nibbling on her tuna melt. "As I was saying, what is so bad about Haven seeing his son?"

Mandy chewed as cars whizzed by on the street outside their window. She finally swallowed and laid her melt back on the plate. "I raised Reece alone for five years, Callie, and I'm tired of it. I'm tired of being a single mom."

"But you—"

"Uh-uh, it's my turn." She shoved her plate aside. "Then Bill comes along and suddenly I'm not alone anymore. Reece has a daddy to look up to, and Bill loves Reece. We've got a family in the making. It's my dream."

Callie nibbled on her sandwich, a sneeze budding up in her nose. That still didn't explain them keeping Haven away.

"The problem is." Mandy sighed. "With Haven in the picture, now all of a sudden, I have visions of Reece going from home to home and not really having a place he calls home. He'll have two daddies that he'll compare and play against the other. Already, I see it happening. Reece is always telling Bill, 'My real dad wouldn't do that or say that.' No way can Bill measure up to this legend Reece has in his head about Haven."

"So, your solution is to cut Haven out of his son's life? What's that going to do to your relationship with Reece? Don't tell me, he'll get over it. This is just going to make him angry, and you've done such a good job of raising him without anger. He's a very well-adjusted child, and the credit goes to you. I hate to see you ruin it over this silly vendetta you have against Haven. Who happens to be a terrific father, by the way."

"Don't you see? That's why this is so hard."

"I see nothing but my friend being selfish. I know there's more to it than that."

"I told you before, Bill and I agreed that we wouldn't put Reece in the two-house situation." Mandy twirled her engagement ring. "Bill means it. If I let Haven have custody, or even visitation, my engagement is off."

AN INDIGO SKY CIRCLED Haven as he got out of his Rogue. He walked around the front and stopped by the passenger door. The evening's fresh air, cooled by the lake's breeze, wiped away the malicious insults of his day job. He leaned against his SUV and looked up at the second story of the Beaumont home. Ten o'clock and lights were still on. His signal to go ahead.

He took out his cell phone and dialed Callie's number. Four infinite rings later, she answered.

"Haven?"

"It's me. You got a minute?"

"Sure. Mom and Dad have both gone to bed. I'm just reading a book. By the way, I need to thank—"

"Hold that thought and look out your window." She peeled back her curtains, and he waved.

She returned the wave. "What are you doing here?" A smile chimed in her voice.

"Do I need an excuse?"

Silence filled the phone as crickets strummed their wings.

"I'll be down in a sec. Meet you on the porch swing?"

"Sounds good."

He put his phone away and walked up the meandering sidewalk and then up onto the porch. He sat on the swing, laced his fingers behind his head, and rocked to the crickets' serenade. What would Callie observe about this evening? The stars were too obvious. Everyone talked about their brilliance. The moon too. She'd see something entirely different, something seemingly obscure.

But nothing created by God should be overlooked.

Callie came out the front door wearing bright green fleece pajamas and a matching robe dotted with Dr. Seuss characters.

How had he overlooked her in the beginning?

She sat next to him tugging her robe tight around her, and she sneezed.

"Bless you. Are you all right?"

"Just a little cold."

Little? She sounded completely stuffed. "Then you shouldn't be outside."

"Yes, mother." She patted his thigh, and he grabbed her hand before it stole away.

She entwined her fingers with his, and his heart did a somersault.

"This is a surprise." With her tippy-toe she restarted the swing's rock.

"A good one?"

She bit into her lower lip and looked down, but it didn't hide the rose coloring in her cheeks. "You beat me to the phone. I was just going to call. I like this much better."

"Me too." He kept rocking to the beat of the crickets and curved his arm around her back. "How is your dad doing?"

"He moved his hand today." With Haven's hand still entwined with hers, she raised them in the air. "I'm embarrassed by what I take for granted."

"Super Cal, you—"

"Stop it."

"—take so little for granted. I'd give anything to see with your eyes."

"Puhlease." Still, she snuggled next to him, fitting perfect against his side. "Did you know that only male crickets make that song?"

Of course, she'd know that, proving his earlier point. She was going to make a phenomenal nature teacher. The kids couldn't help but love her.

Maybe that was the key to capturing the North Shore's beauty. He covered their entwined hands with his free hand. "I have a favor to ask."

"Okay?" Her answer came out tentative as if she feared his request.

"Would it be possible to shadow you next weekend at Gooseberry? I have a feeling that between you and the kids, I might learn a thing or two about seeing beauty."

"You can't photograph me or the kids." Her hand trembled, and he held on tighter.

"No intention. I just want to see God's creation as you do, as Reece does. I want to see more than what the world sees."

"That is so sweet. I'll call and ask, okay?"

"Thank you."

A sneeze yanked her hand from his. "Bless me." She reached into her robe pocket and pulled out a tissue. "I'm sorry." She wiped her nose, a nasal sound in her voice. "This is so not romantic."

He retrieved her hand. "Says who?" The crickets played on as they rocked, as if they were minstrels hired just for this evening. It didn't get any more romantic than this.

Callie squeezed his hand. "Did you know that male crickets play their wings to attract a mate?"

"Really?" Maybe he should bring her back to his place again, tickle the ivories for her. "Would a serenade work for you?"

"It would depend on who's doing the serenading."

"Hmm. I'll keep that it mind." He brushed a hand over her head, tucking it against his shoulder, and he kissed her forehead. Nothing felt more natural, like he could spend the remainder of his life with Callie at his side.

Taking her back to his place could be dangerous. He might not let her leave.

She crossed a slippered foot over his ankle. "Now, can I say thank you for your gifts this week?"

"You're welcome."

"The flowers are beautiful, and those quotes . . . " She breathed in.

"They're just what I needed."

He cradled her chin and turned her head toward him. "And I meant every word."

"And I mean this." Moistening her lips, she angled her chin up.

His lips winged over hers, but his heart raced to the beat of a hummingbird's flight. He took the kiss deeper, savoring her mint-flavored caress, not caring about her cold. Kissing her was worth the risk. But taking her to his place for a moonlight serenade was definitely not an option.

She jerked away and then rested her forehead against his. "I'm sorry. Now I've passed my cold on to you."

"Do I care?" He angled in for more, hungering to taste her again, but she stuck a finger between them. "You need to know . . . " Her heart galloped as her sparkling gaze seized his. "That means you're forgiven."

"Oh yeah?" He smiled, and she looked down. Her shyness was immensely adorable. What he'd give to see her every day. This stolen moment tonight was unsatisfying. "I'm meeting with my editor tomorrow over my lunch hour. Would you have a minute or two to spare for me?"

"Oh, I think I could work you in." She sneezed again and then yawned. "But for tonight, I really should get some rest."

What he'd give to tuck her in and spoil her with homemade soup and hot cocoa, but for now, that had to remain in his dreams. He kissed her again, lightly gliding his lips over hers. More would lead to temptation he wasn't prepared to battle tonight. He stood and offered his hand. "I'll see you tomorrow then."

She laid her hand in his, and he pulled her up.

His gaze centered on her lips, but she looked down. "There's something else I need to tell you."

Uh oh. "Reece?"

She nodded.

The evening's peace abandoned him and tension took its place, tingling through every cell in his body. "Amanda's not budging, is she?"

"I'm so sorry."

He dropped back on the swings' hard slats, and planted his feet firmly on the porch concrete. Why was Amanda being so unrelenting?

He brushed both hands over his hair and stared at Callie's fuzzy yellow slippers. "I guess that doesn't leave me with much choice then, does it?"

"What choice?"

He looked at Callie's innocent face. "I really wanted to avoid this. I thought I could reason with her."

"What are you going to do?"

He stood, walked to the edge of the steps, and gazed outward. "I'm calling her tomorrow to tell her I'm contacting an attorney." He already knew he had an excellent shot of getting visitation, and maybe even partial custody. But he'd wanted to stay away from a legal fight that would only hurt Reece.

Whether or not he called his attorney depended on Amanda's reaction to his threat. And it was a threat. He was done playing nice. "If this is the way she wants to play it, then so be it. I gave up on fighting for Reece before. That's not going to happen again."

HAVEN KNOCKED ON HIS editor's open door and walked in. He handed her his flash drive. "I think this is what you've been looking for." Seeing beauty through the eyes of a child—through Reece's perspective—had done wonders for his perspective. Hopefully, Donna would see things the same way.

She accepted the drive without a comment and plugged it into her laptop.

He sat across from her trying to decode her poker face. The woman was too good at concealing emotions.

Finally, with lips pinched, she turned the laptop around. "Better, much better. Now I'm seeing that spark I believed was there. Now you're taking your art beyond the normal and capturing the area's beauty in a whole new way."

"Thank you." And he owed Callie for helping him see that beauty.

"I have another small assignment for you as well."

Yes. He wanted to pump his fist in the air, but clutched his thighs instead. "What does it entail?"

"We're doing a story on this area's state park naturalists. We want our readers to see and know the people that educate the public. Sean Porter has already begun, but we have a few employees remaining that will be at Gooseberry Park this coming weekend. We'd like to show these men and women at work, not a portrait."

He'd gladly take that out of Porter's hands. "I was planning on spending the day there anyway."

"Wonderful."

Haven glanced at his watch. If he left now, maybe he could have a quick lunch with Callie before returning to work. He couldn't wait to see her response to the red rosebuds he'd sent her today. "Will that be all?"

"Actually, I do have one question for you." She closed out of his flash drive and handed it to him, then clicked an icon labeled 'Haven Carlysle.' "What I need to know is why you kept this picture from me. This one's exquisite." The cursor flicked over a thumbnail picture, and that picture took over the entire screen.

His mouth hung open. "How . . . ?" He'd deleted that shot from the flash drive. No way could Donna have found it. Perspiration mopped his forehead. "We can't use it."

"Come now. This is exactly what we want the world to know about this area." With her pen, she pointed to the shadowed figures of Reece and Callie with Canal Park's lighthouse faded in the background. That morning he'd first met them. Yes, it was beautiful, but the world could never see it.

"No, I'm sorry."

"We want the world to know this area's for families."

"Then I'll find other families interested in posing."

"And you'll end up with a posed picture."

"The subject in that picture does not want it published."

"Haven, you are an expert at bleeding money from the impoverished, certainly you can persuade this woman to comply."

"It's not happening. Sorry." He pushed his chair back. If this meant his fledgling career as a free-lance photographer was over, then so be it.

"That's a shame." Her fingers lingered over the mouse as she stared behind him. Then her eyes brightened. "Callie, would you mind stepping in here for a moment?"

No, no, no. He reached for the mouse, but Donna pulled it from him and skewered him with a piercing look.

"I need your opinion on this picture."

"I'd be glad to—"

He tried standing up to block her view, but the chair flew out from beneath him and he landed on the floor. He reached for Callie's arm and missed. "Callie, it's not that big of a—"

"You didn't," rasped from Callie's mouth. She glared down at him. Red lightning streaked her eyes, and dark clouds hung below them.

He tried to stand, but she pushed him back down. "How. Could. You?" She ran from the office.

"Callie, wait." Using the desk as leverage, he pulled himself up then ran after her. He caught her arm just as she fled into her parents' office. "Please, let me explain."

She shook off his hand and stomped to her desk. She grabbed the vase with the rosebuds and thrust it into his hands. "Pure and lovely? You really are a smooth talker, aren't you?"

"Callie, I . . . "

She dug into her pants pocket and pulled out a handful of papers.

His notes to her.

She laughed amidst tears. "And this one from today? You really had me hoodwinked. *"Shall I compare thee to a summer day? Thou are more lovely and more temperate: Rough winds to shake the darling buds of May, And summer's lease hath all too short a date."* I wonder what William Shakespeare had to say about deception. Oh, that's right, he wrote *MacBeth*, didn't he?"

"Please listen to—"

"No, you listen." She clutched the notes in her hand and ripped them in half. "You come to me, telling lies, getting me to believe I might actually be beautiful." She tore them again. "Did that give you a thrill? Getting the ugly girl to think she was something special?" She made another tear.

"But you are—"

She froze him with a stare colder than a January wind off the lake.

"Mandy was right about you. You're no better than Sean Porter. No, you're worse. He may have used me, but you're using your son, and you can bet family court will hear about this. They're going to know the ugly truth about who Haven Carlysle really is."

# Chapter Twenty-Seven

CALLIE SLAMMED THE DOOR to her mom's office and jutted out her chin. She would not give Haven the satisfaction of a single tear. No, she'd get back to work as if he'd never wormed his way into her life.

She stared at the computer screen and gobbledy-gook leered back as if her brain had gone into hibernation. Organizing didn't require much brain power though, and the top of her mom's desk did resemble a Minnesota forest. Her mom would be mortified if she came in and saw this.

Going through the papers and folders one at a time, she slowly filed the paperwork away, filing away her anger with each piece. She'd relegated Sean to the circular file years ago. That was a perfect place to deposit Haven too.

He'd sworn he'd deleted all the pictures of her. How could he have betrayed her like this?

She jammed paper and mail into the recycle bin and put Haven's love notes—ha! Joke was on her!—through the shredder. Soon the top of the desk became visible again and one small piece of paper remained. How had it eluded shredding along with Haven's other notes?

She picked it up, pinching it with the tips of her thumb and forefinger as if lifting a filthy diaper. She reached beneath the desk, turned on the shredder, and held the note above it. The machine's grinding teeth chomped hungrily, begging to be fed, but she couldn't slide it through. One more look wouldn't hurt, would it? After all, the quotes weren't Haven's, he'd just borrowed them for his ruse.

*"Never lose an opportunity of seeing anything that is beautiful; for beauty is God's handwriting—a wayside sacrament. Welcome it in every fair face, in every fair sky, in every fair flower, and thank God for it as a cup of blessing." Ralph Waldo Emerson.*

*Thank you, Callie, for teaching me this invaluable lesson, for teaching me to see God's handiwork in every flower, every stone . . . every face. And when I see you, I see immeasurable beauty, "fearfully and wonderfully made." You are my cup of blessing, and it's overflowing. You are God's masterpiece.*

She blinked rapidly and fisted her hands. No, she would not cry. She would not let Haven's deceitful voice enchant her again. She grasped the paper and ripped it down the middle, then tore it again and again and again until it lay scattered beneath her desk like the helicopter seeds from a silver maple.

There. Now, Haven was completely eradicated from her life.

So why did it feel as if she'd shredded her heart along with the paper?

HAVEN RESTED HIS FOREHEAD against the wall outside Callie's office, wanting to bang it.

How had this happened? Ten minutes ago, he was flying high.

And now, he'd crash-landed, with Callie as a casualty.

How had Donna gotten a hold of that picture? He'd deleted it long—

Flu-like roiling stewed in his gut. No. He hadn't deleted it. But he'd kept it on his personal files for no one else to see. But no one had access to his personal files. Could he have accidentally left it on Donna's flash drive?

No. He'd have seen it on the slide show.

He fisted his hands and aimed them at the wall, but stopped. Taking his frustration out on plaster wouldn't help anyone. Besides, his fist had taken enough abuse from him this week and the only thing it served to do was turn his knuckles bloody, black, and blue. Exactly how his heart felt.

But being proactive would help.

He spun around and marched back to Donna's office, barging through the closed door without a knock. Jess sat in the chair opposite Donna, and both women looked at him as if he'd sprouted Viking horns on his head and painted his face purple.

The way he felt right now, maybe he had.

"Pardon me, Jess." He stepped in front of her and whipped Donna's laptop around.

"What are you doing?" Donna shrieked at him.

"Just watching out for someone I care about." He moved his finger over the touchpad, highlighted the Haven Carlysle icon, and clicked on it. He scrolled down until he found the picture of Callie and Reece.

"Your career is on the line here." Donna grabbed at the laptop, but he pulled it away.

"If having a successful career means hurting someone I love, then I want no part of it." He clicked on Callie's picture, and then punched delete. It disappeared from his folder.

Into the recycle bin.

He clicked on that, found the picture, and deleted it. "It's all yours." He shoved the laptop back at Donna. "I don't know where you got hold of that picture, and I don't know if you have a copy somewhere else, but I never want to see it again."

Donna sat back in her chair and crossed her arms over her chest, her eyebrows cocked high. "That's precisely the spirit I need to see in your work."

"What?" She wasn't angry?

"Have a seat, Haven."

Keeping her head down, Jess rolled her chair toward the wall while Haven grabbed the extra seat. "You're not upset?"

"Oh, I wouldn't say that. That photograph was precisely what I'm looking for, but it also shows me you've got what it takes to make a dollar in this business. You won't get rich, but you've got the eye, and you see things with a unique perspective. Precisely what I'm looking for. But . . . "

Of course, there was a stipulation. He crossed his arms and frowned.

"You can make it up to me this Saturday." She handed him a list of four names. "These are the naturalists we have yet to photograph. Capture them at work with the same essence, and we'll talk."

He read the names, and his heart nosedived. He shoved the note back to Donna. "Sorry. Won't do it."

"Excuse me." She sat up straight, her arms dropping at her sides.

He pointed to Callie's name. "Don't you understand by now that she doesn't want to be photographed? I don't care what this is for."

"Well then." She pulled the paper back toward her. "I guess that leaves me one alternative. Sean Porter gets your assignment." She pointed to Callie's name. "All of it."

HAVEN STRODE DOWN THE hall, thanking God that he had to go back to work. The sweet, amnesiac stupor of several Heinekens hadn't sounded so good in a long time.

But if he returned to work, he'd probably take his frustrations out on his clients. Not a great temperament to have when needing to talk people into coming current on their mortgage.

Maybe he should call in sick.

And take that short little walk over to Grandma's Sports Garden.

*Bad idea, Carlysle. Don't do it.*

He hurried past Ashley at the reception desk and aimed for the stairs. A little exercise would take his mind off things.

*Call your sponsor.*

He scrambled down the stairs, pulled out his cell, and speed dialed Eric. Voice mail answered. Maybe he should drive down to Minneapolis, show up at Eric's door. Not a bad idea. Maybe he should consider moving back to Minneapolis permanently. He had nothing left in Duluth.

With Callie against him, his chances of getting visitation with Reece were greatly diminished. His photography career was shot too.

And the woman he'd grown to love couldn't stand the sight of him. How could he get her to see it was a terrible mistake?

Feet pounded on the stairs below him. Haven moved to the side as another man ascended the stairs. The man passed him, and then stopped.

"Haven. Is that you?"

Haven turned and looked up. The man walked back down and offered his hand. "Lance Ackermann. Remember me?"

"How could I forget?" Lance, the man who'd designed the landscaping for his and Amanda's yard.

And one of Haven's old drinking buddies.

Haven shook Lance's hand. "How's it going?"

"Can't complain. I've settled down. Got a couple kids even, and the business has taken off."

"Glad to hear it." Lance had been a much bigger partier than Haven.

"And you? What have you been up to? Last I heard you were some bigwig in Minneapolis."

"Guess you could say I took a detour through Duluth on my way back to the cities."

"You're not staying?"

"No reason to." Just like there was no reason for him to head into work today. Let the bank find someone else to do their dirty work. For six years, he'd been the responsible one, and look where it got him. Alone. Stuck in a deeper pit than ever. Why even bother?

"You heading somewhere now?" Lance laid a hand on Haven's shoulder.

"Just home to pack up." After he called the bank and resigned. That was the least he could do.

"Well I can't let you leave without a proper send off, now can I?"

"What have you got in mind?"

"How 'bout we head over to that hole in the wall on Superior Street, Grumpy's. Relive old times."

And erase six years of sobriety. Haven wiped beads of sweat from his forehead. "I don't think that's a good idea."

A heavy door somewhere below squeaked open and closed with a thud. Lance curved an arm around Haven's shoulders as footsteps thudded up the stairs and Jess came around the corner. "Ah, you've got a girl who's keeping you straight, huh?"

"There you are." Jess puffed out a breath and smiled.

Haven locked gazes with her. "My girl just gave me the heave ho."

"She didn't." Her hand flew to her mouth and her eyes widened.

"Then what are we waiting for?" Lance slapped Haven's back. "Let's go celebrate your freedom. Ol' Grumpy's is calling your name."

"You're right." He tore his gaze from Jess. "Let's go." One afternoon of forgetting wouldn't hurt. It was just the medicine he needed.

THE DOORKNOB CLINKED ON Callie's locked office door, pulling her attention away from the computer. Couldn't they leave her alone for just a minute? She massaged her temples to rid the mushrooming headache. "Who is it?"

"It's me. Jess. It's important."

Right. She probably has split ends, or she broke a nail. Ewww. Tragedy. Callie rolled her eyes. But if she didn't let Jess in, she'd pout all night long and complain to Mom and Dad who didn't need any more stress piled on them.

"One second." She took her time going around the desk, shuffling her feet across the low-napped carpet. This better be important.

Grumbling to herself, she unlocked the door.

Jess flung it open and planted hands on her hips. "What did you do?"

Oh brother. Callie returned to her chair and slumped down. "What are you talking about?"

"You broke up with Haven? Are you nuts?"

Callie sighed and looked at the ceiling. "The guy's a big fraud. He was just using me to get to Reece."

"You've gone totally insane!" Jess flung her hands up. "The guy's crazy about you. I don't know why, but he is."

"Sure he is. That's why he went behind my back and gave my picture to his editor."

Jess's face blanched, and her voice dropped several tones. "You think he gave that to her?"

"Who else would have done it?"

Jess pulled a chair opposite Callie's desk and slumped down in it. "Oh man, oh man, I thought I was doing everyone a favor."

"You? What are you talking about?"

"It's my fault, Cal. I gave it to her."

"You? He showed it to you too? See, I told you he's a fraud."

"He is not a fraud! Would you just keep quiet for a second so I can explain?"

"Don't you dare lie for him."

"Give me some credit, Cal."

Callie looked down at her hands fidgeting in her lap. Just because Haven had proven to be a no good, lying skunk—no offense to skunks— didn't mean she had to follow the same route. "You're right. I'm being a jerk."

"That's the first wise thing you've said all day."

"Gee thanks."

Jess leaned forward. "Remember back a few weeks ago, Haven was setting up in his office, and the two of you suddenly decided to go out for lunch?"

How could she forget? That was her first mistake with him. "Yeah? So?"

"Well, he left his computer up. I was just going to shut his door, but then I saw his pictures and . . . and I snooped." Her lips twitched.

"You did what? Our clients expect and deserve confidentiality from us."

"I know, and it's not something I've ever done before, but his pictures were so beautiful. And then I saw that one of you and Reece, and I realized I haven't seen a picture of you in years. You always avoid the camera."

"Some of us aren't blessed with perfect features like you."

"You think I'm perfect?" Jess sneered down at her body. "My agent just told me, I'm too big for plus-size modeling."

"Jess, I'm sorry. I had no idea."

She wiped her eyes. "Yeah, well, you've been stuck in your own self-pity for so long, it's no wonder. You're gorgeous, Cal. You're the only one who doesn't see it."

"Tell that to Mom and Dad. They're always trying to force some plastic surgery on me. It's pathetic when even your own parents think you're homely."

"Girl." Jess shook her head. "They weren't doing that to make you look better. They wanted you to feel better about yourself. You've dumped on your looks for so long, they thought suggesting plastic surgery would boost your confidence. Then Haven came around, and all of a sudden you changed."

Callie looked out the window at the overcast skies, the gulls flocking around the beach, the families riding in bicycle surreys. It was all beautiful, even when the sun was hiding. Why was it she could see beauty in everything but herself? She fiddled with the hem of her shirt and peered through half-closed eyes at Jess. "He made me feel beautiful."

"Darn right, he did. And just now he erased that picture right off his editor's hard drive. Right in front of me. Risked losing his assignment because of it."

"He did?" Callie looked to her lap, nibbling on her lip, and the truth slammed into her. If Jess gave the picture to Donna, then Haven hadn't lied. He hadn't been using her to get to Reece. No, he hadn't erased it like he promised, but he also hadn't shared it with anyone and had no intentions to. How could she have been so stupid? Would he ever forgive her for jumping to conclusions?

"And you know what else he did for you?" Jess pointed her finger at Callie.

"There's more?" she whispered.

Jess leaned toward her. "He said *no way* to photographing you for your Gooseberry job. He said he wouldn't hurt you like that." Jess settled back in her chair and folded her hands in her lap. "But guess who you get instead."

No . . . "Sean," she breathed out and squeezed her eyes shut. She'd never pose for Sean. Never. Not even if it cost her her dream job.

"Now, the question is." Jess crossed her arms. "What are you going to do about Haven? If you're not interested, I—"

"Where'd he go?" Callie whipped out her cell phone and dialed his office number. "He must have gone back to work." Please answer, please answer.

"Oh, you won't find him at the bank."

A strange voice answered the phone and Callie hit 'end.' "What do you mean? He was just taking his lunch hour off."

"I mean, he ran into Lance and apparently the two know each other. They were heading up to Grumpy's."

"Grumpy's!" That old dive known more for its mixed drinks than good food. "Oh, toadstools and tricycles." Callie jumped up from her chair, dialing Haven's cell phone. "We've got to hurry." She made a beeline toward the door.

"What's the big rush?" Jess panted behind her down the hallway. "So the guy winds down with a drink. After what you just did to him, I'd say he's got it coming."

Callie accelerated toward the stairs. "You don't understand. Haven's an alcoholic." And she'd just driven him to make the worst choice in his life.

# Chapter Twenty-Eight

HAVEN STOPPED OUTSIDE GRUMPY'S, his hands shaking, and perspiration bleeding through his shirt. He wiped his forehead with the back of his hand. *Don't be stupid, Haven.*

*Just one. One to calm you down. One to help get through this day.*

And what will get you through tomorrow?

"You coming?" Lance held the door, and the sweet scent of malt seeped out, wrapping around his senses, luring him in.

"Yeah. Sure." His heart beating in double time, he walked across the dark, warped floors forever stained with booze. Cigarette smoke had permanently imbedded itself in walls decorated with peeling paper. He followed Lance to a high-backed wood booth and sat across from his old drinking buddy. They'd thrown enough money into this place for Haven to have paid for his new vehicle outright.

Was that what this one drink would lead to? He could stop anytime. He had for six years, right?

A waitress walked over to their table and slapped a couple of square napkins down. "What can I get for you boys?"

"Just a couple of Heinekens." Lance laid a ten down on the table.

Just.

Haven wiped his hand over mouth, his throat craving that sweet burn.

"So, tell me what's been up with you these past years." Lance folded his hands on the table. "You just up and disappeared after Reece's accident."

"Amanda kicked me out." Because he'd spent the evening in this den, rather than at home where he belonged.

"That's harsh, man."

The waitress returned and set two foaming glasses on the napkins. "Can I get you anything else?"

Lance winked. "We're just beginning."

Beginning his downfall. Haven wrapped his hands around the sweating glass. His mouth watered as his taste buds begged to be satisfied.

Could he really stop at one? If not, could he stop at today?

"Drink up, man. Once upon a time, you could throw 'em back with the best of them."

But that was once upon a time. Wasn't he better off now? Even without Callie? Without Reece?

He strangled the glass between his hands and swallowed an ocean of saliva.

Lance chugged down half a glass. "That Amanda was something else, wasn't she?"

"How do you mean?" Haven slowly raised the glass toward his lips, and it slipped from his hand sending a tsunami of beer over the table and onto both his and Lance's laps. Haven jumped up and grabbed napkins from the holder. "Oh, man, I'm sorry."

Lance laughed as he stood. "Like that hasn't happened before." He looked toward the bar and snapped his fingers. "Hey waitress, my buddy here made a mess."

"Don't snap your fingers at her." He'd forgotten how rude Lance could be. What was he doing here with him anyway?

Forgetting.

At least that was what he was supposed to do, but all he was doing so far was remembering. Haven ran napkins over his pants, but the beer had already soaked in. He'd go home smelling like a brewery whether he drank or not. What would he tell his dad?

Lance pointed to the next booth and raised his hand, about to snap his fingers, but stopped. "That's right. You were always the polite drunk. Hey miss, could we get a couple refills?"

Refill? If he left right now, he'd go home still sober. One more day to celebrate his sobriety.

But he'd go home to a house that wouldn't echo with Reece's laughter. One that would never see Callie's beautiful smile again.

Forgetting was good.

He slumped down in the booth, and the waitress set an overflowing glass in front of him.

"Now, where were we?" Lance threw back another third of his drink like a man accustomed to drinking every day. "That's right, Amanda." A smirk bloomed on his face. "She wasn't the same after that night either, but I didn't expect her to throw you out, I mean she was as culpable as you. If the two of us hadn't hooked up that night—"

"What?" Haven leapt off his seat. "No. Amanda was with her sister that night."

Lance laughed. "That's what she wanted you to know." He raised his glass toward Haven and winked. "Guess the joke was on you."

Haven reached across the table and grabbed Lance by the collar, forcing him to stand. "You were having an affair with Amanda?"

Lance's face turned radish red. "Hey, I wouldn't exactly call it an affair, I mean you weren't married, dude."

"Why you . . . " With one hand still gripping Lance's collar, Haven pulled his fist back.

"Hey, man, I thought you knew. Amanda said that's why you left."

"She did what?" After blaming Haven? After kicking him out, threatening to sic her attorney father on him, and refusing to allow visitation? And she was as guilty as he? Flaming hot anger—even hate for Amanda—rushed through him as he retracted his balled fist and shoved Lance down on the bench. "You're not worth it."

Instead he picked up the glass of beer and saluted Lance with it. "This one's for you."

## Chapter Twenty-Nine

*PLEASE, GOD, HELP ME make it in time.* Callie ran up Superior Street and stopped below the weather-beaten Grumpy's sign. She wouldn't recommend this place to her worst enemy—even to Sean. Haven couldn't be here, could he? Jess must have it wrong. She looked back down the sidewalk as Jess huffed toward her. "Are you sure this is the place?"

"Lance comes here all the time."

And Callie had never even peeked in the window of such a place, much less stepped inside. Oh, peanuts and elephants, this was no time to worry about her reputation. Swallowing a deep breath, she tugged open the heavy wood door, and the stench of stale beer whizzed past her. She stepped into the dark room, blinking to adjust to the low light. All the booths in the narrow room were high backed. She'd have to walk past each one to find Haven.

"There he is." Jess pushed her, and pointed to the end of the row of booths.

Haven stood in front of a table, raising a glass of beer.

"Haven, stop." She ran toward him

And he heaved the contents of the glass onto Lance.

Haven glanced her way, his eyes wide, and he dropped the glass. It hit the edge of the table and cracked, and then shattered on the beat-up hardwood floor. "Callie, what are you doing here?"

"I was . . ." She looked from Haven to Lance, who sat stunned and dripping, then back at Haven. "Stopping you," she whispered.

He stared blankly at her, and then a smile slowly curled up his lips and glistened in his eyes. "From drinking?"

She shrugged, tilting her head to the side.

"What's with this love fest?" Lance stood and shook his hands and arms, spraying beer. He gave Haven a shove as he walked past. "You need to lighten up, man. That always was your problem." He pounded on the bar, drawing the bartender over. "The bill's on him." He jerked his thumb toward Haven.

"Gladly." Haven nodded to the bartender.

Lance stomped out, and Haven grabbed Callie by the arm and gently pushed her toward a clean booth. Well, clean was a relative term. He folded arms on the booze-stained table and rested his head on them.

"Are you okay?" Callie slid in across from Haven and scooted over for Jess.

He sat up and pressed his back into the wood. "I didn't drink, Callie. I wanted to. Badly. But I didn't."

*Thank you, Jesus!*

The waitress stopped by the table. "Get you folks anything?"

"Just a water, please." Though she probably wouldn't touch it. Who knew how well the glasses were cleaned in this dump?

Jess ordered a Coke, as did Haven.

Then Haven reached across the table and took Callie's hand, but fury raged on his reddened face. "I learned something new just now. Amanda wasn't with her sister the night Reece was hurt."

"What?" No. That couldn't be right. That had been Mandy's story from the beginning. She couldn't have been lying all these years. Not to her best friend. "I don't believe it."

She didn't believe or wouldn't. She recalled the few times Mandy had talked about that night, how she'd never looked Callie in the eye. Callie had always assumed Mandy was hiding her grief. Was it because she'd been lying? She shook her head.

"It's true, Callie. She was with Lance."

"No." Callie shut her eyes. Was Haven lying to get her on his side? She'd known Mandy far longer than him and Mandy wasn't a liar. Well, not if Callie excluded all those times Mandy had told little fibs to get Callie to try something new. Those had all been fun times. And not if she excluded the promises Mandy made and broke, all fingering Reece for the reason. Like the promise Mandy made to Haven for his first day with Reece, that he could have two hours with his son. Or the kiss Mandy planted on Haven then lied to Bill about who was really at fault. And so many more times that now cascaded like a waterfall in front of her memory.

Oh Amanda, how could you?

The server delivered the beverages then slipped away.

Callie curved her hands around her glass and stared at it while slowly rotating it back and forth. "I guess that explains why she didn't want you around. You made her feel guilty." Her gaze rose to meet his.

Haven motioned like he was going to slam his fist on the table, but pulled back then gently flattened his palms on the wood surface. "And here I always thought . . . " He sniffled in a breath.

Callie reached across the table and covered his hands, one of which was black and blue. "What are you going to do?"

"Well, after I change." He drew his hands from her and motioned to his drenched shirt. "Thankfully I ended up wearing the beer instead of drinking it. I think I must have had an angel watching over me."

"I was praying the whole way over here."

"God heard you, Callie, and He didn't let me make the worst mistake since Reece got hurt. And now He's showing me a new path."

"You're going to talk to Amanda?"

"I have a feeling she'll be in the listening mood."

"Me too." And it broke her heart. Now, more than ever, Mandy was going to need a good friend. Callie didn't know if she could be that friend anymore.

His gaze flitted from Callie to Jess then back again. "How did you know what I planned to do? How did you find me?"

"Jess." Callie nodded to her sister. "She made me see what I jerk I was to you."

"I was the one who gave Donna the picture." Jess spoke to the tabletop. "It was so beautiful, and I thought she should see it. I didn't know it would get you all in trouble. I wasn't thinking."

"You?" Haven blinked.

"I'll explain later." Callie gave Jess a side hug then nodded toward the door. "Would you mind?"

"Hey, I can take a hint." With a wink, Jess got up and walked out of the bar.

"Do you mind?" Haven nodded to the spot Jess had vacated.

Callie nibbled on her lower lip and shook her head.

Haven came around the table and started to put his arm around Callie's shoulder, but quickly drew away. "Sorry." He motioned to his soggy shirt then gently cradled Callie's cheek instead.

Her face heated at the mere touch, and her heart zoomed as fast as Reece. Try as she might to pull away, Haven's touch had her magnetized.

He inched closer until their faces were barely a book's-width apart. His gaze held hers captive. "Super Cal, you are the most amazing, courageous, loving, fun, intelligent, beautiful—"

"No." She pulled away.

But he tugged her closer. "Yes. Beautiful. Outside and in." He caressed his hand over her check. "You've saved me more than once, and I thank God for bringing us together."

Oh, she did too, but Haven had stolen her voice along with her heart.

"I know I've made a lot of mistakes. I never should have kept that picture of you or lied about it. My heart was in the right place, but my actions weren't, and I'm deeply sorry for hurting you."

Blinking back tears, she reached up to touch his cheek and whispered, "I forgive you."

He sniffled and his gaze went to the ceiling. "Thank you." His voice was coarse with emotion.

Then he brought his head down, and his glossy eyes met her gaze. "You've changed me, and you've captured my heart. I think you stole it with your first quirky saying. You make me laugh, you give me strength, and when I'm with you I'm deliriously happy. How could I not love you?"

She gasped. He *loved* her?

He inched closer and feathered his lips across hers, sending a warm tingle all the way to her toes. "I love you, Callista Beaumont, and I plan to pursue you until you feel the same about me."

She rested her forehead against his and inhaled deep breaths. No, she would not cry, although the joy in her heart was nearly bursting.

Haven didn't have to do any pursuing—he'd already caught her. But there was one thing she had to do before she could repeat those three words back to him.

He had faced his demons and stared them down, now it was Callie's turn. She backed away from him, and worried eyes searched hers. Giving him a reassuring smile, she grasped his hands. "I have a favor to ask of you."

His hands tightened around hers and he swallowed hard. "Name it."

"Meet me at Canal Park tonight? Say, nine o'clock?"

A slow grin crept out. "I'll be there."

She raised his hands to her lips and kissed them. "And don't forget your camera."

# Chapter Thirty

HAVEN STRODE UP TO Amanda's door and rang the doorbell. When he'd called earlier, she'd promised to be home, but her promises didn't carry much weight anymore. Neither did her threats to keep Reece from him.

Two cars zoomed up the hill before Amanda opened the door. Her cheeks were drawn in, and her hair pulled back in a tight ponytail. She pointed to the steps, the very steps on which she'd made a move on him the other night, then lied to Bill about it.

"Sorry. I think I'll stand." He backed up against the railing and crossed his arms.

"What's this about?" Amanda tugged the door shut and matched his crossed-arm stance. "I thought I made it clear that you blew any chance."

He scratched the side of his head. "Funny you should mention that since you're the one who kissed me. You have a habit of kissing men other than your significant other, don't you?"

"I don't know what you mean." She looked down at her hands and picked at her fingernails.

"Does the name Lance mean anything to you?"

Her head jolted up, and she swallowed. "Lance? Should it?"

"He designed the landscape here. Was my drinking buddy. Apparently, your lover too."

Panic widened her eyes, but quickly retreated with the firm set of her jaw. "After you left, I was lonely. You didn't expect me to go through Reece's troubles alone?"

He jerked up straight. "Stop the lying, Amanda."

She backed away and her arms fell to her side. "I . . . I'm not lying." But her confidence had fled.

"I know you weren't with your sister when Reece was hurt." He stepped toward her and she backed away some more. "I know you were with Lance."

Her mouth opened.

"No more lies, Amanda."

Her mouth closed, and she sunk against the front door. "H-how'd you find out?" Her words breathed out in a whisper.

Haven stood straight and walked to the stairs, then turned back to the woman he once thought he loved, and now only pitied. "My lawyer will be contacting you tomorrow." He walked down the steps, his head held high, his shoulders unburdened from the weight he'd carried for far too long.

Very soon, he'd get to be the father he'd always longed to be.

And maybe, just maybe, he'd have a future with Callie.

CALLIE CROSSED THE BEACH, her sandals dangling from one hand and a single calla lily gripped in the other as the nippy waters of Lake Superior leapt up to lick her feet. No gem in her nose to remind her that God found her beautiful. No hat hiding her face. She felt naked, but laying herself bare before Haven and before God made her heart dance with joy.

Nerves still tingled in her hands from what she was about to do, but it was necessary for her to move on, to forgive Sean . . . Jess . . . her parents . . . Mandy . . .

Even herself.

Now hopefully, Haven would forgive her.

She climbed up on a boulder and stared out at the water, its waves blinking the stars' and moon's reflection.

And, of course, crickets provided the background symphony.

An evening orchestrated by God, on a shore fearfully and

wonderfully created. Just as He'd created her. Why had it taken her so long to see that?

She closed her eyes, dropped the sandals, and raised her arms, lifting the flower toward Heaven. *Thank you, Lord, for this magnificent beauty.*

"Callie?" Haven touched her arm and sat beside her, setting the diaper bag on an adjacent boulder.

She spread her arms and scanned the sky, the beach . . . Haven's face. "It's all amazing, isn't it?"

"You're amazing."

"You forgive me?"

"How could I not? You've opened my eyes, Super Cal. You've helped me see the most splendid beauty around me, beauty I was blind to before."

She bit into her lower lip, but didn't look down as she normally would have. "I have a little something for you." She offered the calla lily.

"Ah, my lady's bearing gifts." Grinning, he accepted the flower.

Callie reached into her pocket and pulled out a taped-together note, one she'd painstakingly salvaged from her desk floor and spent a few hours piecing back together. "Confucius once said that everything has beauty, but not everyone sees it." She pressed her palm to his chest. "I always thought I saw beyond people's faces into their hearts, but that wasn't true. You've helped me to see my own prejudice against the perceived beauty of the world. I've been afraid to be beautiful because that meant I was as shallow as I wrongly believed those around me were."

"Callie . . . " Haven cupped a hand on her cheek and leaned toward her, but she put a finger to his lips.

"You've helped me see the Callie God created me to be." She spread open the pieced-together note. "Helen Keller may have been blind, but she understood beauty. Listen to this quote. 'The best and most beautiful things in life cannot be seen, not touched, but are felt in the heart.'" She refolded the note and inserted it into her jeans pocket then splayed a hand over Haven's heart. "When I'm with you, I feel . . . I believe I'm a princess."

He caressed her lips with his thumb. "That's because you are." And he leaned forward, touching his lips to hers, dusting them across as his firm hands roamed over her back. Her lips parted his, and she took the kiss deeper, craving the love in his minty breath, wanting to never stop.

But she had one more olive branch to offer, and this was the most important one, the one that would bridge the gap she'd widened between them with her mistrust and fear.

She pulled away, although his hands resisted the press of her back. Her gaze met his, and she took an arm, pulling it around front, and cradled his hand in hers. "You'll forgive me?"

A grin stretched across his face. "Super Cal, I forgave you the minute you charged into Grumpy's to save me."

"Then let me show you something." She stood up and ran her hands down her jeans, jeans she'd painted for herself long ago but never had the courage to wear. She fingered the one element she'd added today, just above her right knee. A couple walking on a moonlit beach, a child between them, his bionic leg bared beneath his shorts. The three together formed a heart.

Haven traced the heart-shaped trio with his pointer finger. "It's beautiful."

She trapped his hand against the people-formed heart and looked him directly in the eye. "It means I love you."

Haven closed his eyes, but moisture still coated his lashes. "Oh, Callie." He stood up, wrapped his arms around her, and aimed for her mouth. But she backed away and gulped down the Superior-sized lump in her throat.

"First, I have one more favor to ask of you." With her heart threatening to beat out of her chest, she picked up Haven's diaper bag, handed it to him, and then backed away. "Will you take my picture?"

He reared back, and his brows leapt up. "Are you certain?"

Her chin quivered, but she nodded. "More than I've ever been."

"All right then." He removed the camera from its bag, stepped back, and aimed the lens toward her.

Nerves jitterbugged in her stomach as she sat on a boulder.

"You're sure about this?"

She only nodded.

"Okay then."

Hearing the rapid clicking of the shutter, she couldn't force a smile. She looked out at the great lake and lifted her chin in defiance of her fear.

Not once did Haven ask her to smile or pose. Rather, he framed her—loved her—as she was, a broken and beautiful child of God.

After what seemed an eternity, he finally set down the camera then he took her hand, imploring her to stand.

How could she say no?

He drew her against himself, his arms snug around her waist, nearly melding their bodies as one. He pushed a stray hair from her eyes, and his concerned gaze explored her eyes. "Are you okay?"

She nodded. It wasn't a lie.

And he grinned, those brilliant blue eyes sparkling like the night sky. Oh, she could take forever looking into those eyes.

Eyes that closed as he pressed his lips to hers for a toe-warming, hair-curling kiss. Oh, sand on a sandwich, he was a good kisser! Then he tucked his cheek against hers and whispered in her ear. "I love you, Callie Beaumont, and if you'll let me, I could spend the rest of my life capturing your beauty."

THE END

Dear Reader,

*Thank you for reading Callie and Haven's story. Having fallen in love with Haven while writing* Risking Love, *I knew I needed to explore his life more, and* Capturing Beauty *was born.*

*We live in a world that makes judgments on first impressions and values outward beauty over looking deeper and finding beauty within. Hopefully this story will help remind you that each of us is a unique work of art handcrafted by God and the earth is His masterpiece.*

*The* Where the Heart Is Series *continues with one more book,* Planting Hope, *that tells Jess's story.*

*Reviews are vital for authors, so when you get a moment, I'd greatly appreciate it if you'd share a review on your blog, or any of the popular book sites. The review doesn't have to be long or eloquent, just honest.*

*For the latest information on upcoming releases, contests, recipes, what I'm reading, and more, sign up for my e-newsletter. Opt in at:*

**http://eepurl.com/MoZZr**

*You can also stay in touch via my website:*

**http://brendaandersonbooks.com/**

*And via social media:*

**https://www.facebook.com/BrendaSAndersonAuthor/**
**https://twitter.com/BrendaSAnders_n**
**https://www.pinterest.com/brendabanderson/**
**https://www.goodreads.com/BrendaSAnderson/**

*I also love hearing from readers as you are the reason we write! You can send a note to:*

**Brenda@BrendaAndersonBooks.com**

*Thank you for joining me on this writing journey!*

*In Him,*
*Brenda*

# ACKNOWLEDGMENTS

Publishing a book always requires the input of far more people than the single name listed on the cover, and it's important to recognize many of those involved.

*Thank you to* . . .

My awesome Book Booster team who eagerly spread the word about my books!

My fabulous critique partners: Stacy Monson, Stephanie Prichard, Lorna Seilstad, Shannon Taylor Vannatter, and Jerri Lynn Ledford. Thank you for helping to make this story shine.

My sister Gayle Balster ~ Thank you for reading my ugly first drafts and for your honest reflections.

My niece Brianna Balster for that very first colorful Callie-phrase, "Crud on a cracker." That fun expression helped define who Callie is.

Lesley Ann McDaniel, for your hawk-eyed editing.

George at Think Cap Design Studios for another beautiful cover design!

Gay Hartfiel of Portraits from the Heart. You have an amazing gift for capturing every person's beauty—inner and outer—in your portraits! Thank you for making my author portraits shine!

My coffee ~~snob~~ aficionado daughter, Sarah, for schooling me in all things coffee, and for your proofreading help, and for your honest appraisal (rolled eyes) of the first draft of *Capturing Beauty*. Yes, I changed the ending just for you!

My sons, Bryan and Brandon, for supporting and encouraging me on this journey. I can't wait to see where God takes both of you!

My husband Marvin – Thank You doesn't seem adequate to express my gratitude for your unending encouragement and love! You keep me pressing on when I hit too many potholes in this writing road.

And Thank You to the Creator who made each of us unique and beautiful!

Read Jess's story in
**PLANTING HOPE**
A Where the Heart Is Romance
Coming this Fall!

Chapter One

What possessed people to jump out of airplanes? Corliss Morgan slapped the Minneapolis newspaper down on her cube mate's desk and pointed to the headlines. SKYDIVING ACCIDENT KILLS NEWLYWEDS. "Insanity. If I ever think of dating a daredevil, remind me to run far, far away."

Just as she'd like to run far, far away from that fundraiser tonight. She was still hoping, praying even, for something to come up that would prevent her from going.

"Lissa," Rita Dunlap emptied the remnants of a bag of Pop Rocks into her mouth and continued typing, the candy's crackle vying for attention. "A little insanity is exactly what you need."

"No way." Lissa plopped down on her office chair and moved her mouse, chasing away the Fourth of July screensaver, as her eight coworkers' voices buzzed in the background of the bank office. They were all trying to accomplish the impossible: extract late mortgage payments from unemployed people. Talk about insanity. "Give me someone safe, someone who does things the right way, someone like Haven. Now there's—"

"Did I hear my name?"

Eyes growing wide, Lissa slowly swiveled her chair and looked up into her boss's indigo eyes. She swallowed hard, stealing a glance at her chuckling cube mate. Payback would be coming. "Um, we were talking about those skydiving newlyweds and how you'd never do something crazy like that."

"Hmm." He took the newspaper off Rita's desk and rubbed his

Romanesque chin. "Maybe once I would have." He gave the paper back to Rita then handed Lissa a stack of files. "My priorities have changed."

Lissa threw Rita a triumphant smile before thumbing through the files. "Foreclosures?"

"I'm afraid so."

"Gee thanks." She couldn't contain her sarcasm. How many of these foreclosures would be credited to her dad? Good thing he wasn't alive today to see what his generosity had wrought.

"Sorry about that." Haven leaned a broad shoulder against the edge of her gray cubicle and brushed a hand through surfer blond hair. Her heart did a two-step. Handsome wasn't complimentary enough. "But you're the best, Lissa. If anyone can keep those people from losing their homes, it's you." He smiled, lighting a spark in eyes as blue as a Minnesota evening sky.

Heat flooded her cheeks. Now, why did he have to go and smile? If only he weren't her boss. "I'll do my best."

"I have no doubt." He glanced at his watch and slapped the cube wall. "Looks like it's closing time. But before you go, can I see you in my office?"

"I'll be right in." After she regained her composure. The click of associates' fingers on keyboards quieted and the professional phone voices changed to excited personal tones. People couldn't wait to get away from the complaining and hideous words they heard all day. Not that she blamed her coworkers. Trying to collect overdue loan payments always brought out the ugliness in people.

She slid open her desk drawer and secured the files in the To Do slot. Why would Haven want to see her? She wheeled her chair to the left, peeked around her gray fabric wall as he walked past the end cube. His charcoal Hugo Boss suit perfectly accented his six-foot frame. Handsome indeed.

"Hey, sweets, I saw that."

Lissa gulped and focused at her computer screen. "Saw what?"

"Nothing but a little flirtation with the boss."

Lissa spun in her chair and glared at Rita. "I was not flirting."

"Right, and I'm a natural blonde." Rita twirled one of her curly locks as Pop Rocks crackled in her mouth.

"Okay, so the man's cute." More like gorgeous.

"How about hunkalicous?"

Oh yeah. That worked.

"And successful."

"Yeah, so?" Dad was successful too. Until . . . Chin quivering, Lissa snatched a small handful of the raisin, walnut, almond concoction from a bowl on the credenza that separated her workspace from Rita's. She cleared her throat and stilled her chin. "I've got an appointment."

"Uh-huh." Rita shut off her computer. "With a man so straight-laced, word has it his lips are still virgin."

"Please." Not that she hadn't imagined kissing those lips. "The boss is off-limits."

"Wouldn't stop me." Rita drummed a pencil on her desk. "Hmmm, I just might—"

Lissa laughed. "You'd be bored to tears."

"Ahh, but you're so right." With a sigh, Rita gazed at the ceiling and fanned a hand over her chest. "I crave heart-galloping adventure. Something you should try, by the way. Let's face it, the boss is too safe."

*And safe is exactly what I need.* Lissa clicked off her computer and picked up the college graduation gift from her father. A framed list with her sixth grade goals inked on crinkled, yellowing paper: graduate from high school, go to college, and find a job. Three tasks already completed. Next item was to become a boss. Buying a home, getting married, and having children would come in time. God's path for her life written in a tidy package. Step-by-step rules for assured happiness. She set the frame down. The plan had worked well so far.

"Sweets, you definitely need to get a life."

Lissa grabbed her purse from beneath her desk. "I intend to live, all right." If there was one thing her father's death had taught her, it was how to live the right way, and to treat her body as the temple God created it to be.

Rita rolled her eyes. "Mr. Boring is awaiting."

"Yeah, I better go. See you Monday." Lissa dumped the last drops of her water bottle into a bud vase that held a single pink carnation and then strode past the now deserted cubicles. It was amazing how quickly the place cleared out at closing time.

She stopped at Haven's door. 'Hennepin Bank and Trust' was etched into the door's glass, and a mahogany nameplate, engraved with Haven's name and title of Collections Supervisor, hung below the bank's name. The door framed him at his desk, his brows knitted in concentration.

She raised her hand to knock and held it still, nerves jitterbugging in her stomach. What was this about? A pink slip? Probably not. The collections department was the one area in the bank that wasn't lacking for work. Most likely more remnants of her dad's ghost that required exorcizing, more problems created from his granting unwise loans. Regardless, being summoned to the boss's office was never good news.

Gnawing her lower lip, she knocked.

He smiled and waved her in.

The dance in her stomach slowed but didn't stop. He wouldn't smile like that to give bad news.

Would he?

A lingering hint of minty cologne greeted her when she stepped into the room. Focusing on the waterfall photograph on the wall behind Haven, she sat in a chair opposite his desk, crossed one leg over the other, and clutched her purse in her lap, hoping to still her trembling fingers.

"Hi Lissa." He closed his laptop and leaned back in his chair, his face unsmiling.

Not a face bearing good news. She gripped her purse even tighter.

He pointed to a newspaper on the side of his desk. The headline read, JUNE FORECLOSURES IN HENNEPIN COUNTY AT ALL TIME HIGH. "Hennepin Bank and Trust made the paper again."

"Thanks to my dad," she mumbled.

Haven straightened, and a storm brewed in his eyes. "I know I don't always stress this, but with the bank's struggles, your dad's become an easy scapegoat. I'm guilty as the rest when it comes to laying blame, but he was a good man. Don't let anyone tell you otherwise."

She glanced down at her fisted hands.

"Sorry, Lissa, I didn't mean to jump at you, but if you ask me, Theodore Morgan is the main reason this bank is still afloat today."

Lissa's eyes burned, and she blinked back sudden tears. She couldn't recall a time when someone had stood up for her dad.

"And he saved my rear more than once." He toyed with a plastic Snoopy paperweight. "Like you, your father had a heart for helping people."

And if her dad had taken care of that heart, he might still be here for her.

Lissa cleared her throat, reining in her emotions. Breaking down at work was bad enough, but in front of Haven? Sheesh! She squared her shoulders and donned her professional face. "You needed to see me?"

"Uh, yes." He glanced at his watch then set the paperweight next to a framed portrait of Haven's aging beagle, Schroeder. "I've got a commitment tonight that I'd love to avoid but can't." He shook his head and frowned.

"Me too." If raising money to build awareness for heart disease wasn't so vital, she'd gladly skip the evening event.

Haven slid his top desk drawer open and pulled out a sheet of paper. "The bank received this letter today from a customer."

Lissa slumped in her chair and eyed her crimson pencil skirt. It wasn't her fault people got in over their heads with their mortgages, but they sure always found a way to blame her. If it weren't for her occasional successes, the vile language and hate that spewed from people would probably drive her to drink. She didn't need one more vice to deal with.

"You want me to read it to you?" He held out the paper.

Through her lashes, she peered at the dour line of his mouth. "Please." Seeing and reading the words often implanted them in her mind. Maybe in only hearing them, the memory would fade sooner.

Haven took a sip of his bottled water. "It's addressed to the owners of Hennepin Bank regarding you."

"Get it over with." Keeping her head down, she closed her eyes.

"It says, 'Recently, our family went through a difficult time with hourly cutbacks followed by a job loss, then the threat of losing our home. Creditors hounded us, and many used bullying language as if that would somehow help us find a non-existent flow of money. But the collection call we should have feared most was the one that helped steer us out of our situation: the call from Hennepin Bank.'"

Helped them? She stared at Haven.

He winked. "'Your employee, Corliss Morgan, listened to us and sympathized with our plight. She took time to guide us through our finances, helped prioritize our bill paying, and offered ideas on how to save money. It took a few months to get back on track, but without Ms. Morgan's calm advice, we are certain we would have lost our home.'"

Relief washed over her. That was what made her job worthwhile.

"'So, thank you, Corliss Morgan and Hennepin Bank, for being the human side of banking. You have earned our business for a lifetime and we will gladly recommend you to others. Sincerely, Ted and Marla Cockran'."

They'd been a joy to work with. If all people listened like they had . . .

Haven handed her the letter. "We've placed a copy in our files, but you should have the original."

"Thank you." Now these were words she'd love to imprint on her memory.

"We don't get a lot of positive feedback in this department, but when we do, more often than not your name is attached to it. That leads me to another small piece of business." He folded his hands on top of his desk. "I've been offered a new position at a downtown Minneapolis mortgage company."

No. He couldn't leave. Seeing his smile every day always eased the stress of the job and fed her futile hope for something more. "You've decided to take it?"

He shrugged. "I'd be a fool not to."

Of course. "I guess congratulations are in order." Even if she wasn't happy about it. "When do you start?"

"Three weeks. Two weeks here then I'm taking a week off."

"Good for you. We'll miss you around here." *Especially me.*

"I'll miss it too, but it's time to move on. Before I leave Hennepin Bank, though, there's one more very important duty to perform, and that's to help find my successor." Haven slid a manila folder from the side of the desk and opened it.

Not Tyler Abernathy, please! Being unemployed would be better than working under that ogre. His bullying tactics gave all collection agents a bad name. No way would she work for him.

Haven rapped a pen on the open file. A copy of the letter he just read lay on top. "I'm recommending that you apply for my position."

"What?" Her heart sprinted. Others were far more qualified than she. "But I—"

"You, more than anyone in our department, have protected the bank and homeowners from foreclosure. You understand that we don't want to take people's homes away—that we want to find a way to save them. You understand that there's a living, feeling human being at the other end of letters and phone calls. I can't think of a better person to lead this department."

She peered upward and whispered thanks. If she got the promotion, she'd be personally responsible for eradicating her father's mistakes. Life couldn't get better.

No doubt she'd apply, but it was unprofessional to appear overeager. She curled jittery fingers on the edge of his desk. "May I think about it?"

"Absolutely." He closed the file. "I wouldn't expect otherwise."

"Thanks, Haven. Your encouragement means a lot to me." More than she dared let him know. She got up and headed for the door. To think she might be weeks away from achieving the next goal on her list. Owning a house wouldn't be far behind. Too bad she had a commitment tonight. Rita would have loved to celebrate this news with her.

"One second, Lissa." Haven's calm, professional baritone disappeared and was replaced with a wobbly tenor.

She turned on her heel as he stuffed the folder back in his desk drawer.

"One more little incentive to throw in, for you to ponder over the weekend." Resting back in his chair, he rubbed his hands over his thighs.

"Is something wrong?" Never had she seen him anything but confident.

He chuckled and looked toward her, but his gaze didn't meet hers. "I was wondering if, when I left . . ." He rubbed his hand over his chin. "Would you mind if I asked you out?"

Would she mind? Lissa tried to hold in her smile but failed. "I look forward to it." Good thing he couldn't see her heart dancing a samba.

"Whew." He puffed out a breath and grinned. "I listen to people tell me no all day and it doesn't bother me, but if I'd heard it from you . . ."

He pushed away from his desk and shut off all his equipment. "I'll walk you out."

"I'd like that."

Side by side, they walked from the building across the parking lot, sharing small talk. Someday soon, maybe they'd hold hands. Maybe she'd get a chance to kiss those virgin lips.

*Girl, you are getting way ahead of yourself.* She pointed her remote at her Volvo. A clothing store stood out beyond her car. Shoot, she needed panty hose for the night. She nodded toward the store. "I remembered some shopping I have to do." Considering the mush Haven made of her mind, it was a good thing she remembered them now and not once she arrived home.

"Okay, I'll see you on Monday."

Maybe by then her heart would be dancing to its normal beat. With her purse slung over her shoulder, she watched Haven's car head down the road then she floated across the parking lot, imagining Haven's hand protecting hers.

"Watch out!"

Tires screeched. Lissa's body hurled through the air, strong arms tucked around her. With a scream, she landed.

Softly. On top of a woodsy-scented, leather-clad man. A dark-haired, gorgeous one at that.

His arms sprang away, and she pushed herself off the ground, making certain her skirt stayed at her knees. Murmuring shoppers gathered around the two of them

A trail of blood coursed from his temple down his cheek shadowed with whiskers. She retrieved her purse that had flown a car's length away, and dug out a tissue. "Are you all right?" She squatted and dabbed at the cut. "It looks superficial, but you should have it checked out."

He brought a hand to his temple, winced, and looked at his bloody fingers. "I've had worse." He turned in the direction of the sedan that had nearly plowed her down. The car was long gone. "Crazy driver."

And one daydreaming lady. That didn't make for a safe

combination. She stood and wiped off her skirt. She was lucky her handsome rescuer happened to be passing by or she wouldn't just be cleaning road dust off her outfit.

The crowd dispersed as he helped himself up. "Are you okay?"

"Thanks to you."

He shrugged. "I happened to be in the right place."

Right, but how many other passersby would have watched the car ram into her? "In my book, you're a hero." She opened her purse and pulled out a couple of twenties.

He frowned and crossed his arms over his chest. "That wouldn't make me much of a hero now, would it?"

"I feel I owe you."

"Just watch where you're going next time." He winked a toffee-brown eye and grinned. "That'll be payment enough."

*Be still my two-stepping heart.* "I promise." Or was it her two-timing heart? She fanned a hand by her face as her savior sauntered across the parking lot to a bright yellow motorcycle, the streamlined kind that was made for speed.

And danger.

He donned a helmet and zoomed from the parking lot.

She hadn't even gotten his name.

Not that it mattered. He may have saved her, but the man oozed danger. He'd be perfect for Rita.

Besides, now she had Haven's attention—he was made for her.

So why did the thought of gazing into the stranger's deep-set eyes bring a grin to her face and make her heart dance a traitorous tango?

Find **Risking Love** at your favorite online retailer!

# Coming Home Series

 **Brenda S. Anderson** writes authentic and gritty, life-affirming fiction. She is a member of the American Christian Fiction Writers and is currently President of the ACFW Minnesota Chapter, MN-NICE. When not reading or writing, she enjoys music, theater, roller coasters, and baseball, and she loves watching movies with her family. She resides in the Minneapolis, Minnesota area with her husband of 29 years, their three children, and one sassy cat. Learn more about Brenda at www.BrendaAndersonBooks.com.